Besieged

Also by Bertrice Small

BESIEGED

Bertrice Small

𝒌

KENSINGTON BOOKS
Kensington Publishing Corp.
http:/www.kensingtonbooks.com

KENSINGTON BOOKS are published by

Kensington Publishing Corp.
850 Third Avenue
New York, NY 10022

All Kensington Titles, Imprints, and Distributed Lines are available at special quantity discounts for bulk purchases for sales promotions, premiums, fund-raising, and educational or institutional use. Special book excerpts or customized printings can also be created to fit specific needs. For details, write or phone the office of the Kensington special sales manager: Kensington Publishing Corp., 850 Third Avenue, New York, NY 10022, attn: Special Sales Department, Phone: 1-800-221-2647.

Kensington and the K logo Reg. U.S. Pat. & TM Off.

First printing: March 2000
First Kensington mass market printing: July 2003

10 9 8 7 6 5 4 3 2 1

Printed in the United States of America

For all my Irish relatives and friends, both Protestant and Catholic alike. May they learn to live in peace and tolerance.

Prologue

ULSTER 1630

She was coming. Sweet Jesu, she was coming! Coming back to Maguire's Ford. It had been twenty years since he had seen her last, but he knew everything about her there was to know; for her cousin, the priest, had never been chary about sharing her letters. She had borne a royal bastard by the late Prince Henry Stuart. How could a prince not love her? How could any man not love her? he wondered nostalgically. She had married again, to a Scotsman, and had given him three sons. Her eldest daughter by her second husband was a married woman with two children. She had had so much more these last twenty years, while he had only his memories of her. It had been enough until now. He ran a big hand through his thick hair, still a warm red-gold, but less so than it had been those many years back. His eyes, blue as Lough Erne itself, were troubled. He sighed deeply. Why now? Why when he had only recently begun to feel the lack of a family was she returning to Maguire's Ford? He laid her letter to him aside.

"Rory. Rory Maguire!" Father Cullen Butler had entered the hall, an unrolled parchment in his hand. "Jasmine is coming back to Ulster!" he said excitedly. "I had not thought to see her again in my lifetime. Praise God, and His angels!" The years had been good to Cullen Butler. Despite the snow-white hair atop his head, his face was yet youthful. His blue eyes sparkled.

"I cannot be here when she comes," Maguire replied.

"Ye have to be," the priest said quietly, helping himself to a generous dollop of smokey peat whiskey from the decanter on the sideboard. "Yer her estate manager, Rory Maguire. She entrusted ye with Maguire's Ford all those years ago, and now she is coming back. She will expect to see ye here. Whatever is in yer heart must remain hidden, man. I know it was easier when ye didn't have to see her every day, but she will not be here for very long. A few months at the most. Did she tell ye why she's coming?" He sipped at his whiskey.

Rory Maguire shook his head. "Nay," he responded. "She didn't."

"The younger of her daughters, the one conceived and born here, Lady Fortune Mary Lindley, is being brought over to find a husband. There's no man, it seems, in either England or Scotland that's taken her fancy. A headstrong wench, it would appear. The girl is practically past her prime, but she's stubborn," the priest said with a smile. "She sounds very much like her mother was at that age, and I should certainly know for I was her tutor." He chuckled, then grew serious again. "Jasmine wants to give her Maguire's Ford for a dowry, Rory." The priest settled himself into a chair by the fire, motioning his companion to join him.

Rory Maguire sat down, his hand worrying his thick hair again. "Then 'tis surely better that I go," he replied. "The lass will want to choose her own estate manager, or rather, her husband will."

"Now, nothing is settled yet," the priest soothed his companion. "And 'tis unlikely ye'll be replaced by a stranger. Jasmine knows it was yer family who were the lords here before Conor Maguire and his people departed with the earls.

Even to this day you are still considered the lord of Erne Rock Castle, Rory."

"Only because its English owner has not been in residence," Maguire reminded the priest.

"Jasmine would not dispossess ye after all this time," Cullen Butler replied. "I know my cousin. I helped to raise her."

"We haven't seen her in years," was the response. "This is a woman whose second son has a king for an uncle. And what of her Scots husband? Certainly he will have a say in all of this, Father."

"James Leslie has great respect for his wife, and does not meddle in her affairs," came the certain answer. "Now, enough of yer foolishness, Rory Maguire. They'll be here in early May."

"*They?* How many of them are coming?" Rory drained his crystal tumbler, and reaching for the decanter poured them a second libation.

"Jasmine, her husband, and the lady Fortune," the priest answered.

"Her servants?" Rory queried.

"Adali, aye, and little Rohana. Toramalli is a married woman, and will remain with her husband to oversee young Lord Patrick who will remain behind at Glenkirk with his brothers. 'Tis wise. The holding will someday be his, and he will better get the sense of his future responsibilites left alone."

"Erne Rock will welcome them as in my family's time," Rory said with a small smile. "I had best move my belongings back into the gatehouse."

"Aye," the priest agreed. "It would be better. Ye'll probably be living there from now on anyways. As I remember, Jasmine gave it to ye for yer own. I believe my cousin means for Fortune to live in Ireland. She's been in touch with the Reverend Steen regarding Protestant families. Of course, there is only one that he and I both agree is suitable. The

Deverses of Lisnaskea. Sir Shane's heir is a worthy young man of the right age. He is twenty-three, and the lady Fortune will be twenty this summer."

"How can ye be a party to a Protestant marriage, Father. For God's sake, ye baptized the girl yerself!"

Cullen Butler shrugged. "We're a long way from Rome, my lad," he said quietly. "We both know that if Lady Fortune Lindley is to have Maguire's Ford, then she must be wed to a Protestant. Besides, she's been raised by a Scots Anglican stepfather; and Jasmine, like my Aunt Skye, may God assoil her good soul, is a law unto herself where her faith is concerned. If Fortune is her mother's daughter then she will treat all with equality and tolerance. Twenty years ago there were no Protestants in this village, yet now there are, and a church for them as well. We all get on because Samuel Steen and I will have it no other way. My Aunt Skye, who was born an O'Malley, was fond of quoting Queen Bess, who often said, 'There is but one lord Jesus Christ. The rest is all trifles.' I'm sorry to tell ye that the damned woman was right, even if Rome would excommunicate me for even thinking it, let alone saying it aloud. I love the church else I should not have devoted my life to it, Rory, but even the church can be wrong sometimes. And not just our church, but the Protestants as well. How some of them can justify their bigotry, and believe God does too, is beyond me! So I sanction, without publicly saying so, a Protestant marriage between Lady Fortune Lindley and Sir Shane Devers's son. Will it not be good to have a young couple at Erne Rock, and please God, children too?"

"Yer getting sentimental in yer old age, Cullen Butler," Rory Maguire said, but his tone was affectionate, and not at all condemning.

The priest chuckled. "I'm very surprised myself to find I am sixty years of age, Rory Maguire, and ye but ten years behind me for all yer flaming pate. Now, I'll have no more nonsense about yer leaving Maguire's Ford, eh?"

"I'll stay unless I'm ordered to go," the estate manager

said. "I don't know where the hell I would go anyways," he admitted with a wry grin; then he sobered. "But it will not be easy seeing *her* again."

"Nay, I don't imagine it will," the priest agreed, "but ye'll do what ye must as ye did all those years ago, Rory Maguire, won't ye?"

Maguire sighed deeply. "Aye," he said, "but then I'd do whatever I had to to please *her*, Father."

The priest nodded, satisfied, and then draining his tumbler he stood up. "I'll be on my way then. I've Vespers to oversee." He set the crystal down on the sideboard. "I'll be here to get ye through it all, Rory Maguire. God bless ye." He made the sign of the cross over his host, and departed the little hall.

Rory Maguire sat staring into the fire. Jasmine was coming back to Maguire's Ford. He had fallen in love with her the moment he had first seen her in Dundeal, stepping gracefully down the gangway off the *Cardiff Rose,* on her husband's arm. She was the most beautiful woman he had ever seen, then or since. She had taken that obsequious little royal estate agent, Eamon Feeny, quickly in hand. When they reached Maguire's Ford several days later, she learned Feeny had driven off the villagers because they were Catholics. Jasmine had dismissed him on the spot, and sent the vicious bastard packing back to Belfast.

But Eamon Feeny had returned several months later with evil in his black heart. He had attempted to kill Jasmine, but had murdered her husband instead. They had caught him that same day. Jasmine, fierce as any Celtic warrior, had hanged him on the spot. Only when the devil breathed his last did she collapse with her overwhelming grief. They thought she was going to die for she lay unconscious for several days. Then her servant, Adali, the Indian in his neat white turban, and the priest, her own cousin, had come to Rory. She was, they told him, calling out for her husband in her anguish and heartbreak; and they feared she would put herself into the grave unless she could be made to believe that Rowan Lindley came into her bed again.

He was shocked by their suggestion. It was bad enough the servant made it, but that the priest would condone such a thing! But they assured him that she would die otherwise, and perhaps she would anyway. Still, it was worth the chance they were all taking if they could save her. Rory Maguire had wrestled with his scruples, but he had wanted her so desperately. He had known people, as well as creatures, who had willed themselves into the grave in grief. So he had slipped into the castle that night with the aid and complicity of his fellow conspirators. He had made tender love to the unconscious woman. Afterward, she fell into a deep and natural sleep. But he had gone on his way brokenhearted. Though Jasmine would now survive, she would have no knowledge of their single encounter. Nor was there any chance she would ever love him, or know how deeply he loved her.

It had been a terrible burden on his honest conscience all these years. The priest and Adali had borne the burden too, although it didn't really help him to know that. Their love for Jasmine had been of a different kind. His was the heaviest part of the guilt. He wondered what she would say if she ever learned that he had been her lover for that single hour. She would probably be horrified. He doubted her current husband would be too pleased either. Her ignorance had allowed him to remain in his family home, husbanding former Maguire lands all these years. Better she remain ignorant, and he behave like a man of fifty, and not some lovesick boy. Jasmine would never love him. It had not ever been meant to be. He knew it, and had long ago accepted it. The next few months, however, would be the hardest time of his life, but he would get through it. He had to—not just for himself, but for Jasmine too.

Part One

"Drink isn't the curse of the Irish. Religion is."
—Kathleen Kennedy, marchioness of Hartford

Chapter
1

Lady Fortune Lindley drew her soft taupe wool cloak about her, and stared intently as the green hills of Ireland came slowly into view. The May wind was yet sharp, and ruffled the fur edging the hood of the garment against her face. Leaning against the ship's rail she watched as the early morning mists, like pale silver streamers, blew themselves out of existence, revealing a pale wash of blue-white sky. She wondered what Ireland would really be like, and if she would at last find love. Did love even exist for her?

Her gloved fingers tightened about the railing. What on earth was she thinking? *Love?* That sort of thing was for her mother, and for her sister, India. Fortune Mary Lindley was the practical one in the family. Her mother's history was both fascinating and appalling. Two husbands murdered, and one of them Fortune's own father. Her half-brother, Charlie, a royal bastard because her mother and the late Prince Henry had been lovers, but could never have wed because her own mother would have been considered a bastard by English royalty. In India, however, her mother had been a royal princess, courtesy of a grandmother who had been kidnapped, placed in a royal harem to bear the Indian emperor a child before being retrieved by her family, and sent back to her Scots husband.

And her own sister, India, who had attempted to elope with a young man, only to find the vessel upon which she was making her escape attacked and taken by Barbary pirates, had also ended up in a harem. Rescued, she had returned home *enceinte* with her Barbary master's child. Their stepfather had been furious, and had sent her up to the family's hunting lodge in the mountains to have the child. Fortune had gone with India to keep her company. The child had been taken from her sister upon its birth, and India had been married to an English milord. *Love?* Heaven forfend! She certainly didn't want her life filled with such melodrama!

Love was not practical. What a woman wanted was a pleasant man with whom she could live peaceably. He must be reasonably attractive, and have his own wealth, for she would certainly not share hers. That she would keep for her children. They would have their children at reasonable intervals. Two. A son to inherit his father's estate, and a daughter to inherit Maguire's Ford. It was the sensible thing to do. She hoped she would like Ireland, but even if she didn't, she would remain there. An estate of some three thousand acres was not to be sniffed at, and her mother's gift to her upon her marriage would make her not simply wealthy, but very, very wealthy. Wealth, she had observed, was far more preferable than bleak poverty.

"Are you thinking of William Devers?" her mother asked, coming to Fortune's side to look out over the water at the nearing land.

"I keep forgetting his name," Fortune chuckled. "William is not a name that is familiar to me, Mama."

"You have a cousin William," Jasmine answered. "My Aunt Willow's youngest son. He is the cousin who has taken holy orders in the Anglican church. I don't think you ever met him, poppet. A nice young man, as I recall. A bit younger than I." Jasmine's eyes were thoughtful with her concern. Fortune was her privy child. She was never really certain what Fortune was thinking. "If you do not like this young man, poppet, you do not have to wed him," she told her daughter for what must surely be the twentieth time. God! She didn't want Rowan's youngest daughter unhappy. It had been a near enough thing with India.

"If he is presentable, Mama, and kind, I'm sure he will suit me well," Fortune replied, patting her mother's hand in a gesture of comfort. "I am not adventurous like you and India, or the rest of the women in this family for that matter. I want an orderly and peaceful life."

The duchess of Glenkirk laughed aloud. "I do not believe, Fortune, that the women of this family ever sought out wild adventure deliberately. It just seemed to happen."

"It happened because you were all so impulsive and reckless," Fortune said disapprovingly.

"Hah!" her mother snorted with humor. "And you are not impulsive, my little huntress? I've seen you take your horse over a small chasm many a time, sending us all into fits."

"If the stag can take the jump then so can the horse," answered the girl. "Nay, Mama. You and the others sought out exotic climes and places. You associated with the mighty. It was inevitable that you should find yourselves caught up in risky ventures. I am not like that at all. While I did visit France with you and Papa once, I have remained content at home in the bosom of my family. Like Papa I do not like the court. Too many young people who do not bathe regularly, with deceitful tongues, all seeking out the latest gossip, and making it up if they can't find it. *Non, merci.*"

"Even in simple country places, Fortune, there are deceitful tongues all too ready to gossip. Perhaps you have been too sheltered within the safety of our family gathering, but be vigilant, poppet. Always follow your intincts even when they war with your practical nature. Your instincts will be right every time," her mother advised.

"Have you always followed your instincts, Mama?" Fortune asked.

"Aye, most of the time. It's when I didn't that I got into difficulties," Jasmine responded with a smile.

"Like when you took us to Belle Fleurs after old King James ordered you to marry Papa?" Fortune probed.

The duchess laughed again. "Aye," she admitted, "but don't ever tell Jemmie that I said so, poppet. It will be our secret. Ohh, look! We're entering Dundalk Bay. The Irish call it Dundeal. We'll be landing soon. I wonder if Rory Maguire will be there to meet us as he was all those years ago when your father and I first came to Ireland to see our new estates. That dreadful little devil who later killed Rowan had brought him along to drive the coach. Your father was quick to learn that Rory Maguire's family had been the lords of Erne Rock for centuries. They left with Conor Maguire, their overlord, and the earls, but Rory would not leave his lands, or his people. We made him our estate agent, and he has served me loyally and faithfully ever since."

"Shall he remain, Mama?" Fortune asked.

"Of course," Jasmine answered. "Listen to me, Fortune. Maguire's Ford will be signed over to you on your wedding day. It is to be yours alone, and not your husband's. We have been over this, but I cannot make it clear enough to you. A woman who does not possess her own wealth is doomed to a life of servitude. You may want a simple and quiet life, poppet, but you will have neither if you are not your own mistress.

"In Ulster the Protesants and the Catholics have a tenuous relationship at best, but any malcontent can cause trouble easily. That is why we have isolated Maguire's Ford from the estates around it. There are both Catholics and Protestants in our village now. Each attends his own church, yet they work together in peace. That is how I want it, and how you will want it. Rory Maguire has spoken for me for twenty years now. He has kept the peace along with my cousin, Father Butler, and our Protestant minister, the Reverend Steen. You will now be responsible for seeing that the peace continues. Your husband can have no say in the affairs of Maguire's Ford, nor should you be influenced by him to make any changes. The people of Maguire's Ford coexist contentedly. It must remain that way."

Above the two women the wind filled the canvas of the great sailing ship, ruffling it with a faint booming sound. The salt spray faintly misted their lips, and the air was damp with the scent of the sea.

"Why do the Catholics and Protestants fight, Mama?" Fortune asked her parent. "Do we not all worship the same God?"

"Aye, poppet, we do," Jasmine answered, "but the churches have become bases of power for men very much like governments and kings are bases of power. Unfortunately power is never quite enough. Men who have it always want more. To have power you must have a hold on the hearts and minds of the people. God is a most powerful weapon. The churches use that weapon to intimidate the people. Each wants his way of worship to be the right way, *the only way.* So they fight each other, killing, they believe, in God's name, convinced that they are right because they do.

"My father, your grandfather, the Grande Mughal Akbar, long ago brought representatives of all the world's religions into his court. For years they argued with one another about the nature of God, the proper way to worship, and why each was right in his thinking, and the others all wrong. While my father tolerated them, and listened to them with much interest, in the end he founded his own personal religion, but no one other than he was asked to follow it. Faith, my dearest, is a matter between you and God alone. Let no one tell you otherwise."

"So men use God to pursue their own ends, Mama," Fortune said thoughtfully. "I think it very wicked."

"It is," came the reply. "I have raised you to be tolerant of all people and faiths, poppet. Do not allow anyone to change you," Jasmine advised her daughter.

"I won't," Fortune said firmly.

"If you fall in love, you may be influenced by your lover," her mother said.

"I will never fall in love, then," Fortune replied quietly. "Most men today are not, from my small observation, like my stepfather. He respects you, and listens to your counsel. That is the kind of man I would marry, Mama. I hope William Devers is like that."

"Your father respects me because I have made him respect me, but as for listening to my counsel, he may listen, but seldom takes my advice. Men are stubborn that way, Fortune. You must learn to work around them in order to get things done," Jasmine said with a smile.

"I have seen you wheedle Papa," Fortune replied with a rich chuckle. "When we were small, India and I used to wager how long it would take you to get him to do your bidding."

"Did you?" Jasmine said dryly. "Which of you won the most often?"

"I did," Fortune answered a trifle smugly. "India was always in too much of a hurry to win. I, however, bided my time, as did you, Mama. Patience can truly be a virtue when dealing with a man."

Jasmine laughed aloud yet once again. She caressed her daughter's cheek tenderly. "I never realized you were such a wise child, Fortune," she said, chuckling. "I fear William Devers may have more of a woman than he is anticipating."

"The only thing William Devers is anticipating is my dowry," Fortune said sharply. "He will get quite a surprise when he learns that I intend keeping my own wealth. He may not be willing to have such a girl for a wife, Mama."

"Then he will be a fool," came the answer.

"Who will be a fool?" James Leslie, the duke of Glenkirk, joined his wife and stepdaughter at the ship's rail.

"Oh, we were just speaking of men," Fortune said airily.

" 'Tis nae particularly flattering, lassie," the duke answered. "Are ye excited, my pretty? In just a short time, a few days at the most, ye'll meet the young man who will probably become yer husband."

"We will see," Fortune said quietly.

James Leslie drew a slow, deep breath. What was it about his stepdaughters? He had raised them since they were little girls, and they had, for the most part, been amenable lasses until it came to the matter of marriage. Still, he remembered his breach with the eldest, India, only just healed. He had promised India that he would not doubt any of his children ever again. It was a promise he meant to keep. "Aye, yer right, lass. Yer right. We will see. Why the young fellow could turn out to be a terrible dunce, and I'll nae hae my lass wed wi a fool, or a villain," the duke said.

Jasmine Leslie smiled. She had seen the look in her husband's eye, and knew his patience was being tried. He had done the right thing, however. Perhaps it was possible to teach an old dog new tricks.

"We had best go to our cabin, poppet," the duchess said, "and see if all is in readiness for the remainder of our trip."

"Let me stay, Mama, and continue to view the land," Fortune pleaded prettily.

"Very well," Jasmine said, and taking her husband's hand drew him to her side. "She wants to be alone, Jemmie."

He nodded, and together they left the main deck of the vessel.

Fortune continued to lean against the ship's railing lost in thought. This was the land of her birth, yet she had been but a few months old when she had left it. Ireland meant naught to her at all. It was the name of a place. Nothing more. What was it really like? And what was Maguire's Ford like? The castle that was to be hers was not large, her mother had said. It was called Erne Rock, and was set on the lough. Mama said it was a sweet place; that she and Rowan Lindley had been happy there. Fortune's brow furrowed. Could she really be happy in the place where her father had been so brutally murdered? The father she had never known because he had died shortly after she had been conceived.

She had felt his absence her entire life. How often when she stayed at her elder brother Henry's seat at Cadby had she sought out the portrait of Rowan Lindley that hung in the gallery of the house? Tall and big-boned, Rowan Lindley had a square jaw with a deep cleft in its center with a dimple. His hair was tawny and his eyes were golden in color. He carried himself with a faint arrogance, natural to a man whose family had held the same lands since before the time of the Norman conquest. Henry Lindley resembled his father in features, but India, a mix of both her parents, had his famous eyes. Fortune loved the portrait of Rowan Lindley. She drank it in each time she saw it as if she might gain something of her father.

She didn't look like him at all, or her mother either. There was nothing in her that she might say was him. She had her great-grandmother de Marisco's blue-green eyes, and her great-great-grandmother O'Malley's flaming red hair, they told her. Her grandmother Gordon always noted that Fortune was the duck in the swan's nest with her pale skin and wild pate. Fortune smiled to herself. She wondered what William Devers looked like, and if she wed him what their children would look like.

A light rain began to fall, and Fortune drew her cloak more tightly about her. She had heard it said that it rained easily in Ireland, yet the sun would be out the next minute. Looking up she saw the clouds scudding across the sky, yet here and there there were patches of blue. She laughed, deciding that she liked it. Then the sun burst forth, turning the morning bright and faintly warm. The ship moved more slowly now, its sails being trimmed as it glided toward its dockage. Usually ships anchored in the bay, but they would dock today because of the unusual amount of luggage belonging to Lady Fortune Lindley.

As the vessel skid into its berth, and the sailors leapt forth onto the dock to make the ship fast, Fortune saw a tall gentleman standing and watching. She wondered who he was. He was dressed very simply in dark breeches, a doeskin sleeveless doublet with staghorn buttons, a white linen shirt, and fine leather boots. His head was bare, and she noted his hair was almost as bright as her own. Well, Fortune thought, at least I won't stand out so much any longer if this fellow is about. The gentleman stood next to a large traveling coach to which were attached six fine chestnut horses. Fortune noted with pleasure that the coach horses were matched. Since the ship they had traveled upon belonged to her family, and the dock was privately held by them, she knew the coach belonged to them too.

"Why it's Rory Maguire! He has come to meet us. How absolutely wonderful!" Jasmine was by her daughter's side again. She waved quite enthusiastically. "Rory! Rory Maguire!"

He had seen her come to the rail to stand next to the young girl. She was older, yes, but still, he thought, the most beautiful woman he had ever encountered. He waved back at her.

The ship was finally made fast to the dock, and the gangway lowered. Jasmine hurried off the vessel, trailed by her family and servants. She held out her hands in a gesture of greeting to her estate manager. "Rory Maguire! How good of you to come and meet us! How it takes me back. Far too many years than I care to remember," she finished with a smile.

He took the elegantly gloved hands in his and kissed them both. *"Cai mille failte,* my lady Jasmine. A thousand welcomes back to Ireland, and yer family too." He released her hands from his gentle grip.

"This is my husband, James Leslie, the duke of Glenkirk, Rory," Jasmine said, drawing Jemmie forward.

The two men shook hands, each carefully sizing the other up as they did so. Apparently satisfied, they smiled, speaking a greeting.

"My wife has naught but good to say about ye, Maguire," the duke said. "I look forward to seeing the estate."

"Thank you, my lord," came the reply. "I think you'll be

pleased. 'Tis a fair land, Maguire's Ford." Rory turned back to Jasmine. "I've brought the coach, of course, my lady, and there's horses to ride if you prefer. You'll be remembering Fergus Duffy, I'm certain. He's come along to drive the coach for us. As I recall yer servants prefer it to the back of a beast."

"Fergus Duffy, and how is your good wife, Bride?" Jasmine called up to the coachman with a smile. "My daughter is looking forward to meeting her godmother." The duchess drew her child forward. "This is Fortune, Rory. Fergus, this is the lady Fortune."

The coachman tipped his head in greeting.

Rory Maguire took Fortune's slender gloved hand and, raising it to his lips, kissed it. "I welcome you, my lady, and hope Maguire's Ford will please you so that you will want to remain."

Fortune looked directly into the blue eyes assessing her. She felt a sudden and odd sense of recognition, yet she had been but an infant when this man had seen her last. "I thank you, sir," she replied, puzzled as to the strange feelings she was now experiencing.

"I've a lovely little black mare with me you might enjoy," Rory said to Fortune, releasing her hand.

"I'd prefer that fine dappled gray gelding," Fortune said pointing, and quickly recovering from her earlier sensitivities.

"He's a wee bit unpredictable," the estate manager cautioned.

"So am I," Fortune replied with a mischievous grin.

Rory Maguire laughed heartily. "Do you think you can handle him, my lady? I'll not have you being tossed about. 'Twould be a poor welcome home, I'm thinking."

"There's not a horse alive I can't handle," Fortune boasted.

Maguire looked to the duke and duchess, and when James Leslie nodded his approval, the Irishman said, "His name is Thunder, my lady. Come, and I'll give you a hand up."

"My baggage?" Fortune queried.

"We'll need several carts," Jasmine said. "Fortune brought all her possessions as she hopes to remain here in Ireland."

"We can hire them here in town," Rory replied. "I wasn't certain the lassie would be remaining or not."

"Is William Devers a bad catch then?" Fortune asked boldly.

Rory chuckled again. "Nay, my lady. He's considered quite the pick of the district. Tall and handsome, he is, with a fine estate up in Lisnaskea which will one day be his own. Not as big as Maguire's Ford, mind you, but more than respectable. There'll be a lot of disappointed lassies the day he picks a wife and marries, I'm thinking."

Fortune grew silent now. So William Devers was considered desirable by the ladies. He probably had a large head to go with his large estate. She walked across the dock to where the gray gelding stood stamping his feet with impatience. Taking the animal by his bridle she looked directly into his eyes, her other hand rubbing his velvety muzzle. "Well now, laddie, you're a handsome fellow. I do believe we'll get on just fine. Ready for a good long run? I surely am, but you must behave yourself until we get out of the town and onto the high road. Then we'll race the wind, you and I!"

Rory Maguire watched the girl speaking softly with the horse. He had felt a strange feeling when he had first looked upon her. It was as if he knew her, and yet that was not possible. He had not quite yet shaken off the sensation but he approved of her actions with the animal. Cupping his hands together he helped her to mount Thunder. "Up you go, my lady." Only as he boosted her was he suddenly aware that the horse did not have a lady's saddle, but the girl mounted astride, obviously used to riding that way. He untied the animal from its hitching ring.

Thunder danced a bit as he accepted the new weight upon his back. He tossed his head to test her mettle, but she held him firm, her hands resting with seeming lightness upon the reins, her knees pressing against the horse's sides, warning him, guiding him. "Easy, laddie," she soothed him, and his ears pressed back, listening to the soft voice, new but a moment ago, now familiar. He quieted.

Rory Maguire smiled and nodded, pleased. The girl was a natural horsewoman. Turning, he looked to see the boxes and trunks being unloaded off the ship. "Mary, Mother of God," he muttered beneath his breath. "I've never seen such a muck."

The duke laughed. He had had the same reaction when he first saw all of Fortune's luggage. "I've had the captain send into the town for wagons to transport my daughter's belongings. We dinna have to wait. Do ye hae horses for my wife and for me?"

"Aye, my lord. The lady can ride the black mare. 'Twas a black mare you last rode to Maguire's Ford," he recalled with a quick smile at Jasmine, and she nodded. "And I've a fine stallion for you, my lord. He's just trained. I couldn't bear to geld him, and so I must keep him separate from the breeding stock. We'll probably sell him to someone who needs a new breeder. He'll fetch a fine price as do all our animals. The descendants of Nightwind and Nightsong are very valuable animals. Who's to ride in the coach?"

"Adali and Rohana," Jasmine said.

"So they're still with you, eh? What happened to the other little lass you had, my lady?"

"Toramalli is a married woman now," Jasmine answered him. "She and her husband are at Glenkirk, our home in Scotland, making certain our three sons behave themselves. Patrick is fourteen now, while his younger brothers are thirteen and ten. We thought to bring Adam and Duncan with us, but they preferred having a summer without us."

"Then you expect to return home fairly quickly?" Rory asked.

"Aye," Jasmine replied. "William Devers has been recommended by both my priestly cousin and by the Reverend

Mr. Steen. If he and Fortune please each other there will be a wedding before summer's end, Rory. If that happens, the daughter born at Maguire's Ford will make Ireland her home. I hope he will turn out to be Fortune's future, for I should like my daughter to be happy and settled."

" 'Tis every mother's wish," Rory answered her. Ahh, how lovely she was despite her years. He almost sighed aloud.

"Good day, Master Maguire," the voice said, and Rory was pulled from his reverie.

Startled, he looked up, and into the face of Jasmine's faithful servant, Adali. The man never changed, he thought a bit irritably. The light brown face was still bland and smooth. The dark eyes piercing. "I thought not to see you again, Adali," he replied.

"Yet here I am like a bad penny," Adali smiled, showing a row of even white teeth. "All is in readiness for our journey?"

"Aye."

"Then let us depart," Adali said. He turned. "Rohana, get into the coach. I will shortly join you." He swiveled about again, speaking to the duke. "The wagons for my lady's possessions will be here shortly, my lord. Rohana has gathered everything that we will need for the journey and stored it in the coach. The wagons will travel more slowly than we will. I do not expect them at Erne Rock until at least a day after our arrival, but the ladies will certainly want to rest for a few days before entertaining, I am certain."

"Excellent," the duke replied as he swung himself into the saddle of the young stallion.

The day, which had been bright, now turned gray once again as a fine misty rain began to fall.

"A soft day, just like my first day in Ireland," Jasmine said, smiling at Rory Maguire. "Tell me how my cousin fares."

"He is well, and content as a mousie in its winter nest," came the answer. "He's a good man, Cullen Butler, for all he's a priest. He's not judgmental, or small-minded like so many of the others. As he so often admits, Rome would not approve of him at all, but Rome is very far away. At Maguire's Ford he is a blessing."

"And the Protestants we settled with their minister?"

"Good people, and hard working," Maguire replied. "Samuel Steen is cut very much from the same cloth as your cousin, my lady. He's sensible and open-minded. We've had no difficulties although others have, but then we both know the reasons for it."

"Pray God, Rory, that we can keep Maguire's Ford a place of peace for good people," Jasmine told him.

They rode for several hours, finally stopping at a small inn.

"This is a familiar place," Jasmine said, "and yet it was not here the last time. There was a farmhouse. A deserted woman and her poor bairns, Rory. What happened to her?"

He chuckled. "You don't know? Yer late husband, the English marquess, sent me back a month or so after you had settled in at Maguire's Ford. He purchased the farmhouse from Mistress Tully, and then hired her to run an inn here. With the monies he paid she did just that, and was able to keep her land to farm as well. Look at the name of the place, my lady. The Golden Lion. Mistress Tully said that's what the Englishman reminded her of, a lion. Hers is the only decent stopping place between here and Maguire's Ford. A lot of the English don't like it, but there's naught they can do since the place is owned by the most English marquess of Westleigh and his family."

"My son never said anything about this," Jasmine observed.

"He probably doesn't know, either. The administration of the inn and its business was assigned to me at Maguire's Ford. The marquess thought I would be better handling it than an absentee manager."

"My God, all these years, and I never knew! Rowan had such a good heart. I remember that poor woman with her big belly, and those wee ones crowding about her. I remember how poor the place was with its dirt floor and two wooden benches. I remember you telling me that her husband had deserted her to go with the earls, but that she would not leave the land. And yet look at it now," Jasmine concluded as they clattered into the courtyard of the inn. She could just make out the original farmhouse in the quadrangle of buildings that made up the inn.

It was all whitewashed, and neat as a pin with roses and other flowers growing about it. There was a large stable for at least two dozen horses. There was glass in the windows of the place, and several chimneys smoking gently. She could smell the aroma of roasting meat and poultry. The scent of good ale wafted out from the taproom. Several young men ran from the stables to take the horses.

"Come along," Rory Maguire said, helping Jasmine from her mare. "Come in and renew your acquaintance with Mistress Tully. She can speak English now. She quickly found it necessary to her survival."

The duke of Glenkirk found himself a bit piqued by the Irishman's easy manner with his wife. Then he consoled himself with the knowledge that other than Adali and Rohana, Maguire was only acquainted with Jasmine. His was a difficult position. He was not really a servant, having been born to the nobility. Yet he no longer possessed his lands, but rather managed them for an English landlord, who just happened to be the duchess of Glenkirk. I must get to know the man better, James Leslie thought to himself. He seems a good fellow after all, and has been honest with my wife's lands and retainers.

Jasmine scarcely recognized Mistress Tully, who was now plump and rosy-cheeked. The innkeeper greeted her warmly, curtsying and thanking her again for Rowan Lindley's kindness those many years back.

"As you can see, m'lady, his good heart was our salvation. I don't know how I would have managed without it," she said in her soft lilt.

They sat down in a small private room to a meal of

roasted lamb, onions, carrots, and potatoes. There was also a fat duck stuffed with bread and apples; a broiled salmon with dill; fresh bread, butter, and cheese. There were wine and ale both.

"I'm sorry we can't remain the night," James Leslie remarked as he loosed his doublet and pushed his pewter plate back.

"If we did we shouldn't be able to reach Maguire's Ford by late tomorrow, my lord," Rory replied.

"Where will we stop tonight, Maguire?" the duke asked.

"The only place we can, Sir John Appleton's manor," came the reply.

"Is he still alive?" Jasmine wondered aloud. "As I remember he and his wife were terrible snobs, and extremely unpleasant toward the Irish. He had done something minor in old Queen Bess's court."

"He's alive all right," Rory Maguire said darkly, "and he's but grown meaner with the years. His lady died, but his daughter and son-in-law live with him. They're no better than the old man."

"It sounds a right treat," James Leslie muttered.

"Oh, they'll fall all over you and her ladyship, my lord. 'Tis the rest of us that will be given short shrift," Maguire chuckled.

"There's no place else?" James Leslie queried.

Rory Maguire shook his red head, making a mournful face as he did so.

Sir John Appleton was now a fat old man with a gouty foot. His daughter, Sarah, and her husband, Richard, were spare and sour. They were openly flattered to be entertaining the duke and duchess of Glenkirk and their heiress daughter. They sat Fortune next to their son, John, and hoped for a miracle. They did not get it, for John, normally a loud bully, was struck dumb by Lady Fortune Lindley's beauty and air of self-assurance. She was like no other girl he had ever met, and he was frankly intimidated by her. For her part Fortune ignored him. Young John Appleton had a spotty face and damp palms. The fact he was so silent and lacking in interesting conversation did not stand him in good stead with Fortune. She thought him rather foolish.

"The reputation of yer horses is widespread," old Sir John remarked. "I'm amazed considering ye've got Irish Catholics working on yer estates. They've robbed ye blind, no doubt."

"I have both Catholics and Protestants working on my estates," Jasmine said sweetly. "Both render me good service, and I find no difference in them, Sir John. They are all decent people."

"Idol-worshipping papists," the old man said venemously.

"Catholics don't worship idols," Fortune suddenly snapped, highly irritated. "They worship God. What twaddle!"

"Madame! Reprimand your daughter. She is much too forward, and wrongheaded," Sir John snapped.

"Fortune, please apologize to Sir John. He cannot help his ignorance," the duchess of Glenkirk said to her daughter.

"Yes, Mama," Fortune remarked meekly. "I apologize to you for your ignorance, Sir John." She smiled sweetly. Then rising, Fortune curtsied prettily. "I must retire now," she explained, and left the room.

Sir John and his family were not certain at all that Fortune had really apologized, but they dared not argue further with the duchess of Glenkirk. The girl was not at all suitable for their young John, they silently decided. She was much too pretty, and far too bold. Undoubtedly she would come to a bad end. They were not unhappy in the least when their guests announced they would seek their beds.

Rory Maguire, Adali, and Rohana had been grudgingly served a meal in the kitchen of the great house. The servants were suspicious of the Irishman, and his two foreign-looking companions. After they had eaten they were told that Rohana could go with her mistress, but the two men would have to sleep in the stables.

"Master don't allow the likes of ye in the house," the cook said grimly. "We'd all be murdered in our beds!"

"I doubt there is any man who would even get close to *that* woman's bed," Adali said humorously as he and Rory found a spot for themselves in the stable loft. He spread his cloak upon the sweet-smelling hay and sat down. "I've slept in worse places," he decided.

"I, also," Rory agreed, laying his own garment upon the hay. He stretched out, and then said, "She looks happy."

"She is," Adali said.

"Good."

"You have never married, Master Maguire?" Adali asked.

"Nay," came the answer. "There was no point to it. The lands were no longer mine. I had naught to offer a woman. Children would have but complicated my life for they would be Catholics by faith, Irish by blood, and alien in their own land as long as the English occupy it. I cannot be certain of the future myself. I should not want the responsibility of a wife and children to worry over."

"You have no *need* of a woman?" Adali probed.

"After her?" was the reply.

"It was but one hour of one night almost twenty-one years ago, Master Maguire. Are you telling me there has been no other since?"

"Aye. Oh, once in a rare while I have a bout of lust which is satisfied by a village widow of my acquaintance. She is known for being kind to men like me, but as she is discreet, there is none who would call her a whore," Rory said.

"Can you be as discreet as your widow, Master Maguire?" Adali asked him in all seriousness.

"Of course!" Rory exclaimed. "Have I not always been? I know she knows nothing of what happened. I would not distress her."

"Good. She thinks of you as her friend, Master Maguire," Adali told him. "I believe you would not want to lose that friendship. She loves James Leslie, and he loves her. They have built a good life together in Scotland with their children."

"You need not fear, Adali," Rory Maguire said, and there was a dark hint of sadness in his voice. "She never saw me as anything other than a friend. It is the best I can hope for. I will not lose even that small part of her attention on a foolish hope and dream that will never, ever be. Nay, Adali. I would give my life for my lady Jasmine, but she shall never know the part I played in saving her own life all those years ago. It would shame us both."

"Nay, there was no shame, Master Maguire," Adali reassured him. "You, the priest, and I did what had to be done. No more than that. There is no disgrace in it, nor should you feel guilt. Good night now. I will see you in the morning."

"Good night, Adali," Rory Maguire said quietly, rolling himself onto his side, wrapping his cloak about him. Then he thought that the next few months would be the hardest of his life.

Chapter
2

They departed the Appleton estate even before the sun was up. Their hosts were still abed, but they were anxious to remain not a moment longer than was necessary.

"Please tell your master," the duke of Glenkirk instructed the butler, who himself was but barely awake, "that we thank him for his hospitality, but our journey is a long, tedious one. If we are to reach its end by sunset today, we must depart earlier than would be expected."

The butler bowed low, as obsequious as his employer. "Very good, my lord. Sir John will be sorry he had not the opportunity to bid you a proper farewell himself," he replied smoothly.

"He is excused," James Leslie said grandly with a wave of his gloved hand. Turning, he shepherded his wife and stepdaughter from the entrance hall out into the damp and foggy morning.

The coach carrying Adali, Rohana, and their small bit of luggage had already departed. Rory Maguire stood waiting, holding the horses. They mounted quickly and cantered down the gravel drive away from Appleton Hall.

"Good riddance!" James Leslie said.

"Aye, and amen to that, my lord," Maguire responded.

The morning brightened, and the fog slowly lifted, but there was no sun, and it rained once again. Strangely the gray only made the countryside greener by comparison. The green hills over which they traveled rambled gently. The rolling landscape was broken only rarely by a gray stone tower, usually in a state of ruin, or a small village. There were fewer villages, Jasmine noted, than when she had first come to Ireland. Some were deserted and falling into decay; others were gone entirely, their former existence attested to only by a broken and pulled-down Celtic cross in a weed-strewn square. Ulster, never heavily populated to begin with, was now even less populated it appeared.

"What has happened here?" Jasmine asked Rory Maguire.

"Not all landlords are like you, my lady," he replied. "You know the penalties placed upon those who follow the Catholic faith. Many have been driven off their lands because they will not convert to Protestantism. It is that simple."

"But these landlords are not even in Ireland," Jasmine said. "What difference does it make to them as long as the land is worked properly and is prosperous for them?"

"They appoint agents who follow the letter of the law," he explained. "Most are English as are the settlers. We have Scots landlords too, but for now the Scots remain in Scotland, except for those who are able to give up their clan ties to seek lands of their own."

"What happens to the people?" she queried him.

"They go to relations in parts of Ireland where the laws are not so assiduously followed. They flee into the more remote regions, living a more primitive existence. They die. A few emigrate to France and Spain. There are no other choices."

"It is the way of the world," Fortune said quietly, surprising them. "I have learned this in my studies, and Mother has often said that it is so. One tribe conquers another, and another, and so forth. Nothing remains the same forever. Like my mother, however, I see no necessity for what is happening in Ireland. Bigotry is wrong, and it is cruel."

"There's just as much of it on one side as the other," Rory told the girl. "At Maguire's Ford we are fortunate to have two men of religion who are liberal and open-minded, but such a thing is unique. For as many Protestant ministers who tell their flocks that Catholicism is a wicked, idol-worshipping faith, there are an equal number of Catholic priests howling that the Protestants are dirty heretics who ought to be burned, and if not here on earth, then surely in hell, for they are the devil's own spawn. Such thoughts do not lead to understanding, or tolerance, my lady. There are, I fear, and am sorry to say, far more John Appletons upon this earth, than people like yer mam."

"You like my mother, don't you?" Fortune observed, moving her gelding next to his.

His heart contracted in his chest, but Rory Maguire flashed her a casual grin. "Aye, my lady, I do. I always have. It must be the Irish in her for she's got a big heart, does the lady Jasmine."

"My mother says if I remain in Ireland I should keep you on because you can be trusted, and few men can," Fortune said.

"Perhaps yer husband will have other ideas, lady," he replied.

Fortune looked at him as if he had lost his mind. It was a look he recognized, but it was certainly not her mother's look. "My husband will have no say in the management of Maguire's Ford," Fortune said. *"If* I marry William Devers, he will not be in possession of my lands. He has his own. The women in my family do not give over their wealth to the men they wed. It is unthinkable!"

He laughed aloud. "Yer mam has raised you well, my

lady Fortune," Rory Maguire said, vastly amused, but also relieved when she continued.

"If I wed William Devers, you will retain your place, Rory Maguire," Fortune said. "Besides, I will need you to teach me all about the business of the horses. I know little about horses but that I like them very much and enjoy riding them."

"You know how to talk to the horses," he said. "I saw how you conversed with Thunder before you got on his back. Who taught you to do that, my lady Fortune?"

Fortune looked puzzled a moment, and then she said, "No one, Rory Maguire. I have always done it before mounting a strange beast. It only seemed polite. My sister and brothers make fun of me for it, but I've never been thrown, or had any difficulty since my very first pony." Fortune explained to him.

"Ahh, now that's the Irish in you," he said with a smile.

"I like you, Rory Maguire," Fortune told him.

"I like you, Lady Fortune Mary Lindley," he answered her.

"How do you know my full name?" Fortune was surprised.

"Do you not know, my lady, that I am your godfather?" he replied.

"You are? Mama," Fortune called to her mother who was riding just behind her. "Is that true? Is Rory Maguire my godfather?"

"Aye," Jasmine said. "He is."

"Then," said Fortune emphatically, "I shall call you Uncle Rory, and you will call me Fortune when we are in private, *en famille."*

He turned his head to catch Jasmine's eye, and she nodded just barely. "Very well, Fortune," he agreed, his heart warmed by her generosity and her charm. This was no proud m'lady. The people of Maguire's Ford would take to her without question, and they would be able to continue in their

peaceable ways provided that William Devers did not interfere with his bride's authority. Rory wondered how the
young man would take to the notion that Fortune would control her own lands and her own wealth. If Rory knew
Jasmine, the bridegroom would sign a legal document before he took a step down the aisle to claim the flame-haired
beauty.

The rain gradually slipped away, and by the time they had
stopped to rest the horses and eat a bit of bread and cheese,
the sun was shining. From the look of the sky it would be
sunny the rest of the afternoon, Rory decided. Looking
about him he saw several familiar landmarks, and realized
that because of their early start they would reach Maguire's
Ford by midafternoon. Surreptitiously he watched the by-
play between Jasmine and James Leslie. They were so
openly and plainly in love with one another that he felt ac-
tual physical pain in his heart. Whatever he had said to Adali
last night, whatever he said to Father Cullen Butler, there
had always been one tiny secret place within him that yet
hoped she would love him. Now he could see quite plainly
that it would never be. The knowledge was as if something
had died within him at that same moment. He sighed deeply
and audibly.

Hearing the sound Fortune, who was sitting next to Rory
Maguire in the grass, turned. "What is the matter, Uncle
Rory?" she said. "That is the saddest sound I have ever
heard." She laid her head upon his shoulder and took his
hand in hers. "Do not be sad."

Her compassion quite took him by surprise. He felt his
eyes filling with tears which he quickly blinked back. "Ahh,
lassie, we Irish are oft-times subject to black moods that come
suddenly upon us." He gave the elegant little hand holding
his a small squeeze. "It's all right, and now if you are ready
we should be going." He arose and drew her up. "You were
such a wee babe, Fortune Mary Lindley, and now what a fine
lady you have grown up to be."

"I wondered where those dark humors came from, Uncle

Rory. I get them too. That, also, must be the Irish in me," Fortune said. "For a girl whose father was English, and whose mother is a mixture of English and Mughal, I seem to have a lot of my Irish great-grandmother in me," the girl chuckled.

They rode on at a more leisurely pace now, the coach lumbering along behind them. The afternoon was bright, the sun warm upon their backs. Finally they topped a hill. Below was a long stretch of blue water which Rory told Fortune was upper Lough Erne, even as Jasmine explained to her husband. The upper and lower loughs divided the area which was known as Fermanagh, running the length of it before it became the river Erne, which emptied into Donegal Bay at Ballyshannon.

Rory pointed, saying as he did, "There is Maguire's Ford below us, and there on the lough, Erne Rock Castle, where I hope you will want to make your home, Fortune."

"Look in the meadows below, poppet," Jasmine said to her daughter. "See our horses, and look! Sheep. I see the breeding stock we sent from Glenkirk took, Rory."

"Aye, my lady, they did," he replied.

They rode down the hill and into the village. Ahead of them a pack of little boys raced, calling to the villagers in both Irish and in English, "They're coming! They're coming!" People began to appear from out of the cottages and the fields, lining the road to see the absentee landlord of Maguire's Ford, returned after twenty years.

Spotting a familiar face, Jasmine drew her horse to a stop. "Bride Duffy!" She slid from her mount's back and hugged her old friend.

"*Cai mille failte!* A thousand welcomes," Bride Duffy said, her honest face wreathed in a broad smile. "Welcome back to Maguire's Ford, my lady Jasmine!"

The two women embraced again, and then Jasmine drew Fortune forward. "Here is your goddaughter, Bride Duffy. Make your curtsy, Fortune."

Fortune curtsied before the red-cheeked country woman. "How d'ye do, Mistress Duffy?" Fortune said, and met the woman's gaze with her own. "I am pleased to meet you at long last."

"Bless yer heart, m'lady," Bride replied, "and pleased I am to remake yer acquaintance for you were just a wee babe in nappies when I saw ye last." She hesitated just a brief moment, then hugged the young girl. "Now yer back to where you first saw the light of this harsh world, and come to marry, or so I am told."

"Only if I like him," Fortune said quickly.

Bride Duffy chuckled. "Just like her mam, she is."

"Both my daughters have minds of their own," Jasmine said. "Come, Bride, and meet my husband, James Leslie." She drew her friend over to where the duke now stood, and introduced them.

Finally Rory was able to draw Fortune and the Leslies away so they might see the castle. The coach carrying Adali and Rohana had already gone ahead. Erne Rock Castle was set upon a small headland and surrounded by water on three sides. It was almost three hundred years old. To gain entrance one crossed a drawbridge that lay over a moat, which was actually a part of the lough that had been dug out on the land side, and lined with large stones to keep it from collapsing. With its drawbridge raised, Erne Rock was an invincible fortress, small though it was.

They walked their horses across the drawbridge, and upon entering the courtyard they were greeted by several stable lads who took their mounts. Fortune looked about her in order to get her bearings. There were the stables, and there a gatehouse. The courtyard was paved in large flat stones, and not particularly large. She followed her mother up a small flight of steps. There was a red rosebush at the foot of the stairs, growing up from an open flower bed. Fortune cupped one of the roses in her hand and sniffed appreciatively. Then she hurried after Jasmine.

Inside, Erne Rock Castle was a warm and friendly place. There were stone floors on the main level and beautifully polished wooden floors on the upper level. The Great Hall

had two fireplaces alight with bright fires this May afternoon. It was not a large room at all, being no bigger than the
family's private hall at Glenkirk, Fortune noted. There was a
tapestry depicting St. Patrick driving the snakes from Ireland
on one wall. The furniture was of glowing golden oak. There
was a paneled and well-stocked library on the main floor as
well as a room that Rory used to conduct estate business.
The kitchens were located behind and below the Great Hall.
On the second floor of the castle there were several bed-
rooms, each with its own fireplace.

Jasmine opened the door to the large bedchamber, and
stepped back so her daughter might look inside. "Here is
where you were born," she said softly. "Madame Skye's sister, the doctor nun, Eibhlin, delivered you into this world.
You were the hardest of my babies, and were turned about
the wrong way. I wagered Mam a gold piece that you were a
boy."

"Were you disappointed?" asked Fortune, who had never
heard this story before.

"Nay," Jasmine replied. "How could I be? You were a perfect little girl with your grandfather's mole just below your
left nostril above your lip. But more important, you were
your father's last gift to me, Fortune, and I loved him very
much. You, India, and Henry were all I had left of Rowan
Lindley, along with some sweet memories. It was the greatest legacy I have ever received."

"What happened to my grand-aunt Eibhlin?" Fortune
wondered. "Is she still alive? Could we go and see her?"

Jasmine smiled. "Nay, poppet. Eibhlin O'Malley, God assoil her good soul, died almost two years after you were
born." She wiped the tear that had come to her eye, for
thinking of Eibhlin made her think of her grandmother.
Ireland, Jasmine decided, made her sad. Catching herself she
said, "This will be your room now, poppet, for it is the chamber belonging to the head of the household."

"I am not the mistress of Erne Rock Castle yet, Mama,"
Fortune responded. "You and Papa take this room. I want one

that overlooks the lough. *If* I take William Devers for my husband, then after we are wed I shall move into this room, but not now, Mama."

"You are sure?"

"Aye," Fortune replied, and then her look grew distressed. "Will it upset you, Mama, to share a room with Papa that you once shared with my father? Would you prefer to be in another chamber?"

"Nay, poppet," Jasmine told her daughter. "I have happy memories of your father here, but sad ones as well. Perhaps being with my Jemmie will erase those unhappy recollections, and I will come to recall Erne Rock only as a happy place, for you were born here, and will be wed here as well. My grandchildren will be born at Erne Rock."

"Perhaps," Fortune said.

Jasmine took her daughter by the hand, and together they sat upon the chamber's large bed. "Poppet, I have sensed a reluctance in you from the beginning regarding this marriage. It is natural for a maiden to be hesitant when facing her wedding, but I feel it is more than that with you, Fortune. What bothers you, my daughter?"

"You and Papa keep saying that I don't have to wed this William Devers if I do not like him. Yet at the same time you speak as if it is just a matter of time before we meet and are married. I am not you, Mama. I do not want my husband chosen for me. I want to choose my own husband! You have brought me from my home to a strange place, and you expect me to marry a stranger. What if I *really* don't want to marry William Devers? What will happen to me then?" Fortune's blue-green eyes were troubled.

"If you really do not like this young man," Jasmine answered her, "then that will be the end of it, but what makes you think you won't like him? Is it only because you do not know him? Fortune, it is true that my father, the Mughal, chose my first husband for me. I did not not see Prince Jamal Khan until the hour in which we were wed. My parents chose wisely, however, and I was happy with him. My grandmother chose your father, although I did know him beforehand; and old King James chose your stepfather, whom I also knew. Sometimes your elders know better, Fortune, but if you truly dislike this young man, you do not have to marry him. Neither Jemmie nor I want you unhappy."

"None of us knows this William Devers," Fortune said darkly.

"My cousin, Father Cullen Butler, knows of him. The Reverend Mr. Steen knows him. They feel he is a most suitable and eligible candidate for your hand, poppet. Perhaps he is, and perhaps he isn't. Only time will tell. We shall see what we shall see," Jasmine told her daughter. "However, since his family has been approached, it is only proper that we give this young man a fair hearing."

"Aye," Fortune agreed, although not enthusiastically.

Jasmine stood up. "Come, and let us join the gentlemen down in the hall. I imagine that my cousin has arrived by now."

Together mother and daughter descended, coming into the hall arm in arm. Rory Maguire and James Leslie stood speaking with a white-haired priest in his black robes. Jasmine broke from her daughter's side, and hurried forth.

"Cullen Butler! Ohh, I am so happy to see you again! And looking so well, too. Thank you for helping to keep the peace at Maguire's Ford." Putting her arms about her cousin, Jasmine kissed him on both cheeks.

"And look at you, Yasamin Kama Begum," he said. "Yer as beautiful as ever, and you the mother of a houseful of children," he told her, hugging her back, his blue eyes sparkling with pleasure.

"And a grandmother too, Cullen. A little boy named after Rowan, and a baby girl, Adrianna," Jasmine said, smiling.

The priest's eyes went to Fortune, his heart leaping at the sight of her flaming red hair. His face, however, was a mask of calm and welcome. "And this must be Lady Fortune Mary, whom I baptized myself all those years ago. Welcome back to Ireland, my child."

Fortune curtsied, smiling at Cullen Butler. In him she sensed a friend, and an ally. "Thank you, Father."

He raised her up, and kissed her soundly on her cheeks. "Cousin Cullen when we are *en famille,* my child. Well, you surely have grown since last I saw you. And hair like your great-great-grandmother O'Malley, a Scots lass from the Isle of Skye, you have. I never knew her for she died before I was born, but she had hair like a flame, they said."

He is yet quick and clever, Adali thought, standing at the edge of the hall. Madame Skye would be pleased, but then she chose him herself all those years ago, and sent him out to India to watch over my mistress. Still he has put it into their heads that Lady Fortune's hair is a family trait even though none of her siblings, or cousins, have tresses of such an outrageous color. He smiled to himself, satisfied.

"I should like to meet the Reverend Mr. Steen," Jasmine said.

"I invited him to come with me and greet you," the priest replied, "but he felt we should be allowed a small time for a family reunion. He will come tomorrow."

"And the Deverses? When are we to meet them?" Jasmine continued.

"Next week. They have been invited to come and stay for three days so the young people may see if they like one another," Cullen Butler said. Then he turned to Fortune. "Are you anxious to meet yer intended, my child? He's a handsome fellow, I can tell you," he chuckled.

"He is not my intended until I decide if we like one another, and will suit," Fortune responded. "I won't marry a man I can't love."

"Nor should you, lassie," the priest said. "Marriage is a wonderful sacrament, and should be treated with respect, Fortune Mary. Still, I like what I hear of young Master Devers, and I believe you will too."

"Poppet, go with Adali. He will show you the rest of the castle," Jasmine said. "If it becomes yours, then you should know everything you can about it." She waved her daughter off with her faithful servant.

"She's hesitant, and 'tis natural, of course," the priest noted. "How old is she now?"

"Twenty this summer," Jasmine told him.

"A bit long in the tooth to be playing the reluctant virgin," muttered the duke of Glenkirk. "She should hae been wed several years ago, and would hae been but for her obstinate older sister."

"Now, Jemmie, you promised us you would not fuss with Fortune. If you do you will only make her dig her heels in harder. If she and William Devers do not suit it will be unfortunate, but hardly the end of the world, my darling." Jasmine laughed. "There is a man out there in the world who is just right for Fortune, and she will find him in her good time. Of that I am certain."

"Yer beginning to sound more like yer grandmother every day," James Leslie grumbled. "In this day and age a maid must have a husband. We've found her a perfectly respectable young man from a good family, who, I am told, is handsome and well formed; and who is to have a respectable inheritance one day. She's lucky the lad will consider someone as old as she is. Twenty is practically past time to wed."

"Bridal nerves," Cullen Butler assured the duke. "Once she meets with young William she will be reassured, my lord. I guarantee it."

"Rory?" James Leslie looked to the estate manager for some sort of confirmation and reassurance.

"I've heard nothing bad about him, my lord. His mother rules the roost up in Lisnaskea, I'm told, but the young couple will be living here at Erne Rock. He's a fine lad, they say, although I prefer his elder brother myself," Rory Maguire told the duke.

"Elder brother? I was told this William Devers is his father's heir. If he has an elder brother, how can this be?"

"The older brother has been disinherited, my lord," Rory said.

"Why?"

"He is a Catholic, my lord," came the explanation.

"How awful!" Jasmine exclaimed.

" 'Tis the world in which we live," the duke said darkly. "That such a thing should be allowed in our time, and yet it is."

"Even here in Ireland, and especially here in Ulster," the priest said quietly, "we are discriminated against and hounded. The penalties are the same here as in England. Catholics cannot hold public office except in the House of Lords."

"But that is because they cannot in good conscience take the oath of supremacy to the king for they cannot acknowledge him as head of the church in England," Jasmine put in.

"Mass cannot be heard in public, nor can anyone harbor priests," Cullen Butler quickly countered. "Do you not pay the fines to the crown for us here in Maguire's Ford? We would be driven away otherwise. I make certain my people attend Reverend Steen's services several times a month to ease suspicions that we are a nest of traitors here. Failure to take communion on important feast days is subject to a fine of twenty pounds. Three such offences are considered treason."

"You know the reason for that," Jasmine spoke up. "Grandmama herself was in Paris with Grandfather Adam in 1572 when the St. Bartholomew's massacre occured. Pope Gregory XIII openly rejoiced in Rome when he learned of it, and held a public procession of priests and cardinals to celebrate the death of those poor Protestants. Why, he publicly encouraged the murder of good Queen Bess. He even offered absolution in advance to anyone who would assassinate her. Then in 1605 a group of foolish English Catholics plotted to blow up the Houses of Parliament while old King James was speaking. Still, I do not believe that the Catholics should be so penalized and persecuted for the sins of a few fanatics," Jasmine concluded.

"In that, Cousin," the priest chuckled, "I concur, and I know I speak for my whole flock when I say, thank you."

The next few days were quiet ones as Jasmine, James, and Fortune recovered from their journey from Scotland. Fortune explored the estate alone and with Rory Maguire. There would be no changes, she quickly decided, at Maguire's Ford for she liked the Irishman and the way he managed the estate. They seemed to have a great deal in common, particularly their love of the horses. It seemed to her as if they had known each other their whole lives.

On Monday morning the Reverend Mr. Samuel Steen arrived at Erne Rock to greet its mistress, and the bride-to-be. He was a tall man with fine gray eyes. His deep brown hair was peppered with bits of gray as was his imperial, a small tuft of beard that grew from his round chin. His voice was deep and resonant. "Good day, my lady," he said, bowing to Jasmine.

"I am pleased to finally meet with you, Reverend Steen," Jasmine told him. *"Steen.* It is an odd name, sir, although I certainly mean no offense to you. Please, sit with me by the fire on this damp day."

Samuel Steen accepted her gracious invitation. "The name Steen is from Hainault, my lady. My family, who were master weavers by trade, came to England over three hundred years ago as part of Queen Philippa's dowry. There were several families of weavers who came. It was our task to set up a commercial weaving industry for England so its wool would not have to be sent abroad to be woven into cloth. We left England some years ago, and went to Holland because we were being persecuted for our religion. Ten years ago we were offered the opportunity to go to England's colonies in the New World, but alas, our ship, the *Speedwell,*

sprang a leak. We had to put into an English port. We were
then offered the chance to come to Ireland, or be returned to
Holland. We chose Ireland. By God's good fortune Master
Maguire was on the docks the day we landed. He offered us
shelter here at Maguire's Ford if we would but keep the
peace with our Catholic neighbors. How could we not
agree? We know persecution far too well. Some of our people, however, could not manage to restrain their prejudice, so
we left them behind. We have never regretted the day we
came here, my lady."

"Nor have I. My cousin, Cullen Butler, has written to me
of how you have begun a small weaving industry here in the
village, and that you have taught your Catholic neighbors
this trade as well. I am very pleased by your initiative,
Reverend Steen. And tomorrow I shall see if you are a good
judge of bridegrooms," Jasmine smiled.

"I have seen the young lady riding with Master Maguire.
She is a pretty child. Young William will make her a fine
husband," he responded, returning the smile.

"If they suit," Jasmine replied. "I am a modern parent,
and will not force my daughter into an unhappy alliance,
Samuel Steen."

He looked a trifle startled, but the Protestant minister said
nothing. He was certain that the young couple would like
each other. Besides, in the end all the parents would have
their way, and the marriage would be celebrated. "Your
daughter is a Protestant?" he inquired.

"She was born here at Maguire's Ford, the posthumous child
of my second husband, and she was baptized by my cousin.
However, she has been raised in England's church," Jasmine
explained.

"Perhaps I should baptize her a Protestant," he suggested.
"Sir Shane and his wife are very strict, and may be upset by
this knowledge, my lady. I mean no offense, you understand."

"One baptism is quite enough for any good Christian,
Samuel Steen," Jasmine told him. "If the fact my daughter

was baptized a Catholic distresses them then perhaps their son is not for Lady Fortune. My daughter is, after all, a great heiress. She can have her pick of husbands. It does not have to be William Devers. It is providential that Fortune considers him at all." She smiled sweetly at the minister.

She was a strong-willed woman, the minister thought, but he was not in the least put off by it. He hoped her daughter was as strong, for Fortune Lindley's future mother-in-law, Lady Jane Anne Devers, was as tenacious as the duchess of Glenkirk. She was an uncompromising Protestant who had already spoken to him about removing the Catholics from Maguire's Ford when her son became its master. Young William, of course, was more flexible, and if the young couple made Erne Rock their permanent home, he would be under his wife's influence rather than that of his mother, which Samuel Steen suspected would be a better thing. He saw no reason to dispossess the Catholics of the village for their religion. Everyone got on well. If there was no one to interfere, they would continue to get on well.

On the morning that the Deverses were due to arrive, Fortune bathed with the help of her new maidservant, Rois, who was Bride Duffy's youngest granddaughter. She was a slender girl of eighteen with dark braids, large blue eyes, and porcelain skin lightly sprinkled with several freckles across the bridge of her nose. Rois was soft-spoken and diffident towards her mistress. Her grandmother had been training her for several months for this coveted position in what was to become Lady Fortune's household.

"Have you ever had a suitor, Rois?" Fortune asked as she stepped from her tub to be enfolded within a soft, warm towel.

Rois blushed prettily. "Kevin Hennessey and I would like to walk out, my lady, but grandmother says we must keep our attention on our positions. In a year, or two, we may be allowed to court."

"What does your Kevin do?" Fortune was fascinated. It would seem that her servant had no more freedom than she had.

"Kevin helps Master Maguire with the horses," Rois said.

"Does he like what he does? Is he good at it?" Fortune probed further. God's bones! Getting information from Rois was like pulling teeth.

"Aye, he loves the beasties, as he calls them," Rois said, warming now to her subject. "And he is very good with them. They say that one day he may take Master Maguire's place, but that, of course, is a very long way off, my lady."

"Have you ever kissed him?"

Rois blushed again, this time a far deeper hue than previously. "Ohh, my lady," she squeaked. "You shouldn't ask me such a thing."

"That means you have!" Fortune pounced. "Good! What is it like to be kissed? I never have, except by my relations. It is far different with a suitor, I expect, isn't it?"

Rois nodded her head, working furiously to dry her mistress. She wasn't quite certain what to say. "When Kevin kisses me," she said, and then quickly amended, "if he did kiss me, my heart beats a tattoo like a drum, and my whole being feels filled with light. It's hard to describe, but it is wonderful. If, indeed, it actually happened."

Fortune giggled mischievously. "That doesn't tell me a whole lot, Rois," she said frankly. "I guess you have to experience a kiss to know what it's like. I wonder how long before William Devers tries to kiss me. I wonder if I will like this kissing."

"Women usually do," Rois replied. Then she slipped a clean chemise over her mistress's head.

"My mother certainly does," Fortune remarked, straightening the lace edging about the chemise's low-cut neckline, and on the balloon sleeves that came just below her elbow.

Rois rolled a pair of cream-colored silk stockings up Fortune's slim legs, gartering them with gold rosettes. Then she helped the girl into several silk petticoats. Next came the outer skirt of heavy deep green silk, the skirt falling in simple folds with its fullness toward the back, and open in the front to display the skirt petticoat of cream and gold brocade.

"Sit down, my lady, and let me do your hair," Rois said. She unpinned the fiery mass from atop Fortune's head and brushed it out vigorously, parting it in the middle, and coiling it into a flat knot at the nape of her mistress's neck. She tied the single lovelock by Fortune's left ear with a pearl-studded gold ribbon. Stepping back she observed her work, and then smiled. "Come on now, and let's get into your bodice, my lady," she said. She helped Fortune into the square-necked green garment, pulling the cloth down firmly so that the lace from the chemise showed; fastening the sleeves, which came to just below the elbow as did its undergarments, at the armscye, drawing down the lace from the chemise sleeves so that they showed. It was a simple gown, but an obviously expensive one. "You do look nice," Rois said with great understatement. "Shall I bring you your jewelry box, my lady?"

"Aye," Fortune said. When the maidservant opened the case, Fortune chose a long single strand of creamy pearls and slipped them over her head. They lay glowing and perfect upon her gown. About her left wrist she affixed a bracelet fashioned of a double strand of pearls. About her other wrist she wore a bracelet of gold links, each of the rounds studded with an emerald. Contemplating her rings Fortune chose a large baroque pearl, a round emerald, and a simple gold ring with the Lindley family crest, two swans with their necks intertwined to form a perfect heart. "There," she said with a small chuckle. "That should be impressive enough for a first meeting."

"Yer so naughty, my lady," Rois giggled, and taking the jewelry case stored it away.

There was a soft tapping upon the door, but before Rois could answer it, the door opened to admit the duchess of

Glenkirk who was garbed in rich burgundy silk, a necklace of pigeon's egg rubies about her neck with matching earbobs that fell from her lobes, several rich bracelets, and her hands heavy with elegant rings. Her hair was done as was her daughter's save that Jasmine wore no lovelock.

"How lovely you look," she complimented both daughter and maidservant with her words. "The green is quite suitable for your hair, eyes, and skin. You have Irish skin like the O'Malleys, poppet. It is very fair."

"Merci, Mama," Fortune replied. "I see you are dressed for battle," she chuckled. "Is it really fair to intimidate poor Lady Jane at our first meeting? The duchess of Glenkirk is really quite grand."

"I have been informed by those who know that Lady Jane is a very intimidating woman, Fortune. I want her to understand that I am even more intimidating, and by inference, that you will not allow yourself to be bullied. It is important to establish these things upon first meeting, else we have a difficult time doing so afterwards. You must remember it is young William you are contemplating marriage with, and not his strong-willed mama. He is, I have been told, a pleasant young man, as is his father. It is your future mother-in-law that we must put in her place today so you do not have any difficulties later on," Jasmine advised her daughter.

"Listen to her ladyship, my lady," Rois said with sudden unaccustomed frankness. "There are rumors even here at Maguire's Ford about Lady Jane Devers, although my grandmam would skin me for saying so."

"What rumors?" Fortune asked.

"They say she hates Catholics, and will not tolerate any about her. Those up in Lisnaskea must hide their faith, or risk losing everything—their homes, their positions, whatever they may be. Her stepson, Master Kieran, is only allowed to remain in the house because his stepmother will not drive him out for fear of a scandal. Sir Shane did disinherit him when he turned twenty-one and refused to convert to

Protestantism," Rois said. "Most believe her influence was responsible for it."

"How is it that Sir Shane's eldest son is a Catholic?" Jasmine queried the maidservant.

"Sir Shane was born into the one true church," Rois said with complete ingenuousness. "His first wife, may God assoil her good soul, was Lady Mary Maguire, a kinswoman of Master Rory's. She had three children before her death. The eldest was Moire, then came Master Kieran, and finally Colleen, who killed her mother in birthing. The older children were six and four when their mother died. Two years later Sir Shane courted and won the hand of Mistress Jane Anne Elliot, the only daughter of a London merchant who had settled in what the English call Derry.

"She was an heiress of some small means, and Sir Shane was attracted by both her fortune and her person. The only condition to the marriage was that Sir Shane convert to Protestantism, and raise his children as such. The poor man wasn't strong in his faith. He had three motherless children. While wealthy in land and cattle, he hadn't the coin his wealthy father-in-law-to-be could supply to restore his tumbledown manse and buy more cattle. He succumbed to their request, was baptized once again, this time by a Protestant minister, and swiftly married.

"Sir Shane's two daughters were easily cajoled into following their father's lead. Moire was eight, and had been her papa's darling. She wanted to please him, and not lose him to her stepmother, although to be fair to Lady Jane, she has been good to her predecessor's children. Little Colleen was but two when her father wed, and knew no better. Lady Jane is the only mother she ever knew. But Master Kieran was six, and as stubborn as his da's prize bull. He had adored his mother. Now he had but two things remaining to remind him of her. A wee miniature he always keeps on his person, and her faith. While his father and stepmother forced him to attend church with them each Sunday, he would sneak away

afterwards to attend the mass being held in secret somewhere in Lisnaskea. It was years before his father and Lady
Jane discovered it. By then he was a young man, and when
they confronted him he did not deny it. From that time on he
would not attend church with them in their Protestant church.

"Lady Jane gave her husband two children. The girl was
born first when Master Kieran was seven. She is called
Elizabeth. Then came Master William the following year.
There were no more children after that. The rumor is that Sir
Shane has a mistress outside of Lisnaskea, one Molly
Fitzgerald, who has two daughters by him, but it isn't dis-
cussed aloud because she's a Catholic. Finally, when Master
Kieran was twenty-one his father gave him an ultimatum.
Give up his Catholicism, or give up his birthright to his
younger brother, William. 'Tis said that the father and son
had such a terrible fight over it 'twas heard all the way to
Ballyshannon, but Kieran Devers refused to give up his faith
for a piece of land. So, the father disinherited him, and made
young Master William his heir."

"Yet Kieran Devers still lives in his father's house?"
Jasmine was curious about such a thing.

"His stepmother would not allow the father to dispossess
the son for fear of what would be said. She wanted it to appear all her stepson's fault. She wanted to be the good and
gentle lady. So Master Kieran lives in his own rooms in a
separate wing of the house. While there are those who are
saddened by the loss of his inheritance, none can say with
certainty that Lady Jane is responsible. It is very important
to the lady how she appears before others," Rois explained.

"Poor Master Kieran has nowhere else to go. His
mother's family are all gone, and the rest of his father's family are over in Donegal. They are hardly known to him, if
they know him at all. While Kieran Devers is proud, he's no
fool. Me grandmam says she thinks he enjoys remaining just
to annoy Lady Jane, who would appear charitable towards
him but is really not. 'Tis said she attempted to stop her husband from settling a sum on his son so that his wicked con-

science might be salved, but Sir Shane would not listen to her then for he, too, cares what people think. The eldest son is in his will, and is given an allowance each year into the bargain. That generous allowance, I am told, comes from the inheritance the lady was bequeathed from her late father. I háve heard it delights Master Kieran to donate a goodly portion of that allowance to the church just to annoy his stepmother." Rois giggled. "I have never seen him myself, but they say Kieran Devers is as handsome as sin, and as wicked as the devil himself to boot. Yet he is kind, and always ready to help those who need it. Mostly our kind who have been driven off our lands for our faith," she said.

"I have never heard you speak so eloquently before," Fortune teased her maidservant.

"There was nothing to say until yer mam asked me," Rois replied.

Jasmine smiled. "You're a practical puss like my daughter, Rois. Bride did well to choose you for Fortune."

The door to the chamber opened again, and the duke popped his head into the room. "The Deverses' coach is just coming through the village," he told his wife. "Come along, or we shall be late, and appear rude. We want to make a good first impression now, don't we?"

"Do we?" Fortune asked mischievously.

"I obviously didn't beat ye enough when ye were a wee lassie," James Leslie responded.

"You didn't beat me at all, Papa," Fortune said, linking her arm through his, and smiling up into his craggy face.

"Well, I probably should have," the duke teased her. He turned to his wife. "Where shall we greet them, madame?"

"In the hall," Jasmine responded. "Adali will escort them in to us. It sets the proper tone, for our rank is far greater than theirs. They should be honored to even be considered as a possible match for our daughter. The more I learn about the Deverses of Lisnaskea, the less certain I am that they are the right family with which to be allied. Perhaps we did not look closely enough back home."

If James Leslie was surprised by his wife's words he gave
no sign of it. The duke knew Jasmine would have her way no
matter what he said, and much of the time she was absolutely correct. "Nothing is signed, or even agreed to yet,"
he told her. "We can change our minds if Fortune does not
like this young fellow, or we decide he is not at all suitable
for her, darling Jasmine."

"I am glad you see it my way, Jemmie," came the reply.

They descended down into the Great Hall even as they
heard the wheels of the coach rumbling into the courtyard
through the open front door. Adali, garbed in his usual white
trousers, tunic, and turban, was awaiting the visitors.
Stepping out onto the portico, he waited until the Deverses
had descended from their carriage and were halfway up the
steps to the house. It was then he bowed deferentially to
them.

"Sir Shane. Lady Jane. Master William. I am Adali, the
duchess's majordomo. You are welcome to Erne Rock
Castle." He turned. "If you will please to follow me. I shall
bring you to the duke and the duchess who are awaiting you
in the Great Hall with Lady Fortune."

Chapter
3

Lady Jane Devers looked sidewise at her husband, and whispered in discreet tones, "She has a brown-skinned foreigner for a servant, Shane? We were not told she consorted with such people."

"If the man holds a position of such importance in the duchess's household, Jane, then he must be a person worthy of her trust, and the duke's," Shane Devers whispered back. "Now shut yer mouth before you destroy William's chances for this marriage. The girl is quite an heiress."

"I was an heiress," came the icy reply.

"Not like this lass," her husband shot back as they entered the Great Hall. He was a tall man with iron gray hair and dark blue eyes. His face was weathered and ruddy from the outdoors, and his big hands those of a horseman.

His wife was petite with fading blond hair and light blue eyes. Her complexion was yet fair, although her rosy cheeks owed much to the artifice of light rouge which she thought made her appear younger. Her gown was old-fashioned, the

bell-shaped ankle length skirt worn over a farthingale with a
wasp waist, and a long pointed stomacher. It was deep blue
in color, and while of an excellent material, Lady Jane, looking at the duchess's gown, saw at once she was at a disad-
vantage. She almost cried with her frustration. Why hadn't
she found out what Lady Leslie would be wearing. But then
she had assumed that coming from Scotland, the lady would
be no more up on the latest fashions than she was.

Seeing the woman's scrutiny Jasmine felt a surge of triumph.
Lady Jane was obviously already intimidated. Excellent! She
had not yet made up her mind about William Devers, but if
he was indeed to be her son-in-law, Jasmine felt they were
already off on the proper foot with his dominating mother.
She smiled graciously. "Welcome to Erne Rock, Sir Shane,
Lady Jane, and young William. May I present to you my
husband, James Leslie, the duke of Glenkirk; and my daughter, Lady Fortune Mary Lindley."

Sir Shane bowed to his host and hostess as did his son,
while his wife curtsied. Their greetings were acknowledged
with a bow and two curtsies in exchange. Then Sir Shane
said, "I thank you for having us, yer grace. I've always been
curious to see the inside of Erne Rock."

"But I understand your late first wife was a cousin of the
Maguire lords of Erne Rock," Jasmine said sweetly.

"Her kinship was closer to Conor Maguire and his ilk, although the Maguires of Erne Rock shared a great-grandfather
with her," he replied.

"Ahh," Jasmine intoned. The she smiled at the handsome
young man by his father's side.

"This is my son, and heir, William," Sir Shane said. His
wife poked him with a sharp finger. "And my wife, Lady
Jane," he finished quickly.

"How d'you do, your grace," Jane Devers said. Then she
turned her gaze on Fortune. The girl was much too pretty,
and in a rather bold way with that bright red hair. Why she
almost looked Irish. "I am pleased to meet you, my dear,"

she said in dulcet tones. "My dear stepdaughter is a Mary also."

"I am not called Mary," Fortune replied. "I am called Fortune, madame, for my mother considered it good fortune that I was conceived the very night before my father was murdered."

Jane Anne Devers caught her breath in sharply. Had the girl no sense of delicacy using a word like *conceived?* Then she caught herself, saying, "Fortune is a unique name, my dear, but if it is what you are used to being called, then we shall call you that."

"I think it's a wonderful name," William Devers said, and then catching Fortune's hand up in his he kissed it. "Your servant, my lady Fortune." He looked up at her, his light blue eyes assessing her, and smiled winningly, showing a row of even white teeth.

"Sir," she answered, assessing him as openly. Blue eyes, and chestnut brown hair with just a hint of gold in it. He was taller than she was which pleased her for she knew she was tall for a girl. His face and his hands were tanned which meant he spent a good deal of time in the open air. He seemed to be well formed and well made.

"I trust I meet with your approval, my lady," he murmured softly so that only she might hear his words.

"You make a good first impression, sir," she told him.

William Devers laughed. He didn't like shy or prissy women, and had been expecting just that sort of creature. That Fortune Lindley was neither pleased him. It was far more fun to tame a wildcat than to be given a sweet kitten for a pet; and as father had always told him, a wife was a pet to be cherished, protected, and trained to her husband's ways. The training, however, was more fun if the lady in question was a spirited lass, Shane Devers said. Fortune Lindley was obviously a fiery filly.

"Let us have some wine to celebrate our meeting," Jasmine said. "Adali, please see a cask of the Archambault red is broached. It has been aging for some years now in the cellars, and should be quite excellent. And bring some sweet wafers as well."

Adali bowed. "Yes, my princess, at once." Then he hurried out.

"Your serving man," Jane Devers said, quite unable to contain her curiosity. "He is a foreigner?"

"Adali has been with me since my birth. He is half-Indian, and half-French, madame. India was the land of my birth. If you consider Adali a foreigner, then you must surely consider me one too, for my father was the ruler of all India, Akbar the Grande Mughal; and my mother was an English noblewoman with Irish roots. She was his fortieth and last wife. I came to England, a widow, when I was sixteen. My second husband was Fortune's father, the marquess of Westleigh, and the duke is my third husband. Our marriage was arranged by King James himself, and our dear Queen Anne, both gone now, God assoil their good souls," Jasmine finished. *There!* That should give my Lady Jane something to chew upon.

But Jane Devers was not that easily cowed. "Three husbands, gracious! I have always felt one was more than enough, madame. How many children do you have besides dear Fortune?" She smiled again at the young woman.

"Well," Jasmine pondered, and James Leslie held his breath seeing the mischievous look in her eye. "Three by Lindley, two girls and a boy; three boys and a girl who died by my Jemmie." She cast her husband a fond look. "And, of course, my son by the late Prince Henry. He was my lover between my second and third husband. A lovely young man, as I recall. Our son, Charlie Stuart, is the duke of Lundy."

"You bore a bastard?" Jane Devers was pale with shock.

"Madame!" Her husband thundered, mortified by her words.

"The Royal Stuarts have always been generous with their favors, haven't they, Jemmie?" Jasmine said brightly. "Besides, no offspring of a Royal Stuart is considered tainted goods.

The king adores his nephew, Lady Jane. Charlie has been welcomed at court since his birth, and treated like any Stuart kin by the royal family. His grandfather was so pleased with his birth—he was the old king's first grandchild—that he said he would raise my grandfather de Marisco's earldom to a dukedom the day Charlie inherited it, and so he did. Ah, Adali. Come, Lady Jane, Sir Shane. Here is the wine which comes from the estate of my grandfather de Marisco's family in France."

William Devers's eyes were dancing with his amusement. He did hope his prospective wife would turn out to be as amusing as her mother. He almost laughed when his mother, forgetting her manners, took the silver goblet offered her and gulped a great swallow even before the toast was offered. He had been trying all his life to disconcert her vaunted self-control, but had been unable to do so. Even his elder brother, Kieran, could not openly irritate her. How absolutely delicious that his future mother-in-law should prove so formidable.

"To the children," Jasmine said, raising her own goblet. "Let us hope this is indeed a match made in heaven."

"To the children," Sir Shane and the duke of Glenkirk echoed.

Jane Devers weakly raised her own goblet. She was suddenly quite unsure that Lady Fortune Lindley was the daughter-in-law she wanted. Her own brother had a lovely daughter, Emily Anne Elliot, who would be just perfect for William. Thank God nothing was signed! There was yet time to prevent her darling boy from being entangled in this dreadful misalliance. No amount of money in the world could make up for a daughter-in-law whose mother had so shamelessly born a bastard. Then she gasped, her hand going to her heart as a priest walked into the hall in the company of the Reverend Mr. Samuel Steen.

"Cousin!" Jasmine called. "Come and take wine with us. You also, Samuel Steen. Adali, two more goblets."

"Cousin? Shane! She called the priest cousin!" Lady Jane whispered frantically to her husband. "If she is a Protestant, how can she have a Catholic priest for a cousin?"

"I was a Catholic before I wed with you, m'dear," he reminded her. "Many of these Anglo-Irish families are made up of both Catholics and Protestants. Do not distress yerself, Jane. Everything I see tells me this is the right marriage for our William. Look, he and the girl are getting along quite well. He'll win her over in no time, m'dear."

"I am not certain now about this girl. Her mother's loose morals give me pause for thought. Perhaps Emily Anne would be a better wife for William. What if this Fortune Lindley is like her mama? I shudder to think of the unhappiness she would cause our son."

"The girl appears lively, I will grant you, but there is nothing wrong with high spirits among the young, Jane," he answered her.

"Why could she not find a husband in England, or Scotland, Shane? Answer me that! Perhaps she already has a bad reputation that we do not know of, here in our little backwater, and will learn about only when it is too late!" She drained her goblet nervously.

"Adali, more wine for Lady Jane," Jasmine chirped.

"Show a wee bit of mercy, lass," James Leslie murmured softly to his wife. "The poor woman hae already been beaten to her knees."

"This is a mistake," Jasmine said. "I don't want my daughter married to *that* woman's son. You don't know what I learned this morning."

"But ye'll tell me, I'm sure," the duke chuckled. "Forget about Lady Jane, darling Casmine, and look to yer daughter. She and young William are getting along quite well. This isn't our decision, it is Fortune's. She's going to be twenty years old in a few months, and hae already turned down half-a-dozen perfectly respectable young men in England and in Scotland. Every one of them was titled! If this is the young man who will suit her, then so be it."

"We shall see what we shall see," Jasmine responded, but her eye had indeed turned to William Devers and her daughter. He looked nothing like his mother but for his light blue eyes. That in itself boded well, Jasmine decided. He had charm, she could see, but then Fortune would not be dazzled by even the greatest charm. Still, he seemed genuine in his interest towards the girl, and Jemmie was right. Fortune had been uncommonly fussy about choosing a husband. I'll buy them a house in England, Jasmine decided. There is nothing that says they must live here at Erne Rock. I'm sure young Master Devers would enjoy living in England. Perhaps somewhere near Queen's Malvern, or by Cadby where Henry makes his seat. I could be certain of seeing them every year, and it would certainly be as simple for me to come to Fortune's lying-ins as it is with India. Yes! I shall give them a beautiful house in England as a wedding present, along with Maguire's Ford.

"Ye hae that look in yer eye," her husband observed. "What are ye about, my darling Jasmine?"

"Nothing," she murmured back. "I am just deciding that I can possibly have my cake and eat it too, Jemmie."

"God help us all," he rejoined.

Jasmine again became the consummate hostess. "Dear Lady Jane," she said, "you know, of course, our good Samuel Steen. And this is my cousin, Father Cullen Butler."

"My lady." The priest bowed politely.

She gave him the barest nod, and then turned her head away.

"And it is good to see you again, Shane Devers," Cullen Butler said, ignoring the woman's snub. He knew of her reputation, and was not in the least offended. How it must pain her to have to sit quietly in the same room with him, he thought wickedly. I must give myself a penance for my mean spiritedness, he considered. Three Aves at most.

"Father," came the greeting from Sir Shane. "I suppose you've seen Kieran recently." It was said almost bitterly.

"I see him," was the answer. No use rubbing salt into that

wound. He wasn't responsible for Kieran Devers's decisions, nor was the church.

"The young people seem to be getting on quite well," the Reverend Steen noted cheerfully.

"Aye," his companions responded.

"They make a handsome couple, don't they?" Reverend Steen said.

More murmurs of assent followed this observation.

"There should be more to a good union than just two pretty faces," Lady Jane said sharply.

"In that I certainly concur," Jasmine agreed.

"Perhaps," Cullen Butler said, "Lady Fortune would like to take Master William for a ride about the estate."

"What a good idea!" Fortune said. Sir Shane seemed pleasant enough, but she did not like Lady Jane for all her sweet speeches. She wanted a chance to be with the handsome William Devers, and see if he pleased her. If there was any spark that might be ignited between them. "Would you like to ride?" she asked him.

"I have no horse," he said. "We came in the coach." He looked disappointed.

"We have plenty of horses," Fortune laughed. "Adali, go and tell the stables we will need two horses. I'll go change into something more suitable. Is it all right, Mama?"

"Of course," Jasmine agreed. She understood what Fortune was doing, and approved.

Fortune dashed from the hall, returning some minutes later to call to William Devers, "Come on, William!" Then she was gone again.

He followed after her, grinning, even as he heard his mother behind him expressing shock at Fortune's garb.

"Your daughter rides astride? *In breeches?*"

He didn't hear the duchess's answer, but suspected it was pithy. He thought Fortune's breeches rather charming. They were not baggy, but rather nicely fitted, revealing her well-shaped legs and bottom. She was also wearing a sleeveless deep blue silk doublet with silver buttons over a white shirt with balloon sleeves. It was all quite fetching.

The stableboy was holding two horses, one a fine dappled gray gelding that Fortune immediately mounted. The other was a tall, big-boned, shining black gelding. William took the reins from the lad, and swung himself up into the saddle.

"His name is Oberon," Fortune told William. "Come on! Follow me!"

He trailed after her out of the castle's small courtyard, over the drawbridge, and through the village, gradually edging his mount up until they were finally riding side by side. "You do not ride a mare?"

"Nay, Rory Maguire, our estate manager, feels Thunder and I are suited to one another. I like a horse with a bit of spirit, and Thunder has a spritely nature. Do you like to ride?"

"Aye, I do. Sitting about pouring over accounts as my father does isn't my idea of great amusement."

"That's why we have an estate manager," Fortune said.

"Aren't you afraid he'll steal from you? After all he is Irish," William Devers said.

"So are you," she replied. "At least on your father's side."

"I have always thought of myself as British," he said.

"You were born in Ireland. You live in Ireland. Your father is Irish. *You are Irish,*" Fortune told him with perfect logic. "Now I, on the other hand, have a slightly more complicated lineage. My father was an Englishman. My stepfather is a Scot. My mother is Indian on her father's side, and Irish, English, and French on her mother's side. I am the niece of the current Grande Mughal, and my Leslie half-brothers are related to the Ottoman sultan. We have extremely knotty, complex, intricate, and elaborate labyrinthine of a family tree, William Devers."

"You are utterly fascinating," he said. "I have never met a girl like you at all. Why do you want to marry me?"

"I don't know if I do," Fortune said honestly. "I have yet to find a man to love, and love I must if I marry. I suppose that all sounds very romantic and silly, but it is how I feel, William Devers."

"I am known as Will to my friends," he said. "I hope you will learn to love me, Fortune, for I think I am already half in love with you. You are so alive!"

"What a lovely thing to say, Will." She smiled at him, and then, "Oh, look! That is the tree from which my mother hung my father's murderer. That very limb up there." She pointed. "They say my mother never flinched but ordered he be hung with my father's belt, and stood watching as he died. He actually meant to kill mama. She and my father were riding, and had stopped to speak with my sister, India, who was only a small girl. She wanted to be taken up on mama's horse, and when mama bent down for her, it was then the shot rang out. My father was killed instead. The men came from the fields and saw the glint of a musket up upon the hill. They ran as fast as they could and captured the culprit. He was the same man mama had dismissed as the estate's agent, and he was bold enough to admit it was mama he had wanted for kill."

"Why did she dismiss him?" William was curious.

"He was cruel and he was bigoted. He had driven mama's villagers from Maguire's Ford because they were Catholic. He planned to populate the place with only Protestants. He thought mama too forward for a woman, and believed my father was bewitched by her."

"You don't approve of driving Catholics away." It was a statement.

"Nay, I do not. Why would you drive decent, hard-working people from their homes based upon their religious preference?" Fortune said.

"They'd murder us given the chance," he replied.

"I know that, but you'd do the same," Fortune told him in exasperated tones. "Do you think I am a dunce, Will Devers? There is anger and bigotry on both sides of the issue. I understand that, but I belive the English would be better off if they just came to Ireland to rule, and left everyone to live in peace, but no. The English must have their way in all things, and so the Irish will resist with all their might. 'Tis madness."

"You think a great deal for a young girl," he noted as they moved away from the hanging tree.

"Do you not approve of a woman being educated then, Will?"

"I have always been taught a woman's place is in the home, supervising her servants, and her children. She is responsible for their welfare, both temporal and spiritual, as well as pleasing her husband in whatever ways he may desire, and making his home a place of peace."

"Does a woman have to be uneducated to do all those things?" Fortune asked him seriously. She glanced over at him so she might see his face when he answered, and know if he was prevaricating.

"My mother has taught my sisters all manner of household duties," he began.

"Can they read? Or do arithmetic? Do they speak other languages than their own? Do they know the history of their country, or where the New World is on a map? Can they look up in the sky at night, and name the stars, Will?" Fortune waited for his answer.

"Why would they need to know these things?" he wondered.

"If you cannot read or write, how can you truly manage your household accounts? If you do not know arithmetic, how can you be certain that your estate manager isn't cheating you? Knowing other languages allows you to speak with the French, the Italians, the Germans. As for the rest, it is simply fun to know these things, Will. Knowledge gives one power. All the women in my family are educated. I intend educating my sons and daughters, too. You read and write, don't you?"

"Of course!" he replied hastily. "But my sisters do not. Mary, Colleen, and Lizzie are all married women. They have no need of an education such as you describe. My mother certainly didn't. She was my grandsire Elliot's only child, and heiress. My father wanted an heiress for a wife because he was poor in monies though rich in land. My grandfather wanted a man with a goodly estate and cattle. That is how matches are made, Fortune. It doesn't matter if the bride is educated or not. It is her property first, and then her charm that win her a husband."

"I still prefer being an educated woman. The women in my family do not have husbands who stray because they are interesting both in and out of the bedchamber," Fortune said proudly. "I hear it said your father has a mistress."

He flushed. "Young ladies should not speak of such things, or even know about them for that matter." Then he chuckled. "You are a most outspoken girl, aren't you?"

"Would you rather I dissemble? Or be coy, and giggle like so many girls on the husband hunt?" she demanded of him.

"No," he said, surprising himself, but he liked her frankness. His mother would not, but then it was not really her choice, it was his. He had never met a girl like Fortune Mary Lindley, and he found he was totally intrigued by her. "How old are you?" he asked her.

"Nineteen," she said. "And you?"

"Twenty-three," he responded.

"See that hill over there?" she said. "I'll race you!" Then she was off on her gelding, dashing across the terrain like some ancient huntress. Her hair came loose from its chignon, and fanned out, blowing wildly in the breeze created by her speed.

He dashed after her. He was not only intrigued, but excited by this flame-haired beauty with her blunt speech. He could hardly wait to bed her on their wedding night, for he had already made up his mind that she would be his wife. Even if she hadn't had a ha-penny to her name he would want her. Perhaps not as a wife under those circumstances, but he would want her.

Fortune made no pretense of letting him win the race be-

tween them. It was not her way. She played to win. Thunder
covered the ground in great bounding strides, but she could
hear the black gelding close behind her. She leaned low on
the horse's neck, encouraging him to even greater speed. The
wind was cool and damp on her face. The day was beginning
to cloud over. It would soon rain, Fortune thought as Thunder
topped the hill only to come face to face with another rider
coming from the other direction. The two horses came to a
quick halt.

"Kieran!" She heard William Devers say behind her as he
topped the hill. "This is Lady Fortune Lindley. Fortune, this
is my half-brother, Kieran Devers."

The horseman, tall, lean, and dark-haired looked her over
boldly. "Yer a proper hoyden if I've ever seen one," he said
reaching out to finger a lock of her blazing red hair.

"And yer a fool I am told," Fortune responded angrily.

He laughed, and then said to William, "Does your mother
approve of her, Willy?"

"She approves of my dowry," Fortune shot back, "but you
get ahead of yourself, *Master* Devers, for no betrothal has
yet been arranged, nor will it be unless I want it to be
arranged."

"Don't wed her, Willy," his elder brother advised. "She's
too much of a handful for you, I can see it." Then he laughed
again at the look of outrage on Fortune's face. "I think your
cousin Emily Anne Elliot will make you a far better wife
than this wildcat."

"Kieran!" William's voice was anguished. He turned to
Fortune, his face flushed with his embarrassment. "My
brother is naught but teasing, Fortune. He has a rather odd
sense of humor. Please forgive him. He means no harm."

"None at all," Kieran Devers agreed, flashing her a
wicked smile. "None at all, m'lady Fortune."

She glared at him, and his eyes danced mischievously.
They were dark eyes. *Dark green eyes*. And he was outrageously handsome. Even more so than his younger brother.

He had recklessness about him in comparison to Will's civilized manner. She would have never known they were brothers, half-brothers, she amended to herself. William Devers looked like his father. Tall, well-made, and sturdy with his mother's light blue eyes and chestnut-gold hair. He had an elegant nose, a small mouth, and well spaced eyes set in a round face. But his brother, Kieran, was taller, with a long face, squared jaw, a big mouth, and a nose that appeared to have been hewn out of granite. He was craggy and fierce looking while his sibling appeared the epitome of a civilized gentleman. A man like Kieran Devers was dangerous, and not to be tolerated.

"Kieran, why have you come over?" William asked.

"I thought it might help the cause if we appeared the happy family, and the duke of Glenkirk could see I don't give a damn for our father's lands. They are yours with my blessing, little brother. So, m'lady," he addressed Fortune, "William Devers will not come penniless to the heiress bride. Does that please you?" The green eyes mocked her.

"His wealth means nothing to me," Fortune replied scornfully. "My personal riches could buy and sell the Devers of Lisnaskea several times over. I seek a man to love, you lout!" Then yanking Thunder's head about, Fortune cantered off towards the castle.

"Whew! What a firebrand," Kieran Devers said admiringly. "Yer a lucky man if you can win her, Willy. Red hair and a hot temper! She'll be a tigress in bed, you young devil. I'm not certain you deserve such a prize. Yer mam won't like her. She prefers Emily Anne, I'm sure, but poor Emily Anne isn't enough of an heiress, is she?" He chuckled.

"Fortune's the most beautiful girl I've ever seen; and so damned interesting. She says just what comes into her head," William said.

"I've noticed that," Kieran replied with a small smile.

The two young brothers rode down the hillock and across the meadows back into the village. As they traveled down the main street of Maguire's Ford several young women called out a greeting to Kieran Devers, and he greeted them all by name with a smile and a jest. William raised an eyebrow. He had not been aware that Kieran's escapades, as his mother called them, extended as far as Maguire's Ford. In the castle courtyard Kieran was greeted by a red-haired gentleman.

"Kieran, lad, how are you?" Rory Maguire said. "And this will be yer little brother, I'm thinking. How d'ye do, Master William. I am Rory Maguire, the estate manager of her ladyship, the duchess."

"Rory, yer looking well as ever, and aye, 'tis young Willy," Kieran Devers replied as he dismounted his horse.

"You were not in the hall earlier," William said.

"Nay, sir, I wasn't. 'Twas out of respect for your mother's feelings, for we all know how she feels. I felt Lady Jasmine's cousin, Father Cullen, would be just about all she could handle." It was said with good humor, and a twinkle.

William Devers laughed. "Aye," he agreed. He decided he liked this Maguire fellow. Of course his mother had said that once he was master at Erne Rock, his cousin, James Dundas, would be a suitable estate manager, and James was a good Protestant. Still, Fortune had given him pause for thought when she had asked him why anyone who did their job properly should be discriminated against for their religion. Besides, James Dundas knew nothing of horses, and indeed, was afraid of them. He would make a poor manager for a horse breeding estate. William slid from his saddle, saying as he did so, "Come on, Kieran, and let us surprise mother." Then he laughed again.

Jane Anne Devers was indeed surprised to see her stepson enter the Great Hall in his half-brother's company. Still, he was dressed respectably, and appeared in a good mood. She hoped he had not come to cause any deviltry. "Kieran dear," she twittered as he approached her.

"Madame, you are as lovely as always," Kieran Devers told Lady Devers as he bowed and kissed her hand. Then he turned, and bowed quite beautifully to the duchess of

Glenkirk who was sitting with his stepmother. "I am Kieran Devers, your grace. I hope I am not intruding, but my curiosity was, as always, too great. I came to lend my brother, William, support in his pursuit of your beautiful daughter, whom I have just met a while ago." He kissed Jasmine's hand.

"You are most welcome at Erne Rock, Kieran Devers," she replied. "Adali, bring Master Devers a goblet of wine. You will join us, sir?" She motioned him to a seat by the fire. He's a handsome devil, Jasmine thought. What mischief is he up to, or is he indeed just curious? She smiled at Kieran Devers. "Have you ever been to Erne Rock before? I understand your mother was a Maguire before her marriage to your father."

"This is my first visit," Kieran replied. "Thank you," he said to Adali who offered him a goblet from a tray.

"We met Kieran out riding," William said.

"He has already explained that, dearest," Lady Jane said patiently. Lord! Did William have to appear such a dunce before the duchess? "I am certain he cannot stay, especially now that his curiosity has been satisfied. Where is Fortune?"

"Nonsense! Your stepson must stay at least the night," Jasmine replied. "I have always been famed for my hospitality, my dear Lady Jane. It will be lovely to have a family party. Later, I hope to meet your daughters too."

"Only Colleen is in Ireland," Lady Jane said. "Mary and my Bessie are in England where their husbands reside. Colleen lives outside of Dublin in the Pale. Her husband has a small estate there. She is the only one who will be able to come for the wedding."

"*If* there is a wedding," Jasmine amended.

Kieran Devers saw his stepmother pale slightly. So, it was not the sure thing Jane Anne Devers had bragged it was. Interesting. Still, the girl was extremely desirable for her wealth, not to mention her beauty; but Jane Anne had been certain the only reason the Leslies would come to Ireland seeking a husband for their daughter was that she was unmarriageable in England for some reason. After all, according to his stepmother, an English husband was the most desirable husband of all. She had managed English marriages for his elder sister, Moire, who she had called Mary since the day she wed his father; and for her own daughter, Bessie. Colleen, however, had alluded her, falling in love with Sir Hugh Kelly. Hugh, however, had an English mother, and was a Protestant, and so Jane Anne had acquiesced gracefully to one Irish marriage.

"Of course there will be a wedding," William said with a smile. "I intend winning Fortune fairly and squarely. She is a wonderful girl, and I already adore her!"

"Who do you adore?" said Fortune, coming into the hall in a fresh green gown, her hair neatly contained within a pretty golden snood.

"Why you, naturally," William said ingenuously.

Fortune smiled. "You are a fool, Will Devers," she chided him, but her tone was soft, Kieran noted.

That's it, little brother, use your charm on her, he thought. But then as he looked at Fortune Lindley again, the hoydenish and disheveled look gone, to be replaced by an elegant young girl, he thought suddenly that she was far too much for his younger brother. Any marriage between them would force Willy into an untenable position. He would be caught between his strong mother, who had told him what to do and to think his whole life, and a headstrong young wife who obviously ran her own life, and would expect to run his as well. The resulting war between the two women would kill his half-brother, who was really a very nice young man.

Ah, the voice within him said, so that will be your reason. Admit it, Kieran Devers, you're intrigued by the wench, and would like her for yourself. Why you'd have her if she had nothing but her shift to her name. But she doesn't, does she? She's an heiress, and probably thinks herself too good for the likes of you. Fortune Lindley is a proud bitch, but a romantic one. She told you herself she would wed only for love, and no other reason, the voice within said. But he, having lit-

tle, could never wed an heiress. Other men would, but if
Lady Fortune Lindley was prideful, so was Kieran Devers.

"William's brother is going to remain the night, and
visit," Jasmine said to her daughter. "Isn't that nice, poppet?"

Fortune said nothing, but she smiled weakly. The look in
her eyes said she didn't think it nice at all. How dare this in-
terloper push himself into their little group when she was attempting to know more about Will? Fortune was not happy.
William Devers seemed a nice young man, but he had such
old-fashioned ideas, a dreadful mother, and a rogue for a
brother. He didn't set her pulses racing as she had expected
the love of her life would. His older brother aroused more
feeling in her breast than did Will.

Fortune gasped. God's nightshirt! She stole a look at
Kieran Devers, and to her great mortification he met her eye
and winked. She felt the heat suffuse her cheeks, and quickly
lowered her head. This was impossible! Kieran Devers was
highly unsuitable and worse, he was a practicing Catholic.
Will Devers was far more eligible as a husband. He would inherit his father's lands and chattels one day; and if he was a
bit old-fashioned, she would influence him to be less so.
There was no one she cared for at all in Scotland or England.
She was going to be twenty in a few months. If not William
Devers, then who, Fortune wondered? Certainly not that
dark-eyed devil who was his half-brother.

Kieran Devers was not a reliable man, she was certain.
After all, he had given up his position as his father's heir
simply over the matter of religion. What sort of a man was
that big a fool? *An honest one,* a little voice in her head said.
That may be, Fortune thought, but I don't want an exciting
life where I never know what one day will bring. That's the
kind of life a woman would lead with Kieran Devers. I want
stability, not adventure.

"Mama, may Will sit next to me at dinner tonight?"
Fortune asked her mother in sweetly appealing tones. The

sooner she could get over her reticence about William Devers, the sooner they could be wed.

"Of course," Jasmine said, and wondered what it was all about. She had seen Kieran Devers flirting with Fortune, to Fortune's dismay. Then her daughter's face had grown contemplative. What had she been thinking about, Jasmine considered. Then she decided if Fortune were forcing herself to make a match with William when she really wasn't certain, it could only lead to her daughter's unhappiness.

I shall sit William on Fortune's right, and Kieran on her left, Jasmine silently decided. Fortune had recently said she would wed only for love, although there had been a time when her ideas were more sanguine about marriage. What had happened to her practical, sensible child? Still, better love with the wrong man than an unhappy eternity with the right one. If Fortune was attacted to Kieran, better she face it now, and not marry young William because he was the *right* choice. Her daughter could be stubborn. Besides, and Jasmine smiled to herself, a rascal made a far more interesting lover than a proper gentleman. I can't allow her to make a mistake, Jasmine decided. *I can't!*

Of course if Jemmie discovered what was going on he was going to be furious despite his promise to allow Fortune her own decision. She would have to keep the truth from him as long as possible. "Adali," she called to her majordomo. "Put Master Kieran's things in with his brother's. They can share a room and a bed. I'm certain they've done it before. Erne Rock is so small, but it's a wonderful place for a young couple, and their children. Don't you think so, Lady Jane?"

"I had thought William and his wife would live with us at Mallow Court. After all, it is to be William's estate one day, isn't it, Kieran?"

"Indeed, madame, it is," he agreed cheerfully.

"If there is a wedding," Jasmine said, again striking a little bit of fear into Lady Devers's heart. "I think the young couple should have their own home. Fortune should not have

to live with her husband's relations. She will have Erne Rock
in Ireland, and of course, the duke and I intend seeing she
has a suitable house in England, either near her brother's seat
at Cadby, or her half-brother's seat at Queen's Malvern." She
smiled brightly. "We will want to introduce them into the
court."

"Mama, you know I hate the court," Fortune said.

"But you must make contacts, my darling, if you are to be
successful with your breeding farm," Jasmine reminded her.
"After all, you cannot depend upon your share of the family's trading company for your entire support. You surely
didn't think I meant to bring you to Ireland and leave you
here?"

"I didn't know," Fortune said, puzzled by her mother's
speech.

James Leslie and Sir Shane came into the Great Hall.
They had been closeted in the library discussing the terms of
a settlement should there be a marriage between their children. Kieran Devers arose and greeted his father. Then he
bowed to the duke as his father introduced him to James
Leslie. The duke saw an unrepentant Celt like himself in
Kieran Devers, and immediately liked him. The lad was a
fool, of course, to give up his inheritance for the church, but
one had to admire his faith, and his tenacity in holding onto
what he believed was right.

"Yer content with yer decisions then, laddie?" the duke
said.

"Aye, your grace," Kieran Devers replied, knowing exactly what was being asked of him. "Mallow Court is my
brother's, and I happily cede it to him."

"Yet ye remain." James Leslie was curious.

"For now," Kieran responded. "I feel there is somwhere
else for me in this world, my lord, but I am not certain where
it is at this moment in time. I am satisfied to wait, for in time
I will be led there."

James Leslie nodded. Strangely he understood exactly
what the young man was saying. The Irish were even more

fey than the Scots. If Kieran Devers were awaiting a revelation, then he would undoubtedly get it eventually.

"Dinner is served, my lord," Adali said. "My lady says you are to come to table at once."

"Gentlemen," the duke said, and led his guests to the high board.

Chapter
4

It astounded William Devers to learn how quickly he had fallen in love with Fortune Lindley, but he was certain he was in love. She was the most beautiful girl in the world. He liked her flaming red hair no matter what his mother said, and Lady Jane had a great deal to say when they returned home. She kept her peace in the coach as they traveled around the end of the lough back to Lisnaskea. It was as if she were afraid the duchess would hear her unless she was safely in her own home. William was quite surprised that his mother was so intimidated by Jasmine Leslie. He had found her lovely to behold, and quite charming in her manners.

"I will marry Fortune as soon as possible," William announced to his parents when they were gathered about their own fire that evening.

"No," his mother said, "you will not! She is far too outspoken a female. An educated, overbred bluestocking if I ever saw one. She is not the girl for you. Your cousin, Emily Anne, is far more suitable a match for you, William. She

may not have Fortune Lindley's wealth, but no amount of
monies could make up for having that Lindley girl in our
family!"

"I agree with you, madame," Kieran Devers supported his
stepmother. "For the first time in our acquaintance, I agree
with you."

"You do?" Now Jane Devers was suspicious. "Why on
earth would you agree with me, Kieran? You certainly never
have before, although I did my best to raise you properly despite your Catholic leanings."

He laughed. She had indeed done her duty, at least publicly, as his stepmother, and he had to admit to himself that
she had never been a cruel woman. She could not help it that
she preferred her own son, and had encouraged his father
into disinheriting him so William could someday be the master of Mallow Court. Strangely he had no deep feelings for
his home. It had been no loss. There was something else
awaiting him, somewhere.

"I concur with your conclusions because they are correct,
madame. Fortune Lindley is a beautiful, spoilt wench of great
privilege. She would destroy William without ever meaning
to do so. Cousin Emily Anne, however, loves our Willy, and
has since they were children. She is younger than Lady
Fortune by almost three years. She will be delighted to live
at Mallow Court with you to guide her. Lady Fortune would
not."

"You want her!" William accused his sibling. "You want
her for yourself, Kieran. Don't think I don't see it!" His face
was red with his anger.

"Aye, I'm intrigued, I'll admit, but then wild things have
always fascinated me, Willy. Nonetheless, I doubt the duke
of Glenkirk, with his own royal blood, and close ties to the
king, will be willing to match the likes of me with his beautiful, wealthy daughter. Matches among people of our class
are not made that way. I have nothing to offer any respectable woman as you well know. So though I may desire

her, I shall never have her. And you should not be foolish enough to seek her perfumed little hand."

"Make the offer," William Devers told his father. "Make it, or I shall leave this house forever, and never come back!"

"Dearest." Lady Jane reached out, and touched her son's face, but he shrank back from her.

"I will have Fortune Lindley for my wife. When we are wed, we shall live at Erne Rock, and in England, for that will please her. I shall never set foot in this house as its master until you are dead and gone, madame. You will rule me no more!"

"But you will allow *her* to," his mother snapped.

"She has more to offer me than you do, Mama," he replied with devastating effect.

Lady Jane burst into tears. "She's bewitched him!" she sobbed on her husband's sturdy shoulder. "Or else my son should never speak to me in such a terrible fashion. She has bewitched him!"

"Don't be a fool, Willy," Kieran chided the young man. "This girl is beautiful, it is true, but she is not for you. You have absolutely nothing in common with her that I can think of. What would you talk to her about?"

"Talk? I don't want to talk with her. You damned well know what I want to do with her!" came the angry reply.

"Ohhhhhh!" Lady Jane collapsed against her husband in shock.

Sir Shane swallowed back a chuckle. "Mind yer tongue, you young scamp," he half-scolded William.

But Kieran did laugh, receiving a furious look from his overwrought stepmother. "You've raised him honest, madame," he said shrugging.

"If you truly desire it, William, I will tender an offer to the duke of Glenkirk for his daughter," Sir Shane said to his disquieted son.

"If you do, I shall never forgive you," his equally agitated wife cried out. "She is a dreadful girl! Dreadful! Dreadful! Dreadful!"

"Calm youself, madame," Kieran said, and to her surprise he put an arm about his stepmother in a comforting gesture. "It is highly unlikely that Fortune Lindley will accept Willy's offer, and the choice as we all heard, is hers to make."

Jane Devers sniffed audibly. "Do you really think so, Kieran?"

He squeezed her hand. "I do, madame, I do!"

"You mean you hope," snarled William. "Fortune will be my wife! I will not take no for an answer from her."

"You will have to, you young fool!" his elder sibling shot back. "For God's sake, Willy, if you make a spectacle of yourself over this girl, Emily Anne won't have you at all. Behave like a Devers of Lisnaskea, and not some whining, spoiled English milord!" He turned to his father. "Perhaps, sir, this would be a good time for Willy to visit the Continent, and see how the rest of the world lives."

Jane Devers pulled away from her stepson. "Oh, yes, Shane!" she cried to her husband. "He could go to London first, and see his sisters, and their families. And I will go with you, William! I have not been to London since I was a little girl." She clapped her hands excitedly like a child. "We shall all go! You, too, Kieran." Her heart was overflowing with good will at this moment. It was a most wonderful idea. She would get her son away from Fortune Lindley. When they returned the girl would have undoubtedly gone back to Scotland with her family. *And Emily Anne Elliot would be waiting.* "I'll need a new wardrobe, of course, judging by the duchess's beautiful gown. I wonder if Colleen has a good dressmaker down in Dublin who would be willing to come up to Ulster? I must write her this very day." She hurried from the room.

"Make the offer to the duke," William Devers said, implacably.

Kieran Devers went to the sideboard, and poured out three double drams of peat whiskey into small polished pewter cups. He handed one to his father, and one to his younger brother, keeping the third for himself.

Shane Devers gulped the liquid fire down. It seared his throat as it dropped into his stomach like a hot stone. "Hear me out before I go any further," he said to his heir. "I spoke with the duke the first night we were at Erne Rock. The terms of any marriage agreement between you and Lady Fortune would be very odd to say the least. He tells me this is the standard marriage contract for all the women in his family. You would receive a settlement in gold, to be agreed upon by both families. As for the rest of Lady Fortune's wealth, and lands, they remain in her hands. You would have no say in how she managed her property at all, William."

"But what if she frittered her wealth away as any woman would do given such license? Women do not know how to manage their pin money let alone manage great wealth, Da. Look how Mama always comes to you to wheedle additional coins because she has spent her allowance before the quarter is up," William said.

"Lady Fortune has been managing her own wealth since she was a maid of twelve according to her stepfather. Her great-grandmother taught her how before she died. She was the famous Skye O'Malley, who was old Queen Bess's confidante, if the stories be true. The girl has almost doubled her wealth in the past few years, William. She is no fool.

"Do you think you could marry a woman who would not heed your advice regarding her investments? For after all, William, you know nothing of such things. This girl has grown up in a noble and wealthy family, and she is clever. She would not be content to simply sit at home and manage her household while having your children. I am not over-whelmed by jealousy and wild emotions as is your mama, but I, too, agree with her that this marriage would not be a good thing for you. Still, if knowing what I have just told you you still wish me to approach the duke of Glenkirk with a firm offer, I shall do it, my son."

"Make the offer," William Devers said through gritted teeth.

Kieran shrugged, and poured himself another dram of whiskey. "You want to lie with her, and can think of no other way of doing it than to marry the wench," he said scornfully. "I know a lass who would pleasure you so well you would forget all about Fortune Lindley."

"You want her yourself," his brother repeated angrily.

"If I wanted her, little Willy, I'd take her," Kieran Devers said with brutal frankness. "Virgins don't interest me, however."

"You bastard!" William Devers yelled, and tried to hit his brother, but Kieran was too quick for him, and pinioned the young man's arms to his sides, shaking his head wearily.

"Behave yourself, Willy, or your mama won't take you to London Town," he teased his brother wickedly.

"Leave him be, Kieran lad," their father said to his elder son, "and you," he told the younger sternly, "keep your hands to yourself! I'll not have my sons fighting amongst themselves like savages."

"You'll make the offer?" William demanded, shaking himself free of his elder brother's grip.

"I'll send over to Erne Rock in the morning," Shane Devers promised his heir.

"My lord, this message has just arrived from Mallow Court," Adali said coming into the Great Hall the following morning.

The duke took the folded parchment, and breaking the seal scanned the contents. "They've offered for Fortune," he said. Then he turned to his stepdaughter. "Well, lassie? Will ye hae him, or no?"

Jasmine held her breath.

"I know I should accept him, Papa," she began. "It is the sensible thing to do for I am not getting any younger."

"But ye won't accept him, will ye, lass?" James Leslie said.

Fortune shook her head in the negative. "No, I won't. Poor Will. I know he cares not a whit for my money. He is handsome, and has a nice little estate he'll inherit one day; but Papa, he is the dullest man I have ever met in my entire life. And his ideas about women are positively ancient. They are supposed to stay at home having babies, and listening adoringly to whatever their husbands say. He is ill educated for his class, and does not care. He has no interests at all except riding, but horses are only a means of transportation for him. He is not in the least attracted to the idea of breeding, and raising the beasts for sale. That, he says, is for Maguire to handle. I could find nothing of interest to speak with him about, and Lord knows, I tried. If I must remain a spinster, then I will remain a spinster, but I should rather go to my grave a virgin than wed with such a handsome young dunce!"

Jasmine let her breath out in an audible swoosh. "Thank goodness!" she said. "I was so afraid you would do the *right* thing, poppet, and he would have made you miserable, I fear."

"Very well," James Leslie said with surprising calm, "then what are we to do now?"

"I think we should remain in Ireland for the next few months," Fortune suggested.

"Agreed," Jasmine replied. "And we must make certain that poor young William is not embarrassed by your refusal, poppet. It must be put out that you simply didn't suit each other, but that our families have all remained friends despite our mutual disappointment."

"I concur," James Leslie said. "We will deliver our refusal in person. I would not embarrass the Deverses. You and I will ride over tomorrow morning for it is too late now for us to go and return. We must start early. First, however, I would tell Father Cullen, and the Reverend Steen. They had high hopes for this match. Cullen will understand, but it will be hard for Reverend Steen."

"Shall I come too?" Fortune asked.

"I think not," her stepfather said.

Fortune hugged him hard, and kissed his handsome cheek. "Thank you for understanding, Papa," she said. "I realize I am a disappointment to you in that I cannot settle upon a husband, but as nice as he is, Will Devers is not the man for me. I wonder if any man is."

In the morning the duke and duchess of Glenkirk set out for Mallow Court. They both enjoyed the gentle hills and the soft weather as they rode. Mallow Court was a pleasant Tudor dwelling, and the announcement of their arrival brought both Sir Shane and Lady Devers hurrying into their Great Hall where Jasmine and James were already being served wine by the well-trained household servants.

"Forgive us for our unannounced arrival," James Leslie said, kissing Jane Devers's hand, "but we wanted to come personally to give you an answer to your offer for Lady Fortune."

Dear God, Jane Devers thought, agitated. They are going to take my William away from me. She flung her husband a distraught look.

Seeing it, Jasmine actually felt sympathy for the woman, and quickly said, "Your son is a fine young man, and I would be proud to have him for a son-in-law. Unfortunately, my daughter does not believe she is the right girl for William. While Jemmie and I think the boy quite suitable, we will not compel Fortune to a marriage she does not want. We wanted to come and tell you this ourselves because we did not want you to think we were refusing your suit capriciously. Nor did we want any gossip that would reflect badly upon William. I hope you are not too offended, and that you will not think badly of Fortune."

Jane Devers almost collapsed with her relief. William was safe from that girl! Then suddenly she found she was also offended. Fortune Lindley had turned down her son's offer of marriage! Did the baggage think herself too good for William Devers? The words were out of her mouth before she could hold them back. "Then why did you come to Ireland to seek a husband for your daughter if you did not intend she accept a most suitable prospect? It does seem quite fickle to me," she huffed.

"My wife"—the duke began, squeezing Jasmine's hand hard, and warning her to silence—"thought to give her Irish estates to Fortune. We believed under those circumstances an Irish husband would be best."

"A perfectly reasonable conclusion," Sir Shane replied, glowering sharply at his wife as he silently warned her to keep quiet. The duke and duchess of Glenkirk had been more than generous in their treatment of the Devers family. They would not be embarrassed by this situation now despite the fact Jane had blathered about the countryside to all who would listen that their son would undoubtedly marry the heiress of Erne Rock Castle. "Will you be returning to Scotland soon?" he asked.

"Nay, not immediately. We thought to spend the summer here in Ulster," the duke responded. "Jasmine has not been here since Fortune was born. Now with the pain of the marquess of Westleigh's murder long past, she is enjoying Maguire's Ford again. Father Cullen was her tutor in India, and shepherded her from her father's court to England twenty-four years ago. He is her kinsman, and she is fond of him. She had not thought to see him ever again when she left Ireland last. We shall go home to Scotland in the autumn in time for the grouse hunting, and then down into England to court for the winter. Perhaps the right man will make his appearance then. For Fortune's sake I hope so."

"Lady Fortune is a lovely lass," Shane Devers said graciously. "I am sorry she will not be our daughter, my lord."

Bows and curtsies were exchanged all around, and then the Leslies of Glenkirk took their leave of the Deverses of Mallow Court.

"My prayers have been answered!" Lady Jane Devers

cried out when they had gone. "We shall leave for England as quickly as possible. I can have my wardrobe made in London. It will be more up-to-date than with a dressmaker from Dublin."

"William will not be pleased at all," her husband answered her. "I do not know what he will do for he has convinced himself that Lady Fortune Lindley is the love of his life. How he should know that on such short acquaintance is beyond me, my dear. Let us call him now, and tell him. John," he called to a footman. "Fetch my sons, and tell them to come to the Great Hall at once. Find Master Kieran first."

"Why Kieran first?" his wife demanded.

"Because Kieran can help us to control William's assured outburst. I don't want him galloping across the countryside to plead with the girl. It would embarrass Lady Fortune, and shame us."

Kieran Devers came, and was swiftly apprised of the situation. He smiled sardonically. Had he not predicted the haughty wench would turn his younger brother down? Why the Leslies had even considered a Devers of Mallow Court was beyond him. With a duke for a stepfather, a duke for a half-brother, and a marquess for a brother; with a small fortune and rich lands to her name, the Lady Fortune Lindley could have a duke for a husband. She probably had some poor dumb devil back in England dangling while she tortured him by coming to Ireland on a supposed husband hunt. "How soon does the girl go home?" he asked his father.

"They plan to remain for the summer months," was the surprising answer, "which is even more reason for getting William off to England as soon as we possibly can. Are you going with us?"

Kieran shook his head. "I have no desire to see England," he said. "You, William, and Lady Jane go. I'll look after everything here, Da. 'Tis small trouble. The crops are planted. The sheep are flourishing in the meadows. There is not a great deal to do, but I know how closely you mind your accounts, and that I can do for you."

William Devers came into the hall. "You sent for me, Da?"

"Lady Fortune has refused your offer," his father spoke bluntly.

"Of course she would the first time," William answered calmly. "She is a lady, and it would be unseemly for her to jump at my offer."

"For God's sake, Willy," his brother snapped impatiently. "You could offer a hundred times, and the wench would turn you away! She doesn't want you. Her parents came themselves to tell our father and your mother, laddie. Let it go, and marry your cousin, Emily."

"I don't believe you," William Devers said defiantly.

"Faugh! You tell him, madame. Tell your son he has been rejected by a disdainful and arrogant English wench," Kieran said angrily.

"It is true, William," his mother said.

"I shall go to her!" William cried.

"You shall not!" Sir Shane said harshly. "Would you disgrace our family with your lovesick behavior?"

"Take one step out of the hall," his brother warned, "and I swear, laddie, I shall beat you senseless!" His dark eyes threatened warningly as he glared at his younger brother.

William Devers felt his heart sink. *She had turned him down.* How could she? She was the most beautiful girl in the world. She spoke about things he had never heard a woman speak about. He adored her. How could she not understand that he loved her? "You have always planned on me wedding Emily Anne," he said, suddenly turning on his mother menacingly. "Put it from your mind, Mama. I would not have that simpering, treacle-soaked little bitch if she were the last girl on the face of the earth!"

Lady Devers drew herself up, and glared fiercely at her son. "Do not speak to me like that, William. You do not have to marry your cousin if you do not wish to, but Lady Fortune

Lindley will not marry you either. We will leave for England tomorrow to visit your sisters. Perhaps a few months away will free you of the bad influences you have come under these past few days. *No!*" She held her hand up at him. "Do not even attempt to argue with me in this, William." Then she stalked from the hall, her back straight, her head high.

Kieran put an arm about his brother's shoulders, but William shrugged it off. "There is nothing you can say to comfort me," he snarled.

"I suggest you lock him in his room till you're ready to leave, Da," Kieran said mockingly. "If you do not, the young fool may make a run for Erne Rock, and get his backside kicked by a duke for his presumption." He chuckled.

"I'll kill you one day, Kieran," William said angrily.

"Why would you even bother?" his brother returned scathingly. "You already have everything that should have been mine. Not that I care, Willy, but your mama might. Pull yourself together, laddie, and behave like a Devers." Then he, too, departed the hall.

"I don't think I can trust you, William," his father said wearily, and then proceeded to follow his eldest son's advice.

The next morning the Deverses' coach pulled away from Mallow Court, a stony-faced William seated inside with his mother. His father rode alongside the lumbering vehicle with his elder son who had decided to accompany them as far as the Dundalk Road. There Kieran Devers bid them farewell, and headed back cross-country to his home.

Fortune saw him from a distance, but she recognized the large white stallion he had ridden the day he had come to Erne Rock. With its black mane and tail, the beast was quite distinctive. She waved to him. It was bold, she knew, but once she had realized that young William Devers was not really the mate for her, she had also realized that his older brother was the far more interesting man. Now she meant to confirm her first impression. Because she was not marrying his brother did not mean they could not strike up an acquaintance. After all her parents had both stressed the importance of not embarrassing the Deverses by avoiding them, and appearing to snub them. Not that she had any interest in Kieran Devers.

What was the wench up to? Kieran wondered, as he rode toward her. She had certainly been rude enough when they had first met, and then she had made a great pretense of being enthralled by his brother. If anyone was to blame for William's heartbreak and attitude, it was certainly Lady Fortune Lindley. Still, he was rather fascinated by her. A wench who rode a big gelding, and rode it astride to boot. He waved back as he came toward her.

"Good day, Master Devers," Fortune said pleasantly.

"Good day, Lady Fortune," he replied.

"You were coming from the Dundalk Road?" she queried.

"I escorted my parents and William to it. They are going to England to visit my sisters in London," he explained.

"Poor Will. He is a sweet boy," she answered him. "I hope he will enjoy London, although most of the good families leave it in the summer weather. Perhaps your sisters' families have homes outside the town?"

"If it is the fashionable thing to do, then they will indeed have country houses," he told her with a small smile. "If there is one certainty my stepmother has taught my sisters, and my half-sister, it is how to be fashionable, and properly English."

"You don't approve of the English?" she said quietly.

"I don't approve of those who enter a country, take the land from its rightful owners, and attempt to impress their religion and way of life upon a people who already have their own way of life and religion," Kieran Devers said.

"It is the way of the world," Fortune told him as they rode along side by side. "Our tutors taught my brothers and sister and me that throughout history one culture has always conquered and overcome another. Those of you in Ireland today once came from another place to overcome the *Tuatha da Danae,* the Fairy folk, who it is said once ruled this island. It is claimed they now live beneath the earth here because they did not wish to assimilate with the Celtic races. Sometimes these changes are for the good, and other times they are not. I don't approve, however, of how most of the English treat the Irish, but given the opportunity, would you Irish not be as wicked? Given the chance you would pillage and burn in the manner of your ancestors, and drive the English right into the sea itself. You would show no mercy, and are no better than they are."

He laughed, suddenly seeing what had so fascinated his young brother. "Aye," he agreed, "we would do just that, Lady Fortune Lindley. We might keep you though, for I have heard it said there is Irish in you. Is it true then?"

"Aye. My great-grandmother was born Skye O'Malley. She was the O'Malley of Innisfana, and a great woman. She died when I was just thirteen, but I knew her well, and shall never forget her," Fortune told him, and tears sprang into her eyes. "She was always so good to me."

The sky had clouded over as they rode, and now a heavy mist of rain began to fall.

"Let's shelter in that ruin," he said, pointing.

When they had gained the haven of the gray stone and dismounted, Fortune asked him, "What is this place?"

He shook his head. "I cannot say for certain, but they say it was once the hall of a Maguire chieftain several hundred years back. See how thick the moss is upon the walls? This archway, however, should keep us from the worst of it. Sit down, Fortune Lindley, while we wait." He plunked himself upon a shelf of stone that formed a natural bench, and patted the place by his side.

Joining him she said, "May I ask you an honest question, Kieran Devers?" And when he nodded in the affirmative she continued on, "Why have you given up your birthright over a matter as simple as religion? You do not seem to me to be a fanatic like so many others."

" 'Tis a fair question," he replied, "and I will try to explain. You are correct in that I am not a fanatic, and to be most candid religion means very little to me. I'm neither martyr nor saint, but the Catholic faith is all I have left of my mother. She died when I was just a little boy. We were an Irish family then, Moire, Da, and me. Then wee Colleen was born, and our mam lost her life giving our sister life. Da was devastated at first. But he soon began to cast his eye about for another wife to raise his children, and run his house. His other needs he had already taken care of, you see, by a discreet lady named Molly, who has had two daughters by my father. They are called Maeve and Aine, good girls both," he smiled.

"You know them?" Fortune was surprised, considering Lady Jane.

"Aye, although my stepmother is not aware that I do. Maeve was born when I was eleven, and Aine when I was fourteen. Da was wed already to his Lady Jane. A merchant's pretty heiress with firm ideas about everything."

"They say she wouldn't have him until he became a Protestant," Fortune remarked. "They say she made him be baptized again."

" 'Tis true," Kieran told her. "Jane Elliot fell in love with Mallow Court the first time she saw it. She wanted it badly, but she is as firm in her faith as she is self-willed. She insisted Da convert. The local priest in Lisnaskea came, and warned my father he would burn in hell if he did any such thing so, of course, he did. Da and I are alike in that we don't like being told what to do. He was baptized again as were Moire and Colleen. My father sent the priest packing in retaliation for his threats."

"Why weren't you baptized again?" she asked him.

"They couldn't catch me," Kieran said with a mischievous grin. "Everything changed when Lady Jane came into the house. My mother's things disappeared one by one. My mother's faith was erased from our lives. It was as if Jane sought to obliterate my mother entirely, or so I thought. When I grew up I realized it really wasn't that at all. My stepmother is a decent woman, but she lives by her own set of manners and mores, and she expects all her family to live by them, too.

"So even though I was not baptized again, she decided to be patient with me. I was forced to attend church each Sunday, and on other specified days, with the rest of my family. She thought once I was comfortable with her faith, I would acquiesce to her wishes. It was years before they discovered that after I had been to church with them, I would slip off to attend the mass wherever it was being held that day.

"On the day I turned twenty-one, I was told I must either be baptized a Protestant, or Da would disinherit me and Willy would become his heir. I would inherit a younger son's allowance, and I could make my home at Mallow Court, but I would lose the heir's portion of the Devers estate. I tried to explain to my father how I felt. Do you know what he said to me? That he could not even remember my mother's face now. That Jane was his wife, and he would have her content. It was then I told him to give Mallow Court to Willy. I did not want it."

"Did you not allow your pride to overrule your common sense?" Fortune wondered aloud. "I do not think your father was being callous when he said he could not recall your mother's visage. It is difficult to remember those who have died after a time. There is no fault in it."

"The truth is," Kieran Devers said, "that I have no passion for Mallow Court. I know I should, but I do not. It has never really felt like mine, nor has my native land felt like a place I should be. I cannot explain it, but I believe my true home is somewhere else."

Fortune stared open-mouthed at him in surprise. *"You too?"* was all she said.

"But surely you have had a place you love, that is home to you," he replied.

"I was born here at Maguire's Ford," Fortune began, "but I was taken to England when I was just a few weeks old. I have lived at my great-grandmam's house, Queen's Malvern. I have lived in France at Mama's chateau, Belle Fleurs. I have lived in Scotland at Papa's castle, Glenkirk, and at my own father's seat, Cadby, in Oxfordshire, but never, Kieran Devers, have I ever felt truly at home anywhere, though I will admit to loving Queen's Malvern best. There is no place I believe where I really belong. I was hoping Ireland would be that place."

"But it is not," he said.

"Nay, it is not," she admitted. "It would appear that you and I are two lost souls, Kieran Devers."

He looked at her, seeing her really for the first time. She was quite beautiful, but she had a second beauty that shone from within as well. Her green-blue eyes were warm and sympathetic. Her smile was sweet. It was a strange contrast, considering her blunt speech.

"The rain has stopped," Fortune said. "My parents will wonder where I have gotten to, Kieran Devers. Will you ride with me again?"

"Tomorrow?" he asked her softly.

She nodded. "Aye, tomorrow, in the morning."

He led her horse from the shelter, and, cupping his hands together, he helped her to vault into her saddle. When she was firmly seated he took her gloved hand and kissed it. "Tomorrow, Fortune Lindley," he told her. Then he gave her gelding a gentle swat on its rump, and the beast moved off. He watched her go, curious to see if she would look back at him, and when she did he grinned broadly.

Fortune blushed to the roots of her fiery head. The devil! she thought. He was waiting for me to do that, and knows women well indeed that he waited. Boldly she turned about, and stuck her tongue out at him before kicking Thunder into a gallop. She could hear his laughter on the wind, and chuckled. They were surely well matched, she considered.

Then the verity of the thought struck her. *They were well matched.* Or were they? her practical nature asserted itself. What did she really know about him? The fact that they had been able to hold a pleasant conversation was encouraging. At least Kieran Devers was no dunce like his younger brother, Will. Still, Kieran was the first man in all her life who had ever held her interest long enough that she was willing to give him the benefit of the doubt. Had she at last met a man she could love? Only time would tell, Fortune thought. Only time would tell.

Chapter
5

"**W**e were beginning to worry, poppet," the duchess said as her daughter entered the hall, handing her cape and gloves to a servant.

"I was out riding, and met Kieran Devers. We had to find shelter from the rain, Mama. He will be coming in the morning to ride with me. He really isn't so bad a fellow when you get to know him a bit."

"I knew it!" James Leslie said with a grin.

"Knew what?" his wife asked, curious.

"I knew it was Kieran Devers who intrigued Fortune. Tall, dark Celts are far more interesting than civilized Anglo-Irish mama's boys," he chuckled, and then he gave his daughter's cheek a loving pat. "Be careful, poppet. This one's a real man, and, I suspect, unlike any ye hae met before."

"Papa! I am not intrigued by Kieran Devers at all," Fortune protested. "But who else is there for me here at Maguire's Ford? It will be nice to have someone to ride with, and better an attractive man than my mother or father."

"Madame, you hae best speak wi yer daughter," the duke warned his wife. "I dinna want to embarrass her by sending a groom along to chaperone her. I'll nae hae that handsome young devil tampering wi our Fortune, Jasmine."

"Am I such a fool then that I could be seduced, Papa?" Fortune demanded of him angrily. "You think because I am a virgin that I am totally ignorant of what transpires between men and women, but I am not. How could I be, living in your household? And let us not forget the winter I spent with my sister, India, when she was *enceinte* with my nephew, Rowan. Do you think all we did was sit and sigh over lost love, tell stories, and sew infant's garments? While Diarmid courted India's Meggie in our sight? Really, Papa!"

"Fortune," Jasmine cautioned her daughter warningly, but James Leslie was already laughing at his stepdaughter's outburst.

"She's right, darling Jasmine," he said. "Fortune's too old for me to be treating her like a green fifteen year old. She's not our headstrong India, running off, jumping from the frying pan into the kettle. Fortune is our practical child. She will behave wisely."

"I most assuredly will," Fortune huffed. But she couldn't wait to see her chamber, and talk with Rois who, while she might be reticent to chatter for fear of her grandmother, Bride Duffy, could, when coaxed, Fortune had discovered, divulge all manner of local gossip. So she waited patiently through the rest of the day and into the evening as if her life was as it had always been, and it was. *Yet it wasn't.*

An old-fashioned bard, one of the few left in Ireland, had asked for hospitality from Erne Rock that evening. It had been graciously granted. Now the bard, full of good food and drink, sat before the fire and began to strum upon his small harp. He sang of battles and heroes unknown to the duke and duchess of Glenkirk. He sang his ballads in the ancient Irish. James Leslie could understand a few words, but the Scots Gaelic was somewhat different from the Irish Gaelic tongue. Rory Maguire, seated at the high board with them, translated, his rich musical voice making the stories come alive.

When the bard had finished, James Leslie invited him to remain for as long as it pleased him, and sleep in the Great Hall. "We are not a large castle, Connor McMor, but you are more than welcome."

The bard tilted his head in thanks.

"If I am to ride early, I should retire now," Fortune said. She arose from the high board, and curtsied to the three adults. Then she hurried off.

"Make certain you see Kieran Devers in the morning before my daughter does," the duke of Glenkirk said to Rory. "And advise him that Fortune is nae to be touched, unless, of course, he seeks a short life. He is welcome to ride wi her, and pursue a friendship if that pleases them both, but I brought Fortune to Ulster a virgin. I would return her home in the same condition. She must yet find a husband to suit her. You will see he understands?"

"Aye, my lord, I will," Rory said. "Kieran Devers is a decent man. I should trust him with my own daughter if I had one, but I will nonetheless deliver your message."

Standing outside the Great Hall Fortune heard them, and smiled to herself. Her stepfather was really so sweet and protective, even if his diligence was misplaced. He should have been as strict with India, Fortune chuckled. She jumped, startled, as Rory Maguire appeared before her, his gaze amused.

"Eavesdroppers seldom hear good of themselves," he teased her.

"If I am to have Maguire's Ford as a dowry," Fortune reminded him, "you will be in my employ, Rory."

" 'Tis not certain now you will get Maguire's Ford," he replied. "That was supposed to be if you chose young William Devers for a husband. You have turned him away.

There is none other in the area that should suit as well as he. Yer not the lady of Erne Rock yet, but I promise when I speak with Kieran on the morrow, I shall not embarrass you."

"Why does everyone feel they need to protect me?" Fortune grumbled. "I'm almost twenty, and no bairn."

He chuckled. "What a mixture you are," he told her. "The Celt and the Mughal warring with the proper English in you. Go find yer bed, not that you will sleep. I recognize the look in yer eye. Yer mother had that same look many years ago when she thought of yer da."

"I think I love you, Rory Maguire," Fortune said, and kissed his cheek. "Go gently on poor Kieran. I've only just begun to play with him. I may discover I don't like him after all, but until I make my own decision, I don't want him frightened off."

He bowed smartly to her. "As you wish, m'lady," he said.

With a girlish giggle Fortune hurried up the staircase to her chamber. Rois, dozing by the fire, awoke as she entered the room. "I want a bath," Fortune announced. "I'll be riding early with Kieran Devers, and I want to know everything you know, Rois Duffy!"

Rois arose from her chair. "Let's get you bathed first, my lady." She hauled an oaken tub from a cupboard, and going to the door of the chamber opened it, calling down the stairs, "Water for my lady's tub at once, please."

Almost immediately the young male servants began arriving with steaming buckets. Adali knew the habits of the women of the household quite well. The tub was filled, and the serving men were gone. Rois helped Fortune disrobe, pinning her hair atop her head. Naked, the girl stepped into the water, and sat down with a sigh of pleasure. She scrubbed herself quickly as Rois put her clothing away, brushing the dust of the day from it first, and cleaning her boots. Then the serving maid brought out a clean, lace-trimmed night garment for her mistress.

Clean, Fortune stepped from the tub into the embrace of a

towel heated by the fire. Rois rubbed her dry, and slipped the nightgown over her mistress's head, tying the ribbons that held the neckline closed. Then seating Fortune she unpinned her long red hair and brushed it vigorously one hundred strokes before braiding it into a single plait. When she had tucked her mistress into her bed, and drawn the curtains about it, she called for the tub's removal. The serving men came, and lifting the small tub to the open window upended it, pouring the dirty water into the lake itself. They then stored the tub back in its small compartment, and departed a final time.

"Open the curtain now, and sit by me while we talk," Fortune commanded her servant. "Tell me all the gossip about Kieran Devers that you have heard. Hold nothing back! I know about his early years, for he told me so himself this afternoon. Has he a mistress? Does he like the ladies? You hear everything, Rois, and I want to know."

"The lasses like him, aye," Rois began. "He comes from Lisnaskea now and again to visit two here at Maguire's Ford. They are not the kind of girls a man weds, but good girls nonetheless. The gossip is that he is a vigorous lover. Ohh, my lady, I should not be speaking to you of such things, and us both maids yet!"

"I want to know!" Fortune insisted.

"They say he is a kind man with a good heart. One of the women was with child, not his, mind you, and she grew ill. He paid for the physician to come and tend to her, and when the child was born saw she had coin enough to keep her through the winter so she wouldn't have to work, and could regain her health again. The girl was a Protestant too, my lady."

"But no permanent mistress?"

"None that I have heard of," Rois said.

"No bastards?"

"None claimed, none named," Rois replied. "He seems to enjoy a good tumble, but he is not wanton, my lady. He simply has the needs of an ordinary gentleman. After all, he is his father's son."

"And he has courted no lady?"

"It is said he feels he has nothing to offer a woman, being disinherited, my lady," Rois said. "A gentleman of his station likes to be able to offer a woman a home. He is not willing to bring a wife to his father's house as he is no longer his father's heir. 'Tis all I know, my lady. There is really little gossip regarding Kieran Devers."

"Nothing bad," Fortune mused aloud to herself. "Pull out your trundle, Rois. I want to be up with the sun to ride."

Rois did as she was bid, making certain the fire had enough peat to keep it burning through the night, washing herself in a small basin, and disrobing to her chemise. Lying down she was quickly asleep. She had left the bed curtains open for Fortune preferred it that way.

Above in her bed Fortune did not sleep at first. The moon shone through her windows, silvery as it reflected itself in the lough. Kieran Devers was a handsome man with his black hair, and his dark green eyes. He was tall and lean, although Fortune suspected that beneath his doublet his body was hard and well made. He enjoyed women, but was not loose in his behavior. He had a strong will. A very defined sense of right and wrong. He was, to her mind, an ordinary man very much like James Leslie. Why was it then that she was so fascinated by him? What was it about him that made him different from any other man she had ever met?

In a few weeks she would be twenty years old. She had been pursued and courted since she was fifteen, when her breasts had suddenly become obvious. Boys she had known in Scotland and England could scarce keep their hands to themselves, and swore undying love. She had laughed at them all. After all they had played barefoot, ridden, and hunted together since they were bairns. She just didn't see them as husbands. Even though they were all now grown, her childhood companions were friends, not prospective lovers. She couldn't take them seriously, and sent them all packing.

She wasn't India, romantic and headstrong. Not that her sister hadn't been as fussy, for she had. At court young men of good families and old titles had approached their parents with marriage in mind. Both she and India agreed it was their dowries that attracted most. But the Leslies of Glenkirk had always said the choice was up to their daughters in the end. As frustrating as it had been for James Leslie, he had tried to keep his promise to them. India, however, would have driven a saint to perdition. The duke of Glenkirk had finally lost his patience with her, and married her off to the earl of Oxton. That it turned out to be a happy union was another story. And India had made him promise only last summer that he would not do the same thing to Fortune. But could her stepfather, the only father she had ever known, keep that promise? Would Rowan Lindley, the man who sired her, have kept such a promise?

She had come to Ireland fully intending to wed with William Devers as long as he were not an ugly beast with a bad temper. But he hadn't been. Tall, handsome, charming, he had been eager to have her for his wife, and she felt it was not just her inheritance that had attracted him. But in those few days she had spent getting to know Will she had come to realize she couldn't marry anyone just because it was the practical and sensible thing to do. What had happened to her? She was, it would seem, more like her mother and her sister than she had ever thought she was. It was a disturbing revelation.

What was more distressing was her fierce growing attraction to Will's older brother, Kieran. He overwhelmed her senses with the kind of sensual thoughts she hadn't thought herself capable of having. She found this complex man far more interesting than his younger brother. She was frankly relieved that the Deverses had gone to England to escape any possible embarrassment that the proposed match be-

tween their families, gone sour, might have caused them.
Now she had time to be with Kieran, and none to fault her
for it. And Papa had seen her attraction for Kieran Devers
even before she had realized it! Fortune smiled to herself in
the darkness. James Leslie had been a good father to her,
and to the rest of them. Her eyes grew heavy. What was
going to happen? she wondered.

She was up early but much to her disappointment it was
raining. Looking out over the lough that was filled with
heavy fog and mist she wondered if he would come anyway.
A little rain never hurt anyone, she reasoned. She dressed for
riding, and went down into the hall to eat her oat stir-about
and drink her watered wine. James Leslie cast her an amused
look seeing her garb.

"Where is Mama?" she asked, sitting next to him at the
high board. She reached for the cottage loaf, and tore herself
off a small portion, buttering it generously, and then slicing
a bit of cheese from the half-wheel to go on it.

"Ye know yer mother becomes less interested in rising wi
the dawn now that she is getting older," he replied. Then he
sipped his wine, reaching for a hard-boiled egg to peel.

"Do you think he'll come, Papa?" The question slipped
out.

"A wee bit of rain would hae nae kept me from a pretty
lass when I was his age, poppet," James replied.

"I don't even know how old he is," Fortune said.

"I would say he is yet in his twenties, lassie. A husband
should be older than his wife, I believe." He dipped his
peeled egg into the salt dish, and took a bite.

"He is not to be my husband!" Fortune quickly said.

James Leslie popped the rest of the egg into his mouth,
and then he took Fortune's hand in his, looking directly at
her when she turned her face to his. "Now listen to me,
lassie," he said quietly. "Yer a lot like yer great-grandmother in many ways. Madame Skye did nae in her youth,
so I am told, flirt like some court coquette. If a man caught

her eye then that was it. I think it will be that way wi ye, poppet.

"William Devers was a good enough lad, but too soft, too ruled by his family. I could see right away that he was nae the man for ye. His brother, however, is a different matter. He's a real man. Mayhap a bit of a fool to give up Mallow Court, but if he wins ye, he'll hae Erne Rock, and 'twould nae be a bad exchange. So if ye want him, Fortune, then pursue him, and dinna feel shame in it. Happiness is gained, nae conferred upon ye simply because yer a pretty lass wi a grand inheritance."

"Why, Papa!" Fortune was genuinely surprised by his words. "You were not so generous with India."

"India was a bit of a flibbertigibbet when she was on the husband hunt," James Leslie replied. "Ye are nae such a featherbrain, but rather her exact opposite. Intelligence is nae a bad thing in a woman, Fortune, but love is nae a matter one should overconsider. If ye find it, lassie, then grab it, and hold on to it tightly, for it may but come once in yer lifetime. 'Twas that way wi yer sire, and it hae been that way wi me. I loved yer mother from the beginning, and I will love her until I die." He patted Fortune's cheek. "Yer a good lass. Follow yer heart if ye've a mind to, and I will nae complain."

Fortune could feel the tears pricking at her eyelids. She blinked quickly to keep them from escaping. James Leslie had never spoken so candidly, or so lovingly to her as he just did. "Are you sure you are not trying to get rid of me?" she teased him softly.

He smiled a slow smile. "Aye," he said, "I want ye gone, lassie, but only if it is to a man who will love ye even more than I do." Reaching out he brushed the single tear that had somehow managed to escape down her pale cheek.

"My lord." Adali appeared in the entrance to the hall. "Master Devers has just arrived. I thought Lady Fortune would want to know."

"Oh, he did come!" she half-whispered.

"He would hae been a fool nae to come, but I somehow thought he would," the duke of Glenkirk said, rising from his place at table. "He is every bit as intrigued wi ye as ye are wi him, lassie."

"Papa, how can you know that?" she said.

"Did ye nae see the glances he gave ye when he was last here? I saw them, and 'twas then I knew he was already half in love wi ye, lassie. 'Tis fortunate his silly stepmother has whisked her little rooster chick off to England, isn't it?" The duke chuckled richly.

"Aye," Fortune agreed with a small smile. "It 'tis, Papa."

"Good morning, Lady Fortune. My lord." Kieran Devers came into the hall, handing his rain-soaked cloak to Adali. "When I began my journey from home the rain was hardly a mist. Now it is falling quite heavily."

"I will see your garment is properly dried, sir," Adali said. He hurried from the hall.

"Yer welcome nonetheless, Kieran Devers," the duke said. "Do ye play chess by any chance?"

"Aye, my lord, I do," was the reply.

"Then why don't ye and my daughter while away the time until the rains stop in that pursuit? Fortune plays quite well, don't ye, lassie?" He didn't wait for an answer. "I'll hae Adali fetch the chessboard and its pieces, and perhaps some good whiskey to take the chill from yer bones." He walked briskly from the hall.

"Are ye really a good player?" Kieran asked her.

"Aye," she responded, "very good. My mother taught me, and she used to play with her father when she was a girl in India."

"We'll play a game, and then if I find you a worthy opponent," he told her, "we'll wager perhaps, eh?"

"You won't need to test my mettle, Kieran Devers," Fortune told him. "We'll wager from the start. What would you have of me—*if you win*?" Her eyes twinkled mischievously, but his answer caused her to gasp.

"A kiss," he said, his handsome face serious.

"You're bold," she said, recovering her equilibrium.

"*If* you win, what will you have of me?" he asked her.

"*A kiss,*" she responded, surprising him mightily. "I hope it will be worth it," Fortune finished with a wicked smile.

He laughed aloud. He couldn't help it. " 'Tis you who are bold, I'm thinking, m'lady," he told her.

"Why?" she demanded. "Because I didn't blush, and demur, and ask you for a bonnie blue ribbon for my hair? I've been playing with boys my whole life, Kieran Devers. Be warned. I play to win, and am no simpering lass."

The dark green eyes narrowed speculatively as he reassessed her. "No quarter?" he said softly.

"No quarter," she answered him as softly.

"The chessboard, my lady," Adali said, coming upon them. He set a pewter dram upon the table where they would play.

"Damn me, man! You walk on cat's feet," Kieran said.

"Aye, I do, sir," Adali replied, flashing the young man a wide smile. "I was taught to do so when I served in the harem. I find it a useful trait. I often appear where I am least expected." He set the board up on the small square table before the hall's fire. From a rectangular silver box studded with green malachite he removed the pieces carved from ivory and green malachite, placing them with careful deliberation upon the board. "If you will choose your pieces, sir."

"I'll play the green," Kieran said, seating himself, and quickly swallowing down his whiskey.

Fortune sat opposite, immediately studying the board. Then she made a rather ordinary and common move with one of her pawns.

Standing near them Adali smiled softly, then left the hall.

They played at a fairly rapid pace. He was quite pleased by her skill. She was far and away the best player he had ever played with, but nonetheless he was winning. Chuckling he moved one of his two knights. Fortune laughed, and then with a deliberate movement checkmated his king.

"I belive I win, sir," she said sweetly.

His jaw dropped. "How the hell . . ." He looked questioningly at her, surprise all over his handsome face.

"I'll show you if you like," she said, and when he nodded his head quite vigorously she reconstructed their play to demonstrate.

"Madame, that is positively devious," he told her. "Set up the board, and we will play again."

"You owe me my wager," Fortune told him.

Taking her hand in his he kissed it tenderly.

"Nay, sir," Fortune cried, jumping to her feet. "If I had lost, would you have accepted such a paltry reward? I want a proper kiss! I have never had one before, but I want one now!" Leaning forward over the table she closed her eyes, and pursed her lips at him.

God and His Holy Mother help me, he thought. Then Kieran Devers took Fortune Lindley's small chin between his thumb and his forefinger to steady her as his lips brushed her gently, gently. "Is that more satisfactory, m'lady?" he said, releasing her.

Her heart had jumped when he first touched her. Then it had plummeted as his mouth made contact with hers. Opening her eyes she said, "I want more, sir. 'Twas pleasant, but surely there is more to it than that."

"If there is," he teased, "you must win again to find out. Now that I have seen your mettle, I shall not be so easy to beat next time. Sit down, Fortune, and let us set the pieces aright again." His heart was hammering in his chest, and to his shock he had felt a distinct tingling in his nether regions as he kissed her. It was impossible to concentrate although he tried his best to do so. She beat him a second time much to his mortification.

"Pay up, sir," Fortune said, "and this time you will do it properly as I have seen my father and mother kiss. You will put your arms about me, and hold me against you." She stood up, coming around the table.

"Very well, you clever vixen," he growled in a fierce voice, rising. Then he pulled her against him hard, his arms wrapping tightly about her. His mouth found hers, and he kissed her with passion, feeling his lust rising, his heart exploding within him.

She soared! The hunger he communicated, aye, *hunger!* sent her senses reeling. He wanted all of her, she realized, in that kiss. She might be a virgin, but Fortune Lindley knew desire when she faced it. She had seen it in men's eyes often enough. Her arms slipped up around his neck as her lips softened, and she kissed him back with an equal hunger. This was what she had been seeking her entire life. It was delicious!

Suddenly he pushed her away. He was almost trembling. "No!" he said to her.

"Yes!" she countered as quickly.

"You don't know what you are doing to me, sweetheart," he half-whispered.

"Do you know what you're doing to me?" she asked him.

"Aye," he told her, "I do."

"Then why stop, Kieran Devers?" Fortune demanded. She was flushed with her pleasure, and it was all he could do to remain a gentleman.

"Because if we do not, I shall carry you up to your bedchamber, and ravish your sweetness," he said in a hard voice. "Because I have wanted you from the moment I first saw you. Because I prayed you would not want William so I might have you! Because as much as I love and desire you, Fortune Lindley, I cannot have you, for I have nothing to offer. You're not just some lass I have met. You're a girl from a grand family, with a great inheritance. Nothing about me is worthy of you. My lineage, or my worldly goods, which amount to damned precious little. Do you know how angry that makes me, Fortune?" He backed away from her. "I had best return home to Mallow Court."

"The rain has stopped, and you came to ride with me," she countered. She was not about to lose him now, Fortune decided to herself, knowing if she let him go like this, she would never see him again. Remembering her stepfather's advice she plunged ahead. "I will be twenty next month," she said honestly. "I have waited my whole life for you, Kieran Devers. *I will not let you leave me!* What do I care if you are a rich man, or a poor man. My wealth is yours for the taking if you will but have me in exchange.

"As for your lineage, if such things mattered to me, and they don't, yours is a proud lineage. Your father's family descend from the Debhers, the water-finders of the Celtic tribes. They were of high caste, Kieran. Your mother's family, the Maguires, have been the princes of Fermanagh for centuries. There is O' Neil on both sides of your family tree. There is naught wrong with your lineage. You have, I fear, been influenced by your English stepmother, and her disdain for all things Irish."

"How do you know this?" he asked her, amazed.

"I asked Rory Maguire," she said simply. "Do you know that the men of Fermanagh have always been considered the worst swordsmen in all of Ireland?"

"No," he replied with a small smile.

"Well, they have. Fermanagh has been the most peaceful region in all of Ireland. None of the great princes ever considered the men of Fermanagh a threat, for the great families of this region were made up of poets and bards; physicians and lawyers," Fortune told him. "Rory Maguire, being a member of the old ruling family here, knows all the history of the area, and was happy to enlighten me."

"I would not have thought Maguire a historian," Kieran said.

"Because he warned you to mind your manners with me as I am a noble virgin, and not to be taken lightly?" she teased.

He laughed now, for it was exactly what Maguire had said

to him earlier when he had arrived, and stabled his horse. "Let us ride if the rain has stopped, or was that just a way to hold me here longer?"

"Both," she said honestly.

"There is no future in any of this," he insisted. "We're mad to even consider that there is."

"Is that not our decision to make, Kieran?" She put her hand upon his arm, and looked up into his handsome, but troubled face.

"Is it?" he wondered aloud, drowning in her green-blue gaze. He was in love, he thought to his amazement. It had happened so quickly, so suddenly. He had never expected to be in love, and the whole thing was utterly impossible. They would never let him have her.

"I want us to wed before your family returns from England in the autumn," Fortune said frankly.

"I haven't asked you to marry me," he replied.

"Don't you want to?" she demanded.

"Of course I do, but your family will not allow it, sweetheart. Don't you understand? Poor men, even of noble family, do not marry wealthy heiresses. You could have a prince, a duke, or a marquess, Fortune. Your family can certainly seek for a better match than I am."

"Kieran, the choice is mine. It always has been. I choose you. Do you really love me? Even on such short acquaintance?" she asked.

"Aye," he replied softly. "From the first moment we came face to face upon that hill, and you so proud and haughty."

"I was dreadfully rude," she admitted, "but you were as arrogant as I, Kieran Devers. I think my heart knew then even if my mind did not, but I was angry to have you spoil my perfect plans." He had yet to take his arms from about her, and she snuggled against him.

He dropped a kiss upon her fiery head, feeling her young body soft and yielding against his hardness. He wanted her greatly. He wanted to wake up in the morning and find her next to him. He wanted to give her children. Why had he been such a fool to defy his father? Why had he never considered that there might be a moment like this one? Or a girl like Lady Fortune Mary Lindley?

"I was baptized a Catholic by Father Cullen," she said to him, seeming to sense his thoughts. "That means we can be wed in his church. You do not have to give up anything for me, Kieran."

"It still does not overcome the problem of my poverty," he told Fortune quietly, gently pushing her away from him.

"Let us ride while we discuss this further," Fortune suggested.

"I am not a suitable match for you, sweetheart," he replied implacably.

"Adali!" she suddenly called, and the majordomo appeared from the shadows of the hall. "Fetch Papa, Adali. Tell him I need to speak with him immediately."

"At once, my lady," Adali replied, seeing the startled and nervous look upon Kieran Devers's face. He moved quickly from the hall, chuckling to himself as he went. The young man hadn't a chance of escaping Lady Fortune. She had always been a determined child who wanted what she wanted when she wanted it. Since she was not particularly demanding even as a little one, this attitude always came as a surprise to her family when she exhibited it. He found the duke in Maguire's small office going over the breeding schedule. "Lady Fortune would like to see you in the hall, my lord," Adali said.

"Tell her I will be there shortly," the duke responded.

"I think you had best come now, my lord," Adali persisted. "Lady Fortune has told Master Devers that they are to marry, but he demurs, believing he is not good enough for her since he has no wealth."

"God's boots!" the duke swore.

"Well, I'll be damned," Maguire said, a grin upon his face.

Kieran Devers paled visibly as the duke of Glenkirk, followed by Adali and Rory Maguire, entered the hall. They were going to throw him out, and set the dogs on him for sure. He had no right aspiring, even secretly in his heart, to a girl like Fortune. "My lord," he said, bowing. What the hell was the matter with him? He wasn't some damned cotter. He was a Devers with a Maguire mother, and O'Neil cousins. He had little to his name, but the name was a respectable one. Maguire was grinning from ear to ear. What the hell had taken the man?

"I understand ye want to marry my daughter, Kieran Devers," the duke said quietly.

"Aye, my lord, I do, but I know you will not allow it for I am a poor man with nothing but my name to offer," Kieran said.

James Leslie looked to his stepdaughter. "Well, Fortune, what have ye to say to this?"

"I love him, Papa," Fortune said.

"Ahh, yes. And ye do hae enough wealth for the both of ye. Are ye willing to share it?" the duke inquired.

"You know I am, Papa!" she cried. "And Kieran is welcome to whatever I have. There is such a great deal of it."

"My lord, I cannot wed Fortune for her riches," the younger man said emphatically. "I must be my own man, and come to her with something to offer besides my name. I am a man of honor, not some fortune-hunting rogue."

"Ohh, do not be so bloody proud!" Fortune shouted at him.

"Perhaps Willy could wed you for your inheritance, Fortune, but I will not!" he shouted back at her.

"Ye do not have to wed my daughter for her wealth, Master Devers. Ye will nae hae any control over her riches at all, nor would your younger brother hae. The women in this family keep and prudently manage their own wealth. It is their tradition. The men they wed are given a suitable settlement prior to the marriage. Fortune will continue to be very rich. Ye will nae be in comparison. If you wish, ye may take the settlement given you and invest it to increase it. Surely ye canna hae any objection to wedding Fortune now, can ye? Ye will be doing me a great personal favor in taking the chit off my hands. She hae been extraordinarily fussy about choosing a mate."

Kieran Devers had never been so surprised in his entire life. "You are saying that I can marry Fortune, my lord?"

"Aye, provided ye love the lass. Do ye?" the duke of Glenkirk asked, knowing the answer but asking nonetheless for he needed to hear Kieran Devers voice it aloud.

"I love her with all my heart! I could have never married another woman knowing my love for her would never have equaled my love for Fortune. Aye, my lord, I love her!"

Hearing the words Rory Maguire felt his own heart clutch. He knew exactly how Kieran Devers felt. At least the lad was gaining his heart's desire. He never had.

"Ohh, Papa, thank you!" Fortune threw her arms about the duke's neck, and kissed him.

"What is going on?" Jasmine Leslie came into the hall, looking about her.

"Kieran and I are going to be married, Mama!" Fortune said, beaming, and casting a loving look upon her intended.

"This is sudden, even for you, poppet," the duchess said slowly. "Are you sure this is what you want? You didn't want young William, yet you want his brother?"

"I love him," Fortune said. "Why is that so difficult for you to understand, Mama? Will was sweet, but dull. Kieran and I have so much in common with one another."

"For instance?" Jasmine asked her daughter.

"Neither of us has ever felt at home anywhere in this world. We both know there is a place for us we have not yet found," Fortune said passionately.

"You do not feel at home in Ireland? Or here at Erne Rock?" Jasmine was concerned for she knew Kieran Devers had no home other than his father's house, and they could scarcely live there after they were married. Was England the answer? With all the anti-Catholic laws in place Jasmine doubted it. Where then was there a place for her daughter and Kieran Devers to lay their heads? "You know I had thought to give you Maguire's Ford for a wedding gift," Jasmine said.

"It is bad enough that I have fallen in love with your daughter, madame," Kieran said, "but if we lived here at Maguire's Ford my family in Lisnaskea, my stepmother in particular, would burn with envy. Jane Devers adores her son as you saw. She will not be able to bear it that Fortune, having refused William's offer, even though Jane prayed she would, has turned about and married me. She has coveted your lands for some time, although she keeps it from my father. It was she who convinced Samuel Steen to put forth Willy's name. My brother has a tendency to talk to me for his mother has always maintained cordial relations with me for propriety's sake. Willy is a lonely young man, but Lady Jane could turn him against me in a minute if she thought I was in possession of Maguire's Ford. My brother fancied himself in love with Fortune, and is easily led by his mama. 'Tis the land my stepmother seeks. She would do everything in her power to take this estate from its *Catholic masters.* She'll cause terrible trouble over a marriage between Fortune and me."

"He's right," Rory Maguire said thoughtfully. "She's a fanatic, my lady. Kieran and Lady Fortune will have to leave Ireland to escape her anger; and you will have to see the estate is put into the hands of an undisputed Protestant so Lady Devers has no chance of stealing the lands from you."

"Oh, Rory, what about your people?" Jasmine fretted.

"We should be fine with a new *Protestant* master of your choosing, my lady." Damn, she was so good, so thoughtful of them all.

"Duncan and Adam!" Jasmine said suddenly. "We will give Maguire's Ford to our two youngest sons, Duncan and Adam Leslie. They are still boys, but both have been raised in Scotland's Anglican Church. There can be no disputing their loyalties, especially as they are half-brothers of the king's own nephew. The elder can have the castle, and we will build the younger a fine house. Protestants though they may be, Rory Maguire, they are open-minded lads both."

"If they are your sons, my lady, I have no doubt of it," he replied.

"Then Kieran and I can be wed?" Fortune asked.

"Not immediately," Jasmine told her daughter, and held up her hand to stop Fortune's protest before it began. "You and Kieran have been swept up in a passionate whirlwind, poppet. I have no doubt that you love each other . . . *now*. But will you love each other a month from now? A year from now? And where will you live? It cannot be here in Ireland for Kieran is right. His family will be furious that he has snatched up the heiress of Maguire's Ford. England may be a bit safer, provided that Kieran does not flaunt his Catholicism, and obeys the laws laid down by the king."

"The king's wife is a Catholic!" Fortune cried.

"And her faith has already caused a great deal of difficulty because of those people whose minds are closed to the diversity of God's word," the duchess of Glenkirk responded.

"Then what are we to do, madame? What hope is there for us?" Kieran Devers asked Jasmine Leslie.

"There is hope for you," Jasmine said quietly "There is always hope, Kieran. You say you do not feel at home in Ireland even though it is the land of your birth, of your ancestors. Yet you believe there is a place for you. I, too, follow my instincts, which is why I think you are the husband for my daughter, but before I let you have Fortune, you must find a place where you will both be content, and safe. To that end you will come to England with us at summer's end. There is someone I want you to meet there.

"His name is George Calvert, Lord Baltimore. Although his mother was a Catholic, his father was a Protestant, and he was raised in England's church. His family, while respectable and prosperous, were not noble. George Calvert was well educated, and caught the eye of Sir Robert Cecil, the king's Secretary of State. Calvert became his private secretary, and thus began his political career. He married, and his first son was named Cecil after Sir Robert. Slowly, through his diligence and hard work George Calvert rose. He has been here to Ireland several times on royal business, and thus knows the true situation.

"When Cecil died in 1612, the king retained Calvert in his service. He knighted him in 1617, and he eventually became Secretary of State, and a member of the Privy Council. He is a modest man, and very well liked. He has lands here in Ireland himself. He has been involved in the Virginia Company, and the New England Company. However, when his wife, Anne, died in childbirth several years ago, Sir George suffered a crisis of conscience, and turned to the faith of his mother.

"Calvert is a man who possesses great scruples. He publicly announced his conversion, and resigned his positions. The king was heartbroken, and he might have ordered Sir George's death. His love for Calvert overcame his disappointment, and instead the king created him Baron Baltimore in his kingdom of Ireland. Ever since King James' death, the Calverts have managed to retain a friendship, and keep in favor with King Charles.

"Lord Baltimore has a dream to found a colony where all men may worship as suits their conscience, with no interference from others. Whether he can accomplish this I do not know. I have little faith in the good will of my fellow man," Jasmine said, "but if there is anyone who can succeed in this endeavor, it is Calvert. Perhaps his colony is the place for you, and for my daughter. Will you come to England?"

"I will!" Kieran Devers said without a moment's hesitation. He took Fortune's hand in his. "This could be the answer, sweetheart. A place where we could each worship in peace and freedom. It is almost too good to be true."

"It very well may be just that," Jasmine replied. "I have lived long, and seen a great deal of evil done in God's name,

Kieran, but as I told you, there is always hope." She smiled at him.

"But when can we wed, Mama?" Fortune demanded to know.

"When I am certain that your love will last beyond the sweetness of summer," Jasmine answered her daughter.

Chapter
6

Fortune stormed from the hall upon hearing her mother's words. Didn't she understand that they were in love? Certainly Mama had succumbed to love enough times in her life to comprehend the emotion. *I have waited my entire life for this moment,* Fortune grumbled to herself, *and she has spoiled it for me.*

"Sweetheart, wait!" Kieran Devers caught up with Fortune as she half-ran into the open courtyard. "Let us ride. The rain has ceased. We'll talk. Your mother is right, you know."

"What? Are you taking her part then? Don't you want to marry me, Kieran Devers? Has your ardor cooled so quickly? Michael! Saddle my horse!"

He took her into his arms, but Fortune attempted to pull away. "Stop it!" he commanded her sharply. "You're behaving like a child."

There was something in his voice that caused her to obey. She looked up at him, tears in her eyes. "She doesn't understand, Kieran."

"You're wrong, Fortune. Your mother understands all too well." He stroked her hair. "You've been so sheltered, and so wonderfully spoiled, sweetheart. 'Tis you who don't understand, or perhaps you want your way so badly that you don't want to understand."

Fortune sniffled, and put her head against his broad shoulder.

"I am a Catholic, Fortune. I made that decision long ago, and I find no reason to change my thinking on the matter now. Still, I will be neither martyr nor bigot regarding religion. That is the one thing the church was never able to drum into my head. I worship as a Catholic because I am comfortable doing so. You worship as a member of England's Anglican church because you are content that way. Each of our faiths has enemies who would destroy the other. It would seem in order to live in peace we must choose one, or the other. Your mother offers us the possibility of a place where we may each be able to worship as we choose, and not how someone else tells us we must worship."

"Such a place does not exist now," Fortune said sadly.

"If Sir George Calvert could found a colony where such a way of life was possible, would you not want to live there, sweetheart? Perhaps it is that place each of us has been seeking all our lives."

"But where would such a place be?" she asked him.

He shrugged. "I am not certain, but I think, perhaps, in the New World across the ocean. Let us spend the summer here in Ireland, falling more and more in love with each other, Fortune. Then come the autumn we will go to England with your parents. We will meet Sir George, and see what he has to say to us about this wonderful world he wants to make where we may worship freely as we choose."

"But when will we wed?" she persisted.

"Hopefully before we leave for England," he replied. "Your parents are not against us, sweetheart. They simply want to make certain that we truly love one another. I am willing to be patient, and so must you. Now, here is Michael with our horses. Come, my love, and let us ride out over the hills where we first met."

They rode out together, slowly through the village, then racing across the meadows, the sheep scattering before them. Fortune laughed, the sound echoing on the wind. Finally they topped the hill where they had first met. Below them the lough spread itself blue, melting into the blue-green hills hovering mistily towards the west. They dismounted, and stood looking out over the land.

"It is beautiful," she said, "but 'tis not home." Removing her cloak, she spread it on the grass, and sat down.

"Nay," he agreed, sitting next to her. "I've looked out over these hills all my life, and never felt the kinship with it that I should." Putting his arm about her he drew her down, and then leaning over her he kissed her, tenderly at first, and then with more passion.

How odd, Fortune thought, her mind hazy, I have absolutely no desire to hit him. She slipped her arms about his neck, drawing him closer, feeling her breasts give way beneath the hardness of his chest. *This was really kissing!* Surprisingly, it seemed to come quite naturally to her even if she had no real prior experience before today. The pressure on her mouth increased, and her lips seemed to part almost of their own volition. She felt the tip of his tongue encircling her lips. It was a delicious sensation. Boldly she reached out with her own tongue to touch his. It was as if she had been struck by lightning!

Raising his dark head Kieran smiled a slow smile at her. He rolled onto his back, and stared up at the sky. His male member was quivering with rising excitement. She really had no idea what was happening to either him or to her. How far, he wondered, would she allow him to go? He turned back to her, lying on his side, propped up by a single elbow. Then with his other hand he reached out and unbuttoned the silver buttons on her doublet.

She watched him through half-closed eyes, her heart

beating a bit faster as the last button slipped through its buttonhole. His hand reached out to very, very gently caress the soft swell of her bosom. She drew an audible breath, her blue-green eyes widening at the burst of excitement that rippled through her body. How far would he dare to go? she considered nervously. Was she willing to allow him greater liberties? Would he stop if she asked him to?

His fingers played with the lacing on her silk shirt. Swiftly he loosened it. The ribbons of her chemise lay within reach of those fingers. His eyes met hers, silently asking permission to proceed further. He bent a moment, and lightly kissed her mouth.

Her whole body felt leaden. She couldn't move. She couldn't say no to him. She wanted him to open her chemise. She wanted him to touch her breasts. Once when she was small she had seen her mother's lover, Prince Henry Stuart, caress Jasmine's bare breasts. The look of pleasure upon both their faces and her mother's heartfelt sigh of delight had remained in Fortune's memory her entire life. She wanted to know that same joy. Sighing, she closed her eyes.

She had spoken not a word, and yet she had given her consent to him to proceed further. His fingers practically tore the ribbons from the delicate fabric which he spread open to reveal Fortune's bosom. He almost whimpered with sheer gratification for she was so beautiful, absolutely perfect in form. Her breasts were small, and fully round with delightful little nipples that looked like tiny fruits atop a bowl of fresh cream. His hand was unable to help itself, and tenderly cupped one of those small breasts.

Fortune's eyes flew open, and she stared down at the hand. A small sound squeaked from her throat. Her eyes grew wide again.

Kieran smiled at her again. She was such a fierce creature, but she was also far more innocent than either of them had anticipated. Still, he could not help himself for she was simply too tempting. He laid his cheek against her breast, and heard the frantic beating of her heart beneath his ear.

"Forgive me, sweetheart," he said low, "but I cannot help myself. You are so lovely, Fortune. So damned lovely!"

She touched his dark head with her hand, gently ruffling his thick hair. There was something so natural about this even if she was a little frightened. Kieran loved her. He would not harm her. Passion, her mother had always warned her, was a powerful thing. She was only just beginning to understand at last what her mother had meant. "I love you, Kieran Devers," she told him.

He raised his head from her bosom. "And I love you, lambkin," he replied. There was something in his look she did not understand.

"What is it?" she asked him.

"I am not used to playing love games, Fortune," he answered her honestly. "I am burning with my desire for you."

"Oh." Her voice was very small. She was wise enough to know precisely what he meant. She drew the halves of her chemise together herself, and laced the ribbons. Then her silk blouse. Finally she did up the buttons upon her doublet. "They can be dangerous games, Kieran, can't they?" she half-whispered.

In reply he took her hand, and placed it upon his breeches. "Aye," he agreed, "they can, sweetheart."

Beneath her fingers she felt a hard length that simply radiated heat, and almost seemed to throb at her touch. She looked at him wonderingly. "Your manhood is a fine thing," Fortune told him. "You will give me great pleasure one day."

He laughed, the tension suddenly broken between them. It was such an outrageous remark from a virgin, yet he would have expected no less from Fortune. "Aye," he agreed with her. "I will give you a great deal of pleasure, lambkin. Now, take your wicked little hand away from me before I burst with my lust for you."

Giving him a teasing pat she said, "I did not place my hand upon you of my own volition, sir. 'Twas you who wished to boast." Then she moved her hand away from him.

"Next time I would see it unclothed as you viewed my breasts today. Turnabout is considered fair play."

Laughing he took the hand that had touched him, and kissed it, both upon its back, and upon the palm. "Must I beat you to make you behave, sweetheart? You are a most naughty lass, I fear."

"You may beat me if it gives us pleasure," she shot back.

He raised a quizzical eyebrow. She had absolutely no idea what she was saying, he realized. Laughing again he struggled to his feet, and quickly caught the horses who had been grazing peacefully nearby. " 'Tis past time, sweetheart, that we rode home. Your parents will wonder where we have gotten to, and Maguire will set the dogs on me, I fear, if he thinks I have dishonored you in any manner." He helped her to mount, refraining from caressing her temptingly round bottom as she climbed into her saddle.

They rode home slowly even though the clouds were now beginning to scud quickly across the skies. A small rumble of thunder caused them to hurry the horses, and they reached the courtyard of Erne Rock just as the rain began to fall. There wasn't a stable lad in sight, and so they rode their mounts directly into the stables, dismounting there, and leading their beasts to their stalls. Efficiently they removed the animals' saddles and bridles. Fortune took up Thunder's own brushes, and began to curry him. He snuffled and danced gently as she worked. Kieran watched her, smiling. Then making himself useful he poured a measure of oats into the horses' individual troughs.

When Fortune had finished grooming her gelding she hung up the brushes and came out of his stall, closing the door carefully behind her. "I don't know where Michael has gotten to," she said. "Perhaps he went to the kitchens to be fed." She looked out of the open stable doors. The rain was coming down in sheets. "I suppose we must remain here until this shower ceases, or at least eases." She looked at him coyly. "What shall we do to while away the time?"

He chuckled wickedly. "You are really quite shameless, lass," he told her, backing her against the wall of the stable. His body not quite touching hers he reached around her, and cupped her buttocks in his big hands, fondling them teasingly. "What would you like to do, sweetheart?" he leered at her.

She was mesmerized by him. By the dark green eyes that devoured her face. By the strong fingers kneading her bottom. By the almost uncontrollable urge she was having to be made love to by him. She heard herself giving voice to her very thoughts. "I want you inside of me, Kieran Devers. I want you hard, and hot, and hungry for me."

"Jesu!" The word exploded from his mouth.

"I shock you because I am a virgin, and virgins shouldn't know such things, should they? But I have a mother who had a prince for a lover. I have a stepfather who is not shy about showing his passion for my mother. I have an elder sister who lived almost a year in a harem. And, Kieran Devers, I have eyes to see, and ears to hear. I know what happens between a man and a woman. I want that to happen between us. I am bold. Aye, I am, but I'm mad for you, and I want to be your wife," Fortune told him, her cheeks flushed with her daring.

He kissed her. He didn't know what else to do with her in the face of such frankness. She hadn't said anything to him that he hadn't been thinking himself. She wanted no more of him than he wanted of her. His hands moved to take her face between his two palms. His mouth moved over her soft skin hungrily, touching her lips, her nose, her eyes, her forehead, her cheekbones. She smelled of horse and heather. The nearness of her sent his senses reeling. He wanted the moment to go on forever. It didn't.

Rory Maguire's voice cut into their reverie. "Yer mam sent me to see where you were, m'lady Fortune."

Her eyes opened, and she smiled up at Kieran Devers as his hands released their hold upon her heart-shaped face. She looked past Maguire through the open stable door. "Ah, the rain has stopped," she noted. "We were waiting for it to cease, Rory."

"And well occupied you were, I could see, while you waited," he said dryly. Then his gaze fixed itself upon Kieran. "Her ladyship wants you to remain at Erne Rock for the interim, Kieran. Do you think you can behave yerself if you do? Frankly I think this is the best place for you—where we can keep our eye on you at all times."

"I'm not a maid of sixteen, Rory," Fortune said sharply.

"Nay, yer not, which means you should know better than to be making love in the open where every servant and gossip can see," he replied as pithily. "Next time, lass, try and be a bit more discreet. Word of your indiscretions with the handsome rogue will be distorted enough when they finally reach Lisnaskea. And you may believe me when I tell you that they'll be repeated in salacious detail to Lady Devers upon her return. She will not be happy to hear them, particularly as you will probably be wed to her stepson by then, having first spurned her lad. Her immediate thoughts, good Christian woman that she is, will be upon revenge."

"Mama should let us wed now," Fortune snapped. "Then there would be no cause for gossip."

"Yer mam is wise. Where's the harm in waiting if you truly love one another?" he demanded of her.

Fortune tossed her head in a gesture that was oddly familiar to him. "The harm may be in my belly if Mama makes me wait too long!" Then she dashed from the stables, heading for the castle steps.

Kieran Devers held up his hands in a gesture of surrender. "I will not seduce her," he promised the older man.

"Nay, but she'll do her best to seduce you," Maguire said with a shake of his head. "I had a younger sister, Aoife, who was just as headstrong as the lady Fortune. You had best be on yer guard, Kieran Devers. You could find yerself on yer back being ridden hard by that young vixen. A virgin she may be, but she's also an impudent wench."

The two men parted, Kieran Devers going into the castle.

Rory, however, left the stables, and walked to the small gate-house that Jasmine had given him years ago. He had not lived in it until she returned to Erne Rock, but it had long ago been furnished with family heirlooms dear to his heart; and Bride Duffy had seen that it was kept clean and aired should he ever need it again. Entering the house, and seeing his things, he was overcome with nostalgia. He climbed to a little attic beneath the pointed roof. There in a trunk was a rectangular box made of ashwood, its corners banded in silver. Removing the box he brought it down into the main room on the first floor of the gatehouse that served as his day room. A servant had already lit a peat fire against the damp.

Setting the box down on a table near the fireside chair, Rory poured himself a small dram of smoky whiskey. Then sitting down he sipped it appreciatively for several long moments before setting the tumbler aside, and reaching for the box. He had not seen, or opened this particular box in years. It contained individual miniatures of his family. Looking on them gave rise to a deep sadness, for Rory Maguire remembered that time long ago when his family had been in possession of Erne Rock, and Maguire's Ford. They had held their modest holding for several hundred years for their more powerful Maguire kin.

When their chieftain, Conor Maguire, had left Ireland with the northern earls over twenty years ago, Rory Maguire's father, mother, younger brother, along with his three sisters, and their families, had followed. He had been the only one not to go for he could not bear to leave their people to the mercy of the English. It had only been God's blessing, or the devil's luck, that their new English master turned out to be Jasmine Lindley, marchioness of Westleigh; and that she, even knowing his history, had made him manager for her new estate.

He had been able to remain in his home. While some might have been too proud to humble themselves as he had, Rory believed he had done the right thing in staying. His parents were buried in France, far from their native soil.

What had happened to his sisters and their families he did not know. His younger brother, Conan, had gone to Russia and become an officer in the Tzar's Imperial Army. He had last heard from Conan ten years ago. He might even be dead for all Rory knew. The box with its miniatures was all he had left of his family.

Slowly he raised the box's lid. There were the seven oval miniatures, each sitting in its little recessed velvet indentation. He smiled seeing his father's face for he realized he now looked like his father although he hadn't seen it when he was younger. There was his mother with her elegant long nose, and bright blue eyes. And there he was at eighteen, and Conan, the second son, and next to the youngest at fourteen. His sisters, Myrna, the eldest of them all at twenty-one; Aoife at sixteen, and Fionula at twelve. Those had been happy times, he thought sadly as he prepared to close the box.

But then suddenly his eye returned to Aoife. The artist had painted her in what had once been to him a familiar pose—an impatient toss of her head. It was a gesture he hadn't seen in years . . . *until today.* Rory lifted the miniature from its case, brushing the thin layer of dust from it. He stared unbelievingly at the face staring back at him. It was Aoife's face, yet he had long ago forgotten it. *It was also Fortune Lindley's face.* But he had not until now recognized the two faces as identical, yet they were without any doubt one and the same.

Reaching out he grabbed the tumbler in his fist, and swallowed its remaining contents down in a single gulp. He felt as if he had been felled by a giant blow. *How could it be?* How could Lady Fortune Lindley and his sister, Aoife, have the same face? The same gesture? The same flaming red-gold hair that in all the family only he and Aoife possessed? *Fool!* The voice in his head mocked him. You know the answer to your own question. Did you not lie with Jasmine Lindley all those years ago? *Fortune is your daughter.*

He groaned as if he had been injured. His mind raced back twenty-one years ago. The marquess of Westleigh had been murdered. His wife had fallen into a fit from which she could not be aroused. She had cried out for her husband to love her but one more time. She was dying, or so Adali and the priest had claimed. They sent him to make love to the delirious woman in hopes she could be drawn back from the brink of death. While he had loved her secretly from the first moment he had seen her, he had known she would never love him.

Rory remembered he had been shocked by the suggestion made to him. Especially since the priest harried him every bit as much as Adali, who could be forgiven, being a foreigner. Still, he could not resist the opportunity they offered him to make love to her, even if she would never know that he had done so. They had not had to struggle too hard to convince him, he realized. And if she lived he would have the secret satisfaction of knowing he had saved her. If she died, he would die too. So he had done their bidding, and then slipped from her chamber back into the shadows of his loneliness. But Jasmine had survived, finally awakening the following morning. Discovering she was with child several weeks later, they had all rejoiced that her beloved Rowan Lindley, who had himself made love to his wife the night before he was killed, had given his darling this final gift of a third child.

But Fortune was not Rowan Lindley's daughter. She was Rory Maguire's daughter. Who else knew? Did Jasmine? No! She would not know because she never knew of his part in saving her life. Adali would know. His damned sharp eye would miss nothing. And Father Cullen? Aye, he probably knew too! And they had managed to keep it from him all these years. Had he not felt the need today to look upon his family's faces again he might have never known the truth. And now that he did, what was he to do with it? He pocketed Aoife's miniature before closing the box and setting it aside. His hand ran through his red hair in a gesture of despair. *What was he going to do?*

A serving girl entered his day room with a covered tray.

"Master Adali sent you some supper, my lord, since you did not come to the hall. He asks if you are well." The girl set the tray down on a small table and lifted the linen cloth from it.

"Tell Adali I am not well, and would see him before he retires this night," Rory Maguire said. "And I would see Father Cullen too." Then seeing the horrified look on the servant's face he laughed. "Nay, lass, I am not dying. Just under the weather a bit. I need the priest's advice on another matter. Be discreet as you do my bidding, for I would cause no unnecessary disturbance." He gave a wink.

The girl hurried out giggling, and Rory looked at the meal on the tray. Trout. Several slices of beef. Bread. Butter and cheese. A dish of new green peas. He ate out of habit, but he tasted nothing. Pouring himself more whiskey he drank it down. He was cold. So damned cold. *He had a daughter.* A beautiful daughter who was the image of his favorite sister. A daughter who would be absolutely horrified to learn she was not the posthumous child of the marquess of Westleigh. He sighed. For twenty-one years he had kept the secret of Jasmine's survival after Rowan Lindley's death. It had not been easy, but he had done it, putting Jasmine from his mind, although she had always remained in his heart.

It had been a burden, but he now had an even heavier burden upon his shoulders. The knowledge of Fortune's true parentage. How could he not have known her? But Aoife had been gone from him so long, she had faded from his memory. They had all faded. He had put the box with the miniatures in his attic because it had been too painful being reminded of happier times and the loving family he had once had, and then lost. He might have gone with them, but he had refused to be driven from Ulster. He remembered how his mother and sisters had wept as they departed Maguire's Ford. The memory of it pierced his heart even now, some twenty-five years later.

He had strongly disagreed with the northern earls who had deserted their homes, and their people; for more people had been forced to remain than had been able to go. He had thought the earls selfish. He remembered arguing with his father, whose loyalty to his cousin, Conor Maguire, was greater it seemed than to his own immediate family. Only his mother's intervention had kept the two men from coming to blows. In the end, of course, his father's will prevailed. The family left Ulster in the earls' wake, but Rory Maguire had remained to protect, as best he could, the people of Maguire's Ford. That he had been able to was nothing short of a miracle, but in doing so he was bereft of a family. He had never married because he had fallen in love with Jasmine, and no other woman would do. She, of course, had never known the depth of his affections. Now, suddenly, he had a family; but how could he ever claim his daughter without causing Fortune and her mother irreparable harm?

The serving girl returned to take his tray, saying, "Both Master Adali and the priest will come, m'lord. Yer really all right, aren't you? Her ladyship asked that I inquire."

"Just a small flux upon my belly, lass," he told her with a smile. "I should be right as rain by the morrow."

"I'll tell her ladyship," the girl said, picking up the tray and leaving him alone once again.

He was not alone for long, however. Both Adali and Cullen Butler entered the room one after the other.

"Yer ill," the priest said. "The servant girl told my cousin."

"My illness is one of the soul, Cullen Butler," Rory responded. Reaching into his pocket he withdrew the oval miniature, and handed it to the priest.

Cullen Butler looked at it casually. Then he asked, "Where did you get this charming miniature of Fortune?" He handed the oval to Adali.

The majordomo looked at the small painting, saying quickly, "This is not the Lady Fortune, good Father. She does not bear the princess's birthmark between her left nostril and her upper lip." He looked directly at the Irishman. "Who is it?"

"My younger sister, Aoife," Rory Maguire replied.

"Of course," Adali said quietly. "The resemblance is utterly amazing, my lord Maguire. Both are beautiful women."

"You knew?" Rory's tone was accusatory.

"I knew," Adali said.

"And you, priest? Did you know also?" Rory's voice was hard.

"I knew," Cullen Butler admitted, "may God have mercy on me, on us all, Rory Maguire."

"But *she* does not know?"

"How could she?" Adali answered him. "She knew nothing of what transpired between you that night. Therefore she would not know the truth of her daughter's parentage. Nor would you have known but that you found that miniature of your sister."

"How could you have kept this secret from me? How could you have not told me that I had a daughter?" Rory asked his two companions brokenly. His blue eyes were filled with pain, and wet with his tears.

Cullen Butler looked stricken, but Adali was far more pragmatic than the guilt-ridden priest. "And if we had told you, Rory Maguire," he said, "what would you have done? What could you have done? *Nothing!* Who would have believed the manner in which my Lady Fortune was conceived? The knowledge of her true sire would have brought shame upon my princess, and the stain of bastardy upon Lady Fortune. You could have never expected to be a part of Lady Fortune's life, my lord Maguire. What happened twenty-one years ago was known to but four people. Madame Skye saw the truth, and questioned me. I did not lie to her. She is dead these seven years now, and only we three remain with our knowledge. What you did was a noble thing, my lord Maguire, and because I knew that you loved my princess I used you to save her. I felt no shame in my actions, nor should you have.

"I never knew my Lady Fortune would grow up as she did. I hoped that she would never see this place again, or you. But my princess has been determined for some years now to give this daughter Maguire's Ford. It was not up to me to tell her no, and it was only by unfortunate happenstance that you discovered the truth. I am sorry for you, my lord Maguire. 'Twill be a heavier burden for you to bear than any you have ever had before, but bear it in silence you will, or I will kill you myself. I will not have my princess, or her child, hurt by anyone. We will soon be returning to England, and that will be the end of it."

"Aye," Rory said quietly, "there is nothing I can do but sigh over the daughter who doesn't know she is my daughter; but that will not be the end of it, Adali. You cannot expect me to go on as if none of this ever happened. In the future I shall expect a letter from you twice a year telling me about my daughter, and how she gets on. That is only fair under the circumstances."

"Agreed," Adali said. He was a practical man, and this was a sensible solution to a rather unfortunate incident. "Remember, however, that my knowledge will not be first-hand once she is wed. There is talk that Lady Fortune and young Devers may go to a colony in the New World where all may worship as they choose. I will have to rely upon the letters sent to her mother, my lord Maguire."

"Fair enough," was the reply.

"I will pray for us all," Cullen Butler said, "especially you, Rory. Can you ever forgive me?"

"For what, Cullen Butler? You saved me from myself, and I fear Adali is right when he says I could never have been a part of my daughter's life without shaming both her and her mother."

"Then it is settled?" Adali said briskly.

"It is settled," Rory responded.

"And should you feel any bursts of foolishness overcome you, my lord Maguire, you will come to either me or the priest, eh?" A small smile creased Adali's brown face.

"I will," Rory agreed. Aye, I will be practical, but you cannot prevent me from dreaming about what might have

been, the Irishman thought to himself. You cannot prevent
me from protecting my child if need be. I have missed all of
her life but those first two months, and these past few weeks.
I will take what little happiness I can before she is gone from
me again, this time probably forever.

"I will return to the castle then," Adali said, and turning
he left his two companions.

"Stay, and have a bit of whiskey with me, Cullen Butler,"
Rory said. "You look as if you could use it. Strangely I think
this is harder on you than on Adali and me." He motioned
the priest into the other chair by the peat fire, and pouring
him a tumbler of whiskey handed it to him. *"Slanta!"* he
said, downing a goodly dollop from his own tumbler.

"Slanta!" the priest nodded, swallowing down half his
portion. Then feeling stronger he said, "You are truly content
then, Rory?"

Maguire shrugged. "What else can I do, good Father?
God's blood, when I saw Aoife's face for the first time in all
those years, and then recognized it as Fortune's face too! I
thought at first I was imagining things. Then I realized I was
not. So I do not die entirely alone one day. My daughter and
her children will live on for me. It is a better fate than I had
hoped for, Cullen Butler."

"I am so sorry, my friend," the priest said. "That I should
have been drawn into such a plot all those years ago still as-
tounds me. Yet that plot saved my cousin's life though she
knows it not. I remember asking my Aunt Skye how an ac-
tion so wrong could be right. Do you know what she said to
me? That the church was often wrong. That the laws to
which they clung so determinedly were made by men, and
not by God. She believed if mankind used more common
sense we would be a great deal better off." He smiled with
his memory; then he sobered once again. "But you were hurt
by our actions, I know, Rory. I had thought it all behind us,
and it might have been but that you sought out those miniatures. You must be discreet now, and I know it will be difficult for you for young Fortune is a willful lass."

"So was Aoife," Rory replied with a small chuckle. "And now I know where Fortune gets her passion for horses from, for my sister had that same passion, and like Fortune was a marvelous horsewoman. She is not her mother, priest, but a headstrong Irish lass, I fear."

"I will warn my cousin, Jasmine, to watch the lass more carefully," Cullen Butler replied.

"And I'll be watching my daughter too," Rory told him. " 'Tis a good, if unfortunate, match she wants. Her desire for Kieran Devers has cost her Maguire's Ford. Still, I would not want her living under the constant threat of a charge of treason because of her husband's faith, which will happen if she remains in Ireland. When are the two young Leslie lads arriving to claim this gift from their mother?"

"Next spring," the priest said. "Jasmine has told me she wants to have them confirmed by the king in their rights to Maguire's Ford so that none can gainsay them. I am more than aware that Lady Devers has long had her beady blue eyes on this estate. She thought to gain it through Fortune, and while I will admit I thought William Devers suitable, I feared *that* woman's influence over her son. We may thank God that she herself has destroyed all chances of a match between Fortune and young Will; and we may praise God that Fortune is a wise lass who saw the danger in such a mother-in-law."

"Aye," Rory agreed, "but she'll have made an enemy of that fine lady when her preference for Kieran Devers becomes public knowledge. Lady Jane will find it hard to stomach the fact that Fortune preferred her stepson over her son."

"She cannot have her cake and eat it too," Father Cullen answered him. "She feared Fortune's influence while coveting the girl's dowry. Now she'll have neither, and my cousin, Jasmine, will make certain she does not gain Maguire's Ford and Erne Rock by foul means when she could not acquire them by fair."

"I hope yer right," Maguire said, "but she's a determined woman, Jane Devers, for all the fact that she's English."

Cullen Butler laughed. "Now, Rory, my friend, even the English have their good side, or so I'm told, although the holy mother church might disagree."

"And there's one time I'd be in agreement with the church myself," came the dry reply. " 'Twilll not hurt to keep an eye on the Deverses when they return from England. Remember, the Leslie lads will not come until next spring, and they are young. We'll have to watch them closely lest *that* woman attempt to cause any mischief."

"We'll watch together, you and I, my friend," the priest said. "We'll watch together."

Part Two

ULSTER AND ENGLAND
1630–1631

"All I know about love is that love is all there is."
—Emily Dickenson

Chapter

7

Midsummer's Eve on June twenty-first marked the halfway point in the growing season between May Day and Lammastide on August first. In Ulster this year it dawned unusually sunny. Kieran Devers rode that day from Erne Rock to Mallow Court to make certain his father's estate was being managed properly in his absence. He was very surprised to find his sister, Lady Colleen Kelly, in residence.

"When did you get here?" he asked her, giving her a kiss.

"Mama wrote from England that I should come and check on you," she told him with a smile. "Where have you been, Kieran? I have been here three days already, and the servants were most mysterious." She was a pretty young woman with black hair like her brother's, and fine blue eyes. "Mama is still smarting over the fact that Willy was turned down by Lady Lindley, and yet she is already planning his wedding to Emily Anne. She says he is coming around, which of course means she has finally badgered him into submission." Colleen laughed. Then she said, "Was Lady Lindley really as awful as Mama says she is?"

"Fortune Lindley is independent, headstrong, intelligent, clever, and beautiful," he replied. "She would have made Willy absolutely miserable, for he would have found himself torn between her and his mother. She was wise enough to see it, and so she sent him away, albeit gently for she is not unkind."

"You seem to know her well, big brother," Colleen Kelly said softly, her blue eyes curious.

"I'm going to marry her, Colleen," came the surprising reply.

"Oh, Kieran," his sister said breathily, her hand flying to her heart with surprise.

He put an arm about her shoulders. "I know, Colleen, I know. Fortune and I have done the unthinkable. We have fallen in love. We will not be forgiven by Lady Jane, or Willy, for our recklessness, but there it is. It is impossible to control the direction of the heart as I have found much to my surprise." He smiled at her wryly.

"Mama has had her eye on Maguire's Ford ever since she learned from the Reverend Steen it was owned by a duchess with an eligible daughter. For you to steal that girl from under her nose is an insult she will never forgive, Kieran," his sister warned him.

"Once she met Fortune she didn't even like her, and did all in her power to remove Willy from the girl's influence," he replied.

"But for you to acquire Maguire's Ford, which is so much bigger, and more prosperous than Mallow Court, after Willy has been sent down by this heiress is a terrible affront. You know it as well as I, big brother. If Mama would not allow you to inherit Da's holding one day unless you became a Protestant, do you really think she will be content to sit by while you snap up a larger and richer estate from under her nose?"

"Maguire's Ford does not belong to Fortune," Kieran told his younger sister. "It belongs to her mother, the duchess of Glenkirk. It was only to be Fortune's if she married a

Protestant. Lady Leslie is no fool, Colleen. Fortune and I will go to England, and from there we will probably go to the New World. Neither of us has ever felt at home in any place we have lived."

"Why can you not simply become a Protestant? Just think if your Fortune managed to bring you to our church how frustrating it would be for Mama after all her years of trying," Colleen chuckled.

"You know why I will not convert," he said quietly.

"Kieran, our mother has been dead these twenty-seven years. You have made your point. I hate it that you will have to leave Ireland! We will never see you again. If you did not have that tiny miniature of our mother you would not even remember what she looked like," Colleen told him desperately.

"She looked like you, Colleen," he replied with devastating effect. "She was fair with her blue eyes, and raven's wing hair, and she was but twenty years old when she died birthing you. I do not blame you for what happened, Colleen. You were only two when Da remarried. I do not blame Moire, for she didn't want to be cut out of Da's life. As for me, I made my decision long ago. I see no reason to change it."

"But you aren't even particularly devout, or prayerful," his sister noted. "Why you even care is beyond me."

"Come with me over to Erne Rock Castle, and meet Fortune," her brother said. "The Leslies are very hospitable folk."

"Nay," Colleen said, shaking her head vigorously. "If I go I shall have to tell Mama I knew what you were up to, and I don't want to do that, Kieran. You recall our mother, but remember that Lady Jane is the only mother I have ever known. She made no distinction between me, or Mary, or the children she bore our father. And even when I disappointed her by marrying an Irish Protestant rather than an English one, she never deserted me. Even Mary loves her. You were the only one of Da's offspring who could not get on with her, Kieran."

"You'll be going back home," he wheedled her, "and not see our dear stepmother until Willy's wedding to Emily Anne. By then it will be known that Fortune and I are to be wed. Our stepmother will be so torn between her joy over getting Emily Anne as a daughter-in-law, and her outrage at my own marriage, she won't think to wonder if you met the Leslies while you were here in Ulster checking up on me. She will assume I slyly kept it from you because you would certainly have told her had you known. You've always been so good, Colleen; our stepmother would never suspect you of a subterfuge." He grinned mischievously at his younger sister, then grew serious again. "It will probably be the last time we see each other, Colleen, and the only opportunity you will have to meet Fortune. I want you to know the girl who is to be my wife. You are my favorite sister, and our true mam's last gift to her family."

"Damn you, Kieran," she said, tears in her eyes. "You have the tongue of the devil himself. Very well, I will come and meet your lass, and then I shall flee south to my own home. Mama will be home shortly after Lammastide for Willy's wedding which is planned for Michaelmas."

"I need a few hours to go over the estate books for Da," he told her. "I'll remain the night, and then tomorrow we'll ride over to Maguire's Ford."

"I'll have to pretend I'm departing for home," Colleen said. "I don't want Mama's servants gossiping when she returns, and they will. It doesn't matter to you, I know, but it does to me, Kieran."

"Aye," he replied. "I really do understand, Colleen, but I wanted you, of all my siblings, to know that Fortune is not the terrible creature Lady Jane claims she is."

"God's blood, Kieran," his sister swore softly. "You're in love! Really in love! I would have never thought it of you."

"Catholics fall in love, too," he remarked dryly.

She laughed. "Now, big brother, do not paint me with the

same brush you do Mama. I am not that close-minded thanks to you."

He chuckled. "If Lady Jane ever knew that you occasionally attended the mass with me she would have disowned you entirely. And worse, you met our half-sisters, and Da's kind Molly. I knew I could trust you. Not Moire, for she would have never done anything to earn our stepmother's disapproval, but you had a bit of an adventurous spirit unlike the others."

"It's a wonder I wasn't caught. I almost was when Bessie was eight. She got very curious about where you and I used to roam. I told her we were searching for a leprechaun and his gold. She was so like Mama, and made fun of me for believing in such things, but it quelled her curiosity. Not Mary, however. She followed us one day when we went to visit Molly and the girls. When I got back she threatened to tell Mama. She was so mean! I said if she did, you would put an Irish curse on her, and she would grow a wart on the very tip of her nose so she could never find a husband. She scoffed at me, but she was afraid, I know, for she never told Mama."

"So that is why you never went back to Molly's," he said.

Colleen nodded. "I thought it better I didn't. Mary was never certain if the visit she spied upon was a one time thing, or not. It was better that way."

That evening brother and sister watched as the bonfires were lit upon the hills in honor of Midsummer's Eve. There would be dancing and feasting in the nearby villages. Kieran gave his permission for the servants to celebrate if they chose to do so. Without the presence of Lady Jane, or her disapproval, the house was emptied by late afternoon. A cold supper had been left for the siblings in the larder. Colleen had instructed her coachman and her maid that they would be returning south the following day, and she should like to leave as early as possible.

In the morning they departed Mallow Court, but no sooner were they out upon the high road than Colleen sig-

naled her coachman to stop. Exiting her carriage she untied
her mare from the rear of the vehicle, mounted it, and said to
her driver, "I have a stop to make before we go south,
Joseph. Just follow along after my brother and me."

By midafternoon they were within sight of Maguire's
Ford. Fortune came to meet them, riding her great gray gelding, her red hair flying as she galloped across the hills to
greet them. They stopped to await her as Fortune drew
Thunder to a halt.

"If this is your wife, and you've lied to me, Kieran Devers,
I'll cut your black heart out!" she said to him, grinning.

" 'Tis my sister, Colleen, and I've brought her to meet
you so at least someone in my family could defend your reputation. Now, however, you bad-tempered wench, you've
disgraced youself," he teased her back.

Fortune's blue-green eyes swung to meet Lady Colleen
Kelly's gaze. "You're Mary Maguire's last child," she said.
"Welcome to Maguire's Ford, m'lady. You'll remain a few
days?"

"I think I will," Colleen heard herself reply.

"Good!" Fortune responded. "Come on, you two, and I'll
race you home. I hope you're better at racing than your
brother. He always whines, and cries foul when he loses,
which is more often than not."

"I never whine," Colleen said, and kicking her mare she
raced off down the road away from them.

With a delighted whoop Fortune followed her. Shaking
his head Kieran dashed after the two young women, catching
up to them only when he arrived in the courtyard of Erne
Rock castle where they stood, already dismounted, laughing
madly, their arms about each other.

"I suspected you were two of a kind," he said, sliding
from his saddle.

"Come into the house," Fortune said, linking her arm
with Colleen's. "My parents will be delighted to meet you."

Jasmine and James Leslie were in the hall of Erne Rock.

She seated by the fire, and he standing next to the stone mantel. Introductions were made, but Fortune suddenly realized that her parents seemed rather subdued and perhaps even a bit distracted.

"What is wrong?" she asked. "Is everything all right?"

"Your mother has some rather startling news," the duke said, putting a hand upon Jasmine's shoulder, and giving it a small squeeze.

"Mama?" Fortune's beautiful face was concerned, and she knelt by her mother's side.

"Perhaps this is not a good time for uninvited guests," Colleen said.

"Nay, my dear, you are more than welcome," Jasmine said. "It is just that I have gotten a bit of a surprise today. It seems that I am going to have a baby."

"What?" The color drained from Fortune's face. "Mama! It cannot be! You are much too old to have another baby!"

Jasmine laughed, and patted her daughter's cheek. " 'Tis exactly what I thought, poppet, but it would seem I am not too old after all."

"And I am certainly not too old," James Leslie replied.

Fortune blushed, clearly embarrassed by her parents' behavior, and yet the thought of another baby was rather nice. It would keep Mama and Papa from missing her too much when she and Kieran went away. "When is this baby to arrive?" she asked her parent.

"Sometime in November," Jasmine said.

"Madame, you have my warmest felicitations," Colleen said. "I have three of my own."

"How can you be certain?" Fortune asked.

"I am certain because I have borne eight children previously," Jasmine said, "although I will admit when my moon link broke, I thought it was the autumn of my years come upon me. But then I noticed . . ." She stopped. "I do not think this is a conversation for mixed company, poppet. Let us just say I am certain, and Bride Murphy, who acts as the village midwife, has confirmed my suspicions."

"Then we must go back to Glenkirk right away," Fortune said.

Jasmine shook her head. "Nay. Bride has advised me against traveling because of my age. This baby will be born here as you were. I have already sent home for Adam and Duncan to come so the people of the estate can learn to know them even sooner. Your brother, Patrick, will have to remain at Glenkirk on his own. I have sent down to Edinburgh for Uncle Adam and Aunt Fiona Leslie to come and watch over him. He enjoys their company, and will not feel quite so bereft of his family with them there. I know Adam and Fiona have grown quite bored with the city in recent years. I believe they will welcome the chance to return to Glenkirk. So, my dears, we must settle ourselves in for a bit of a stay here," Jasmine concluded.

"Then Kieran and I must wed immediately," Fortune said. "Colleen tells me the Deverses will return from England by Lammastide. Will is to marry his cousin Emily Anne at Michaelmas."

"Then you most certainly cannot be wed to Kieran until after his brother has married, Fortune," James Leslie said firmly. "The Deverses will not be pleased by what has transpired while they were away. If they return to find you married to Kieran it will make bad blood between the people of Maguire's Ford and the people of Lisnaskea. William Devers asked you to marry him, and you turned him down. Nicely, but it was still a refusal. If you and Kieran publicly declare yourselves, and wed before William marries his cousin, it will be an even greater insult. You know you have our permission to wed Kieran. All we ask is that you wait until after Michaelmas, and William's nuptials."

"I agree with you, my lord," Kieran Devers said quickly, forestalling any vocal outburst by Fortune, to whom he now turned. "Your father is right, sweetheart. I love my father, and my brother. I don't want a feud between us over our decision."

"But they will be offended anyway," Fortune reasoned.

"But their offense will be less since Willy married first," Colleen interjected. "My stepmother will fume, I guarantee you, but with Willy wed she will be able to put a far better face on the situation than if she returned to find you and Kieran a *fait accompli*. What worries me is her desire to possess Maguire's Ford which she had hoped to gain when Willy married Fortune." Colleen turned to the duchess. "Kieran says the estate is yours, my lady. Is it so? Please understand that while I love my stepmother, and would not be disloyal to her, I love my older brother too. Lady Jane is acquisitive. She will not like the idea that Kieran will have this place through marriage to your daughter who spurned her son."

"Kieran will not gain Maguire's Ford," Jasmine said quietly. "My two younger Leslie sons have been raised Protestants. Being the younger in our family, they have nothing to recommend them but their good name. My eldest son is the marquess of Westleigh. My second son, the duke of Lundy. My third son will one day inherit his father's dukedom. Only Adam and Duncan are titleless, and landless. They can well live without the former, but it is difficult to live without the latter. I shall divide Maguire's Ford equally between them. To steal this estate away from me on *any grounds* would require a great deal of influence at court. I do not believe your stepmother has that particular resource, *but I do*."

"But then where will Kieran and Fortune go, especially given his intransigence regarding the matter of religion?" Colleen wondered. "He has said something to me about the New World."

"Aye. Sir George Calvert is attempting to found a colony in the New World based on the principles of religious freedom. He is a Catholic himself, well-liked, and well respected. The king is very fond of him. If anyone can succeed in such an endeavor, he can. I believe there is a place for Fortune and your brother in his colony. When we return to England we will see what progress he has made. In the meantime I shall write to my son, Charlie, who is at court. He will obtain whatever information I need. Do not worry about Kieran, my dear. There is a safe harbor for him, and for Fortune. Now, however, we must make a berth for you. Our guest chambers are small, but very comfortable. I'm certain Adali has already shown your maidservant where you will lay your pretty head." She smiled at Colleen.

"You are most gracious, my lady," the younger woman said, curtsying. "I am so glad that Kieran insisted I come to Erne Rock to meet Fortune, and her family. My mind is at peace now knowing my brother will be safe."

Lady Colleen Kelly did not depart Erne Rock for several days despite her good intentions to do so. She found she liked the duke and his wife. Fortune frankly delighted her, despite her outspoken ways. She could well understand why her stepmother had not taken to the girl, but she could also see that while Fortune had been the wrong lass for Willy, she was absolutely the right girl for Kieran. Lady Jane lived a rather insular life in Lisnaskea, Colleen realized, for she herself had been gone for several years, and knew that in Dublin Fortune Lindley would have been much appreciated for her wit, her beauty, and her intellect. Her older brother and Fortune were a perfect match although she knew that their marriage would bring trouble for them. Her stepmother would find some way to exact revenge.

"Have you chosen a wedding day?" she asked the couple the night before she was to finally leave for her own home.

Kieran looked to Fortune.

"A few days after William is wed," Fortune said. "When Lady Jane learns we are remaining here at Maguire's Ford for the next few months, she will have no choice but to invite my family to the wedding, for to exclude us would be a dreadful faux pas as my parents are of high rank, and friends of the king. And we will have no choice but to go, lest we appear to either be snubbing the Deverses, or our absence give rumor to the lie that it is Will who turned me away in favor of his cousin, Mistress Elliot. Such a thing would be unthinkable."

"Mama would like that," Colleen said candidly. "When will you tell the family of your own plans?"

Fortune's brow grew troubled. "I do not know," she said. "I am frankly at a loss how to broach it. I do not want to spoil your younger brother's wedding day, and I fear such knowledge would."

Colleen nodded. "Kieran will have to go back to Mallow Court," she said. "If he remains here at Erne Rock there will be no stopping the gossip. It will certainly come to my parents' ears when they return. Mama's servants love Kieran, but now that he is not the heir, they are loyaler to my stepmother and Willy, mindful of their own futures. I cannot blame them."

"Lady Kelly is absolutely right," the duke of Glenkirk said. He put a comforting arm about Fortune. "I know you love each other, poppet, but until the day you are wed, you and Kieran must be separated. The Deverses will be angry enough when they learn of this turn of events. However, Sir Shane is a reasonable man. I shall be able to make our peace wi him, but his wife, and her son will be mortally offended. There will be nae forgiveness there, poppet. If I am nae mistaken, they will go out of their way to make difficulties."

"But Lady Jane is getting what she always wanted. Will will wed his cousin, Mistress Elliot," Fortune said despairingly.

" 'Twas not *you* Mama wanted for Willy, Fortune," Colleen said. " 'Twas your rich estate. She thought she could stifle her disappointment over her niece, and accept you as a daughter-in-law because you would bring her son Maguire's Ford, and Erne Rock castle. But once she met you, saw how beautiful you were, how willful, and determined you were to run your own life, she knew she could not bear you, for you would have taken Willy away from her, which is something that poor Emily Anne will never do."

"How astute you are," the duchess said quietly.

"Please, do not think me disloyal, madame," Colleen replied. "I love *all* my family, and would have them happy. Mama cannot help herself. She is ambitious for all her children. Using some of the inheritance her father left her she arranged marriages for my sisters, Mary, and Bessie, with minor lordlings in England. She was very proud of those matches. Only the fact that my Hugh's mother is English placated her and enabled her to give her consent to my marriage. She doesn't really like the Irish even if she is the wife of an Irishman. She means no harm. She has done her best to be a good wife to Papa, and a good mother to all of his children. Only Kieran escaped her vigilance, but because he has been so amenable about Willy being made Papa's heir, she is willing to tolerate what she refers to as his *impossible behavior.* Every family, she says, has at least one bad penny."

"Kieran isn't a bad penny," Fortune said indignantly. "He is a man of strong principles."

"Unfortunately my principles are not those of my stepmother," Kieran Devers said with a wry grin.

Colleen laughed. "Nay, they are not, brother."

In the morning, Lady Kelly departed Erne Rock Castle for her home outside of Dublin. "I may offend Mama, madame," she told Jasmine, "but if Kieran's wedding to your daughter is shortly after our brother Willy's wedding, then I would be there to see it. Will you write, and let me know what date they have chosen? If I am not mistaken, Papa will be there with me. He says nothing for he does love Mama, but he loves Kieran too, even though my older brother's intransigence hurts him deeply."

"I will write," Jasmine promised.

Lady Kelly's coach moved out of the courtyard and across the little drawbridge. Kieran and Fortune rode alongside of the vehicle as far as the Dublin road. There the coach stopped for a minute while brother and sister bid each other a tender farewell, and Fortune kissed Colleen's cheek lovingly. Then the carriage rumbled away, Kieran and Fortune waving after it until it was out of sight around a bend.

The late June morning was cloudy and warmish. It was obvious that a storm would threaten by late afternoon. They rode a ways without speaking, heading for their favorite place, the ruins of the hall of Black Colm Maguire. Fortune had asked Rory about it after the first time she and Kieran had sheltered there. Black Colm had been so called not for his dark hair, but his black heart. When he carried off the wife of his chieftain, and raped her, his enraged relations had finally had enough of him. They had stormed Black Colm's hall one moonless night. He had disappeared, however, gone to his master, the devil, so it was said. He was never seen again. His unfortunate victim was rescued and brought back to her home, but never again did she speak a word to anyone to her husband's sorrow. Black Colm's hall was pulled down and razed.

" 'Tis an unhappy place," Rory said, but Fortune did not find it so, for it was here she and Kieran might be alone, free from spying eyes. To her the ruined hall was a place of happiness. The summer rain came suddenly with a small rumble of thunder. It poured down in sheets, obscuring the lough, and the hills beyond. The horses huddled beneath a wide stone arch, almost dry. Nearby Fortune and Kieran sat within their sheltered alcove, arms about each other.

"We should choose a wedding day before you leave me," she said.

"You need but tell me, sweetheart" he replied, "and I will be there." He kissed the top of her red head, his arm tightening about her.

She snuggled against him, rubbing her cheek against the

leather of his doublet. "October," she said. "As soon as possible after Willy marries his cousin. October fifth?" She looked questioningly up at him.

"It sounds as good a day as any, my love." He brushed his lips against hers softly. "Sweet, sweet," he murmured low.

"Kieran, I cannot bear it that you are to leave me," Fortune whispered. "I am behaving like a child, I know, yet the thought of not seeing you every day is hard." Her hand cupped his dark head, and drew him to her so she might kiss him softly.

"It is not forever, my love," he soothed her, nibbling on her lower lip. She was so damned exciting in her innocence.

"Could we not meet here where there is no one to see us?" she cajoled him sweetly, her tongue sweeping around his lips.

"The family is due back at Lammastide, and that is just a little over a month away, Fortune. Once they return it will be difficult for me to disappear too often without rousing suspicion. When my dear stepmother orchestrates a family celebration, we are all pressed into her service, and expected to be at her immediate beck and call. Willy's wedding will be the triumph of her life to date, for he is the heir to Mallow Court. If poor Emily Anne thinks it is to be her day as the blushing bride, she will find herself sadly mistaken, and overshadowed by her mother-in-law," Kieran chuckled. "We can meet here several times a week until the preparations begin. After that I cannot say when I will see you, sweetheart."

For a long moment Fortune felt overwhelmed with her disappointment, but then she laughed. "I suppose I will be so busy preparing for our own wedding that I will not miss you at all. Well," she amended, "almost not at all. Won't they be surprised when we marry just a week after Will and his Emily?" Her eyes danced wickedly.

"Shocked is more like it," he said with a grin. "You don't want to give them any warning?"

"Nay, Kieran! There is simply no good time to tell your

family. 'Twould but spoil Will's wedding, and cause such an uproar that we would be the focus of everyone's attention, and I do not think that would please Lady Jane. Besides, while I dislike your stepmother, I do like Will, and would not deliberately cause his unhappiness."

"Our marriage will not please my stepmother," he said.

"Nay, it will absolutely not, but then it is not really her concern, is it?" Fortune said with complete logic. "You are not her son, and she has, in her bigotry, done you a great disservice, stealing your inheritance from you for her son. I hold no sympathy for Lady Jane."

"You are so strong and so fierce," he said, wrapping her in his embrace, and kissing her hard so that her lips felt almost bruised.

"Make love to me, Kieran," Fortune murmured into his ear. She tickled it with the pointed end of her tongue, and breathed softly into the whorl of it even as she moved her body provocatively against his. "You want me, Kieran. I know that you do." She slid a hand up to caress the back of his neck, entwining her fingers through the thick dark hair at the nape. It felt silken yet rough to her touch.

"You're a wicked wench," he told her through gritted teeth. He could feel his male member beginning to stir with serious interest.

In response Fortune took her other hand, slipped the buttons on her doeskin doublet, and unlaced her shirt front. She smiled as, unable to help himself, he slid his hand into her blouse and cupped her breast within it. "Ummmmm," she murmured as he fondled her. "Ohhh!" she squealed as he teased at her nipple, pinching it lightly.

He backed her hard against the stone wall of the alcove. "You mustn't tease me, Fortune. You don't know what you are doing," he told her. He was beginning to throb with his need for her.

Her head was spinning with the nearness of him. "Yes, I do know exactly what I am doing, Kieran," she told him breathlessly. "I am tired of being a virgin! *Make love to me!"*

"No," he said. "You will come to me on our wedding night a proper virgin, Fortune, but since you are so damned curious I will offer you a small lesson in passion. I wonder if you are brave enough to manage it." Then before she might answer he pulled off her doublet and her shirt, baring her to the waist. "Ahhh," he breathed. "How lovely you are, sweetheart." His big hands encircled her waist, and he lifted her up onto the stone bench where he might view her at his leisure.

Fortune was surprised at first, but then she smiled very seductively down into his handsome face, and loosening her belt she pulled her breeches down, letting them fall to her calves where her boot tops stopped them. "Just how brave are you, sir?" she asked him.

"Jesu," he groaned, seeing her, for all intents and purposes, naked. Her skin was pale and flawless. Her Venus mont was hairless. He had heard that great ladies denuded themselves in this manner but he had never seen such a sight before. His country lovers had sported curls where her mound was pink and smooth. Her cleft was mauve shadowed, a long tempting slash that seemed to beckon him to his destruction. "Cover yourself," he begged her. "You are too beautiful, Fortune." He could not restrain himself. His hands reached up and caressed her.

With a deep sigh of pleasure Fortune closed her eyes, not in the least afraid when he cupped her buttocks in his palms, drawing her near so that his face pressed into her soft belly. She gasped softly as he covered her flesh with little kisses. Then his hands slid upwards to grasp her breasts in a hard embrace. Her body arced itself, pressing harder against his face, feeling the sandy roughness of his cheek against her.

Kieran Devers was shaken to the core of his very being by her beauty, and her obvious willingness to give herself to him without reservation. His manhood was iron hard now. Why not? he thought to himself. Where was the harm in it? They were to be wed soon. Then his conscience began to niggle at him. Aye, they were to be wed, but he held Fortune in the deepest love and respect. What if he got her with child? What if, God forbid! he were killed in an accident, and their child was born a bastard? She was not her mother, a royal Mughal princess, nor was he a Stuart prince whose bastard child had been welcomed as if he were every bit as legitimate as that prince himself. He felt himself begin to tremble as he reached the outer edge of sanity, and restraint. With a groan he pulled her breeches up, and buckled her belt. "Clothe yourself," he growled angrily at her.

"What is the matter?" Fortune asked him. "How have I displeased you, Kieran, that you do not want me?"

"Put your shirt on, and we will talk," he said harshly, turning away from her as he saw the tears in her eyes.

Confused, and burning with feelings she had never felt before, and certainly didn't understand, Fortune picked up her silk shirt, and pulling it over her head, tied it. Her doublet followed, and she buttoned it up. "I am dressed now," she said, still standing upon the bench.

He turned, lifting her down, and enfolded her tightly in his arms. "I love you," he said. "When I take your virginity, I want it to be in our marriage bed. I want the leisure to caress and admire your loveliness. To kiss you long and sweet kisses, not just on your lips, but all over your fair body, Fortune. If anything should happen to me before we said our marriage vows, and you were with child, *our child,* a child created from our love for each other; our innocent offspring would be considered bastardborn, shunned. I will not do that to you, Fortune. I will not do that to our child. Do you understand?"

She nodded her head against his chest, then said, "But I long for you so much, Kieran. My body aches with its need for the unknown."

"As mine burns for you, and the thousand pleasures that will come when we are joined together, sweetheart," he told her. "I see now it is better that we be separated else our passions overcome us."

"But we will continue to meet here?" she begged him. "At least until Lammastide?"

"We Celts in Ireland call it *Lugnasadh,*" he told her. "It is a harvest festival, but in ancient times it was the yearly celebration of the many-skilled god, Lugh."

"You know the ancient stories, don't you?" Fortune said. "And yet you claim to have no place here in Ireland. Are you certain, Kieran?"

He smiled down at her. "I like the old history, and the old tales, sweetheart, but it does not mean I feel at home here. Nay, my sweet Fortune, our future together is somewhere else. Perhaps in that new colony your mother's acquaintance, Lord Baltimore, seeks to found. I like the idea of starting afresh in a new place where we will be accepted for ourselves, and not judged by others."

"There will always be those who judge," Fortune replied cynically.

He laughed. "You are so innocent on one hand, yet on the other you are very worldly, my love."

"I have had a rather eclectic upbringing," Fortune said dryly. "Whenever Mama went to court we were left behind at Queen's Malvern with her grandparents. It was, frankly, my favorite place, for Madame Skye was so interesting, and so knowledgeable. We were very small then. I was just four and a half when my great-grandfather de Marisco died. After that Madame Skye was never quite the same, although she never stopped loving us, or involving herself in our lives. I have lived in France, and in Scotland. I saw the proxy marriage of King Charles in Paris. I have never been bored, Kieran. I look forward to finding this new place with you, for although I have never thought myself adventurous, and I wish only for a good marriage, there is something in me that longs to leave this old world and see the new. I have always been considered practical. Yet of late I have discovered that I am, perhaps, a bit more like the women in my family than I had previously believed. I have never really wanted to be like them. They are too impossible, and wildly passionate to the point of disaster."

He burst out laughing. "And you do not consider removing your clothing before a man in a stone ruin in a driving rainstorm impossible, or wildly passionate?"

"But I wanted you to make love to me," she wailed. "I don't really know what lovemaking is all about, and yet I know I must do it, or die of this terrible longing that has engulfed me," she told him.

He hugged her hard. "I adore you, Fortune Lindley. You are mad, and marvelous! I never thought to find a girl like you, but now that I have I shall not let you go!"

Fortune sighed happily. "I don't care where we go, Kieran, as long as we are together," she told him.

"Go home, you adorable temptress. I will be here at this same time in three days," he said. "If my family is due home at the beginning of August, there will shortly be a message from England for me. My stepmother is extremely organized. If Willy is to be married on September twenty-ninth, she will already have certain instructions for the staff; and she will want me to be her liaison between the Deverses and the Elliots before her return. Poor Willy! His whole life is now quite neatly mapped out."

"Your brother will be happy that way," Fortune replied. "He does not appear to me to be a venturesome lad. That's why I was so certain that he would suit me. Then I discovered I wasn't a demure and retiring girl after all."

He chuckled. "Demure is not a word I would use to describe you, Fortune. Wild and willful is more like it." He ducked the blow she aimed at his head. "Come on, lass, and up on your great Thunder. I've a longer ride than you to get home." He caught her gelding, and helped her to mount.

"I'll be glad when home is the same resting place for us both," she told him softly. She had almost succeeded in seducing him today. She intended trying again. She knew her mother had some concoction she took that had been handed down from generation to generation that prevented conception. She didn't want to wait until October to feel his hard body on hers, loving her as she had never been loved before. *She wanted him now, not later!*

"Three days from now, sweeting," he told her, wondering what that light of battle in her eye had been about. He took her gloved hand in his, and kissed it, then smacked Thunder's rump hard. The gelding bolted off, Fortune clinging to his back like a burr. He smiled watching her go, his wild and willful lass. She had almost tempted him beyond perdition today, but he would not allow it to happen again. He was older, and the responsibility for her reputation rested in his hands. He loved her too much to fail her.

Chapter

8

"What is it that Mama uses when she wants to prevent babies?" Fortune inquired of her mother's serving woman, Rohana. Then she giggled. "She obviously hasn't been using it lately, or she would not be with child again."

Rohana's dark eyes were expressionless as she carefully folded her mistress's newly laundered chemises. "Your mother thought herself past the time of bearing new life, child," she replied, and closed the storage chest. "As for your question, it is not for me to answer you. Ask your mama, but I am sure she will tell you before you wed with Master Kieran."

Fortune stamped her foot. "Damn it, Rohana, you know! Why will you not tell me?"

"For the very reason you will not ask your mother," was the sharp reply. "You are a grandchild of the Mughal, and your blood runs hot, Fortune. You seek to seduce your beloved, and escape any of the consequences of your bad actions. I will not help you."

Fortune shrugged. "It matters not. I shall have him when I want him anyhow," she said petulantly.

"What is the matter?" Rohana demanded. "You have always been the one child my lady did not have to worry over. What has made you turn into such a heedless and willful girl?"

Fortune sighed. "I know, I know," she said. "I do not understand it myself, Rohana. I am the sensible and practical one, but I do not want to be either of those things any longer. I just want to be with Kieran. What has happened to me?"

"Love," Rohana replied sanguinely, her dark eyes suddenly alight with comprehension. "You are in love, child. It tends to make the women of your family reckless. Still, it is now the month of July, and you will be wed in three more months' time. Be patient."

"But what if what I want is a disappointment to me when I finally obtain it?" Fortune worried.

Rohana laughed. "It will not be, and certainly not with that great, handsome, dark, and glowering Celt who has stolen your heart, my child. A word of warning to you. If the cow should give away her cream to a prospective purchaser, and he decides he does not like it, then perhaps he will not want the cow, eh? Master Kieran is a man in every sense as several of the girls in this village will attest to, Fortune. You are but an inexperienced virgin. Save yourself until you have his ring on your finger else he lose interest."

"I had not thought of it that way," Fortune considered. "I have allowed my passions to overwhelm me, and am behaving foolishly. You are right, Rohana. Best his ring is on my finger, and my ring in his nose before I give myself to Kieran Devers."

Rohana chuckled. "Aye," she agreed. "Tease him if you will to keep his interest up, and to keep him eager, but wait until your wedding night to let him get between your legs, child."

"How can you know so much, and you still considered a maiden?" Fortune wondered.

"A maiden? At my age?" Rohana snorted. "I know because I have in my day had my little adventures. I know because I have a married sister. I know because I have been your mother's servant since she was born. *I know."*

"Why have you never wed?" Fortune asked her.

"Because I never wanted to marry," Rohana answered. "I like the freedom I have being *a maiden.* I like serving your mother. This makes me happy, Fortune, and every woman has the right to be happy." She put a loving arm about the girl. "Now, child, no more questions, and promise me that you will cultivate your patience, and behave yourself."

Fortune nodded. "Will you tell Mama?"

"Nay. I know I can trust you, and that this conversation was just between us. Do not disappoint me, child," Rohana said softly.

"It won't be easy," Fortune admitted.

"I know," came the sympathetic reply.

The next few weeks seemed to pass quickly. Fortune spent most her time out of doors riding Thunder. She saw Kieran but briefly now and again. Her appetite ceased. She was restless at night, and sleep, when it did come, was unsettled, and filled with confusing dreams that she could only just vaguely recall when morning came, but she could never really remember what she had dreamed. Toward the end of July Kieran and Fortune met at Black Colm's Hall.

"This will be the last time we see each other for awhile," he told her. "My brother will be home on the first. My dear stepmother is, as always, prompt and efficient. The Elliots will arrive from Londonderry on the fifth to finalize the marriage agreement, and the wedding plans. It will be impossible for me to get away, sweetheart. Every moment of my day will be taken up by my father and his wife in pursuit of the perfect wedding day for Willy and his cousin. I'll try and come if I can get away, but I'll be unable to send word. If you are not here, I will leave a message for you beneath our bench, held down with a large rock. You do the same."

Fortune nodded bleakly. Weeping and bemoaning this turn of events wouldn't change anything. "It will be hard, Kieran," she said.

He took her in his arms, holding her against him. "I know." He kissed her lips softly. "You have not attempted to seduce me in our last meetings, Fortune. Do you yet love me, or have you had a change of heart?"

"Do you think me that fickle then?" she demanded half-angrily. "And what do you mean I haven't tried to seduce you? When did I ever attempt to seduce you, Kieran Devers? It is said that women are vain, but I think it is you men who are filled with conceit!"

He laughed wickedly. "If I offered to make love to you now, this very minute, what would you say, sweetheart?" he teased her.

"I would say you are a pompous ass!" Fortune snapped at him.

He laughed all the harder. "I love you, my wild wench," he told her, "and in a bit over two months you will be my wife. I can hardly wait, Fortune, and that is the truth."

She pulled his head down to hers, and kissed him slowly and deeply. Her firm young body pressed itself seductively against him as her lips worked themselves against his lips. She ran her tongue over his mouth, then pushed it into his mouth to stroke his tongue sensuously, nipping at that tongue when he played too fiercely with hers. Her fingers kneaded the nape of his neck, and she rubbed herself suggestively against him. It grew more difficult to remember her promise to Rohana as each minute passed. Her riding trousers did not offer the kind of protection that her many skirts would have, and she could feel him, hard and eager, against her belly.

His head was spinning. He held her so tightly that he wondered if she could breathe, and yet she writhed and twisted in his arms easily, arousing his basest passions. It was all he could do not to push her to the ground, and ravish her as he desired her so terribly. He could feel the full softness of her young breasts, and the flatness of her tender belly pressing against his muscled body. He wanted her as he had never wanted any woman, yet he felt something was different. A month ago she would have succumbed to his erotic blandishments. Now, however, he sensed the steel in her. She would not seduce him, nor would he be able to seduce her. His arms dropped from about her, and Fortune stepped back.

"Remember me until we meet again, Kieran Devers," she said softly, and then turning from him she mounted Thunder, and without a backward glance rode off.

He watched her go. She was his, he knew, and would eventually become more woman than any he had known, but he had been right. She would have destroyed his younger brother. Willy would be angry when he learned the truth of Fortune's passions, but Kieran Devers knew in his heart that Emily Anne Elliot was a better match for the heir to Mallow Court. His hand went to his groin, and he rubbed himself. The little witch who would shortly be his wife had roused him mightily. He walked slowly back and forth across the ruins of Black Colm's Hall, quieting his lust. His passions finally eased, he mounted his own stallion and galloped off towards his home.

In early afternoon on the first of August the Deverses returned to Lisnaskea, their coach rumbling down the drive of Mallow Court to stop before its front door. The footman hurried from the house to open the door, let down the carriage steps, and help his mistress from her traveling equipage. Jane Anne Devers looked about her with a pleased smile, and shook her skirts which had become crumpled within the confines of her vehicle.

"Welcome home, madame," Kieran said, coming forward

to greet his stepmother, a smile on his handsome face. "I trust my sisters and their families are all well. Will they be coming home for Willy's nuptials?"

"Unfortunately no as both of them are breeding again. They are more like Catholics than Protestants in their desire to have large, and rather unwieldy, families," his stepmother replied. She glanced about. "All looks in good order, Kieran. You have done well, and I thank you for husbanding your brother's patrimony so diligently." She then swept past him into the house.

His father descended from the coach followed by his younger brother.

"Thank God we're home," Shane Devers said. "May I never have to go more than five miles from Lisnaskea ever again, laddie. Yer sister, Colleen, wrote well of ye, and as you can see, yer stepmother is pleased. Now, laddies, I want a good sup of my own whiskey."

"The tray is awaiting you in the library, Da. Coming, Willy?" Kieran looked to his sibling who was oddly quiet.

"I'm marrying Emily Anne," William Devers said dully.

"I know," his brother answered.

"I don't love her," William replied.

"Ye'll learn to love her," his father said impatiently. "Come along now, and let's have a drink." He hurried into the house.

"I suppose the Leslies have returned to Scotland," William said. "I'll never see Fortune again."

"Nay, they're still here," Kieran told William. "The duchess has, much to her surprise, found herself to be *enceinte*. It was quite a shock. The child is due in November, and her ladyship has been advised not to travel. It's quite the gossip in Maguire's Ford. As you know, I have several *friends* in that most hospitable little village."

"If they are here then they must be invited to my wedding," William Devers said, horrified. "I do not think I can bear to see *her* on the day I wed another woman."

His elder brother took him by the shoulders and shook him hard. "Get ahold of yourself, Willy. You are no longer a little lad denied a toy you desired. You're a man. Lady Lindley turned you down. Move past it and be glad you have such a faithful and devoted young girl as Emily Anne willing to marry you. Stop feeling sorry for yourself, and whining about what might have been. You have agreed to marry your cousin, who is, whether you realize it or not, the perfect wife for you. Do not hurt Emily Anne by your selfish and childish fantasy that there was something between you and Lady Lindley. There wasn't. There could never be, and there will not be," Kieran told him harshly. "Now come into the house, and have that drink with Da."

"Have you seen her?" William asked as they walked together into the house.

"Aye, out riding," Kieran replied.

"Was she alone?" his brother probed.

"Aye, she was alone. There was no gallant with her, Willy. I suspect she doesn't fancy the Irish."

"I'm not Irish," William said.

"Of course you are," Kieran told him. "Our father is Irish. You live in Ireland. You are Irish."

"*She* once said very much the same thing to me," William said.

"Then she has more sense than I ever gave her credit for," Kieran noted. He opened the library door. "Here we are, Da."

Their father, now seated before his own peat fire, his boots off, his stockinged feet turned towards the blaze as he sipped his whiskey. He waved them both to the sideboard where the decanter sat upon a silver tray. "Help yerselves, laddies, and come sit with me," he said. "Ahh, now, I've been waiting for this since yer mam hustled me from here in June. Both yer sisters live in the country, and their homes were intolerably damp the summer long. Mary is the mother of five, and Bessie has four. Such noisy, ill-mannered children I have never met, and even yer mam agreed with me on that even if they are our grandchildren. What unruly households yer sisters run. Children, and nursemaids, and dogs running all about, and never a moment's peace. There were five of you, but my house was never in such an uproar, thanks to my Jane," Shane Devers said.

Kieran Devers laughed. "I will have to agree with you, Da. My stepmother has always managed to keep an orderly establishment, and whatever good manners I may have, I will lay credit at her feet."

Shane Devers looked up from his whiskey tumbler at his eldest son. The look was piercing. "If only . . ." he began.

Kieran held up his hand to silence his father. "I will gain what I want on my own, Da," he said softly. "I am not suited to your life. Willy is. I have no regrets, nor am I filled with any choler. Everything is as it should be, and the Devers bloodline will continue on at Mallow Court."

"You're so damned noble!" William Devers suddenly said angrily.

"Go to the devil, little brother," Kieran replied pleasantly.

"You don't have to marry someone you don't love!" came the petulant reply. "I do. My whole life has been mapped out for me!" He angrily smashed his crystal tumbler into the blazing fire.

Kieran Devers's dark green eyes narrowed with annoyance. He grasped his younger brother with one hand at his neckline, and yanked him forward so that they were face to face. "Listen to me, wee Willy," he said in a menacing voice, "you have nothing to complain about. You are heir to a fine estate, and bear an ancient respected name. You are to wed a girl you have known your entire life. A lass who is utterly devoted to you, and will make your life happy if you will but let her. What the hell is the matter with you? You don't want adventure, or excitement in your life for you are too much your mother's son. Now, hear me well, little brother. If you make Emily Anne's life miserable, I will personally beat you to a pulp. That girl comes to this house bringing her hopes and dreams. *You will not destroy them!*"

"Why should you care?" William sneered.

"I care because I so generously gave you all you have,

and will have one day. If I should decide to become a Protestant, Willy, do you really believe Da would keep you on as his heir? A second son isn't usually as fortunate as you have been. All that could change in the blink of an eye should I will it, little brother. Even your formidable dear mama couldn't stop it. Now, accept your good fortune, and be kind to your cousin. You really don't deserve either Mallow Court or Emily Anne, for you are truly a callow youth. Try to change for all our sakes." He loosed his grip on his brother's shirt, and pushed him away.

William Devers stormed from the room, slamming the door behind him as he went.

Kieran laughed, and sat opposite his father. "I hope you will live a good long life, Da, for it is obvious our Willy isn't ready for all the responsibilities that you will pass on to him eventually." He gulped his whiskey, enjoying the satisfying warmth it spread through his veins.

"I intend living a very long life, laddie," Shane Devers replied. "I can see the youngster needs seasoning. Traveling with him was no joy, I can tell you. He did nothing but bemoan his *loss* of Lady Lindley. I wish to God the wench had never come to Ulster! She must be a witch to have such a hold over William. I do not understand it, Kieran."

"Fortune Lindley is exerting no hold over William, Da. It is all in his imagination, I fear. How in the name of God did my stepmother get him to agree to marry Emily Anne Elliot?"

"She told him he had no other choice since there was no other young woman of his acquaintance he fancied who would have him. She told him it was his duty to wed and sire another generation of Deverses for Mallow Court. You know your stepmother, Kieran. When she wants something she will not be denied. At first William resisted her, but when Mary and Bessie agreed with Jane, he could no longer fight against his obvious fate. Even I have to agree 'tis best for him."

"You had best be certain Willy is pleasant, and affectionate toward his cousin when the Elliots arrive in several days, Da."

"I'll speak to him myself, and so will his mother. He'll treat the lass properly, or Catholic or no, you'll find yerself heir to my estate once again," Shane Devers said bluntly.

"God forbid!" Kieran chuckled. "With that threat hanging over me, Da, I'll speak to my brother myself!"

The two men laughed. Shane Devers loved both his sons, but he truly liked the elder. Kieran was strangely sensible for a man with such a stubborn nature, and he was honorable to a fault. It saddened Shane Devers that his eldest son had so easily given up his patrimony, but in a strange way the older man understood. Kieran, with his Celtic heritage, harked back to their more adventurous ancestors. William, with his English mother, was truly more suited to Mallow Court, particularly in their world which was changing so rapidly. Ulster, with its farms and its Scots and English immigrants, was gaining a smooth veneer more suited to the midlands of England than to the north of Ireland.

Jane Devers was horrified to learn that the duke and duchess of Glenkirk remained in residence at Erne Rock Castle. There was no way she could avoid asking them to William and Emily's wedding. There were none of greater rank currently in the vicinity, and everyone knew the Deverses knew the Leslies because of the match gone awry. While no one was particularly surprised that William and Emily were marrying—it had always been a given despite the Deverses' try for the Lindley heiress—the scandal that would ensue if the Leslies of Glenkirk were not invited to the Devers wedding would be impossible to live down.

The invitation was dispatched, and accepted. A large silver punch bowl, embossed with grapevines, leaves, and clusters of fat grapes, along with twenty-four matching silver cups, and a large silver ladle engraved with the family crest, arrived in the care of Adali himself. Lady Devers could scarce contain her excitement as the bowl and its accoutrements were carefully lifted by the white turbaned majordomo from the velvet-lined, polished ebony box with its silver corners and silver *Devers* nameplate. She managed to contain herself long enough to say, "Thank the duke and the duchess for their generosity. The bride will certainly write them when she arrives from Londonderry next week. We look forward to seeing his lordship and his family at the wedding." She smiled faintly.

Adali made his most elegant bow. "I shall convey your kind words to my master and mistress," he said. Then he backed from the room.

When he had gone Jane Devers made no attempt to hide her delight. "Shane, will you look at it! It's magnificent! William, is it not wonderful? Dearest Emily will be so pleased. It will provide a point of conversation for anyone who admires it. You shall be able to tell them it was a wedding gift from the duke and duchess of Glenkirk, who are related to the king himself! What generosity, especially considering . . ." Her voice ceased. "It is lovely," she finished weakly.

"I shall think of Fortune each time I see it," William said.

"Stop it!" his mother screeched. "I truly believe you have lost your mind, William. I can only pray for you. Stop thinking of yourself! Think of Emily Anne. You hardly spoke to her when she was here in August. The Elliots thought it strange, but I told them you were just exhausted from your travels in England. When your cousin and her family arrive next week I expect you to behave lovingly toward Emily, and with dignity and respect towards her family."

"Come on, laddie, and ride out with me," Kieran said, with a quick wink towards his stepmother. "The September air will clear your head, and you'll be thinking straighter."

Jane Devers gave but an imperceptible nod of her head to her stepson. Kieran had been so helpful of late, and while he had certainly never been difficult with her except in the matter of religion, she wondered about his attitude. Still, she was grateful for he seemed to be the only one that William would listen to these days. She watched from the window of her salon as the two brothers rode off together.

"Can you feel her watching us?" William said as they set their horses into a canter. "She is so afraid that I shall cry off at the last minute, and spoil her dreams, but I won't. I have no choices left to me at all. I shall marry my cousin, sire children, and do all that is expected of me. And why? Because I fully believe Da capable of turning about and giving you back your inheritance," he concluded.

"I don't want Mallow Court," Kieran replied.

"But I do," his brother said, for the first time admitting what Kieran had always known. Willy was indeed his mother's son.

The two brothers rode in silence for some time, and then Kieran realized they were coming up on Black Colm's Hall. From the opposite direction another horse and rider were visible. Kieran recognized Thunder, and attempted to distract his brother, and turn about, but William, too, had recognized Fortune's gelding. He spurred forward eagerly. Cursing beneath his breath Kieran followed.

Fortune recognized the brothers, and swore softly. She could hardly turn and run at this point. At least she would get to see Kieran even if he was with Will. She had only managed to see him once since the end of July, and then but briefly because he wanted no questions asked as to a lengthy absence. As they drew abreast of her Fortune smiled, drawing Thunder to a halt. "Hallo!" she greeted them. "What a surprise to meet you two out here. Will, how was England? Your sisters are well, I hope. My most hearty felicitations on your upcoming marriage. I look forward to meeting your bride."

"I love you!" William Devers cried. "But say the word, Fortune, and I will tell my cousin our wedding is no longer possible!" His blue eyes were pleading with her.

Fortune glared at him as if he had insulted her deeply. Kieran had warned her about Will's continuing infatuation. She had to stop it right now for all their sakes. "You stupid puppy!" she snapped. "I do not want to marry you! Did my family not make it clear? If they did not, then I will. You are a nice young man, Will Devers, but I would not wed you were you the last man living on the face of the earth."

"But why?" he wailed at her.

Fortune sighed. It was obvious her blunt tact had not worked, and was not going to work. She continued on in battle mode. *"Why?* Because you bore me, Will. You are the dullest fellow I have ever met. Why even Mama's estate manager, Rory Maguire, has more vitality than you, and is far better read to boot. *Why?* Because we have absolutely nothing in common. I am educated. You care naught for knowledge. I believe a woman can do almost anything. You think women are only good for running a household, and having babies. I could never marry a man like you. Now, do you understand?"

He stared at her, astounded by her words. "You do not love me?" he said bleakly.

"Nay, I do not love you, nor could I ever love you, Will," Fortune replied.

"Then why can I not get you out of my heart and soul?" he demanded of her. "You haunt me, Fortune, both when I am awake, and when I am asleep. Why have you bewitched me?"

"I have not bewitched you, Will. You have simply been loved your whole life by your family, and never been denied anything. I am probably the first thing you thought you wanted that you cannot have. You are most fortunate to have your cousin to wed. I am told she is perfect for you, and will be a good wife to you. Be satisfied with that, Will Devers."

He stared at her blankly and then, turning his horse, spurred away from them.

"You were hard on him," Kieran said softly.

"Should I have been otherwise?" Fortune replied.

"Nay. You knew just what had to be done, and you did it," he told her. "I miss you, sweetheart!"

"And I you, but you had best follow your brother lest he

grow suspicious. I will see you in a fortnight at the wedding." She turned Thunder about and rode off. She didn't look back. She didn't dare. The longing for Kieran had overwhelmed her when she had first seen him riding towards her. It was only in afterthought that she had noticed Will. Until today she had felt pity for him. Now, however, she felt irritation. William Devers was a fool. Her parents had refused his suit. He had spent a summer away from Ulster so he might forget. He had returned supposedly ready to wed his cousin. Poor girl, Fortune thought.

But to everyone's delight William Devers greeted his bride-to-be enthusiastically when she arrived a week before their wedding. She was a pretty young woman, just turned sixteen, with a round, sweet face, and large blue eyes. Her strawberry-blond hair was styled in bunches of corkscrew curls that bobbed about her face. She had a straight little nose, and a cupid's bow of a mouth. Her skin was the peaches and cream tone so currently in fashion. William kissed her heartily upon the lips, and left her blushing.

"Ohh, William!" she managed to gasp.

"Welcome home, dearest Emily," he greeted her, and taking her by the arm led her into the house.

"What has caused this turn?" Shane Devers murmured to his eldest son.

"We ran into Lady Lindley several days ago out riding. Will made a perfect fool of himself, and she gave him a tongue-lashing the like of which I have never heard. I believe the words fool and bore were used several times, Da. She left him absolutely no maneuvering room, or any doubt that she didn't love him, never loved him, or ever could love him. She shattered his dream entirely, and I believe it brought him to his senses rather abruptly. He was quite surprised, for you know he has harbored this boyish infatuation for months now."

"Thank God!" Sir Shane said softly. "Your stepmother has been hell to live with of late because she has been in fear that William would cry off at the last moment. She wants this marriage, and always has. She was only willing to give it up for Maguire's Ford, but once she met Lady Lindley, she saw an enemy who could actually take William from her, and was relieved to have her son turned down."

"But she still covets Maguire's Ford," Kieran said.

"Aye," his father admitted.

"They say Lady Leslie is dividing it between her two younger Leslie sons, who are both staunch Protestants. They are already here from Scotland, I have heard," Kieran told his father. "I expect we will meet them at the wedding."

"Yer stepmother knows," Shane Devers replied. "She is hoping that William will impregnate Emily with a daughter first. Then she hopes to match that child to one of the Leslie lads. If she cannot have all of Maguire's Ford, she is willing to settle for a half."

"I stand in awe of your wife, sir," Kieran Devers responded.

"As we all do," his father replied dryly. "As we all do. Praise God this wedding is but a few days hence. I do not think I can stand much more of this *tarah*, laddie."

Kieran chuckled. He knew just how his father felt for he felt the same way, although for different reasons. But six days after his brother wed Emily Anne Elliot, he would marry Lady Fortune Lindley in the ancient church at Maguire's Ford. He longed for that day. He had thought the Leslies overcautious regarding his wedding to Fortune. He had wanted to share his happiness with at least his father, but today he had seen that they were right. William's infatuation for Fortune made it impossible. He didn't trust his brother now, for despite the severe put-down he had received, Kieran suspected Willy still harbored feelings for Fortune Lindley. His attitude toward young Emily was only partially sincere. When William Devers learned that his older brother, Kieran, had married the woman he secretly coveted, all hell could break loose. He would have to wait until Willy was safely off on his wedding trip to Dublin before saying a word.

Still, he suddenly found the need to speak with someone,

and so he rode to the north edge of the village of Lisnaskea to see his father's longtime mistress, Molly Fitzgerald, and his two half-sisters. Molly's home was always referred to as a cottage, but it was in actuality a fine brick house that Shane Devers had built for his mistress. Molly's old servant, Biddy, opened the door when he knocked, and seeing him her face broke into a wide smile.

"Master Kieran, and 'tis it truly you now? Come in, come in! The mistress will be happy to see you, and so will yer sisters." She ushered him into the front salon where a good peat fire was burning in the fireplace. "Ye know where the whiskey is, Master Kieran. I'll go and fetch the mistress." She bustled out.

He poured himself a whiskey, swallowing it down, for the ride had been chilly. Hearing the door to the salon open he turned with a smile. "Molly, you will forgive me calling unannounced."

"Always, Kieran Devers, always," she said in her husky voice. She was a truly beautiful woman with thick dark hair, and warm amber eyes. "The lasses have missed you, but I am told you ride with the English girl at Erne Rock, and meet often at Black Colm's Hall."

He laughed. "I had thought we were being discreet, Molly," he said. "Thank God no one has gossiped aloud lest I be in a great deal of trouble at home. You know she turned Willy down. Well, she didn't turn me down. Father Butler will marry us on the fifth of October."

"And your father doesn't know?" Molly looked concerned.

"How can I say anything right now?" Kieran replied. "William still fancies himself in love with her although she gave him a severe set-down the other day when we met out riding. He now pretends he is content with his cousin, but I know Willy. He still harbors passions for Fortune. We didn't want to spoil my brother's wedding by announcing our betrothal. I'll tell Da when Willy and Emily are safe off on their wedding trip to Dublin. If Da wants to come to our wedding we'll be glad to see him. If not, then we'll still be married."

"I trust your sisters and I will be invited," Molly Fitzgerald said quietly. She took his hand in hers and led him to an upholstered settle by the fire.

"Of course!" he said, sitting by her side.

"So, Kieran Devers, you'll be the master of Erne Rock and Maguire's Ford," she said. "Her ladyship won't like that, I fear."

"Nay, Moll, I'll not have either Erne Rock or Maguire's Ford. Fortune's mother understands the situation here in Ulster. She knows if she gave the estate to Fortune, and I married her, that my stepmother and brother would cause all kinds of difficulty, trying to take those lands away from me because I remain a Catholic. Instead she has arranged for her two youngest sons, Protestants both, to have Maguire's Ford. Fortune and I will not be remaining in Ulster. We'll go to England first, and then to the New World. The duchess says there is a gentleman, high in the king's favor, who is founding a colony for Catholics and others who suffer persecution, in the New World. We will go there to start our new life together."

"The duke and duchess don't object to you marrying their lass? I had heard they were strange people; and they say she is a foreigner with a servant who wears a funny white pudding of a hat on his head. Is it all true then, Kieran?"

He chuckled. "The funny hat is called a turban. Adali is half-French, and half-Indian. The duchess was born a princess in another land, and is the daughter of a great king. She came to England when she was sixteen, and has lived here ever since. She's very beautiful, and very kind. Her husband is a decent gentleman who adores her. Fortune is a daughter of her second marriage. The duchess was widowed twice before she wed the duke of Glenkirk. She has seven living children. Does that satisfy your curiosity, Molly-O?"

"It's a start," Molly Fitzgerald replied with a smile. "I hear the duchess is expecting another child."

"Aye, and quite a surprise it was to her, I can tell you," he answered with a chuckle. "They plan to remain in Ireland until next summer when the child will have been long born, and be ready to travel."

"Will you and Fortune remain with them?"

He shrugged. "I don't know. I haven't been able to go over to Erne Rock and discuss the matter since the family returned home from England. They'll do whatever needs to be done, Moll, and I'll have to be satisfied with that for now. It's rather odd, for I'm used to running my own life."

"You will again, Kieran. Now, tell me how your da is. I haven't seen him since he returned. 'Tis the wedding preparations that keep him away, I know. Tell him I miss seeing him, as do the girls."

"Where are Maeve and Aine?" he asked her.

"In the kitchen learning how to make fine soap," Molly answered. "I'll not have them running about the village getting a reputation. There are enough small minds out there who think because I'm not considered respectable, my girls are fair game. My daughters will make respectable marriages, they will!"

"There are few Catholic lads about any longer, Moll," he said quietly. "You may have to settle for a pair of Protestants, or ship the girls to a convent in France, or Spain." He grinned at her.

"A convent?" Molly Fitzgerald snorted. "My girls are meant to be wives and mothers. Protestants, or Catholics, I don't care as long as the banns are read publicly, and the ceremony performed properly before all of Lisnaskea. I want grandchildren from those two!"

"Kieran!" His two half-sisters burst into the salon. They were pretty girls with long dark hair. Maeve had her mother's amber eyes, but Aine, the younger, had their father's bright blue eyes. He kissed them heartily upon the cheeks, and hugged them warmly. Maeve was seventeen now, and a husband should certainly be found for her soon, he thought. She

looked ripe for the picking, and he understood Molly's concern. Aine, however, was just fourteen, and only now growing out of her coltishness. She snuggled next to him on the settle.

"They say you have a lover," Aine said.

"Aine!" Her mother was mortified.

"Well, they do, Mam," Aine replied defensively.

"I'm getting married, but you must keep it a secret, Mistress Minx," Kieran said to his youngest sibling.

"Why?" Aine demanded.

"Because I am marrying Lady Fortune Lindley on October fifth, and you shall be invited only if you behave yourself," he told her.

"The lass who was to marry William Devers?" Maeve said, surprised.

"The lass who turned down brother Willy," Kieran said, "but we don't want to spoil his wedding to Emily Anne Elliot; nor do I want him challenging me to some sort of duel because he still secretly harbors feelings for Fortune."

"She's a fickle wench to have toyed with him, and then chosen you," Maeve remarked scathingly.

"She isn't fickle at all," Kieran defended Fortune. "She was brought to Ulster for the purpose of seeing if she and Willy suited each other. She saw they didn't, and told her parents, who immediately spoke with Da and Lady Jane. They took Willy off to England to prevent any scandal arising, for he was ready to make a fool of himself. Fortune did not lead our brother on, or promise him anything. Willy is infatuated with her, and has behaved like a perfect simpleton. The other day out riding we met her, and he declared himself in love with her. She was forced to tell him exactly how she felt, although she had attempted to spare his feelings in the past. Fortune Lindley is everything I could ever want in a woman, and you will like her."

"Kieran is in love!" Aine singsonged. "Kieran is in love!"

He grinned at her, and ruffled her dark hair. "Someday

you will be in love, Mistress Minx. I am only sorry I won't be here to see it." He turned to Maeve who stood by the fire. "Well, Maeve-mine?"

"I don't often agree with Aine," came the reply, "but she does seem to be correct. You're in love, Kieran Devers. Never did I think to see the day that would happen."

He chuckled. "Anything is possible, Maeve-mine," he told her. "Why even you might fall in love one day."

"I don't believe I have that luxury, brother," Maeve said seriously. "I must be respectable, and wed a respectable man, or so Mam is constantly telling me, even if she did choose love."

"I was a respectable widow when yer da came to me," Molly said spiritedly. "I was a grown woman who knew exactly what she was doing, and what the consequences of her actions would be. Yer a girl, Maeve, with no experience. You'll do what I tell you, lass, for I'm yer mam, and I'll tolerate no disobedience from you!"

"Now, lasses, now," Kieran interceded. "I came to see you, not to bring discord into the house. Tell me, Molly-O, what will you be giving me for my supper? I'm a big man, and I've ridden a ways in the chill damp." He smiled winningly at the older woman.

"You don't fool me, Kieran Devers," she said. "Yer nothing but a charmer like yer da. God help yer lass. Will you bring her to see us, and meet yer half-sisters?"

"I will," he agreed, "but it can't be until after Willy's wedding. Today I can remain with you just long enough to eat. Then I must get back up to the hall for my stepmother will be wondering where I have gotten to, and why I was not there to be at her beck and call."

" 'Tis to be grand doings, I'm told, by those who have been called into temporary service," Molly said.

"I wish we could go," Aine said wistfully.

"Well, we can't!" Maeve snapped. "The shock would echo around Fermanagh for years should Da's two pretty bastards appear at the wedding of his most legitimate son and heir. Be grateful Lady Jane hasn't had us driven out of Lisnaskea, and our mam with us."

"She wouldn't do that!" Aine cried, distressed.

"She wouldn't? She would if it suited her, just like she convinced Da to disinherit Kieran if he didn't become a Protestant," Maeve said. "She's a devil, that one!"

"Enough," Kieran Devers said quietly. "Maeve-mine, listen to me, for you're old enough to understand. I didn't want Mallow Court. If I had, I would have done what was necessary to keep it. Now set your anger aside, lass, and go see what Biddy is fixing for my supper." He stood, and held out his arms to her.

Maeve flew into them. "Don't go, Kieran! Don't leave Ireland, or if you do, take Aine and me with you! Mam holds her hopes and dreams high, but there are none here who would marry Sir Shane's bastard lasses. We need to make a new life every bit as much as you do!"

Kieran held his half-sister tightly in his embrace, looking over her dark head to Molly. "She could be right, Molly-O," he said quietly. "If this colony is indeed a safe place, it might be a better place for your two lasses."

Tears began to roll down Molly Fitzgerald's face. She nodded slowly. "I have always known that I would end my days alone," she said to him. "You could be right, Kieran, but would you be willing to take on the responsibility of these two, and what will yer Fortune think?"

"We won't know until we ask her," he replied, "but she's a practical lass, and has a good heart. Let her meet you first, Molly-O, and then we'll see, eh?"

Chapter
9

"Madame, you look lovely," the duke of Glenkirk complimented Lady Jane Devers. "What a happy day this is for you, and Sir Shane. I regret my wife canna be wi us, but at this time her condition forbids even a short journey, you understand." He bowed, and kissed her hand.

How handsome he was, Jane Devers thought. And so very elegant and distinguished in his bejeweled doublet and black velvet breeches. The tops of his boots were turned down to reveal the broad lace fold of his boot hose. He would add such prestige to the wedding gathering. She smiled, and then her eye swung to his companion.

Fortune curtsied. "What a fine day for a wedding," she said sweetly. "It was kind of you to include me, madame."

"How could we not?" Jane Devers said in return, her eye sharply assessing the girl.

She was beautifully garbed in deep purple velvet; the gown was cut very wide on the shoulder with a low neckline and an exquisite broad draped lace collar that extended low on the shoulder. Her sleeves were divided by lavender ribbons into two paned puffs. Fortune's skirt fell to the floor in loose folds, its fullness towards the back, the skirt open to display a cream-colored petticoat delicately embroidered with gold-thread butterflies and daisies. Her red hair was coiled into a knot at the nape of her neck, a single lovelock tied with a lavender silk ribbon. She wore a long rope of perfectly matched pearls and pear-shaped amethyst earbobs. She was supremely fashionable, certainly more so than any other woman guest; and yet her garb was not ostentatious, nor was it so splendid that it would draw attention away from the bride.

Lady Jane Devers had to admit that it would appear young Lady Lindley had dressed with utmost propriety. And, her manner was most discreet. Her hand rested upon her stepfather's arm, her eyes modestly lowered. In a way it galled Jane Devers that Fortune would appear so perfect to their guests. She had hoped people would not wonder why such a paragon had turned her son's proposal of marriage down. It could reflect badly on them all, but there was nothing she could do about it now, worse luck! She smiled as the duke and Fortune moved on, and turned to greet the next guests.

The wedding itself was to be held in the main salon of Mallow Court as the church at Lisnaskea was too small to contain all the guests who had been invited. The bride was lovely in her rose satin, taffeta, and lace gown. Her head was topped with a wreath of delicate Michaelmas daisies. The groom was somber in his sky blue velvet suit. There was an almost sullen look upon his handsome face although the bride smiled constantly, obviously unable to contain herself. Her responses were clear. His, muttered and low. When the couple were finally pronounced man and wife, the guests cheered. William Devers dutifully kissed his new wife.

Fortune felt absolutely no regret at the union. Her eyes were fixed upon Kieran, elegant in forest green velvet that matched his eyes. She could barely wait until they could be alone. It had been so long. She sighed aloud, and then blushed at James Leslie's chuckle.

"Easy, lassie," he cautioned her, having noted the direction her gaze was taking. "You've managed to be circumspect for weeks now. Dinna gie the game up now when the finish line is so near."

"Papa!" Her cheeks felt so warm.

"Discretion, my lady Lindley," he said softly. "We hae to remain here until next summer. I want nae feuds between our families."

"And you don't think our marriage will cause ill will?" she asked him, almost mockingly.

"They'll nae be happy at first, I agree, but we'll work around them, lassie, especially as yer husband will nae hae Maguire's Ford," the duke responded. "You know the truth of what Lady D. really wanted."

The wedding feast had been set up in Mallow Court's grand dining room, which had once been the house's Great Hall. Servants hurried to and fro carrying platters of salmon, beef, capons, ducks, and small game birds. There were hams, and plates of lamb chops; artichokes swimming in white wine, braised lettuces, bowls of peas with shredded mint, breads, sweet crocks of butter, fine English cheddar, and soft French cheeses. The goblets were kept filled with the best wine that the Deverses had been able to import. Some of the men grumbled that there was no ale, but Lady Devers did not consider ale a refined beverage.

The guests thoroughly enjoyed themselves, and toast after toast was raised to the newlyweds. A bridal cake, decorated in spun sugar, was carried in to much cheering. This was quite an unusual luxury, but Lady Devers had learned while in England that it was the latest and most fashionable extravagance at important weddings. It was therefore imperative that such a cake be served at her only son's marriage feast.

Now the guests were invited to partake in the dancing in the large salon where the marriage ceremony had been celebrated. The furniture had been cleared from the room while they ate, and a dais for the musicians had been set up at one end of the room. In the corners at the opposite end of the chamber were painted screens behind which the guests would find the necessary chairs and chamber pots for their convenience. The dances at first were mostly country style; the dancers executed the steps either holding hands in a circle, or in a line. Lady Devers, frowning, spoke with the musicians, and they began to play a spritely galliard.

Kieran Devers led Fortune out onto the floor. His hand was warm in hers, and their eyes met in silent passion. The music for the galliard was bright and quick. Only the young people danced. All but the bride and groom. Williams Devers glared at his brother and Fortune. He had not been forced to notice her until now. But as she flaunted herself before him with his brother, he could not help but stare. Her bosom was so white against the purple and lace of her gown. How he desired her!

"Who is that beautiful girl dancing with your brother?" his bride asked him innocently.

"Lady Lindley," William replied tersely.

"Oh," Emily Devers said softly. Her mother had been most honest in explaining the situation with Lady Lindley before she would allow her daughter to accept her cousin William's proposal of marriage. William Devers had asked Lady Lindley to be his wife, and she had turned him down. He had been most distraught over her refusal, Mistress Elliot told her daughter. It was possible he still loved her.

"I will make him forget," Emily Anne had answered her parent with the pure innocence of youth. But now seeing her one-time rival in the flesh, the new Mistress Devers was not at all certain that she could make William forget the beauteous and fascinating Fortune Lindley. Emily Anne felt the beginnings of jealousy starting to gnaw at her vitals.

The galliard was over. Fortune laughed up into Kieran Devers's face with delight. He was an excellent dancer, she had discovered to her enjoyment. Her own visage was flushed with her exertion, and her cheeks pink. The neat coil of hair at the nape of her neck had become undone, allowing the flaming red-gold curls to tumble down her back in a most disorderly fashion.

"You are so beautiful," he said, bending to whisper the compliment in her ear. "Were I not an honorable man I should take you off into a dark corner, and make love to you, my darling."

Fortune blushed deeper with the pleasure his words gave her.

The musicians took up their instruments once again. The notes of the gracious and courtly pavane sounded. Kieran caught Fortune's hand in his again, and they danced, suddenly so absorbed in each other that they were oblivious to anyone else in the salon. They were so absolutely perfect together that the other guests stopped dancing, stepping back as the young couple swayed with the elegant steps of the dance.

Her head was turned looking up at him. Her face was alight with her love for him. Her blue-green eyes glittered like fine jewels. Her lips were slightly parted, and there was a faint, secret smile upon them. His dark head, turned towards hers, was bent so low that their mouths were close to touching. They twisted and turned with every nuance and beat of the sensuous music; their bodies curled gracefully into each other with the dance. As he gazed upon her his love was unmistakable, his passion palpable. They were one, and the obviousness of it swept through the salon like a brush fire.

Jesu! James Leslie thought looking at them. The secret will be out now for certain. His eyes swung to the bridegroom, and as he saw the look of sudden realization and naked fury upon the younger man's face, it dawned upon the duke of Glenkirk that he was unarmed.

Then William Devers' voice broke the magic that had surrounded them all, stopping the music with his venom. *"You bastard!"* he snarled. "You lying bastard! You have wanted her all along though you denied it! *I could kill you!"*

"William!" his father's stern voice warned.

"If I couldn't have her, why should you?" William Devers said, his tone anguished. He was almost weeping.

Jane Devers thought she would die then and there so acute was her embarrassment. Now all of Fermanagh, nay all of Ulster, would be gossiping with this outrageous scandal.

"You bitch!" William cried, his anger rising again to encompass Fortune. "You led me on, and all the while you were whoring after my brother!"

The guests' heads snapped back and forth between the trio. Kieran Devers had remained silent in the face of his brother's charges. Fortune, however, was not so restrained.

"How dare you, sir?" she said in her most regal tones. Her voice was scathing, and dripping with contempt. Then she turned away from him and walked over to Emily Devers, who stood pale and trembling. She spoke more gently to the girl. "Madame, I apologize that my presence has upset your wedding day. I shall withdraw now in the hope that normalcy may be restored to this festive gathering." Then Fortune curtsied, her violet skirts brushing the parquet floor.

James Leslie was immediately at his stepdaughter's side. He bowed to the bride, to Lady Jane and Sir Shane, but he said not a word, and his look was stern. Then he led Fortune from the salon, his large hand laid comfortingly over hers, which she had placed on his velvet-clad arm.

When William made to follow, Kieran Devers reached out, and grasped his younger brother by the arm. His strong fingers dug into his sibling's flesh. "Are you not satisfied, Willy, to have broken young Emily's heart, and spoiled her wedding day with your obsession?" he said low through gritted teeth. "Go and apologize to your wife, or she'll be widowed before you can have her virginity, for I'll kill you myself to restore the family's honor, which you do not seem to care about at all." His head turned, and he signaled to the musicians to begin to play again. They took up a lively reel, and Kieran Devers shoved his brother toward his bride. Then he walked over to where his stepmother stood, ashen, and kissing her hand led her out onto the floor. "Come, madame," he said softly to her, "and let us try and smooth over this discomfiture that your son has brought upon us all." For the first time in his life he actually felt sorry for her, Kieran thought.

"Oh, Kieran, do you think we can?" Jane Devers whispered, her voice tremulous.

"We must, madame," he told her sternly.

Sir Shane, over his initial shock, bowed to Emily's mother. "Shall we join the dancers, ma'am, and allow our children to settle this foolish matter?" He led the abashed Mistress Elliot onto the floor to join the circle of dancers that was now forming. Her husband, with not a backward glance at his daughter and her bridegroom, chose a nearby lady, leading her off to join them.

Bride and groom were now alone in their corner of the room. "She has bewitched you," Emily Anne said calmly to William. "I can see that, my poor dear. She must be a very wicked girl, but I love you, William. I will help you to overcome her sorcery if you will but allow me." Standing on her tiptoes she leaned over and kissed his cheek. "You will never have to see her again. Tomorrow we shall leave on our wedding trip down to Dublin. When we return your mama will see that Lady Lindley is not allowed at Mallow Court any longer, or at any gathering which we may attend. I was shocked by her open, and most lewd behavior with your brother." She patted his cheek gently. "I think we must see that Kieran is no longer welcome here either, eh? Your mother has been very generous in her tolerance of his presence, but he will not change, and we cannot have a Catholic about influencing our children, my dear. After all, one day this will be your house. He would have to go then at any rate. Everything is going to be just fine, dearest. We shall have a perfect and happy life together."

He stared at her, astounded. He had not realized how strong-willed she was until this moment. Still, he suddenly realized he needed her strength. "Emily," he began, "I am so sorry."

She stopped his mouth with her slender fingers. "It is forgotten, William dearest. You were led on, and bewitched by a noblewoman of loose morals. It was before our marriage and, therefore, of no importance to me at all. While I do not generally approve of public displays of affection, I think it would help to put our guests at ease if you would kiss me on the lips, my dear. Then we will join the dancing." She held her pretty face up to him.

He kissed her tenderly, and in leisurely fashion. Emily was right, he thought. Fortune had indeed bewitched him. She was a wicked and libertine bitch, who probably had no more control over her lustful desires toward his brother than she had had over her quick tongue. "You are the perfect wife for me, Emily dear," he told her as their lips parted. "And you have said a great deal that makes sense to me. Kieran must indeed leave Mallow Court. He is every bit as wicked as *that woman*. I do not want him around the children we will have." Then, daringly, he kissed her again, and she blushed prettily. "Thank you for forgiving me, my dearest wife," he said, and then he led her out to join the dancers.

It was as if nothing at all had happened. Seeing the well reconciled bride and groom, the guests relaxed. The celebration continued on into the night. The bride and groom were put to bed with as much decorum as was possible. The guests departed. The servants cleared away the debris of the celebration. Lady Devers sought her bed with a rather large carafe of wine, while Sir Shane sat with his elder son over full whiskey tumblers in his library before a blazing peat fire.

"A successful day, Da," Kieran said to his parent.

"Aye," the older man answered. "No one was maimed or killed despite our William. 'Twas fortunate the duke of Glenkirk was unarmed, or he might have defended his stepdaughter's honor after your brother insulted her so gravely.

She's got a cool head, that one," Sir Shane remarked. "I don't know of any young woman so affronted who would not have caused an even greater scene defending herself, or castigating your brother before everyone with the plain truth. She's a strong lass."

This was the perfect moment for it, and Kieran knew it. "We're being married on October fifth, Da," he said quietly. "I'd like you to come, but I'll understand if you don't. Willy isn't to know until he and Emily have returned from Dublin. You understand why."

Shane Devers nodded. "Aye, I do."

"You don't seem surprised," Kieran said.

"After seeing you two together today, I'm not, laddie," his father responded. "How did it happen? Did you want her from the start, Kieran? Was William correct in his accusations?"

"I honestly don't know, Da. Fortune and I met up the day you left for England, and I was just returning from the coast road. After that . . ." He shrugged. "We fell in love."

"We can't tell your stepmother about this until after the fact," Shane Devers said. "There's going to be hell to pay when she learns you are to have Maguire's Ford and Erne Rock."

"But Da, we're not," Kieran said. "The estate really is going to the two younger Leslie sons. My stepmother can dream her dream of matching Willy's first daughter with one of those lads. Mayhap it will even come to pass. Fortune and I will go to England with the duke and duchess. Lord Baltimore is mounting an expedition to the New World in order to found a Catholic colony where all faiths may live together in peace, *especially the Catholics*. Fortune and I intend to join that expedition, and start over. We will not be anywhere in evidence where my brother, or my stepmother can see us, and be chafed."

Shane Devers said nothing for a long moment, but finally he spoke. "That it should come to this," he said sadly. "That my eldest son should be driven from his heritage, and the land of his birth." He slowly drank down the tumblerful of whiskey, and held the crystal out for more, tears running down his weathered face. "I saw the handwriting on the wall when I married Jane, but I didn't want to fight. I just wanted peace and comfort for us all. Now yer leaving us."

Kieran poured the amber liquid into his father's tumbler, and then set the decanter aside again. "Da, you know that I never felt truly at home here. I don't understand it, but there it is. Ulster is not where I belong. Fortune feels the same way. She has lived in England, in France, in Scotland. She is well loved by her family, and yet she, too, never felt comfortable anywhere. We are two like souls, drawn together in spite of ourselves. The New World beckons to us, Da. We must be together. We must go away from this old world."

"You're certain, laddie? This isn't just a compromise because you've fallen in love with Fortune Lindley?" Sir Shane looked directly at his son, seeking the truth.

Kieran smiled. "We're certain, Da."

"Then God bless you, laddie, and your lass too. I'll be at your wedding no matter your stepmother's outrage afterwards."

"Colleen will be there too," Kieran said softly.

The older man nodded his head. "This will be the first secret I ever kept from my Jane, laddie. I love you greatly to do so."

"Ah, Da," Kieran told his father, "in all the years since my mam died, the one certainty I've always believed in was your affection for me. I return it, sir, and thank you for your blessing upon Fortune and upon me."

"I tell you, laddie, I am grateful I have lived most of my life when I see how the world is changing about us," Shane Devers mourned.

"Changing with the world while holding fast to your ideals and ethics seems to be the only way to survive," Kieran said quietly.

"The young can change," his father replied fatalistically. "The old cannot, or do not want change."

Kieran chuckled. "You're not that old yet, Da," he said.

"I'm old enough to want peace in my house, and peace in the land," Sir Shane said. Then he downed his whiskey, and stood up. "I'm off to my bed now, laddie. I would suggest you not be around in the morning when your brother leaves with his bride for Dublin."

Kieran nodded. "I agree, Da. Perhaps I will ride over to Erne Rock tonight. There's a fine moon rising, and there's no rain. Tell Colleen I will see her on the fifth. Molly and the girls will be there too." He chuckled. "All your black sheep, Da."

His father laughed. "Black sheep are far more interesting than the docile white ones," he noted, and then left the library.

Kieran sat for several more minutes before the peat fire; then he arose, and set his crystal tumbler on the silver tray by his chair. Going out into the empty antechamber of the house he looked up the staircase. His father would be in his own bedchamber now. His stepmother would have been lulled into sleep with wine. William would have, by now, it was hoped, breached Emily Anne's virginity. He would do little more, Kieran suspected, and smiled to himself. He wondered if there was any depth or passion to his pretty sister-in-law, or his brother. No matter, he thought, leaving the house, and going to the stables where he saddled his horse.

Riding out he thought his wedding night with Fortune would be more interesting and active than his brother's. Willy, however, would do his duty, and provide Mallow Court with children for the next generation. They would be more English than Irish though, Kieran realized, and sighed sadly. There were some changes he didn't like either, he realized.

The ride was uneventful, although he did spot the shifting shadows of several local poachers. They, however, recognized his horse, and ignored him as he passed by. He rode down the main street of Maguire's Ford, passing two cottages where he knew he would be more than welcome. His horse clopped across the little drawbridge of Erne Rock, and

Take A Trip Into A Timeless World of Passion and Adventure with Kensington Choice Historical Romances!
—Absolutely FREE!

Enjoy the passion and adventure of another time with Kensington Choice Historical Romances. They are the finest novels of their kind, written by today's best-selling romance authors. Each Kensington Choice Historical Romance transports you to distant lands in a bygone age. Experience the adventure and share the delight as proud men and spirited women discover the wonder and passion of true love.

Get 4 FREE Books!

We created our convenient Home Subscription Service so you'll be sure to have the hottest new romances delivered each month right to your doorstep—usually before they are available in book stores. Just to show you how convenient the Zebra Home Subscription Service is, we would like to send you 4 FREE Kensington Choice Historical Romances. The books are worth up to $24.96, but you only pay $1.99 for shipping and handling. There's no obligation to buy additional books—ever!

Save Up To 30% With Home Delivery!

Accept your FREE books and each month we'll deliver 4 brand new titles as soon as they are published. They'll be yours to examine FREE for 10 days. Then if you decide to keep the books, you'll pay the preferred subscriber's price (up to 30% off the cover price!), plus shipping and handling. Remember, you are under no obligation to buy any of these books at any time! If you are not delighted with them, simply return them and owe nothing. But if you enjoy Kensington Choice Historical Romances as much as we think you will, pay the special preferred subscriber rate and save over $8.00 off the cover price!

We have **4 FREE BOOKS** for you as your
introduction to
KENSINGTON CHOICE!
To get your FREE BOOKS, worth up to $24.96, mail
the card below or call TOLL-FREE 1-800-770-1963.
Visit our website at www.kensingtonbooks.com.

Get 4 FREE Kensington Choice Historical Romances!

💗 **YES!** Please send me my 4 FREE KENSINGTON CHOICE HISTORICAL ROMANCES (without obligation to purchase other books). I only pay $1.99 for shipping and handling. Unless you hear from me after I receive my 4 FREE BOOKS, you may send me 4 new novels—as soon as they are published—to preview each month FREE for 10 days. If I am not satisfied, I may return them and owe nothing. Otherwise, I will pay the money-saving preferred subscriber's price (over $8.00 off the cover price), plus shipping and handling. I may return any shipment within 10 days and owe nothing, and I may cancel any time I wish. In any case the 4 FREE books will be mine to keep.

Name_____

Address_____ Apt._____

City_____ State_____ Zip_____

Telephone (___) _____

Signature_____
　　　　　　(If under 18, parent or guardian must sign)

Offer limited to one per household and not to current subscribers. Terms, offer and prices subject to change. Orders subject to acceptance by Kensington Choice Book Club. Offer Valid in the U.S. only.

KN073A

into the courtyard. A sleepy stable lad came to take his mount, leading it away as Kieran Devers mounted the staircase, and entered the castle.

He found his future father-in-law awaiting him in the hall.

"I thought you'd come tonight," the duke said.

"I've told my da I am to wed Fortune," Kieran replied.

"And?"

"He'll be at the wedding, and gave us his blessing," the younger man replied. "My stepmother is planning to match a granddaughter with one of your lads."

James Leslie laughed aloud. "She doesna gie up, does she? Well, Leslie men, nae matched in the cradle, tend to wait to wed. She could hae her wish in the long run. I want nae feud between our families, Kieran. 'Tis yer brother who is the difficulty. 'Twill be up to yer da and his wife to keep William in line. I'll nae hae my lass insulted by him again. 'Twas fortunate I was unarmed this day, or the bride would hae been a widow before she was deflowered."

"I suggested the same thing to my brother Willy," Kieran said.

The duke nodded. "Yer a good man, Kieran Devers. I'll be proud to call ye my son. I only regret that yer stubborn nature will take Fortune from her family, but if she's content to go wi ye, then we must be content also."

"Were not your family once Catholics, my lord?" Kieran asked.

"Aye," James Leslie replied. "But times change, laddie, and what good does it do to argue over semantics in the matter of religion? Faith is what counts, Kieran. Our good Lord Christ once said that in his father's house were many mansions. Surely one road alone canna lead to all those mansions. But while I will nae condemn ye for the manner in which ye worship, there are those who will, and laws to punish ye if ye do nae conform. I dinna agree with such laws, but I will follow them until they are changed. When we are in England ye must obey the king's law for all our sakes. Yer nae the stuff martyrs are made of, laddie; and I'll nae hae my family endangered by yer rebellion. Is that understood, Kieran Devers? If ye want my help, ye must play my game by my rules. Ye do understand that, don't ye?"

"Aye, my lord, I do. I will do whatever I must to see that Fortune and I can make a good life together. I swear it!" he said.

"Good," James Leslie said, well pleased. He thought the lad would behave himself if importuned. "Now, I see nae reason for yer returning to Mallow Court other than to obtain yer belongings. Can ye find the room which ye shared wi yer brother, and which was yers the last time ye visited wi us?"

"I can, my lord," Kieran replied with a smile.

"Then welcome to Erne Rock, laddie, and welcome to this family of ours. Ye hae nae idea what ye've let yerself in for, Kieran," the duke chuckled. "Oh, try not to let Fortune seduce ye before the wedding. She's ripe for trouble, but then I suppose a day or two will nae matter." Then James Leslie laughed for his about-to-be son-in-law actually blushed. "Go to bed, laddie," the duke said. "I'd be a fool if I didn't know the women in my household well, and yet they sometimes surprise even me."

Kieran bowed to the older man, and hurried from the hall and up the stairs to the guest chamber where he had twice stayed in the past. The hall was chill with late September. The torches lighting the passageway flickered eerily. Entering the chamber he closed the door behind him, and then turning caught his breath with surprise.

"I knew you would come tonight," Fortune said softly. She was lying naked upon his bed, her red-gold hair her only adornment.

"So you mean to seduce me, do you?" he said in equally soft tones, walking across the small room to stand over her.

"Aye," she replied. "You want to be seduced, don't you?" Reaching up she drew him down upon the bed.

"You are the boldest virgin I have ever known," he told her.

"I didn't know you knew any virgins," Fortune responded with a wicked grin. "Kieran, you know I'm mad for you, and I know that you love me. In less than a week we will be man and wife. Why must we wait until then to enjoy each other?" Her lips were dangerously close to his, temptingly moist, and half-parted.

I'll never be a saint, he thought, as he kissed her slowly, deeply, his mouth working against hers. His head spun with the nearness of her. The perfumed scent from her body surrounded him. "One taste, sweetheart, and then no more until our wedding night," he said sternly. "I'll not have you coming to the altar looking too sated and well satisfied. Do you think that's a secret you could keep, my bold innocent?" His hand swept down the curve of her body slowly, sliding around to fondle the cheek of her bottom.

Being touched so suggestively was entirely different than she had anticipated, Fortune considered. It had seemed to her the right thing to do when she had decided to await him in his bedchamber. Now she wasn't certain she was ready for such intimacy. When he pushed her back upon the pillows her heart began to hammer wildly. Fascinated she watched as his fingers trailed lightly over her silken flesh. It was utterly delicious, but now she wondered if she gave herself so freely to him before they were married whether he would marry her at all. His big hands were lightly holding her shoulders as he bent his dark head and began to kiss her breasts with tiny, feathery kisses that set her all a-shiver. His tongue laved her nipples gently, and they grew taut in response. Fortune clenched and unclenched her fingers nervously. *This had been a mistake.* She had to tell him to stop right now. She whimpered nervously as a hand brushed over her belly, tensing as it rested itself, palm down, upon her Venus mont.

Kieran could feel Fortune trembling with both her fear

and her rising desire. He half sat, removing his doublet and
his shirt. Her eyes widened at the sight of his smooth, broad
chest. Now he leaned forward again to press his bare flesh
against her bare breasts. His tongue teased her ear, and he
murmured hotly, "Do you like that, my sweet Fortune? Ahh,
lambkin, you are so soft and warm against me."

It was wonderful! Fortune sighed, and boldly put her
arms about him. She could not for the life of her, however,
speak. The moment was far too intense. She loved him. They
were together as lovers should be. Shyly she let her palms
smooth down his back. Then suddenly she stiffened. He had
pressed his length against her, and she could feel the hard
ridge within his britches pushing into her naked flesh.

"I can't!" Fortune gasped.

He immediately sat up. "It took you long enough to decide it, you damnable little tease," he growled at her, taking
her hand and putting it against what to her eyes seemed an
inordinately large bulge. When she sought to pull her hand
away he held it firm. "Your touch will soothe it," he told her.
"It's either that, or . . ."

"How did you know?" she demanded, rubbing him gently.

"Because I am experienced, sweetheart," he told her, "and
while you may be a passionate creature, you're no wanton,
Fortune."

"But I don't want to be a virgin any longer!" she wailed.

"You won't be in a few days," he told her.

"Are you being soothed?" she inquired, her hand caressing him, and realizing that she was becoming curious again.

"Aye," he grinned at her.

"Well, I could use some comfort too, Kieran Devers!"
Fortune told him. "Isn't there a way to pleasure me without
spoiling our wedding night? There must be *something* you
can do."

His eyes twinkled. "How brave are you, Fortune?"

"I don't know," she told him.

"Lie still and trust me, lambkin," he said softly. He turned onto his side, and one hand reached out to touch her Venus mont again. He began caressing it with teasing fingers in a provocative manner.

Fortune closed her eyes, half-afraid, but determined to learn exactly what he was about. His touch began to engender ripples of excitement within her. She squirmed slightly, unable to help herself, but forcing herself to concentrate on the sensations he was loosing. A single finger began to stroke at the slit between her nether lips. It pushed between the tender folds of pink flesh, and Fortune tensed.

"It's all right, sweetheart," he promised her. *"Trust me."*

Fortune made herself relax, but then she suddenly gasped as he touched her in what was apparently the most sensitive spot on her entire body. *"Kieran!"* she managed to gasp.

"It's called your love button," he told her. "Touched in just the right way, it can give you extraordinary pleasure." His finger flicked back and forth over the swollen nub of flesh. "Do you find it pleasurable, Fortune?"

"Ohhh, yes!" It was wonderful. Why hadn't he introduced her to this delight before? A frisson of enjoyment washed over her. This was heavenly. She murmured softly as the pleasure broke over her like a wave, and then gasped once again as the digit, only recently teasing at her, suddenly penetrated her. *"Ohhhh!"* The finger began to move back and forth within her. *"Ohhh! Oh! Oh! Yesss!"*

He bent and kissed her just as she peaked. His tongue found hers, stroking it fervently. The kiss deepened, and he thought he might explode with his own desire for her. He would not take her until she was his wife, but dear heaven, it would be difficult!

"I'm not afraid anymore," Fortune said, pulling her head away, from his. "I don't want to wait, Kieran. *Please!*"

He withdrew his finger from her wet sheath. "No, lambkin, not until we are properly wed will I properly bed you." He kissed her gently, avoiding the disappointed look in her blue-green eyes.

Fortune rolled away, putting her back to him. "I hate

you!" she muttered. "I don't think I want to marry you at all, Kieran Devers!"

He looked at her delicious little rump, and unable to help himself fondled it. "Having tasted your charms, lambkin, I don't intend letting you get away now," he told her. "In just a few more days you and I will be man and wife, and then, my darling, I will satisfy all your naughty little desires, and even some you don't know about yet." He gave the tempting rump a little smack.

Fortune rolled back onto her back again, glaring up at him. "I suppose you want me to go back to my own chamber now," she grumbled.

"I think it might be a good idea. Try not to awaken Rois. She'll be very shocked, I fear. You understand why I'm doing this, don't you, Fortune?"

She shook her head in the negative. "Why?"

" 'Tis an old custom to hang the bloody sheet from the wedding bed out the following morning for all the neighbors to see that the bride was indeed pure. Tomorrow at Mallow Court Lady Jane will proudly display the soiled linen that lay beneath Willy and his bride. 'Tis not a custom she likes, but she knows it is expected, and gossip would surely ensue if that bloody sheet didn't fly. I want no one, especially my foolish brother, saying that you were not as pure as the vaunted Emily Anne on your wedding day. I don't want to have to fight my brother, because if I fight him, I will kill him. And I will be forced to it if he ever slanders you again, Fortune."

Reaching up she drew his head down to her breasts. "I don't want Willy's death on my conscience either," she said. "I would never allow you to be put in such a position, Kieran. *But,* if your little brother slanders me again, I will kill him myself, and my conscience be damned!"

Startled by her tone he sat up, and looked at her. He could see she was most serious.

"I'm an excellent swordswoman," Fortune explained.

Kieran Devers laughed aloud. "You'll never bore me,

lambkin," he said. "Now, put something on that luscious body of yours, and go back to your own chamber. You did wear something, didn't you?"

With a mischievous grin Fortune arose from the bed, and walking across the bedchamber opened the door, closing it behind her as she disappeared out into the darkened hallway.

"Jesu!" he swore, and then he laughed all the harder.

Chapter

10

"Stand still, m'lady," Rois pleaded with her mistress as she brushed Fortune's long red-gold hair.

"I don't see why I must wear my hair all long and flowing," Fortune grumbled. "Emily Anne certainly didn't when she married Will."

"The English don't follow proper customs," Rois sniffed.

"I'm partly English," Fortune reminded her maidservant.

"That may be," Rois replied quickly, "but you were raised by a Scots father, and he knows what's right as does your mam. Now stand quiet for a moment longer while I get these last tangles out."

Fortune remained silent now, letting her eyes wander to the glass to gaze at her reflection. It was her wedding day. Her garb couldn't have been more fashionable than if she were being married in London at the court. While low, square necklines were still the mode in Ireland, her neckline extended low on the shoulder which Fortune found far more elegant. The gown was a rich golden brown velvet with a creamy draped lace collar. Her sleeves were divided by gold ribbons into two paned puffs, the upper sleeve being decorated with topaz-colored paste buttons that rivaled in quality the semi-precious stones after which they were fashioned. The cuffs of her sleeves were double ruffles of lace, and a gold silk galant tied at the side encircled her waist. The underskirts showed through the opening of the gown, a spiral motif of gold thread on a creamy silk taffeta. The skirt fell in simple folds with its fullness towards the back. Fortune's stockings were golden-colored silk, and her shoes were decorated with pearls. In her ears she wore pear-shaped pearls that seemed to have a gold tint, and matched the long strand about her neck that fell onto the bosom of her gown.

"There!" Rois's voice broke into her thoughts. "You surely have the most beautiful hair, m'lady. It seems to have a life of its very own. Are you excited?" Rois's bright eyes danced with her own anticipation of the wonderful day to come. "He's a handsome devil, Master Kieran, and"—she lowered her voice—"the lasses who know say he's a grand lover. All fire and yet tender too. How have you been so patient, m'lady?"

Fortune laughed weakly. "It hasn't been easy," she told her servant. "I think I've wanted to lie with him since the first moment I saw him even if I couldn't admit it to myself." She sighed lustily.

Rois giggled. "You'll gain your heart's desire tonight, m'lady, and come the morrow your mam will fly the bedsheet proudly for all to see." She sniffed audibly. "We're all so happy for you! You came to Ulster to find your love, and you did! I'll surely miss you when you're gone back to England, m'lady," Rois told her mistress.

Surprised, Fortune turned to look at her servant. "But I want you to come with me," she said. "I couldn't do without you, Rois."

"I cannot leave my Kevin," the girl answered.

"Then the two of you must be wed, and he shall come

too," Fortune said. "There will be far more opportunity for you both with us in the New World than there is here in Ireland, Rois. Your Kevin is good with the horses, and it is said the part of the Americas to which we are going is a fine place for horses. I intend taking a goodly number of the beasts with us. Kevin shall have charge of them. Isn't that better than waiting around for Rory Maguire to grow too old? I doubt he ever will," she chuckled.

Rois's pretty face was thoughtful. To be able to marry her sweetheart sooner than later was an enticement to be sure. She wasn't certain she was brave enough to travel all the way to the New World, but if Kevin was by her side she believed her courage would quicken. "I'd have to ask Kevin," she said slowly. " 'Tis a fine offer, m'lady."

The door to the bedchamber opened, and Jasmine entered. "Let me see how you look," she said. "Ahhh." Her turquoise eyes filled with sentimental tears. "You are beautiful, poppet," the duchess of Glenkirk told her youngest daughter. She sat down heavily upon the bed. "I do not know where the years have gone," she lamented almost to herself. "It seems like only yesterday you were born here at Erne Rock. Rowan would be very proud of you, Fortune. I know it in my heart."

Fortune half bent, and embraced her mother, her own eyes damp. "I am so happy," she said softly.

The duchess patted her daughter, and then said, "Rois, go and tell them down in the hall that we will come shortly. You remain, child. There is no need for you to come back upstairs again."

"Yes, my lady," Rois said, curtsying, then closing the door behind her as she departed. She was no fool, and wondered what it was the duchess wanted to impart privately to her daughter. They had already spoken on a wife's marital duties, Rois knew.

"Why did you send Rois away?" Fortune asked.

"Because what I have to say is for you alone," her mother

replied. "For over a month now Rohana has, each morning, been bringing you a cup of what she has called her strengthening posset. The liquid you have drunk has nothing to do with strength, Fortune. It is a recipe, given to your great-grandmother, Skye O'Malley, by her sister, Eibhlin, the physician nun. It is to prevent the conception of children. I did not want you going to the altar today with a secret in your belly."

Fortune blushed beet red, her fair white skin growing mottled with her embarrassment "We didn't . . ." she began.

Jasmine laughed. "I know," she said. "He is a very stubborn young man, isn't he? And honorable as well. Still, a wee bit of precaution didn't hurt," she told her daughter. "Now you are to marry Kieran Devers. I know you will both want children, Fortune, but if you will accept my advice, do not have them until you have left Ireland far behind. I do not trust the Deverses, for Sir Shane, poor man, desires peace at any price. William still believes himself in love with you which makes him a dangerous enemy despite his marriage. Lady Jane will yet covet Maguire's Ford despite the fact I have given it to my two youngest sons. I wrote to your brother, the duke of Lundy, a month ago to speak to the king regarding Maguire's Ford, and to have him confirm Adam and Duncan Leslie's rights to it.

"Only yesterday I received a missive from him saying the king had agreed, and that the new patent was being drawn up, but it will probably not be here before the spring. Until such time as I can publicly display that document, I believe the Deverses, mother and son, will use our lack of legal proof as an excuse to harry us, and cause difficulty because of your marriage to the Catholic Kieran. We must protect Maguire's Ford, and all its people, both Protestant and Catholic, from the fanatics, Fortune. Your father was murdered by one such, and they have not changed in the years since. Fanatics never change. I should send you and Kieran to England now, but I am selfish. I want you by my side a bit longer. When you depart for the New World, it is unlikely we shall ever meet again, my daughter. Besides, the autumnal winds have begun to blow from the north, and crossing to England or Scotland would be dangerous now," she reasoned.

"I would stay with you as long as I can, Mama," Fortune replied, "and I agree with you that now is not a good time for me to have a child. Kieran, of course, shall not know. I suspect Papa never did, and 'tis better that way, isn't it?" She smiled mischievously at her mother.

Jasmine nodded. "You were ever my practical child," she said fondly with a small smile. She hugged Fortune warmly. Then she arose. "Let us go downstairs, poppet. Father Cullen is waiting to marry you in private before your most public marriage ceremony, which is to be performed by the Reverend Steen. Rohana will continue to bring you your posset each morning, and when the time comes for you to leave us, she will give you the recipe, and the ingredients. You must decide if Rois should eventually know, or not."

"Why did you cease taking the potion, Mama?" Fortune asked.

Jasmine placed her palms over her large belly, and smiled. "I thought I was past babies growing in my womb," she said with a chuckle. "My Jemmie and I have enjoyed a generous and bountiful bedsport for two years now without any restraints. Bride Murphy tells me, however, that this can happen to a woman at my time of life. I shall be more careful in the future, I promise you. I had forgotten how hard it is to carry a child the nearer one gets to its birthing. This last sibling of yours is an active creature."

Mother and daughter descended the narrow stairs to the main floor of the castle. There in a small room off the hall Fortune Mary Lindley and Kieran Sean Devers were married in the rites of the Holy Mother Church. Father Cullen then absolved Kieran of the sin he was about to commit by being publicly married again, this time by the very Protestant Samuel Steen, in the little stone church that served the village's non-Catholic population, fast becoming the majority in Maguire's Ford. All the Catholics who would be attending the ceremony had been previously absolved, and Cullen Butler, his priestly vestments put aside, joined his cousin, Jasmine, and her family, for the happy occasion, dressed in a very fashionable black velvet suit.

Fortune walked through the village on her stepfather's arm. Her mother followed in a pony cart along with the priest; Rory Maguire, and Bride Duffy, in her best gown, strode proudly along behind their godchild. The church was filled to overflowing. Sir Shane, his daughter, Lady Colleen Kelly and her husband were in a front pew. Behind him sat Molly Fitzgerald, and her two daughters, Maeve and Aine. If any thought it odd, those thoughts were kept to themselves.

The bride was led up the aisle by the duke. One slender hand rested upon his arm. In the other she carried a small bouquet of creamy, late roses tied with golden ribbons. The Reverend Samuel Steen smiled upon the young couple. There was, after all these years, hope for Kieran Devers. His bride, schooled properly by her parents, would lead him safely into the right church at long last. He would be saved from the wicked and sinful ways of the papists. Love could indeed move mountains. Inspired by this happy turn of events, his rich voice intoned the words of the Anglican marriage rite, the elegant language rising to fill the church. Well-schooled, the bridegroom spoke his part in a calm, clear voice. Even the beautiful bride's voice was heard quite distinctly throughout the church.

Finally they were pronounced man and wife. Kieran Devers took his wife into his strong arms, and kissed her heartily. The church erupted into cheers. Samuel Steen smiled, well pleased by today's turn of events as he watched the happy couple hurry back down the aisle, followed by the duke and duchess, Sir Shane, Lady Colleen, and the others, even that wanton Fitzgerald woman, who despite her licentious behavior seemed to have raised two decent daughters, for all they were Catholics.

The day had been unusually fair, and the sun shone brightly upon the newlyweds. The village had been invited to the wedding feast in the hall. Archery butts were set up in the castle courtyard as well as bowls. In a small field outside on the lake, a group of young men began a rugged game of wind ball, using the inflated bladder of a sheep for their ball.

In the hall tables and benches had been set up below the high board which sat upon a raised dais. The smell of roasting beef and lamb filled the hall. Platters of salmon, trout, ducks, and geese were passed. There were fresh trenchers of bread at every place as well as polished wooden spoons. Game pies, steaming hot and rich with winey gravy, were offered. Roasted capons stuffed with fruit, and broiled rabbit were set out. There were bowls of carrots, peas, and braised lettuces. Sweet butter and fine cheeses were on all the tables. Those at the high board drank rich wine from Archambault. The other guests were well pleased with the casks of brown October ale and cider.

The old bard who had come into Erne Rock's hall some months prior had remained. His days of wandering were over, and he now had a permanent home. He entertained the guests with his songs and tales of an Ireland past that had been filled with giants, fairies, glorious deeds of honor, and great battles. He played upon his well-worn harp, and when he tired, a piper took up a tune. Soon all were well fed, and many pleasantly drunk. Toast after toast was raised to the happy couple. The tables were pushed back against the walls, the piper joined by musicians who played upon flute, cornet, and drums; and the dancing began. Because the guests were mostly country folk, the dances were those most familiar to them: the rounder, the jig, and the somewhat slow and melancholy dump. Many of the women were eager to dance with the bridegroom, but the bride did not lack for partners.

The sun set early, it being October. The fires in the hall burned high. The bride and her groom were suddenly gone. The guests, well-fed and filled with good ale, slowly staggered out, thanking the duke and his wife for a fine time. The family sat by the fire talking together. Lady Colleen had not seen her half-sisters in many years. Now she regretted having been put in the difficult position of having to choose between them and her stepmother. These two younger women were her blood kin, and that had meant something once in Ireland.

"It's too dark now for you to return home," the duke noted to Sir Shane. "You'll stay the night, of course."

Sir Shane nodded. "Aye. Jane will not fret as I've stayed away before, and she thinks Colleen gone home to Dublin with Hugh, but my son-in-law is every bit the rebel Colleen is, aren't you, Hugh?"

Hugh Kelly grinned cheerfully. "Aye, Da," he agreed. "Nonetheless, we'll be on the road to Dublin tomorrow, and 'twill be awhile before we're back. I can only imagine how put out Lady Jane will be when she learns of this rather unique gathering to celebrate the marriage between Kieran and Fortune." He chuckled. "You'll be taking the brunt of her anger, I fear, Da."

"My eldest son is entitled to his happiness too," Shane Devers said quietly. "For expediency's sake I became a Protestant, and for expediency's sake I disinherited my eldest son; but I never disowned him, nor would I deny him his happiness. Jane has gained for her son what she sought. There is no more." He chuckled. "And, James Leslie, my lad doesn't come to your family a pauper. I have arranged for him to have now what would have been his upon my death one day. It has been sent to my goldsmith, Michael Kira, in Dublin. He has had it sent to his Kira cousins in London. Do you know of them?"

"Aye," the duke replied with a smile. "The Kiras have been our bankers for well over a century."

"Well, then, my lad will have his own monies," Shane Devers said. " 'Tis not a great deal, of course, but neither my wife or younger son will be able to deny him what is now his, and I believe they might have done so. Jane has a strict sense of ethics that does not extend to Catholics, I fear." He chuckled again. "She'll not know what I've done until after my death, but I'll not be here then to be scourged by her scolding tongue." He looked at his daughter and son-in-law. "You've heard none of this," he told them sternly.

Colleen threw up her hands. "Indeed I haven't," she said. "I shall be in trouble enough with Mama for months to come for having attended this wedding, but I wouldn't have missed it for the world." She arose from her place by the fire. "I think Hugh and I had best seek our beds as we are leaving early."

"Adali," Jasmine called. "Show Sir Hugh and Lady Colleen to their chamber." She smiled at them. "I am so glad you were with us for I know how much it meant to Fortune. Thank you."

The Kellys departed the hall, and Shane Devers looked to his longtime mistress. "I've provided for our lasses too," he told her. "All know I've never denied them."

"I'm sending them to the New World with Kieran," Molly told him. "No matter our relationship, they are still considered bastards in Lisnaskea. How can they find respectable husbands with such a stain upon them? They say in this new colony being founded, their Catholic faith will not be counted against them. In such a faraway place, with Kieran as their guardian, their birth may be concealed, and my lasses will be able to find good husbands, Shane. 'Tis what I want for them."

"When they go to England they will have their portion," he promised her.

Jasmine saw the devotion and love that the two had for each other. How sad, she thought, that Shane Devers could not have married Molly Fitzgerald instead of his English-born Jane, but then it was Jane Devers's wealth that had saved Mallow Court. She rose from her place, feigning a yawn. "Adali will show you to your rooms," she said. "I am exhausted, and will retire now. I will see you in the morning."

The hall had emptied and only a few servants were left to clear the last bits of debris from the wedding feast. No one noticed Rory Maguire seated in the shadows by the fire, a wolfhound's head upon his knee. Staring into the flames the Irishman considered how fortunate he had been to learn that Fortune was his daughter, and to see her happily married this day. That no one else but the priest and Adali knew was comforting in that they, too, were forced to bear his burden.

She had been such a beautiful bride, the golden brown velvet of her gown bringing out the gold in her red hair. He sighed. Only a few more months, and she would be gone from him forever. Gone from Maguire's Ford, which should have been hers, not just through her mother, but through her blood tie to the Maguires themselves. Gone to a new world across the vast ocean; a place he couldn't even imagine. Then Rory Maguire did something he hadn't done in years. He prayed from his heart. Prayed that his daughter would be happy and content for the rest of her days.

Happy. She had never been happier in her entire life, Fortune thought. In the midst of the dancing Kieran had taken her hand, and they had slipped away from the hall, running wordlessly up the stairs to her chamber, stealing into the room, and locking the door behind them. He had put the key on the window ledge with a great show of ceremony.

Fortune laughed softly. "Dare I ask you if you know how to help a lady remove her gown?" she said.

Kieran grinned, and turning her about began to unlace her bodice even while Fortune undid the tapes holding her skirts up. In short order she stood in her chemise and petticoats. Pulling the garments up she held out a slender leg to him. Kneeling he slid the silk rossetted garter off, and then rolled the gold silk stocking down the shapely limb, and over her foot, kissing her kneecap as he did so. She giggled. He repeated the procedure on her other leg, but then he surprised

her for his hands glided smoothly beneath her skirts, clasping her buttocks in a firm grip as he drew her body forward,
his face pressing itself against her belly, rubbing insinuat-
ingly.

Fortune could feel the heat through the fabric of her undergarments. She could acutely sense the longing he felt.
Her hands touched his dark head, and gently caressed it. His
hair was thick, and silky to her touch. He looked up at her,
and the passion she saw in his deep blue eyes took her breath
away. Instinctively she loosed her petticoats, letting them
slide down, drawing her chemise over her head, and drop-
ping it. He released his grip upon her long enough to allow
the silk to fall away; then he grasped her once again, but this
time he bent his head slightly, his lips touching her plump
Venus mont.

Her head spun, and her fingers tightened in his hair. She
couldn't speak for a long moment for her throat was so tight.
Her heart beat wildly against her chest as a burst of heat
washed over her.

"Fortune! Do you mean to tear the hair from my head?"
she heard him say in a strangled voice.

She looked down and saw that she was gripping him
fiercely. "Ohh!" Her fingers loosed their hold on him.

His blue eyes danced now with amusement. "You have a
strong grip, wife," he told her. Then he stood up.

"I like it better when you kneel at my feet," Fortune
replied pertly, the delicious shock of his intimate kiss reced-
ing.

"You are utterly charming without your clothes," he told
her.

" 'Tis time you had yours off, sir," she replied wickedly.
Then her fingers began to undo his doublet, casting it aside
in a heap with her wedding gown and petticoats. She loosened the ties on his shirt, her hands glossing beneath the fabric to press against his chest. Pushing the shirt from his
shoulders so that it fell to his hips, she bent her fiery head

and began to kiss the warm flesh with tiny, feathery kisses. Unable to restrain herself she let her tongue smooth over his skin.

Kieran gritted his teeth. She had the manners of a courtesan, and yet he knew she wasn't a wanton. "I'm going to remove my breeches," he warned her. When she didn't answer him, but instead kept on kissing and licking at him, he loosed and then lowered the garment in question.

Fortune's head shot up. "You aren't wearing any drawers!" she squeaked. Her eyes were riveted on his manhood as his shirt slid by it to the floor. She had brothers, and was not surprised by his possession of a manhood, or even its location. *It was the size of it.* She stared, fascinated, a bit frightened, yet enthralled. Then she spoke. "It's wonderful. Why don't you wear drawers?" Her hand was itching to reach out and touch him.

"They're a waste of time, and material," he said, intrigued by her reaction. Then he pulled her to him. She melted into his body, feeling the hard length of him against her thigh. His fingers brushed over her mouth. He saw the innocent desire rising in her eyes. He wished she weren't a virgin for he wanted nothing more than to plunge himself into her sweetness right now.

"Hurry!" she whispered into his ear.

"You're not ready yet," he told her. "Don't you think I want to take you right now, Fortune? But I won't hurt you. I want this first coupling between us to be perfect. I have waited a lifetime for you!" His mouth came down fiercely on hers, kissing her deeply, taking her breath away as he plundered her lips, kissing and nibbling upon them until she was gasping. His tongue found hers, stroking it sensuously. He could feel the little nipples of her breasts hardening, and pushing against his chest. Lifting her into his arms, he stepped from the puddle of velvet and silk that was his breeches and shirt. Walking across the room he laid her gently upon the bed.

Looking up at him she held out her arms. He smiled, and lay next to her, taking her hand in his, and kissing first the palm, and then each finger. "You are the most beautiful girl I have ever known," he told her quietly. "And you are the only girl I have ever loved."

"In practical terms you are the most implausible man I could have married," Fortune replied softly, "but I love you, Kieran, and I have never loved any man. Not even an infatuation, my darling. I want to please you, but I have absolutely no real idea of how to do so. Mama would tell me nothing except the mere rudiments for she says, as did my sister, that passion between two people who love each other is wonderful, and indescribable."

He smiled into her eyes, and Fortune was suddenly filled with an incredible sense of well-being, knowing that she was loved. "Just be quiet, lambkin, and let me adore you in my own fashion. There is nothing to fear from me, Fortune." Then he kissed her lips again, but briefly, his mouth brushing over the pure white column of her throat, nestling into the tiny hollow beneath her ear. He nibbled upon her lobe.

"Do you mean to devour me then?" she teased.

"In very tiny bits that will last forever," he replied. His lips then found the soft hollow of her throat. He could feel her pulse throbbing excitedly beneath his mouth. He rested there a moment; then raising his dark head again he laid it upon her chest, listening to her heart which beat a tattoo beneath his ear.

Fortune caressed his head once again with her fingertips. She hadn't known what to expect, and while this was lovely, it really wasn't very exciting. Still Mama and India seemed to enjoy lovemaking. Was there something wrong with her? Then Kieran raised his head, and began to kiss her breasts. The sharp intake of her own breath was very audible, and almost painful. She lay helpless as he cradled her in the curve of an arm. Then his big hand began to fondle her tenderly, but firmly. His fingers lightly crushed the supple flesh, leaving brief marks she could see in the shadows of the firelight. A frisson of sensation ran down her spine when he pinched a nipple, and a small *"Oh!"* of surprise escaped her lips.

He rolled onto his back, drawing her atop him. She felt her cheeks flaming with the exquisite intimacy as their naked bodies touched from shoulder to toes. His hands caressed the length of her, brushing over her suddenly sensitive flesh. Then those hands fastened themselves about her narrow waist, and lifted her up so that her breasts hung over his face. Raising his head just slightly he licked at her nipples, and a little moan slipped from her lips, to be followed by a gasp as his mouth closed over a nipple, and he suckled upon it. *Now this was definitely more exciting,* Fortune thought, and then she gave herself up to the delights he seemed to be engendering within her by his actions. She sighed deeply as he transferred his mouth to her other nipple.

He was rolling them again. She found herself upon her back once more. He began to stroke her breasts and belly. Waves of heat again coursed through her body. There was a distinct tingling in that forbidden spot between her legs. Unable to help herself she squirmed slightly. He smiled knowingly, putting his hand upon her Venus mont, and pressing down. A bolt of sensation shot through her. A single finger began to run up and down the shadowed gash between her nether lips. She could feel the moisture beginning to ooze from between those fleshy folds as his finger glided back and forth.

"You will be ready soon, sweetheart," he murmured against her mouth. He was as hard as granite now, his male member throbbing with excitement and anticipation.

"Do what you did before," Fortune begged him. *"Please!"*

"Little wanton," he laughed, and then he pushed his finger between her nether lips to find her love button.

Fortune gasped with pleasure as he attained his goal. This was what she had wanted. Not the caressing, but the excitement of her own lust. *"Ohhh, yes!"* she cried to him. *"Don't stop, Kieran! Don't stop!"*

He had no intention of stopping. He played with the sentient nub of flesh, exciting it, rousing it, making her squirm with her own rising passions. Her lust boiled over once, but he did not cease the sweet torture until she was whimpering with another burst of delight. It was then he growled into her ear, "Open yourself for me, Fortune!"

"Not yet," she pleaded, wanting more.

"Now!" his voice said harshly as he forced a knee between her thighs, levering them open. *"Now,* you honied little bitch, before I explode with my desire for you!" Reaching down he positioned himself, and then with two fingers he pinched her love button hard, sending Fortune into a paroxysm of pleasure. At that moment he plunged deep into her eager body, feeling her maidenhead explode with the force of his fierce thrust, hearing her astonished intake of breath.

"Ahhhh!" she gasped. His initial entry had been painful, but now the pain was quickly gone. She became awakened to his possession of her. Her first reaction was to be frightened, but then she was acutely aware of how he filled her. It was so natural. So perfect. She sighed deeply, her arms wrapping themselves about him.

"Look at me," he commanded her.

She opened her eyes and stared into his which were so filled with his love and his passion that she was near to weeping. "I love you, Fortune," he told her once again. *"I love you!"* Then he began to move within her. With each stroke of his love lance she became more and more conscious of a new pleasure that was rising within her, reaching up to claim her very soul. Her gaze locked itself on his until the intensity of her emotions was so great that her eyes closed of their own volition, and for the first time in her life Fortune soared among the stars.

He drove deeper and deeper into the sweetness of her. Her fingers dug strongly into the flesh of his muscled shoulders. *"Please! Please!"* she said huskily, and he understood the delights she was experiencing because he was savoring those same delights as their bodies, one now, peaked together in a fierce firestorm of satisfied passion.

"Kieran! Ahh, 'tis sweet, my darling! Sweet!" Fortune cried as she was swept up in a maelstrom, and then hurtled down into a pool of warm darkness.

His hunger burst, flooding her secret garden with his juices as he collapsed upon her lush body. He could scarce catch his breath, but he quickly realized his weight on her was much too much, and rolled from her. He lay gasping, feeling the moisture from his exertions oozing from every pore of his body. As his heart slowed he heard it. A soft weeping. Stricken he turned toward her. "Fortune? What is it, sweetheart? Why do you weep? Have I hurt you?" He was a beast! he thought. So wrapped up in his own pleasure he hadn't even considered her. He gathered her into his arms. "What is it, lambkin? Tell me!"

"I am so happy," she wailed, and wept all over his smooth chest. *"I have never been happier in all my life, Kieran!"* she sobbed. "You were so worth waiting for, my love. I didn't think love would ever find me. When I met your brother, and knew almost at once he wasn't the one, and thought I might have to take him because it was expected. . . ." A fresh flow of tears poured forth from her blue-green eyes.

He wanted to laugh at her innocent confession. He wanted to shout with joy at it. Instead he held her tightly. "I didn't think love would find me either, Fortune, but then I saw you, and knew I could not let Willy have you. I would have stolen you away in the manner of my Celtic ancestors if you had chosen him. *You are mine!* You always were, and you always will be. Now, cease your weeping, my love, and kiss me," he told her, turning her to face him.

Their lips met in an almost desperate embrace. Then drawing away from him she said candidly, "Can we have each other again tonight?"

He nodded. "Aye, but let me rest awhile, and you also, my

darling. I have much more to show you, and to teach you, Fortune. I hope you will not be disappointed."

"I want to know how to pleasure you," she said. Then she climbed from their bed, and padded across the bedchamber to where a silver ewer had been set next to a small pile of soft cloths. Bringing them back to the bedside she set them down, and first washed herself, then bathed his manhood carefully. "Mama calls these love cloths. She says it is advisable to bathe after each encounter with passion because then we are ready for more."

He had never heard of such a thing, but it seemed quite sensible to him, and he certainly had no objection to the procedure. "I like it," he said. "Will you always care for me so tenderly, Fortune?" He reached up, and fondled her breast, rubbing the nipple with the pad of his thumb.

"Aye," she said, carefully putting the basin and cloths aside, then climbing back into their bed atop him. His two hands began to caress her two small round breasts. Fortune clasped him between her two milky thighs as she would her gelding. "I can ride you, sir, even as I do Thunder. Will you prove as lusty a mount?" she teased him, almost purring as he squeezed her breasts. She arched away from him, and his hands glided down her torso, sliding around beneath her bottom to fondle it suggestively. "Ohh!" she squealed, and wiggled herself against his outspread palms.

He chuckled, and looked up at her, his eyes twinkling. "So, you're not afraid of my lust, my beautiful wife." His strong fingers kneaded her flesh. He could feel his love lance hardening with each of her very provocative movements. She had wondered if they could make love again tonight. He now wondered if he could stop. He had never known such desire for a woman as he had for Fortune. Usually his lust was easily satisfied with one good tumble, but not with his young bride.

She could feel the throbbing of him, and raising herself above his manhood she slowly lowered herself onto it, a gusty sigh escaping her as she couched his lance entirely. He groaned, and pulling her forward so he might kiss her again began to move rhythmically within her. Their lips tasted each other. Their hearts beat frantically. "Oh, God!" Fortune cried desperately as he drove once again with unrelenting insistence until the stars were exploding within her head, behind her eyes, and in her very heart.

"Fortune, my love!" he cried out as his desire peaked once more, his arms tightening about her as she yielded herself to him again.

And afterwards as they lay together, fingers entwined, he insisted that she sleep for a time. "You are so fierce a lover, my darling," he told her, "but you must rest, and so must I."

"Yes, sir, my lord husband," Fortune replied sweetly, sated, and replete with her contentment. "But can we please do it again when we awake? *Kieran?* Why are you laughing? Have I said something amusing?"

He somehow managed to restrain his mirth. "Are all the women in your family this passionate, Fortune?"

"Isn't passion with your husband a good thing?" Her look was honestly questioning.

"You will never hear me complain, my love," he told her, "but this thought suddenly comes to mind. I don't have to worry about my little brother killing me when he learns I have married you, Fortune. You will probably kill me with your wickedly delicious lustful nature before much longer. Willy doesn't know what a narrow escape he had." And he laughed again.

"Villain!" she scolded him. "And you have yet to answer my question. Can we make love again after we have rested?"

"Aye," he said, and then, "I wonder if I shall live to see the morning, you delightful wanton."

Fortune leaned over him, and ran her tongue along his lips before kissing him quickly. "Now that you have shown me the delights of passion, my love, I intend keeping you alive," she told him.

"Keeping you content will be a lifetime occupation," he replied, pulling her against him so that she could hear the steady beat of his heart.

"You will have to work very hard," she told him.

"Oh, madame, I will," he responded. "You may be certain that I will."

Chapter

11

"What do you mean Kieran has married Fortune Lindley?" Jane Devers stared at her husband uncomprehendingly.

"They were wed yesterday by the Reverend Steen at Maguire's Ford's church," her husband replied. "I was there, and witnessed the ceremony."

"You allowed this thing?" She could feel her anger beginning to rise. "You let that Celtic bastard of yours marry the greatest heiress in all of Fermanagh? *How could you?"* Her fair skin was mottled with her ire, and she was practically gasping.

"How could I prevent it?" he asked her quietly. "The duke of Glenkirk and his wife were content with the match. And do not ever again refer to my eldest son as a bastard, Jane." His look was hard.

"What else is he?" she shrieked. "Your Catholic marriage was illegal. That is the king's law! Your children by that creature you called a first wife were not legitimate, and yet I looked the other way, raising them as if they were my own. When you recognized William as your legitimate heir, I thought we were of one mind, Shane."

" 'Twas you, my dear, who said unless Kieran became a Protestant I must disinherit him if Mallow Court was to be protected, and remain in the Devers family," he replied. "Are you now telling me that if Kieran had complied, and became a Protestant, you would have claimed he was illegitimate because my first marriage to Mary Maguire was celebrated in the Catholic Church?"

"Yes!" she told him bluntly. "Yes, I would have! We did not marry for love, Shane. You married me for my inheritance, and I married you for Mallow Court. Did you really think I should let Kieran have it after my William was born? And if I had not borne you a son, but only a daughter, I should have wanted it for Bessie. Mallow Court does not belong to you, Shane. My father bought it with his gold, and I sealed the bargain when I let you grunt and sweat over my body in order to give you a daughter and a son. In the eyes of the law they are your only legitimate heirs! Do not ever forget it!"

"I am not such a fool that I believe ours a love match, Jane," he said, "but I did think we had an affection for one another after two children, and all these many years. I am saddened to learn I was wrong."

"You Irish are such romantics," she sneered. "Marriage, like anything else, is a practical business, Shane. Now, let us discuss this disaster that has come upon us. Kieran cannot be allowed to have Erne Rock, and Maguire's Ford. It would give the local Catholics who persist in remaining here too great an advantage."

"Kieran and Fortune will not be remaining in Ulster, Jane. They are not to have Maguire's Ford. You have already been told that. The estate is to be divided between the duke's two youngest sons, Adam and Duncan Leslie, who are already in residence at the castle. The duke, his wife, Fortune, and Kieran will be leaving next spring after the duchess has had her child, and it is safe for them to travel."

"That is what they tell you," Jane Devers said venomously. "I am not so great a fool that I do not realize what Kieran has done. He quite deliberately set out to entice the Lindley wench so that William could not have her. William suspected it all along. Why else would Kieran have married *that* girl but for her vast estate? What else could she possibly have to recommend her? Kieran is an Irishman and to him land is important. He planned to gain a larger and richer holding than his younger brother. That is why he was so willing to give up Mallow Court. Ahh, you Irish are a wickedly devious lot, but Kieran will not succeed, I promise you, Shane! The law will not allow a treasonous Catholic to have such a prize."

"Jane, do not meddle! I forbid you to do so else you bring disaster on my house. Kieran and his wife are *not* to have Maguire's Ford. The Leslies of Glenkirk are no fools to throw away a rich holding like that on a Catholic son-in-law. They have a friend in King Charles, and a certain small influence at court. The duchess's son is the king's nephew. *If* they wanted Maguire's Ford and Erne Rock for their daughter and Kieran, they would have the king's protection no matter the law, *but they do not.* They are wise enough to know the difficulty it would cause, and wish no harm to their people. The two sons who will divide the holding are Protestants. You cannot take Maguire's Ford from the Leslies of Glenkirk, Jane. You have no grounds on which to base any accusations. Let it be, and consider how we are to tell William when he and Emily Anne return from their wedding trip in a few weeks."

She paled. "Ahh, my son! What will he think of this turn of events? Poor William!"

"Poor William?" her husband said almost mockingly. "Why would you feel sorry for him, Jane? He is the heir to all I have. He has married a young girl who genuinely loves

him, and will one day bring him all her father has, which is considerable. Why would you feel sorry for him, Jane? Because he retains a foolish passion that was never returned for a girl who saw nothing of value, or to love, in him? He had best get over his childish lust, for that is all it ever was. And he had best not covet his brother's wife." Then he looked hard at his own spouse "And you will not spoil William and Emily Anne's wedding trip by sending a message to him in Dublin. Let them have these few weeks together to find some happiness before you begin to infect them with your bitterness, my dear.

"Kieran has wed Fortune in the rites of the Anglican Church, *the king's church*. There is nothing you can do about it, Jane. The match is legal, approved of by the Leslies, and the bloody bedsheet flew this morning over Erne Rock Castle in proof of the consummation of the marriage. Kieran has never done you any harm, Jane. Like William, he is entitled to his happiness. *You will not interfere.*" His look was stern.

"Your Catholic son allowed himself to be wed in the Protestant Church?" she jeered at him. "Then the girl is no more than a whore to him, for his marriage could only be sanctified in the foul rites of the Roman Church." Her eyes narrowed. "Unless, of course, they were first married by that priest the duchess claims as her kin. Were they, Shane? Did your precious son and his whore flout the king's law first, then make a mockery of our true church?" She glared at him.

"If there was another ceremony, Jane, I was not aware of it, nor was I present at any such ceremony," he told her. No, he hadn't been present. Bride Murphy and Rory Maguire had been the witnesses. He had already been seated in Maguire's Ford's little stone Protestant church with Colleen, Hugh, Molly, and their daughters. God help him when Jane learned of that, and she would eventually. "The Leslies of Glenkirk are Protestant, Jane. It is natural their daughter, brought up in England's faith, would be married by Reverend Steen. And pray, my dear, do not call my daughter-in-law a whore."

Frustrated, and angered beyond all reason, Jane Devers lost her calm demeanor and vaunted control. Her fingers closed about the wine decanter, and then she flung it at him. *"I hate you!"* she screamed.

Shane Devers ducked the missile and burst out laughing. "Why, my dear Jane, 'tis the most passion I have ever seen you show in all our years of marriage. It quite becomes you."

Open-mouthed, she stared at him, her pale blue eyes almost bulging from her head. Then with a cry of despair Jane Devers fled her husband's library. She was appalled by the situation; appalled by her inability to manage it; appalled by her loss of control. She began to weep, but after a moment she ceased. She needed to know more about this wedding. Hurrying to her apartments she called to her maid, Susanna.

"See if one of the household servants has kin in Maguire's Ford," she said "My stepson married Lady Lindley yesterday, and I want to know everything there is to know about the wedding."

"Yes, m'lady," Susanna said, showing no emotion at all. Her ladyship did not like any show of feelings, but Susanna was very surprised by her mistress's news. "The undercook has family in Maguire's Ford, m'lady. Shall I speak to her?"

"Yes," Jane Devers replied. "Tell her there is a silver piece in it for her if she is forthcoming."

"Yes, m'lady." Susanna curtsied, and hurried off.

Several days later Jane Devers had learned all she needed to know about her stepson's wedding. It had been a happy occasion, and the duke had invited all in the village to celebrate it with his family. Learning this made her even happier William had not contracted an alliance with Fortune Lindley. That the duke could associate himself and his fam-

ily with those bog trotters was disgusting. The Leslies might
be wealthy, but they were obviously not people of real quality. How could they be when the duchess had no shame in
the mongrel she had borne a dead prince?

More interesting, however, was the knowledge that her
husband's mistress had been at the festivities with her two
bastards. And that they had all spent the night at Erne Rock.
While Shane knew it not, she had seen those two young
hussies in Lisnaskea on several occasions. And she had made
it quite clear to the Reverend Mr. Dundas that no respectable
family should take either of those two woods colts to be a
wife for their sons. They were baseborn. *They were Catholics.*
But that Shane should have consorted with them publicly at
Kieran's wedding was an insult she would not forget. He
would pay for his misbehavior. Kieran would pay for his
treachery as well.

She hardly saw her husband at all now. They had had separate bedchambers for years. They only met over the dinner
table, except that Shane was away in the evening more often
than not of late. Probably with his blowsy whore and her two
brats. Consequently there was little exchange between them
anymore. She didn't care. William would be home soon with
Emily Anne, and then they would decide what was to be
done about Kieran and the estate at Maguire's Ford. No matter that Shane said Kieran was not to have it. She didn't believe him. Why wouldn't the duchess give the lands given
her by her late husband to the child born of that marriage?
Surely she would. She wouldn't give it to sons born of another husband. Jasmine Leslie would use her influence with
King Charles to give Maguire's Ford to her daughter and
Kieran. Bringing her two youngest sons from Scotland was
but a ruse. Well, it wouldn't work, and Kieran Devers wasn't
going to have the chance to lord it over her son!

Blissfully unaware of Jane Devers, Kieran and Fortune
spent the days following their marriage making love and riding out together. Their passion for each other was so great

that they could scarcely wait to leave the hall each evening. Finally Jasmine told them to not even bother coming into the hall, but to have food sent to their bedchamber to eat when they realized another hunger other than the one they had for each other's bodies.

"Mama!" Fortune blushed, embarrassed, but Kieran just laughed.

"I thank you, madame, for your understanding," he said with a rakish grin, and a wink.

Both the duke and Rory Maguire chuckled at his reply, and Father Cullen hid a smile.

"The quiet from Lisnaskea is a wee bit deafening," the duke noted.

"I heard that Lady Jane and her good husband had quite a row over the marriage here," Rory noted. "The undercook at Mallow Court was given a silver piece to obtain all the information she could from her kin here. Now they say Sir Shane and his wife do not speak to each other except when they cannot avoid it. It should get a bit more interesting when young Willy comes home with his bride."

"Surely he won't make a scene," Fortune said.

"You turned him away, and married his brother, lass," was the answer. "Kieran can tell you, young Willy has never been one to easily let go of something he wanted."

"We'll talk, my brother and I," Kieran said.

Maguire raised a sandy eyebrow. "If you can get within shouting range of him, Kieran Devers, for he'll be out for blood unless that simple lass he has married has been able to turn his heart."

"Do you think he's dangerous?" Fortune asked her husband later that evening as they lay abed. They were naked, and seated, he against the pillows, she against his chest. His big hands played with her sweet round breasts, teasing them lightly.

"I don't know," he answered her, one hand moving to push her hair aside so he might kiss the soft nape of her neck. "I've never seen him driven so far as he was with you." He nipped at her, then soothed away the sting with his wet tongue.

She took his other hand from her breast, and mouthed the fingers, finally taking one finger into her mouth and sucking on it seductively. Her tongue swirled about the finger in an almost thoughtful motion, and then releasing it she said, "Does his wife have the ability to rule him as his mother did? Perhaps we should try to make our peace through Emily Anne."

"I am not certain it will be possible for Emily Anne loves Willy with all her heart, and she is yet very young. She will say and do what she believes will please him. Nay, I think there is little chance of a reconciliation between me and my family."

"Your father will not desert you," Fortune reminded him.

"Nay, he won't, but neither will he do anything else. He must live with my stepmother and my siblings long after we have gone."

"Than we shall ignore them all," Fortune said. "I see no other way. In six months' time we shall be gone, and with the winter coming, I see little chance of your stepmother causing difficulty."

He turned her about so he might kiss her, but did not answer her. His bride did not know Jane Devers as he did. Even now her troublesome mind would be twisting and turning in an effort to find an excuse to make mischief of some sort for the Leslies of Glenkirk, and to justify that wicked behavior as right, based upon her religious beliefs. Not that the Catholics weren't as bad; for they were. How they could all excuse their viciousness toward one another, and still claim God favored them alone defied logic, Kieran thought.

Toward the end of October Maeve Fitzgerald rode over from Lisnaskea to tell her half-brother that William Devers and his bride were expected home that same day. "Da says to be on your guard as that woman he's wed to is surely plotting some deviltry."

"I had heard Da wasn't at Mallow Court a great deal now," her brother remarked.

"He's there enough," Maeve said sharply.

Kieran put an arm about his half-sister. "What is it, lass?"

Maeve sighed deeply. "I don't want to leave our mam, and yet she wants us to go with you in the spring, and the truth is that she is right. There is nothing here for us. We're being driven from our home by the likes of Jane Devers, and her Protestant ilk. And what will happen to Mam when we are gone?"

"Da will protect her," Kieran said in an effort to comfort his half-sister.

"And when Da is gone? Do you think your younger brother will respect the fact that Da built Mam her house, and gave her an income? He'll drive her from it, and send her from Lisnaskea, the only place she's ever known, and all because she's a Catholic. God help her!"

"We'll make a plan," Kieran promised her. "If that should ever happen, she will come to us in the New World, Maeve."

"I hate the Protestants!" Maeve declared. "They may hold sway here in Ulster now, but they'll all burn in the fiery pits of hell one day for their impiety and false religion. I'm glad for it!"

"My wife is a Protestant," Kieran reminded Maeve.

"Fortune is different, and at least she was once baptized a Catholic. With your help, Kieran, she'll return to the true church one day, especially when you have children," Maeve reasoned.

"Don't waste yourself in hating, little sister," he told her. Then he sent her back to Lisnaskea, and went to tell his in-laws that William Devers would shortly be home.

He came early the next day, riding through Maguire's Ford as if the devil himself was on his heels. He stormed into Erne Rock Castle, pushing past a startled servant. He found the family in the Great Hall, breaking their fast of the previous night. They did not see him until pointing a finger at Fortune he shouted at her, *"Whore!"*

Before James Leslie, Kieran, or the two younger Leslies might respond, Fortune was on her feet, coming down from the high board to stand in front of William Devers. She slapped him with all her might. "How dare you insult me?" she demanded of him. "Who do you think you are, William Devers, to come into my mother's house and slander me? You have no rights over me, and you certainly never did!"

"You were to marry me!" he cried, taken aback by her fury. His mother and his wife had spent all the previous evening telling him what an affront Fortune Lindley's marriage to Kieran was. He had right on his side, damn it!

"There was no marriage contract between us, or our families, Master Devers. I came to Ireland to seek a husband, and you were the first candidate for my hand presented me. I refused you."

"So you might whore with my bastard brother!" he accused her. "All the time I courted you so tenderly, you were thinking of him!"

Fortune slapped him again to his surprise. "If you keep calling me foul names, and maligning my husband, Master Devers, I shall go to the local magistrate and register a complaint. Do not think that because Kieran is a Catholic I shall be ignored. I shall not. I am a Protestant, and my brother is the king's well-loved nephew. As for the king, his wife is a Catholic. Whose side in such a matter as this one do you think the king will favor, *Master* Devers? That of a very unimportant Irish landowner's son, *or mine?"*

"I loved you, Fortune." His voice was low.

"You were fascinated by me. What you loved, Will, whether you knew it or not, was Maguire's Ford, and this castle. Even as your mother had taught you," Fortune said with devastating effect.

"Kieran shall not have it," William Devers said, his voice now hard, his eyes filled with anger and hate. "My bastard half-brother shall not have Maguire's Ford and Erne Rock. I will not allow any Catholic to lord it over me, madame!"

"You know the disposition of this estate, Will," Fortune said. "It is to be equally divided between my brothers who even now sit at the high board, their daggers at the ready to slit your throat," she mocked. "Now, apologize to me, and to your brother, who is my husband. There is no reason for strife between us."

"Go to hell, you bitch!" he snarled, and turned to go.

At that moment Kieran Devers leapt from the high board, and dashed across the floor to beard his younger brother. Grasping him by his doublet he said fiercely, "I'll not kill you lest I have the sin of Cain upon me, Willy, and because I promised my wife I should not; but if you ever insult either of us again, *little brother,* I will forget my promises, and the consequences be damned. My father's marriage to my mother was a legitimate one even as his marriage to your mother is. If I were the bigot you are I should claim otherwise for is not the Holy Catholic Church the one true church? Some say it is so, Willy, although the Protestants would disagree. Like Fortune and her family I desire no animosity between us, but so help me God I shall beat you senseless if you ever come to Erne Rock again uninvited to cause trouble!" He loosed his hold on the younger man. "Now, get the hell out of here, Willy!" Spinning William Devers about he applied his boot to the seat of his antagonist's breeches, and pushed.

Stumbling, William Devers almost ran from the hall, but as he reached its entrance he turned, raising a fist to shake it at them. "You will be sorry for what you have done to me, Kieran! I'll see you dead, and that witch you've married who haunts my dreams with you!" Then he was gone.

"He's mad," Fortune declared. "There was never anything but a possibility between us. Now he is a married man as I am a married woman, and he can still not let it go."

"You were his first love, sweetheart," Kieran said. "In a strange way I cannot blame him. How could any man love you, and then be married to another, Fortune?"

Hearing his words Fortune smiled up at her husband. "I do love you so," she said softly.

At the high board James and Jasmine Leslie smiled fondly at the pair, but Adam Leslie and his brother, Duncan, rolled their eyes at each other, and snorted their derision.

Hearing them their sister turned about. "You'll be just as bad one day, my laddies," she told them.

"Never!" Adam swore. "We dinna like lassies."

"You will," chuckled his father, "and sooner, I fear, than later."

"And make a fool of myself like that William Devers? I dinna think so," Adam replied scathingly. Then he quickly apologized to his brother-in-law. "Yer pardon, Kieran. I know he's yer brother, but . . ."

Kieran smiled at the boy. "I take no offense, Adam Leslie, for I fear you are wiser than Willy."

"Poor William," Jasmine said sympathetically.

But William Devers didn't need the duchess of Glenkirk's sympathy. Filled with righteous anger he returned to Mallow Court quite determined to see that his brother and Fortune were punished for what he had decided were their offenses against him. He was encouraged in this pursuit by his mother and his wife, for like her mother-in-law, Emily Anne Devers had little tolerance for Catholics.

"They must be rooted out of Lisnaskea for good and all," she said to her husband. "Certainly your father can be made to see reason, William. These people are a danger to us all for they hate us."

"I will speak with him," William told her, but when he brought the subject up, Shane Devers was taken aback.

"What do you mean we must drive the Catholics from Lisnaskea?" he demanded of his son. "Are you mad? The peace between Protestant and Catholic is fragile enough as it is. And where are these people who have lived here in this place for centuries to go?"

"The Catholics put us all in peril, Da," William answered him. "Their popish ways can taint our children."

His father snorted with derision. He had just about had enough of his wife, his son, his daughter-in-law, and their bigotry. He had become a Protestant to gain Jane's hand, and her fortune, but he had never discriminated against his Catholic neighbors.

But a passing servant heard the argument between father and son. He gossiped to his fellow servant, whose sweetheart, a maidservant in the house, had overheard a similar conversation between Lady Devers and the young mistress. The rumors began to fly from Mallow Court into Lisnaskea. Neighbor began to look upon neighbor with suspicion even though only the day before they had been friends.

The priest in Lisnaskea, Father Brendan, began preaching against those who would come into Ulster with its traditions of greatness and put that heritage with its wonderful myths and legends and history to scorn, calling the Irish barbarians, and papists who needed to be taught better. The Protestant minister, the Reverend Mr. Dundas, began to sermonize that only the Protestant faith was the true faith, and any who stood against it must be either brought forcibly to the truth, or destroyed. To worship other than in the proscribed manner was outright treason.

Then one evening as Shane Devers sat quietly with his mistress in her house, sipping his whiskey, the sound of cries reached their ears. Rising from his place by the hearth he went to the door, opened it, and looked out. To his shock he could see several fires burning in the village, and hear the shouts and cry of voices. "I had best go and see what is happening, Molly. Lock the door, and do not open it to any but me. I'll be back." He hurried off.

Molly Fitzgerald barred the door as she had been instructed, and called her daughters from their bedchamber, bringing them down into the parlor with Biddy, her servant. "There is some trouble in the village," she said. "Your da has gone to investigate."

" 'Tis been coming all week," Biddy muttered darkly.

"What have you heard?" her mistress asked.

"No more than you, but I can tell you that young William Devers has been going about stirring up the Protestants, telling them we're a danger to them, and if we were gone 'twould be heaven on earth in Lisnaskea. And there are those who would listen, mistress."

"Filthy dissenters! May they all burn in hell!" Maeve said angrily. "I wish I were a man so I might fight them for the true faith."

"Don't be a little fool," her mother said impatiently. "This is William Devers's outrage at his brother marrying Lady Fortune. He covets Maguire's Ford."

"But Kieran isn't to have it," Aine, her younger daughter, said. "Surely he knows that, Mam."

"He won't believe it, nor will his greedy mother until Kieran and Fortune are gone from Ulster," Molly said fatalistically.

The sound of shouting seemed to be drawing nearer as the four women huddled by the fireside. Without a word Biddy got up, and drew the draperies shut. She had seen the shadowed figures of men moving toward the house in the light from the fires, but she said nothing, instead going to the front door of the house, and setting the heavy oak bar across it. Then she went to the back of the house, and did the same with the door into the pantry. Molly watched her elderly servant silently, exchanging a questioning look with Biddy who but shook her grizzled head cautiously.

The smell of burning began to seep through into the house, but Molly was not concerned for her own house was made of brick with a fine slate roof. The angry yelling was close now, and the mistress of the house wondered where Sir Shane had gotten to, and if he was all right. She looked to her two daughters seated by the fireplace, their arms protectively about each other. They were unusually silent, even the usually outspoken Maeve. Suddenly a thunderous pounding came upon the front door. Biddy slid back into the shadows of the room while Molly put a warning finger to her lips as she caught her daughters attention.

Then the glass in one of the windows was smashed violently, and unable to help themselves the women screamed in fright as the draperies were yanked aside, and a man climbed into the room. He glared at them, but said nothing, and going into the hallway unbarred the front door to allow a mob of howling men into the house. They crowded into the elegant parlor, and Molly recognized many of them as her neighbors. The girls were sobbing, terrified.

"How dare you break into my house!" Molly said angrily. "What is this all about? You, Robert Morgan, and you, James Curran! Why I recognize most of you. What is going on?"

The two men she named looked shamefaced, but remained where they were. The others shuffled their feet uncomfortably.

"The whore is bold, is she not?" William Devers moved forward from the crowd of men who stepped aside to let him come. "My father's Catholic whore thinks she can lord it over us all. Well, you cannot, whore, and you will not ever again." Raising the pistol he had concealed in his hand William Devers shot Molly Fitzgerald through the heart, killing her instantly.

With a shriek Maeve arose to cradle her mother's lifeless body. "You Protestant devil," she screamed at him. "How could you? I shall tell our Da what you have done, William Devers! I hope he kills you himself!" Sobbing she held Molly's body against her chest.

His face expressionless, William raised his pistol once again and shot his half-sister through her head. Maeve's body jerked once, and then she fell over her mother's still form. Then his icy eyes turned to Aine who cowered in the corner near the fireplace. An unholy light lit William's face. Reaching out he pulled Aine up. "Now here's a pretty little wench, and every bit the whore her mother was, I'll wager. Let's take her upstairs, and have her entertain us. You'd like that, wouldn't you, wench?" Reaching out William ripped Aine's bodice open, and fondled her little breasts.

The girl looked at him with shocked blue eyes. "You're my brother," she said weakly. She was shaking all over.

William slapped Aine hard, and she cried out surprised. "You cannot claim kinship with me, wench. You're a common whore's brat, and, now, up the stairs with you! You'll ply your mother's trade this night before I kill you. What's one more dead Catholic bitch more or less. By morning Lisnaskea will be free of your kind." He dragged Aine from the parlor, turning to invite his companions along. "Come on, lads. She looks like a tasty morsel, and we'll all have at her."

Not all the men followed William. Most drifted from Molly Fitzgerald's house silently, not even daring to look at her body and that of young Maeve as they went. They had only wanted Lisnaskea to to be a wholly Protestant town. They hadn't wanted murder, and rape. Yet in the hour since Reverend Dundas had exorted them to follow William Devers, and cleanse Lisnaskea of the Catholics, they had seen death too many times to be able to cry their innocence any longer. They felt guilty, and their guilt made them only angrier at their Catholic neighbors. Then they heard a terrible scream-ing, peal after peal of pure terror crying out from the upper floor of Molly Fitzgerald's house. They heard unholy laugh-ter, and the shouts of encouragement from those who had re-mained behind to violate the young girl. Many had daughters Aine's age. The men hurried off into the darkness to escape the sound.

Then a young lad ran from out of the darkness shouting, "The dirty Papists have fired the church, and locked Reverend Dundas and his family inside. Our women can't get the doors open!"

"Go on," Robert Morgan told his companions. "I'll fetch Master William, and the others."

And then Molly Fitzgerald's house was silent again. The door, hanging from its hinges, swung open. From her hiding place old Biddy crept forth, tears streaming down her worn face. Her old legs shaking she climbed the stairs, and sought Aine. She found the young girl, stripped naked, and spread open on her mother's bed. Her throat had been cut from ear to ear. Her blue eyes were open, and filled with utter terror. Her sweet little face was already showing signs of bruising, and her milky thighs were smeared with blood, evidence of her violation. Biddy gently closed Aine's sightless eyes, and drew a coverlet over her although she was certainly past all modesty now.

The old servant wiped her eyes once more with her apron, and then a look of grim determination crossed her face. Looking down on young Aine, whom she had helped to birth, Biddy crossed herself and said a prayer. Then she descended the elegant small staircase of the house, reentering the parlor. She prayed again over the bodies of her mistress and Maeve. Then she departed the house through the rear entry and went to the stables. Biddy was deathly afraid of horses, but she bravely saddled Aine's fat pony, heaving her wiry frame into the saddle and riding off, away from the town, and into the darkness.

She knew the way for she had spent her entire life in this region. She was not of Lisnaskea, but a Maguire's Ford woman. Slowly, carefully, she guided the pony as it picked its way through the darkness on the rocky path toward safety. The night was only just beginning to give way to the day when she finally made her way into the village of Maguire's Ford, and across the small drawbridge of Erne Rock Castle. She practically fell into the arms of the young gatekeeper.

"Fetch the Maguire," she wheezed at him, shaking the lad off. "I can stand. *Get the Maguire!* There's murder about!"

Rory Maguire came from his gatehouse, half-dressed, but

struck by the gatekeeper's urgency. He recognized Biddy immediately.

She didn't wait for him to ask. "There's murder at Lisnaskea! My lord himself was with us last evening when it began. I don't know where he is now. William Devers shot my mistress, and young Maeve. They are dead. What he did to our wee Aine I am too ashamed to say. She is dead now too, for which I thank a merciful God."

"So it's finally come," Rory Maguire said, almost to himself. Then he took the old woman by the arm. "Come into the hall, Biddy. I must fetch the duke and his wife. You must tell them what happened."

"And what will they do, these Protestants, to avenge my poor mistress and her daughters?" Biddy demanded angrily. " 'Twas their kind who killed them, and God knows how many others in Lisnaskea!"

"Nay," he told her quietly as he led her into the castle. "Not all Protestants, like Catholics, are the same, Biddy. That is why I have been able to remain here all these years with our own folk. That is why Maguire's Ford is a place of peace. Lady Jasmine is a good woman who holds no prejudice against any faith. I will admit that in that she is rare, but it is she who possesses Maguire's Ford, and her will has ruled us peacefully for a long time. Remember, her own dear daughter, born here in this castle, is wed to Kieran Devers. She knew your mistress, and her children. She will be horrified by your tale."

They were in the hall now, and Rory sent a servant for the duchess and her husband. They came almost immediately, James Leslie helping his wife who was now very full with their child.

"What has happened?" Jasmine asked, sitting heavily.

"This is Biddy, Molly Fitzgerald's serving woman," Rory said. "I'll let her tell you her tale, my lady, but be warned. 'Tis a terrible one."

The Leslies listened with growing horror as the old lady

spoke of the terror, the violence, the murder, and the rape that had occurred the previous evening in Lisnaskea. "I am ashamed that I hid, that I could not aid my mistress and those two sweet lasses I helped to raise," Biddy wept as she came to the end of her tale, "but I knew that someone had to remain alive to tell the world of William Devers's perfidy."

"You did exactly the right thing," Jasmine said, rising to embrace Biddy. "Without you we would never have known, but I am concerned for Sir Shane. You say he left the house when he heard the uproar begin, and you saw him not again? What could have happened to him?"

"He has probably been murdered by the English bitch's offspring," Kieran Devers said coming into the hall, for the same servant who had gone to fetch the Leslies had gone to find their son-in-law as well.

"Surely not!" Jasmine cried.

"William was never particularly patient when he wanted something badly," Kieran said. "If he would kill poor Molly, and our half-sisters, why not our father? My stepmother has now gotten almost everything she ever wanted. What use has she for Da now? She has his home, and his lands. The girls are gone. She has managed to drive me off, and married her son to the girl she wanted for a daughter-in-law. I'm quite certain it is she behind this trouble in Lisnaskea, but I want to know what happened to my father before I kill William Devers."

"There will be nae further killing," James Leslie said sternly "I'll nae hae Fortune the wife of a convicted felon, and convicted and hanged ye'll be, Kieran, if you kill yer brother, no matter what he's done."

"He'll go free then, my lord," Kieran replied. "No court in Ulster will accept the word of a Catholic, let alone a Catholic serving woman, against the word of a Protestant gentleman."

"Be patient, laddie. There are ways, and in time ye'll hae

yer revenge, but for now we must find out if yer da is alive. We'll ride to Mallow Court this day, you and I."

"Nay, Jemmie," Jasmine cried. "I do not trust the Deversés now to allow you and Kieran to come and go in safety."

"I must go," James said firmly. "If I dinna, darling Jasmine, the same evil that infected the people of Lisnaskea could infect the people of Maguire's Ford. Do you want that to happen?"

Jasmine Leslie pressed her lips together in frustration. She knew her husband was right, and yet she had suddenly been overcome by a sense of foreboding. It wasn't that she thought Jemmie or Kieran would be killed, for she didn't; but she could sense the wickedness in the air about them, and for the first time since Rowan Lindley had been killed here, she was uncomfortable at Erne Rock. She looked to Rory Maguire. "Will they be safe?" she asked him.

"Aye, but he can't take a large party with him, m'lady. That would be considered a harassment in this tense situation. A few of your own clansmen, my lord, as you would normally travel."

The duke of Glenkirk nodded in agreement.

"You must go with him," Jasmine said.

"He canna," James Leslie replied. "He's the Maguire no matter the fact you legally possess this land, darling Jasmine. 'Twould be thought a provocation for the Maguire to ride into Lisnaskea after such a massacre. I want Rory here in the event there is any attempt to start difficulties here as there. This sort of trouble is like a canker that grows, and becomes more poisonous wi every passing hour."

"What has happened?" Fortune came into the hall, her hair flying. "Rois says the Protestants have murdered all the Catholics in Lisnaskea. That they're coming here to kill us all!"

"Jesu!" Maguire swore. "It's started already. I had best get the rest of my clothes on, and calm the village before all hell breaks loose." He turned to Jasmine. "With your permission, of course, my lady." He bowed to her.

"Go," Jasmine said, "and you two also," she told her husband and her son-in-law. "Fortune, come with me, and I will tell you everything. Biddy, I'll want you to remain here in the castle with us for your own safety's sake. Adali will see you are fed, and a warm place is found for you to sleep. You must be exhausted after your ride."

"Thank ye, my lady," Biddy replied. Then she turned to Maguire. "You were right, laddie. All Protestants aren't bad," she said.

Chapter
12

The duke of Glenkirk and his son-in-law rode into Mallow Court. Dismounting, they entered the house to be greeted by Lady Jane.

"How dare you enter this house after what your filthy Papist brethren did to my husband!" she screeched at her stepson.

The duke put a warning hand on Kieran, and said, "We have only just learned of the troubles in Lisnaskea last night, and came as quickly as we could to see if Sir Shane was all right, madame."

"He lies abed, barely alive," she snapped. "His whore tried to murder him, but William managed to save his father."

"Indeed," the duke remarked. "We should like to see Sir Shane, madame. You will understand that Kieran is deeply concerned for his father. We had heard a very different story of the happenings in Lisnaskea."

"My husband is too ill to be disturbed," Jane Devers said loftily. "Come back another time, my lord."

James Leslie looked about him. There was no one else in the hall, and he knew the Devers household had no men-at-arms. "Madame, as I have told you, 'tis another tale I have heard. We will see Sir Shane now, so that I may ascertain he is indeed alive. How dare you refuse my request! You will either take us to him, or I shall have my clansmen search the house until he is found," the duke told her half-angrily.

Jane Devers wanted nothing more than to send the two men before her packing, but the duke was a man of authority. She dared not, even if William had said his father was not to be disturbed. She had not seen her husband since their son had brought him home, and William held the key to Shane's bedchamber. "My son has locked his father in for his own safety," she told the duke. "I do not have the key to his room, my lord, and William is not here right now."

"Show me where Sir Shane is confined," the duke commanded her. "We will break the door down, madame. Such treatment of your husband is outrageous, and I am astounded that you would have allowed such a thing. You are mistress here, are you not?"

Flushed with irritation Jane Devers led the way to her husband's bedchamber. She was surprised that her stepson had been so silent in all of this. William had warned her that he would come tearing into Mallow Court with some wild tale, yet Kieran had said nothing. Still, his silence and his angry eyes made her more than aware of his fury. She stopped before her husband's rooms. "He is in there," she said.

Without a word Kieran Devers put his shoulder to the door, and after a minute or more, it sprang open. He and the duke hurried into the room. There they found Sir Shane Devers, bound hand and foot, a gag tied about his mouth, upon his bed. Swiftly they loosed the gag and his bonds, and helped him to sit up. There was a nasty bruise upon his temple, and a small crusting of blood at the back of his head.

"Da!" Kieran embraced his parent.

"He killed Molly!" Sir Shane said "He told me himself, the young devil. And my lasses too, God curse him!"

"We know," Kieran replied grimly. "Biddy hid herself, and afterward came to Erne Rock to tell us, Da."

"He tried to kill me too," Sir Shane declared, "and he might have done so had you not come to seek me out, my lord. I thank you."

"What are you saying?" Jane Devers quavered. "How can you accuse our boy of such a terrible act as patricide?"

"Your son, madame," Sir Shane said coldly, "coldly murdered the woman I love, along with our two daughters, his half-sisters. He attacked me, and then when he found I had not died so he might blame my death upon the hapless Catholics of Lisnaskea, he brought me home, trussed up like a Christmas goose, and told me quite plainly he intended killing me so he might have his inheritance sooner than later. He is a viper, *your son,* and I will drive him from my home as soon as I can."

"You have been injured, dearest," Jane Devers said, reaching out to touch the bruise on her husband's temple. "You have surely misunderstood our William. He would never harm you, Shane."

He pulled away from her hand. "Madame, I am not so injured that I could not understand *your son* when he boasted of how he had shot Molly Fitzgerald and our two daughters. Maeve was seventeen, and our wee Aine just fourteen, madame. They were to go with Kieran and his wife to England, and then the New World next year. We knew they had no future in Ulster. What harm did any of them ever do to William that he would murder them with such icy disdain? Innocent lasses, madame! I rue the day I ever wed you, and brought you into my house, Jane! I regret the son I fathered on your passionless body. He is a monster!"

"He is not!" she defended her son. "If he killed that woman he did it to protect my honor. That you would take a mistress was bad enough, but a Catholic mistress? And those two brats you fathered on her brought me nothing but shame, flaunting themselves about the village. I was pitied for your follies, and had it not been for the kindness of the Reverend Mr. Dundas, I should have been a laughingstock in Lisnaskea. Now poor James is dead along with his wife and children thanks to your bloody murdering Papists!"

"It was Dundas who encouraged the mayhem last night, and at your bidding using your son as a cat's paw, I have not a doubt," Kieran Devers said. "Willy is not that clever, madame, but he is certainly vicious enough given the proper encouragement. I imagine both you and his wife fostered his baser nature. What in the name of God did you hope to gain by your mischief?"

"I will have no Catholics in the vicinity tainting my children," William Devers said, suddenly entering the room. "My wife is with child, and it was past time these Papists were driven from our lands." His cold blue gaze swept them all. "Ah, Da, I see you are up now."

"You're no son of mine," Shane Devers replied angrily. "I want you gone from this house today!"

"What?" William mocked. "You would send me from my birthplace? And what of my little wife, ripening with your first grandchild, Da?"

"Take her with you, and this bitch who bore you as well," Shane Devers said furiously, his color now high with his choler. "I'll not have the man who shot my Molly and our girls in this house even one more night!" Shane Devers then hit his son a mighty blow that staggered him, and sent him to the floor.

Surprised, William struggled to his feet, aided by his mother. "I only shot your whore and her eldest brat," he said cruelly. "The other one, the littlest, I had on her back. How she struggled and screamed when I savaged her maidenhead. I meant to give her to my men to enjoy as well, but then came the word the church was afire with poor old Dundas in it. I cut her throat. I wonder if she was as lusty a fuck as her mother, your whore?" He smiled at his father.

Shane Devers stared hard at his younger son. *"You raped your half-sister?"* he said, horrified. "Aine was but a child."

"She had nice little tits," William replied. "Besides, I count her no kin of mine, Da. Surely your whore could not be certain which of her lovers fathered her children." He smiled again.

Shane Devers heard the mighty thundering of his heart in his ears. His temples throbbed fiercely. The world was red before his eyes, and then he felt a violent sharp pain slam inside of his head. With a cry he fell to the floor. He knew he was dying. His eyes desperately sought his eldest son. His breath was coming in shallow, short pants. He struggled to speak a final time. *"Forgive me, Kieran,"* he rasped, and then he died with his last heroic effort.

There was a long silence, and then William Devers said, "Well, that is that, is it not? Get out of my house, Kieran, and do not come back ever again. Be warned. I have taken care of the Catholics in Lisnaskea. I shall come to Maguire's Ford next."

James Leslie caught the young man by his shirt front. "Ye be warned, William Devers, put one foot, ye or yer minions, on land belonging to my wife, and ye'll be driven off wi nae mercy. I canna prevent ye from causing trouble here, but ye'll cause nae difficulties in Maguire's Ford. Trust me, laddie, ye dinna want Jemmie Leslie for yer enemy. I hae only just hae word from my cousin, King Charles, that he hae approved the transfer of the properties belonging to my wife to my two sons, Adam and Duncan Leslie. Yer a fool if ye think ye can rob my lads of their lands. I'd happily use that as an excuse to kill ye for what ye did to Mistress Fitzgerald, her lasses, and yer own da. Yer responsible for the death of Shane Devers, *Sir William.* Try to place the blame on anyone else, and I'll see the world knows the truth. For yer brother's sake, for the sake of the Deverses' good name, I'll say nought for now. I will nae hold yer family responsible for the actions of one villain, for the Deverses hae always been an honorable family. Do ye understand me, *Sir William?"* He loosed his grip on his antagonist's shirtfront, pushing him away with a sound of disgust.

William Devers's cold eyes surveyed the duke, half-afraid. His glance flicked swiftly to his elder half-brother, but Kieran's face was grief-stricken with their father's death. He knelt by the body, tears streaming down his handsome face, his hand tenderly protective on his father's head. Let him mourn the old man, William thought. He's gone, and good riddance. *I am now master of Mallow Court.* The knowledge sent a frisson of pleasure down his spine, but then Kieran looked up at him. His gaze was filled with both anger and pity.

"Don't look at me like that!" William almost screamed.

"God help you, Willy," his elder sibling said wearily. "God help you. I'd not have this sin on my conscience for all the world."

"Get out!" Sir William Devers shouted at his half-brother. *"Get out, you filthy papist bastard!"*

Kieran Devers arose from their father's body and struck his brother a blow upon his elegant chin, knocking him to the floor. His stepmother screeched, and ran to her son.

"I'll have the law on you, Kieran Devers," she threatened.

"Oh, pray do, madame, and I shall tell them the truth of what happened last night in Lisnaskea. There are enough of your Protestants feeling burdened by their guilt who would gladly unload the onus of the horrors committed there on *your* son. Willy was never particularly popular for his arrogance would always overcome him when dealing with those good souls he considered his menials. The authorities may not believe the Catholics, although I suspect they would believe me, but they will certainly believe their own Protestant fellows. Remember, your precious son raped his fourteen-year-old half-sister before his companions, and then murdered her. 'Tis not a pretty picture, madame, especially as Aine Fitzgerald was known to be a decent lass. Many in the mob have daughters her age. Now, madame, I am going into your village to take the bodies of my half-sisters, and their mother, for burial. Should you, or that mongrel you bore my father attempt to stop me, I shall kill you. Is that quite understood, madame? Willy?" Kieran kicked his younger brother with his booted foot. "Do you understand me, laddie?"

Sir William Devers groaned weakly.

"Good!" Kieran said. Then he bowed to his stepmother. "Madame. I shall be at my father's funeral. If you try to prevent it, you will live to regret it." He turned and left the room, the sound of his footsteps echoing as he descended the staircase.

A sardonic smile touched James Leslie's lips. This was a side of his son-in-law he had hitherto not seen. Kieran Devers was tougher than he had thought which boded to the good, for it would not be an easy life in the New World. Reaching out he aided William Devers to rise. Then he, too, bowed first to the mother, and then the son. "Good day, madame, Sir William," he said, and departed them. He found his son-in-law outside awaiting him. "Do you think they will tell you when the funeral is to be, laddie?" he asked.

"They'll try to keep it from me, but I have allies in the house who will keep me informed," Kieran said stonily.

"I'll ride wi ye into Lisnaskea to fetch the bodies of yer sisters and Mistress Fitzgerald," the duke said.

"I'm grateful for the company, and the help," came the reply.

They came into the village, and were shocked by the ruin they saw. Houses burned to the ground, half-burned, the church totally destroyed. The smell of death was everywhere, and yet the people were already rallying to rebuild. The Catholic families who remained alive had been gathered together in a cattle pen. James Leslie was appalled, and insisted they be set free at once.

"What the hell did ye intend doing wi them?" he demanded angrily.

"Sir William says they're to be killed, my lord," Robert Morgan, the village blacksmith, said.

The duke looked into the pen which contained mostly women, children, and old men. "Open the damned gate, let them gather what belongings they own that may have escaped the carnage, and allow them to leave Lisnaskea unharmed. Are ye such fools that ye truly believe God has smiled on yer murder and violence?"

"But my lord, they are papists. God doesn't care about the papists," the smithy reasoned.

"And who was after telling ye that?" the duke said scornfully. "For God's sake, man, we worship the same God, albeit in different ways."

"Their God is an idol, my lord, and not our true God," came the reply. "Surely you understand that?"

James Leslie closed his eyes briefly. It did no good arguing with fools, he thought wearily. Would this kind of thing ever stop? His eyes snapped back open, cold and determined. "Free those poor souls at once!" he thundered. "I have far more authority than yer damned Sir Willy, and I'll fire what's left of this place if ye do not obey me at once!" Behind him his dozen clansmen glared with equal determination at the smithy, and the small group of men who had gathered about him.

The smithy considered defiance against this Scot, but then to his horror the duke spoke again, and his words were chilling.

"Would ye like to hae yer daughters suffer the same terrible fate as poor wee Aine Fitzgerald, man?"

"Open the pen and let them out," Robert Morgan said. "Let them take what is theirs, and leave Lisnaskea."

"And nae harassment," James Leslie cautioned the villagers. "These are women, and bairns, and the old ones. Ye lived in peace wi them for years until ye were infected by others wi prejudice. Ye shared happy times, and mourned together over yer dead. Ye birthed children, and danced at each other's weddings. Remember those times, and nae what happened last night." Then he turned to his own men, and ordered six of them to remain to oversee the freeing of the Catholic survivors while he, Kieran, and the others went to fetch the bodies of the Fitzgeralds.

They reached the lovely brick house and saw that its front door still hung open. Entering they were surprised to be greeted by Father Cullen Butler. The priest in Lisnaskea, he explained, had been murdered last night along with the Protestant cleric. It had been the death of Father Brendan that had enraged the Catholics to commit their own murders. Until that moment they had been too busy defending themselves but when their priest had been killed, they had erupted with fury.

"Someone had to come and pray over these poor women," Cullen Butler said quietly. "You won't be able to bury them here. The burial ground has been destroyed. And you cannot bury them at Maguire's Ford for their graves would be a terrible reminder of the hate between the Protestants and the Catholics. They will have to lie in some quiet place, unmarked, but safe," the priest said. "I will consecrate the ground myself, and say what needs to be said. Best your men do it, James Leslie, for then no one will ever know where Molly Fitzgerald and her daughters have been laid to rest. When Kieran is gone there will be none left to mourn them."

Kieran Devers looked at the two bodies in the parlor. The priest had untangled the two from their deathly embrace, and laid them out upon the floor. Molly's blue bodice was darkly stained with her blood. Maeve's wound, being in the back of her head, was not visible to her half-brother. "Where is Aine?" he asked the priest.

"Where William Devers left her," came the reply. "Biddy covered her before she left."

Without another word Kieran Devers climbed the staircase of the house, and entered the chamber where Aine Fitzgerald lay dead. Below they could hear of a sudden, the sobs of grief that wracked him. All knew that next to

Colleen, Aine had been Kieran's favorite sister. Then they heard his footsteps descending the staircase, and he reentered the room, the young girl wrapped in the coverlet Biddy had thrown over her, cradled in his strong arms. "Willy must pay a price for this," Kieran Devers said quietly.

"God will judge him, and God alone," Cullen Butler said. "You have a wife now, laddie, and a bright future. Do not allow yourself to be trapped here in the past that is Ireland, Kieran Devers. Do not endanger your immortal soul for the sake of a moment's vengeance."

"You can ask me that even while looking upon the body of this innocent lass?" Kieran said brokenly. "He violated her. *His own half-sister.* She was barely out of her childhood, and as pure as a spring day. And then he murdered her. How can I forgive him any of it?"

"You must for the sake of your own soul," the priest counseled. "Aine, Maeve, and Mistress Fitzgerald are safe now in God's kingdom, for surely the manner of their deaths spared them the trial of Purgatory. Your half-brother has blackened his soul, and will answer for it, I promise you, Kieran Devers. Do not darken your own soul by preempting God's authority over us all. Vengeance is mine, saith the Lord."

"Let us bury them," Kieran said, still holding Aine.

"Commandeer a cart," the duke said to one of his men, and when the cart was drawn up outside the house the bodies were carefully laid out in it for transport to their burial site.

"Give me but a moment," Kieran said, going back into the house.

When he had emerged again they went on their way, moving back through Lisnaskea so the duke might ascertain the surviving Catholics had been freed, and were safely gone. They were, and the duke's men joined the funeral train. The Protestants of Lisnaskea lined the village's only street watching them go. Some were stony-faced, and grim, but a few wept. One fresh-faced young lad ran to the cart to look in, and seeing the women he said but one word, *"Aine."* Then he dashed away.

James Leslie stopped the procession, and looking sternly on the people there said with a sweep of his hand, "This is what your hate, and your intolerance hae brought you. I hope you can live wi it." Then he signaled his men and the cart to move on again. Behind them Molly Fitzgerald's brick house was completely engulfed in flames, for Kieran had set it afire, determined that those who had killed her would not have her house or her possessions.

They traveled until they were halfway to Maguire's Ford, and there, in an ash and oak wood, they dug one large grave, laying the mother and her two daughters side by side. The grave was filled in carefully, and then camouflaged carefully with a blanket of moss and dead leaves. The priest had consecrated the ground before the trio were laid to rest, and then he had spoken low, in his soft Latin, the words of the burial service. Kieran prayed with him, his handsome face grim. James Leslie wondered how much to heart his son-in-law had taken the priest's words on the matter of revenge. He would keep a hard eye on Kieran for he would not have his daughter widowed and unhappy. Ulster, he decided, was an impossible place. One murder led to another, and another. There seemed to be no room for compromise.

It was just past sunset when the duke and his party returned to Erne Rock Castle. Biddy dozed by the fire where Jasmine sat with her daughter.

Fortune jumped to her feet as they entered the hall. "Sir Shane? Is he all right? God's boots, Kieran, you are pale." She hurried to her husband, and put her arms about him.

"We have buried Molly and her girls," he said.

"Your father?"

"Dead. Willy killed him," Kieran responded.

Jasmine gasped, shocked.

"He's a devil, that one," Biddy muttered, suddenly awake. "He'll roast in hell for his wickedness, and sooner than later, I'm thinking."

"We found Sir Shane a prisoner in his own home," the duke said to his wife and daughter. "We freed him, but then William came. His father told him he must leave Mallow Court, taking his wife and mother wi him. He was furious for William hae bragged to him about how he hae killed Mistress Fitzgerald and her lasses. William then told his father how young Aine had died, sparing him no vile detail. Sir Shane grew apoplectic, and fell to the floor. He died almost immediately thereafter," James Leslie told them.

Fortune burst into tears, and clung to her husband.

Jasmine's eyes were moist. Her hands went to her belly, and she said, "How terrible. Thank God Fortune did not marry that man. He is obviously mad."

Night had fallen outside the Great Hall's windows. Rory Maguire joined them, and he was obviously concerned. "There are hotheads among some of the Protestants here," he said. "The good Reverend and I have had all we could do to keep the peace this day. I think some of the younger men from Lisnaskea have infiltrated Maguire's Ford with their poison, and are trying to stir up our people against one another."

"Surely the Protestants cannot be so foolish as their brethren in Lisnaskea," Jasmine said. "We allowed them a refuge in this village when they were homeless, and the English were insisting they return to Holland after their ship, the *Speedwell,* sprang a leak in the Irish Sea. They are far more comfortable here than they would have been in the Plymouth Colony. We *must* keep the peace in Maguire's Ford! I will not allow intolerance to destroy my sons' inheritance!"

Rory looked at her, and at the daughter he could not acknowledge. This same prejudice that had caused the massacre and misery in Lisnaskea was responsible for sending Fortune and Kieran from Ulster. His old age would be as lonely as much of his life had been. He would never have the pleasure of watching his grandchildren grow up, even if they did not know who he really was to them. "The Catholics are just as bad, but I swear to you that *I will keep the peace here, my lady Jasmine,"* he promised her fiercely.

"We will keep it together, Rory," she told him. "We won't allow anyone to destroy what we've done, what you've done all these years. Cullen, you'll speak to your people again?"

"Aye, Cousin, I will," the priest said.

For the next few days an almost eerie calm surrounded them. The duchess of Glenkirk had proclaimed her will personally in each church at Maguire's Ford. "If you cannot live in peace with your neighbors as you always have," she told the people, "then you must leave here. I will not have happen here what happened in Lisnaskea. Good people, both Protestant and Catholic died, and for what? We all worship the same God, my friends. Do you truly believe our God condones violence and murder of those who are different than we are? Does not the Bible preach love, and peace? Is not the fifth commandment, *Thou shalt not kill?* That commandment does not say thou shalt not kill except for. . . ."

Sir Shane was buried without incident, Colleen Kelly and her husband standing like a buffer between Lady Jane, William, and Emily Anne, and Kieran, Fortune, and the Leslies. She had told her half-brother quite frankly that she would never forgive him for what he had done to their father, or to the Fitzgeralds. "You were always more one of them," Sir William sneered at her. "You are no longer welcome at Mallow Court, or your family either."

"You are beyond hope, William," she replied quietly.

The peace in Maguire's Ford held despite the rumors that were passed about daily, and despite the infiltrators from both faiths who sought to stir up trouble. Several survivors from Lisnaskea with family at Maguire's Ford had come to beg refuge of their kin and were taken in, which frightened some of the Protestants who were worried they might seek revenge upon any non-Catholic.

Kieran Devers spoke to Father Cullen, for he had the

germ of an idea that he thought might solve part of the problem. "The duke tells me," he said, "that I will have an easier time of being accepted in Lord Calvert's expedition if I have my own vessel, and colonists who can help in building the colony when they settle upon a place. Since this is to be a colony for Catholics first and foremost, why should I not bring a shipload of good Irishmen and women with me?"

Fortune heard her husband's suggestion, and was in full agreement with him. "I have two ships of my own that ply the trade route," she told him. "There's a wonderful old, but quite sturdy vessel called the *Cardiff Rose* that brought Mama from India long ago. It should soon be returning from the East Indies run. Then I have a newer ship, the *Highlander,* in the Mediterranean. It will be returning to England come spring." She turned to her stepfather. "Could we not outfit both of these vessels, Papa, and sail them to the New World?"

"I should purchase my own ship," Kieran protested.

"Don't be foolish," his wife chided him. "We'll need the monies you have to outfit our ships. If it would make you feel better you may pay me a fee for leasing my ships."

"It's quite practical," the duke told his son-in-law, "and I know both the *Cardiff Rose* and the *Highlander* are well-maintained both above and below the water line. You cannot be certain of that if you buy a strange vessel, unless, of course, you have the ship dry docked for inspection before you purchase it, and it is doubtful its owner would allow you to do so because of the expense involved."

"And the *Cardiff Rose* has the most wonderful master cabin for us to travel in," she murmured at him, her eyes bright with her love.

James Leslie chuckled at his stepdaughter. How like her mother she was although she could not know it, he thought. "I am sorry to spoil your romantic dream, poppet," he said, "but it is unlikely many women will be allowed to go with Lord Calvert's expedition until it is decided where he will settle the colony, and housing is built."

"That's ridiculous!" Fortune said.

"Nonetheless that is the way it will probably be," the duke told her. "You have no choice, I fear."

"Then we shall not go," Fortune replied firmly.

"And where will you live then?" he asked her.

"We shall buy a house near Cadby, or Queen's Malvern," she said with what she thought was perfect logic, "or perhaps near Oxton so I may be near my sister, India."

"With your Irish Catholic husband?" the duke posed.

Fortune's face fell. "Oh dear," she said, suddenly realizing how foolish she must have sounded. "The Puritans in England are every bit as bad as the Protestants in Ulster where the Catholics are concerned, aren't they?" she reasoned aloud, not needing an answer to her own question. "We could go to France, or Spain," she suggested.

"Where you, my darling wife, would be every bit as discriminated against as I am in Protestant lands," he told her. "There is no help for it, Fortune. If we are to live together in peace we must go to the New World; and if Lord Calvert will have me, I may have to go alone until the colony is safe for women."

Before Fortune might protest further Adali came into the hall. "Father Cullen just sent word there is a large party of horsemen coming down upon the village from the direction of Lisnaskea, my lord. I thought, perhaps, that you would want to know. Your preparations are all in effect."

"What preparations?" Jasmine asked her husband.

"For the defense of both the village and the castle," her husband told her. "We canna allow that rabble from Lisnaskea to destroy Maguire's Ford as they did their own nest." He arose from his seat. "I must go and join the others."

"What others?" Jasmine demanded, struggling to her own swollen feet. "I am coming with you, Jemmie. These lands are, after all, still mine, and I think it important that I am seen."

He wanted to argue with her, but he knew she was correct in her reasoning. Besides, he considered with a small chuckle, he would not dissuade her no matter what he said. "Come then, madame," he said.

"We're coming too," Fortune told them.

The duke of Glenkirk burst out laughing, but led the way without another word. They assembled in the square of Maguire's Ford with its tall stone Celtic cross at its center. The Reverend Mr. Steen, Father Cullen, and the town's leaders, both Protestant and Catholic, were awaiting them. About them the houses were shuttered and barred. Not even a dog or a cat wandered the street this day. Above them the skies were gray with the clouds of an impending autumnal storm, but on the western horizon a slash of blazing red and gold shone with the setting sun from beneath the clouds. Not a breeze stirred. Not a bird called. There was silence but for the faint hum of the mob which grew louder as it approached them.

Down the road into Maguire's Ford they came, led by William Devers upon a fine bay gelding. They carried torches, and the faces of the men behind Sir William were stone hard and without pity. Seeing the welcoming party ahead of them they stopped, and their master moved his mount slowly forward until he stood in front of the duke and his wife. He glared down at them.

"If you come in peace, Sir William," Jasmine said, "you are welcome here. If you do not come in peace, I would request you depart."

He pointedly ignored her, directing his speech to James Leslie instead. "Is it your custom, my lord, to allow a woman to speak for you?" he asked the duke insultingly.

James Leslie laughed mockingly at the young man. "Maguire's Ford and its castle belong to my wife, Sir William. I cannot speak for her any more than she would speak for me in matters pertaining to my possessions. Now, sir, my wife has asked you a question. Have the courtesy to answer it lest you betray your mother's base heritage."

William Devers flushed. He was being made a fool of before his own men, and he did not like it. He heard a faint snickering behind him, but did not turn about for he had too much pride. "We have come for your Catholics," he said. "Give them to us that we may cleanse Maguire's Ford of their foul popery, and we will go in peace."

"Get off of my lands, and take your rabble with you," the duchess of Glenkirk said in an even, cold voice. "Am I Pilate that I would betray innocent people into the hands of your intolerant mob?" She stepped forward so that his horse was forced to move back a pace. "How dare you come here and attempt to cause trouble? The Protestants and the Catholics have lived in peace at Maguire's Ford for years. The Catholics here took in the Protestants ten years ago when they had nowhere else to go. They built a church for them, and all have lived in equanimity ever since. How presumptuous you are, William Devers, to think that you have God's permission to come here and cause murder and chaos on this All Hallows' Eve. You are more the devil's disciple than you are God's, I believe. Go now before I set the wolfhounds on you, and your men!"

"Madame, I will have what I came for," he replied stubbornly. "Search the houses, and bring out the Catholics," he commanded.

Suddenly a flaming arrow arced into the darkening skies above the town, and the bells in both the churches began to peal furiously. The doors of the holy houses at either end of the village opened, and the population of Maguire's Ford streamed forth from their separate ends of the town, surrounding the Lisnaskea men. All were armed with something, from ancient blunderbusses to scythes to frying pans and iron pots.

"Our people will not allow you to turn them against one another," Jasmine told Sir William. "We all worship the same God."

"Hear me!" her opponent cried out from his vantage point upon the back of his mount. "How can you live in the same place as these dirty papists, men of Maguire's Ford?

We have cleansed Lisnaskea of their kind, and now with your help we will do the same here! Join us!"

The Reverend Steen spoke for his people. "We will not join you, William Devers. *Go home!*"

"Have you joined the legions of the damned, Samuel Steen?" Sir William asked him.

The Protestant minister laughed aloud. "Do not presume to judge me or mine, William Devers. You have broken more than one of God's commandments. Thou shalt not kill! Thou shalt not covet thy neighbor's wife, or lands! Honor thy father, and thy mother! You are no fit leader. You are a bully, and a bigot. Get you gone from here!"

William Devers suddenly kicked his horse, and the beast leapt forward, startled, knocking both Jasmine and the Reverend Mr. Steen to the road. A cry of outrage arose from the Maguire's Ford people, but then to everyone's surprise a single shot rang out. With an absolutely astounded look in his eye, Sir William tumbled forward from his horse and onto the ground.

"They've shot Sir William," the cry arose among the Lisnaskea men. "We must be avenged!"

"Nay, the Maguire's Ford men did not shoot him. I did," a voice from among the Lisnaskea mob said, and surprised, they parted to allow a young lad forward.

" 'Tis Bruce Morgan, the smith's son," came a faceless cry.

The Reverend Samuel Steen pulled himself to his feet while the duke helped his wife up. "Why, lad?" the Protestant cleric asked the youngster. "Why have you killed Sir William, Bruce Morgan?" Gently he took the ancient pistol from the lad, amazed it had fired at all let alone with such deadly accuracy.

"For Aine," came the devastating reply. "For Aine, and because of what he did to her. I heard it, but I could not believe it, and so I crept into the house while they were all trying to rescue those in the church. *I saw what he did to my lass.* We were to be wed one day, you see. I loved her."

"Do you think I'd let you marry some damned Catholic wench, a whore's fatherless offspring?" his father, the smithy, Robert Morgan said, pushing forward angrily. "And now look what you've done, you stupid boy! You've killed our leader. You're no son of mine any longer!"

"Sir William was an evil man, Da," Bruce Morgan replied, drawing himself up to his full height now, and they suddenly saw the boy was almost a man. "And do you think I would have let you stop me from marrying Aine? I never cared about her religion, Da. I cared about her!"

"Faugh!" his father snorted. "I'll hang you myself to take the shame of what's been done here off my name."

There was a faintly audible groan at their feet, and Reverend Steen cried out, "Sir William is not dead! He is injured, but alive."

Kieran Devers quietly reached out to touch young Morgan's shoulder while the others were distracted. "Go to the castle, laddie," he said. "I'll not see you hanged. Hurry before they remember you again. *Sir William* will not be generous in this matter. Go now!" He watched with a faint smile upon his lips as the lad did his bidding.

"Fetch something to use as a stretcher," the duchess of Glenkirk, finally on her feet again, said. "I'll not have this man in my home, but perhaps Reverend Steen you will see the physician is fetched, and you will shelter Sir William until he is fit to travel again." She looked into the mob before her, forcing herself to stand as tall as she might, but the pains wracking her were difficult to ignore. Still, Jasmine reasoned, just a moment more. "Men of Lisnaskea, are there any of you here who saw Bruce Morgan fire the shot that has injured Sir William? If not, for his father's sake keep silent, I beg of you. You will not see the lad again, and by the time Sir William and his family stop to consider who fired the shot, Bruce Morgan will be long gone from Ulster. He is but a boy, and he loved a young girl who was foully abused and then murdered by Sir William. You know in your hearts what he did to Aine Fitzgerald was an evil iniquity, and a sin as well. Do not compound his sin or the lad's with one of your own. Now go back to Lisnaskea. I will not permit you to wreak havoc in Maguire's Ford." She stood glaring at them until the men had the good grace to turn slowly about, and start making their way home, their torches lighting the darkened road before them as they went. Jasmine Leslie gasped loudly, and fell to her knees. "Yer bairn will be early, Jemmie," she said through gritted teeth.

"Mama!" Fortune ran to her mother's side.

James Leslie didn't bother to wait for help. Pushing his stepdaughter aside, he lifted his wife up in his arms and carried her through the village, across the drawbridge, and into the castle.

Seeing him enter the hall old Biddy called out, "Have you a birthing table, my lord?"

Rohana came running. "I will take care of my lady," she said. "I have been doing it since she was born."

"Let Biddy care for the bairn after it is born," Jasmine said so the old woman would not be offended by Rohana. "And she can help you now too, for she has had the experience." Then she groaned. "This child will wait for no one now it has decided to be born! It will not be like you, my Fortune, taking forever, and then having to be turned about so you could come properly. Ahhh! I can feel the child's head! *It is coming now!"*

James Leslie knew just what to do. He deposited his wife on the high board, and braced her shoulders so the other women might aid her. There was absolutely no time for niceties. Jasmine groaned with her labor. She had never had so quick a birthing, but she could quite distinctly feel the child's head pushing down. "Rohana?"

Her serving woman pushed Jasmine's skirts up, and peered between her mistress's legs. "You're correct, my lady, the head is coming. Push with the next pain. Ohh! 'Tis almost here. Gracious, I have never seen a baby born this quickly, my princess. Ohh!" Rohana caught the infant as it slid easily from its mother's body. The child began to howl almost immediately, waving its small arms protestingly at having been pushed so rudely from its dark and warm safe haven.

"What is it?" Jasmine demanded.

" 'Tis a lass!" James Leslie crowed, delighted. " 'Tis a fine, hot-tempered wee lassie!"

"Well, Jemmie, you wanted another daughter to spoil, and damn me if you haven't gone and gotten your way," his wife said with a chuckle.

Fortune had stood staring at her mother's very brief travail, and had actually seen her new half-sister born. She was fascinated, and asked her mother, "Do they all come so quickly, Mama?"

Jasmine laughed weakly. "Nay, poppet, they do not all come so swiftly. 'Twas my fall earlier, I believe, that brought my early labor on, although from the sound of her this child is strong."

"A fine lass," Biddy said, handing the cleaned and swaddled baby into her mother's arms. "A *Samhein* lassie!"

"What are we to call her?" James Leslie asked his wife.

Jasmine considered a long moment, and then she said, "Autumn, because she was born to me in the autumn of my life, in the autumn of the year." Then she saw the bowl of late roses on the sideboard. "Autumn Rose Leslie," Jasmine decided. "Our daughter's name will be Autumn Rose."

Part Three

ENGLAND AND MARY'S LAND
1632–1635

"Love God, and do what you please."
—St. Augustine

Chapter
13

Sir William Devers survived his wound, but he would never walk again. As soon as it was feasible he was moved from the Reverend Samuel Steen's house in Maguire's Ford back to Lisnaskea. He was only in his mid-twenties, and as he lay in his bed, or sat in the chair that had been fashioned for him, he grew angrier and angrier. He wanted to hold the Catholics responsible for his infirmity, but they had not shot at him. He had been shot from behind, and the Catholics of Maguire's Ford had been facing him. Still, Sir William Devers reasoned, if they had not been at Maguire's Ford then neither would he have been there, and he would not be the invalid he was now. Who had shot him he did not know, nor did anyone else seem to know.

And so he did hold the Catholics answerable for his helpless state, and encouraged by his wife and mother, plotted a revenge he would never be able to carry out against the Catholics in general, against his half-brother, Kieran, and against Fortune, for he reasoned, had she never come to

Ulster, none of this would have ever happened. It was all *their* fault.

No one came to visit Sir William and his family. The servants gave notice but for a few. He was condemned, it seemed, to spend the rest of his days at Mallow Court with only his mother and his wife for civilized company. Sir William Devers took to drinking anything that would free him from his pain and his boredom.

At Maguire's Ford Autumn Leslie, born on All Hallows' Eve, the *Samhein* celebration of the ancient Celtic races, thrived. Jasmine knew instinctively that this was absolutely her last baby, and so she nursed her daughter devotedly, declining a wetnurse. Fortune adored the baby, and spent much of her time with Autumn and their mother.

"She is so sweet," Fortune sighed. "I should so like a little girl like her . . . one day. I know this is not the right time, Mama."

"If Kieran goes alone to the New World," Jasmine suggested, "perhaps you should be with child then. That way I could be with you when the child was born. Then when it is safe for you to join your husband, the baby will be old enough to travel with you, but wait until we return to England before you make that decision."

Fortune sighed again. She wanted a normal life like her mother and her sister, India, had. A home, a husband, babies, and peace. Why could she not have these things? But she knew the answer to her own unspoken questions. She had married a man whose faith was not acceptable. They would have to make a new life in a place where his faith and hers were acceptable. But when? Why must it all take so long? She cuddled her baby sister closely, marveling that everything about Autumn was so perfect. Her dark hair with its faint auburn tints, her eyes which were beginning to hold distinct glints of green even at two months of age when she was baptized by the Reverend Samuel Steen, her half-sister, and brother, Adam, standing as her godparents.

Christmas and Twelfth Night had come and gone. The

winter had set in hard. Maguire's Ford was quiet, and there was no longer any threat of violence from Lisnaskea, the excesses of the previous October having drained all choler from them. To Kieran's delight there were several families who had decided that they would like to go with him and Fortune to the New World, including young Bruce Morgan. They saw the opportunities available to them there despite the dangers involved. The older folk, of course, could not find it in their hearts to leave Ulster. They had always survived somehow, and would continue to do so, they reasoned.

January gave way to February, and then February gave way to March. The green hillsides were dotted with the white coats of the lambs born the month before. The duke began to make plans to leave Maguire's Ford for Scotland. They would depart the estate the fifteenth day of May, the day after Adam Leslie's fifteenth birthday. The two Leslie sons had settled quite well into Maguire's Ford. The Reverend Steen had been engaged as their tutor. The king's patent was expected before they departed, and Jasmine had already had the estate boundaries redrawn, dividing the land equally between the two boys. When Duncan turned sixteen in another four years, a house would be built for him on a site he had already chosen.

March departed, and halfway through April the royal warrant arrived, transferring Maguire's Ford from Lady Jasmine Leslie, the duchess of Glenkirk, to her sons, Adam and Duncan Leslie. Each boy was gifted with a peerage from the king since their father was a duke. Adam became Baron Leslie of Erne Rock. Duncan became Baron Leslie of Dinsmore, which meant *from the hillfort,* the site of his future dwelling. A copy of the document was posted publicly in the village square, and Kieran took the second copy to Mallow Court to show his half-brother and his stepmother.

Jane Devers, looking worn, greeted him sourly. "You were told not to come here again," she snapped at him as he entered the house.

"It will be my last visit, madame, I promise you. Where is

William? Take me to him, and fetch your daughter-in-law too."

Jane Leslie brought her stepson to the rear parlor of the house where he found William Devers seated in a padded chair.

"Kieran!" William's voice was almost welcoming.

"I am sorry to intrude unannounced upon you, Willy," Kieran said, "but I feared you wouldn't see me if I sent ahead. I have brought you a copy of the royal patent for Maguire's Ford." He handed the document to the younger man. "You will note it transfers ownership of the estate, which is to be divided equally between Adam and Duncan Leslie, now Sir Adam and Sir Duncan. There can no longer be any doubt as to the disposition of Erne Rock and its lands. They are in the hands of two Protestant milords whose tutor is Reverend Steen."

"But Maguire is still there," William said, "isn't he?" His tone was now sour.

"Aye, and he will be until he dies," Kieran said. "He causes no trouble, and he's a genius with the horses, Willy. He is needed."

"He's a Catholic," came the stubborn reply.

"His masters aren't. Do not trifle with Glenkirk's boys, Willy. Scotland is not that far away, and James Leslie will kill you."

"I'd be better off dead," William Devers replied bitterly. "I cannot feel anything below my waist, Kieran. The physician says the child Emily Anne will shortly have is the only child we will ever have. What if it is not a son? I sit here all day long with only Mama and my wife for company. Their cheerfulness and their nobility sicken me. The physician informs me, other than the fact I am dead in my legs and my manhood, I am as healthy as a horse and shall live a long life. Are you pleased to hear that, brother? I shall probably outlive you."

"I am sorry, Willy, but the truth is you have no one to blame for your situation but yourself. Oh, the Lisnaskea

Protestants gladly followed you once you, your mother, and the late Dundas had fired them up, but afterward they deserted you. Seeing you reminds them of what they did to their neighbors and friends just because they followed Catholicism. And each time they see you, they are reminded of what *you* did to our half-sister, Aine Fitzgerald. I am truly sorry for you, Willy. Yet I cannot help but think you got exactly what you deserved."

"You weep for a whore's brat, but not for your own brother!" he snarled. "I'm glad our father died else he might have given you back your inheritance, you bastard!"

"I wouldn't have had it, Willy. Ulster is a place of sorrow for me. I do not belong here. You may have Mallow Court for yourself, and your heirs, and good luck to you, little brother."

"What is it you want?" Jane Devers and her daughter-in-law entered the room. The voice was Emily Anne's. She was very full with her child, and Kieran wondered if it was a son or a daughter, and if he would ever learn that fact. The child looked ready to be born.

"Good day, madame," Kieran said pleasantly, and he bowed to her. "I have brought a copy of the royal patent with its seal for Maguire's Ford so you may see the legal and official transfer of the estate from my mother-in-law to her two younger Leslie sons is complete." He took the document from William's hands, and passed it to Emily Anne and Lady Jane. "When you have properly perused it, I shall take it back. I have also come to bid you farewell. My wife, the Leslies, and I will be departing for Scotland in mid-May. It is unlikely that I shall ever return to Ulster."

The two women read the warrant carefully, finally returning it to Kieran.

"She was not lying, Lady Jasmine, when she said she was giving Maguire's Ford to her sons," Jane Devers said, sounding surprised.

"No," he replied, "she was not lying." Then, there being nothing else left for him to say to any of them, he kissed the women's hands, shook his brother's reluctant hand, and departed his childhood home for the last time. At the crest of the hill he turned to look at it a final time. He would not see it ever again.

At the end of April word was brought to Kieran that his sister-in-law had prematurely delivered a female child who would be christened Emily Jane. The child was healthy, and the mother had survived her ordeal with courage. Kieran Devers sent the niece he was unlikely to ever see a small silver spoon and cup. He had sent to Belfast for the items several months ago, and they had only recently come.

"Poor William," Fortune observed. "But at least they have a child. Do you think it is time for us to have one, sir? We must try harder, I fear. You have neglected me shamefully these past weeks." Fortune was soaking in the large oaken tub before the fireplace. The tub took up much of the room that the bed did not.

He chuckled at her, stripping his own clothing off as he prepared to join her. She was adorably tempting, her red hair piled atop her head, her cheeks rosy with the heat of the bath. "We must take a fine tub like this to the New World," he said with a grin. "I am willing to give up much to find a land where we may live in peace, free of prejudice, but I do not intend giving up our baths, madame."

Fortune giggled. "Thank heavens we are not Puritans. I hear they consider bathing a great sin of the flesh. Some of the gentlemen I have met at court are not pleasant to be near. Get in gently, Kieran, else you'll splash water on the floor."

He waggled his thick black eyebrows at her as he slid effortlessly into the tub. "Did you not know, madame, I am part silky?"

"What is a silky?" she asked, curious.

"A man who can take the shape of a seal. Or perhaps a seal who can take the shape of a man. Or so the legends go."

"Ahh," she said, and she reached beneath the water with her hand to tease him. "And just when do you become a seal, sir? And if you become a seal, how shall we ever conceive a child?"

He felt himself hardening as her provocative words taunted him, and the brush of her nipples on his chest inflamed his desires. "Would you like to see how a silky mates?" he goaded her wickedly. He turned her about, and cupped her breasts in his hands, his thumbs tantalizing the hard little nipples. Fondling her he nuzzled at her, nipping at her earlobes, and the nape of her neck. "The silky," he said, "exhibits dominance over his mate."

"Does he?" Fortune returned, grinding her buttocks suggestively into his groin. "Just how does he do this, sir?"

He didn't answer. Instead his arm encircled her waist, drawing them even closer. A hand slipped beneath the water to find the little jewel of her womanhood which he teased unmercifully.

"Silkies don't have *those,* or such naughty fingers," she gasped.

"But their human mates do," he reasoned. He was afire with his lust, and he knew she was too. The oaken tub was wide enough for what he wanted to do, and so he bent her forward until her face was almost touching the surface of the water. Then grasping her hips in his big hands he slipped into her female passage in a manner in which he had not previously taken her.

Fortune gasped, surprised, and would have fallen into the water face first had he not been holding her. He began to move with a slow, almost stately rhythm within her, his long, thick manhood stroking the walls of her sensitive passage, stoking the fires of her own hunger for him. She caught the cadence of his movements almost immediately, and moved with him. Her head was spinning with the pleasure he was affording her. Her breath was coming in short, hard pants that sent ripples across the water before her face.

"This," he ground out in her ear, *"is how the silky mates!* He covers his female's body with his own, and takes her." He thrust deeper, and Fortune murmured with her open delight.

"Ahhh, Kieran, *yes!"* she encouraged him, wiggling her bottom into him. His own breath in her ear was hot, and fast.

"Oh, witch, you have unmanned me, and I am not yet satisfied!" he complained to her. His juices had burst forth, but he was still hard, and filled with a hungry lust. He withdrew from her, and exited the tub, pulling her behind him. Flinging her upon their bed he entered her once again, thrusting, thrusting, thrusting, until Fortune was desperately stuffing her fist in her mouth to stifle her cries.

The room was cold, yet she was burning up. If he could not get enough of her, she could not get enough of him now. Wrapping her long legs about him she drew him closer, her teeth sinking into his muscled shoulder, her nails raking the flesh of his back. *"More, damn it! More!"* she commanded him, and he complied, pushing himself as far as he could into her eager body. She screamed softly as their possession of each other became so intense she thought she was dying, would die from the extreme excess of pleasure she was now experiencing. The world dissolved behind her eyes, shattering into an explosion of color, and then she was soaring, soaring. As quickly she was falling into the sweet darkness that arose to claim them both from their excesses.

When she was in control of herself again some minutes passed. She became aware that he was bathing her gently with the love cloths. She watched him through half-closed eyes. "I have taught you well," she murmured softly.

He looked at her, his eyes dark with unconcealed passion. "Now, 'tis I who wants more, Fortune." He knelt over her, and taking his manhood in his hand, he rubbed it against her lips. Back and forth, back and forth, and then her little tongue shot from between those tempting lips, and began to lick at him. "Yes, my poppet, that's it," he encouraged her as his manhood began to tingle in anticipation. She opened her mouth now, not protesting at all as he guided himself in, and sighed deeply when she began to nurse upon him, at first tentatively, and then more strongly. "Ah, God, Fortune, 'tis sweet." He began to harden and swell until he more than filled her dainty mouth. Slowly he withdrew himself from the hot, wet cavity.

Fortune was trembling with her own desire now. What they had done had been incredibly exciting for her. She wondered if other women serviced their husbands in such a manner. Her breasts felt hard and aching, as if they would burst. Her pleasure place was already wet with her juices, and so filled with sensation it almost burned. She gasped when her husband slid down her body, and spreading her open brought her legs over his shoulders so he might service her as she had him. *"Ohh yesssss!"* she breathed, encouraging him. *"Please!"*

She was all musk and honey. Hot and slick, and so eager. Her little jewel was swollen and visibly throbbing. He touched it with the tip of his facile tongue, and she shrieked with its sensitivity. Now he played with it, flicking his tongue back and forth while she writhed and moaned with her rising pleasure until the first wave of her lust burst. It was then he entered her body, pushing slowly inside her as her legs wrapped about him once again. "Wanton, little witch," he taunted her, his love lance flashing back and forth with increasing speed. *"I love you!"* His lips found her, and he kissed her hungrily.

His mouth bruised hers but Fortune didn't care. Their passion was incredible, and unlike anything she had experienced with him before. "You are so randy, my husband," she told him. "I hope you will not change as the years go by. Ah! Ahh! *Ahhhhhh!"* The pleasure was rising, rising, rising, and then it burst again leaving her shaken with her joy and delight. *"I love you too, my darling!"* she told him as she yanked the coverlet over them.

They awoke again to the glowing light of a spring dawn coming soft, and faintly golden into their chamber. The fire had long since gone out, the great oak tub blocking whatever warmth it might have provided had it been ablaze. Fortune sneezed, and then she sneezed again. Her husband crawled, swearing softly, from the bed, going across the room to push the great oak tub from before the fireplace, but there was little room. He knelt, and poked among the coals, but their life had been long extinguished. Kieran sneezed.

"Merde!" He swore more volubly now. "I think I am catching an ague."

"I know I am," she responded. "Can't you get the fire going?"

"I'll have to go down to the hall and fetch some live coals, for these are dead." He sneezed a second and third time.

Fortune couldn't help herself. She chuckled aloud, and then as quickly explained to her aggrieved-looking spouse. "I think there is a lesson in this, Kieran. Do not make love wet, and then sleep in a damp bed on a chilly spring night. I think we had best get some clothing on, and then go down to the hall to get warm. The servants will take care of the chamber, and empty the tub for us, but I could use some oat stirabout, and some hot mulled cider, sir."

"I concur," he said. Then a twinkle lit his eyes. "But 'twas a grand evening's entertainment we had, my lusty wife, was it not?"

Fortune laughed aloud.

April came to an end, and their time in Ulster was growing short. Kieran had gathered several Catholic families as well as individual men and women who were willing to leave their homeland and go to the New World. There were fourteen men. Most were farmers, but for Bruce Morgan, who had been his father's apprentice and was a good blacksmith. There was also a cooper, a tanner, a shoemaker, two weavers, two fishermen, and a female physician, Mistress Happeth Jones, who came from Enniskillen. She had been driven out by her Protestant neighbors who suggested she might be a witch. Before they might act on their assumption, Mistress Jones had packed her belongings and fled to

Maguire's Ford. Mistress Jones had no declared faith, but she had heard that in Maguire's Ford there was more tolerance than in the rest of Ulster, and so she had come.

"Do you practice witchcraft?" Kieran asked her bluntly.

"Of course not," Mistress Jones answered him indignantly. She was a plump, sweet-faced woman with dark hair, rosy cheeks, and bright blue eyes that surveyed him with a level gaze. "The ignorant always try to explain what they cannot by crying witchery, sir. I am a physician as was my father who taught me. I am a healer, as was my mother, who had *the touch*. I have it also. My success in Enniskillen succeeded in arousing jealousy in the town's two other physicians, and its surgeon. 'Twas they who started the rumors. Not only was I a better doctor than they were, but I was a woman, and we all know that women are only good for bearing children and keeping a man's house," she finished with a twinkle in her eye.

"You have no husband?" he pressed her.

"I have no time for a husband," she replied tartly.

"Jones is not an Ulster name," he said.

"My parents came from Anglesey," she told him. "My grandfather was a physician at Beaumaris. My mother's people were merchants who traded with Ireland. Since my grandfather Jones had two sons, and both followed in his footsteps, my father, who was the younger, had no choice but to leave Anglesey to seek a place where his skills would be needed. Anglesey is a poor place, and one physician and his elder son were more than enough. I was my parents' only child, and a wee baby when we came to Enniskillen," she concluded her explanation.

"It will not be easy in the New World, Mistress Jones," Kieran told her. "Have you no one to go with you?"

"There is Taffy," she said quietly. "He is part of the reason it was so easy to believe witchcraft of me."

"Why?"

"He is a dwarf, sir, and he is mute, but he is intelligent, and understands everything said to him. His mother aban-

doned him when she saw what he was going to be. I have
raised him as I would have my own child. He assists me, and
is my apothecary. He is not ugly, just tiny. And there are my
dogs, sir. I do not keep a cat for obvious reasons," she finished with a chuckle.

He laughed. He liked her, and knew Fortune would too.
"There are certain things you must bring," he said. "Have
you the coin to purchase them? We can help if you do not.
Your skills, and that of your assistant, will be valuable assets
to us."

"When do we leave?" she asked him.

"My wife and I will depart for Scotland, and then
England in a few days' time," he explained. "Then I must be
introduced to Lord Baltimore, who is heading this expedition, and convince him to take us with him. My people will
remain in Ulster until I send for them. It may be this summer, or it may not be until next year. We have the ships, and
they will take our party from here. There is no necessity to
travel to England," Kieran said. "The horses will come with
the rest of you."

Adam Leslie celebrated his fifteenth birthday on the four-
teenth day of May. He was as tall as his father now, and
openly eager to be his own master. Jasmine, however, took
her second Leslie son aside.

"You must keep the peace here," she said. "You cannot
allow *any* persecution of either Catholic or Protestant in
Maguire's Ford. There will be those who will come and attempt to make you choose sides, Adam, *but you must not
give way.* No faith is better than another, whatever certain
men may say. St. Augustine said, *Love God, and do as you
please.* It is good advice, my son. I hope you will go down to
Trinity in Dublin in another year, or so. As long as Rory
Maguire is here to see to your interests you are free to edu-
cate yourself fully."

"I've hae all the education I can stomach, Mam," he told

her. "Duncan is the one who hae a love of book learning. I can read, write, and keep the accounts. I can speak French and Italian, although what good that will do me, I dinna know. Now I would learn from Maguire how this estate is managed, and how to breed the horses. Free me this day forever from the good-hearted, but dull Samuel Steen."

His mother laughed, and ruffled his dark hair. "Very well, Adam, you are freed. 'Tis better, I suspect, that you learn the business of life now that you have such a responsibility on your strong shoulders."

"Do I hae charge over Duncan?" the young man asked.

Jasmine thought a moment. Duncan Leslie was now twelve years old. Still a boy. Adam was yet young enough to be a bully. Jasmine did not see the Reverend Mr. Steen, a well-natured man, as having the final authority over Duncan. Mr. Steen could be easily led as he was, by nature, a peacemaker. "Cullen Butler will have charge over your brother," she told Adam. "And if he is not here, then Rory Maguire. You do not need any more responsibility than I have given you, Adam," Jasmine concluded, softening her decision.

"If there is trouble," Adam said, "there are some who will nae appreciate that you appointed two Catholics to hae charge over one of your sons, Mam. What are we to do then?"

"Then," Jasmine said, "the final authority will rest with your father, Adam, and as he will be over the sea in Scotland, no decision of any importance regarding Duncan can be made until Jemmie Leslie decides it, eh?"

Adam Leslie grinned. "Yer a clever slyboots, Mam."

Rory Maguire watched them as they spoke. Would he ever see her again? he wondered. *Or their daughter?* It was Fortune he feared for now. The New World was an ocean away, yet he would not brave the journey. His lass was a fine combination of her Celtic ancestors and her Mughal ancestors. And how she loved Kieran Devers! He smiled to himself. She had every bit the fire and passion her mother had. And she was so eager to begin this grand adventure with the man she loved.

I hardly know you, he pondered silently. And you know even less of me, my daughter. Mine is a secret that will go with me to my grave. Only on the day we meet in heaven will you know the truth, Fortune Mary, but I'll miss you, lass. This year has been the best in all my life because you were here for me to see, and to be with, but you cannot know that. Once, long ago, I bid your mam farewell, and then I wept all the while telling myself that men did not cry. I'll weep twice as much and as hard this time, lassie, but at least I know you are loved. Not just by your mother, and James Leslie, but by that wild Ulsterman you've gone and married yourself to, Fortune Mary Devers. And my love will go with you, my daughter. You will always have my heart, even as your mother has had it all these years.

The last loose end to be tied before they might leave Maguire's Ford was Rois's marriage to Kevin Hennessey. The ceremony was performed in the castle's wee chapel the morning of their departure. The young couple would be going with Fortune and Kieran as their personal servants, although once they were in the New World, Kevin would take over the responsibility of the horses that would be coming with them. Kevin's parents were long dead, which had played a part in his decision to come. Rois's parents and grandparents saw her wed to her childhood sweetheart. Michael Duffy wiped a tear from his eye to see his daughter married, but his mother, Bride, wept openly and noisily as her granddaughter spoke her vows. All knew that Bride's tears were because this would be the last time she was likely to see her youngest granddaughter, and Rois had always been a particular favorite of Bride's.

In the hall the bride and groom were toasted, and wished every good fortune. The time had come to depart Maguire's Ford. Jasmine bid her two sons a tender farewell, promising to return in a year or two to check on them. This knowledge cheered her many friends who had thought never to see the duchess of Glenkirk again once she left them.

"Nay," laughed Jasmine. "I must make certain these two

scamps do what they ought. Then, too, one day I shall have to find wives for them, won't I? This one"—and she tousled Adam's hair—"is already sneaking about looking at the lasses. Didn't think I knew?" she teased Adam. "Even from Scotland I shall know what mischief you are up to, my darling laddies." Then she hugged her sons. Now she turned to Rory.

"Continue as you have in the past, old friend," she said. "I made no mistake the day I put my trust in you, Rory Maguire. I thank you for all you have done, and for all you will do. I shall be back, I promise you." Then Jasmine surprised him by leaning forward and kissing him on the cheek. "I think I may do that, mayn't I?" she queried the blushing man. Then she patted his hand. "Farewell, Rory, until we meet again."

"Why you're red as a beet, Rory Maguire," Fortune said with a chuckle as she put her arms about him, and hugged him, kissing his other cheek heartily. "Mama did surprise you, didn't she? But I haven't. You should know by now that I love and adore you, Godfather. I shall miss you, Rory. Are you certain you don't want to come to the New World with us? What fine horses we shall raise from the fine stock you will send us. Ulster is such a sad place, I fear, and growing sadder."

Rory held Fortune tightly in his arms, for a moment, savouring the sweetness of her, *his daughter*. Then he said, "I would not leave the people of Maguire's Ford when my family departed Ulster with the earls all those years ago, lassie. I will not leave it now, though I thank you for the offer." He kissed her cheek. "You're leaving with a fine husband, Fortune Mary, and that is, after all, what you came to Ulster for, didn't you?" He set her back from him, and smiled into her beautiful face. "Go with God, and go in peace and safety," he said. "If you were to send me a missive now and again, I should not mind, and I might even answer it." Then holding her by the shoulders he kissed her a final time upon her smooth forehead.

Fortune felt a terrible sadness suddenly overwhelm her, and her eyes filled with tears. Looking momentarily into his eyes she saw that they, too, were filled with moisture. "Ohh, Rory, I shall miss you! And I will write, I promise you!" she half-sobbed.

"Take your wife, Kieran Devers, for she is about to weep all over my good doublet," Rory said gruffly as he handed Fortune off to her husband.

Kieran Devers put a protecting arm about Fortune while holding out his other hand to the Maguire. "Farewell, Rory Maguire. You know what I would have of you, don't you?"

Maguire nodded. "Aye, laddie, I'll watch over the graves, I swear it," he said, shaking the younger man's hand.

Now James Leslie came, and bid Rory Maguire good-bye. "Watch over my lads," he said. "I know you'll teach Adam well, Maguire."

"I will, my lord," came the expected answer.

Bride Duffy, still weepy, bid them all a farewell. Fergus Duffy would be driving the coach to the coast where their ship was waiting.

Jasmine had a final word with her cousin, Cullen Butler. "Tread lightly, Cullen. I want no martyrs on my conscience," she cautioned him. " 'Tis a very delicate part of me, and I'll not have the ghost of Mam rising up to chide me."

"Have I not done well all these years, little cousin?" he said.

"Times have changed even in the year we have been here, Cullen," Jasmine reminded him. "The militant Protestants become more vociferous with each passing day. England rules Ireland, and in England the king himself is struggling with the Puritans to maintain order. He must be very careful lest his French Catholic queen be accused of influencing him. It is not an easy time, and it does not appear things will be getting any easier soon. Foresight, even in a priest, is not a bad trait."

"God will watch over me," he said quietly.

"God helps those who help themselves," she said with a small smile. "Watch over my lads, but if anyone would force your hand, remember, the duke of Glenkirk is the final authority in *any* matter concerning his sons, Cullen."

The priest kissed her hand. "God bless you, Cousin," he said. "Now, depart, else you meet yourself returning."

The Leslies and the Deverses departed for the coast. The great baggage train they had brought with Fortune the year before had now increased in size, and gone ahead of them the day before. There was a single travel coach, but for now it held only their necessary luggage, Rohana, and Adali. The two other servants, like their masters, preferred to ride rather than be confined to the coach. They avoided the Appleton estate on their return journey, traveling a bit longer distance so they might stay at Mistress Tully's Golden Lion Inn overnight.

Reaching the coast they found their baggage carts already upon the docks, and being loaded upon the ship that would return them back to Scotland. Slowly the carts were emptied, the trunks and the boxes being carried up the gangway to be stowed in the ship's hole.

" 'Tis fortunate you warned us to come empty, my lady," the ship's captain said with a grin, "but at least the young mistress got what she came to Ulster for, eh?" He chuckled.

The duchess of Glenkirk smiled. "Aye," she said in reply. "Fortune has probably gotten more than she bargained for, captain."

The voyage was a short one. Seeing the coastline of his native land disappearing Kieran Devers had a mild pang, but he felt no regrets. They were doing the right thing in leaving, and he relished the adventure ahead. He had never in all his life been out of Ireland, unlike his young wife for whom travel was a commonplace thing. He wondered what awaited them. He wondered what they would do if Lord Baltimore would not have them. He hoped his father-in-law's small influence would aid them, and if it did, what would this New World be like?

Kieran Devers looked to the coast of Scotland that was now in his view after two days at sea. His arm rested lightly about Fortune's slender shoulders. She smiled up at him.

" 'Twill be all right, Kieran, my love. I feel it in my heart. The New World is where we belong, you and I. There is where we will carve out a grand life, and a wonderful future for ourselves, and for our children. Lord Baltimore will have us. How can he refuse?"

"I have never before in my life felt such responsibility as I do now, Fortune," Kieran admitted to her. "All my life I was answerable for no one but myself. I lived in my father's house, safe and secure. Now it is all different. I have you to love, but we have no place that we may call our own, where we may live together. I am not afraid, yet I am concerned, my love."

"You needn't be, Kieran. I told you that in my heart I know what we are doing is the right thing. The world is ours!" And her confident smile convinced him that all would truly be well.

Chapter
14

George Calvert had been born to Leonard Calvert, a well-to-do country gentleman, and his wife, Alicia, in Yorkshire in the year 1580. While his father was a Protestant, and he had been raised as one, his mother was a Catholic who quietly practiced her faith. Calvert had been educated at Trinity College, Oxford. Concluding his studies he embarked upon a tour of the Continent as did most young gentlemen of his station. At the English embassy in Paris he had the good fortune to meet with Sir Robert Cecil, the queen's Secretary of State. Cecil liked the circumspect young man, and offered him a position on his staff.

Elizabeth Tudor died, and James Stuart became king. Cecil remained in his position, and made George Calvert his private secretary. By this time Calvert had contracted a marriage with Anne Mynne, a young woman of good family from Hertfordshire. The Calverts named their first child, a son, Cecil, in honor of George's patron. Other children followed. Three more sons and two daughters.

Sir Robert became the Earl of Salisbury which but increased George Calvert's stature and visibility. When the king and queen made a visit to Oxford in 1605, Calvert was one of five men to be awarded a master's degree from the university. The other four gentlemen were all nobles of high rank. Now the king began to send Sir Robert's secretary on his own official business to Ireland, for he liked him personally, trusted him, and knew him to be very competent.

When Cecil died in 1612 the king kept George Calvert on, and five years later knighted him. Shortly thereafter Sir George Calvert was made the king's Secretary of State, and a member of the Privy Council. The country gentleman's son had come far indeed.

A hard worker, and genuinely modest, Calvert was very well liked by the men with whom he came in daily contact. Unlike many at court he had no enemies. As his fortunes rose he and his wife planned a large house at Kiplin in Yorkshire where he had grown up. But then Anne died in childbirth with their sixth child, and devastated, George Calvert turned to the Catholic religion of his mother for solace and comfort. He kept his new faith a secret, obeying the strict laws imposed upon England's citizens in the matter of religion.

Unfortunately it was at this time King James asked his loyal servant to officiate on a committee that was being formed to try a group of men who refused to belong to the Church of England. Some were Catholics and some were Puritans. Now George Calvert's conscience and ethics came to the forefront. This was not a task he could take on under his changed religious circumstances. So he first spoke to his master, the king, and after publicly announced his conversion to Catholicism. He resigned his offices, including that of Secretary of State. This, despite the fact the king had offered to release him from taking the oath of supremacy so he might continue in the royal service. Trustworthy, capable gentlemen of Sir George Calvert's kind were difficult to find.

Still, James Stuart was an honorable man who valued the few real friendships he had. He knew that despite his

Catholic faith George Calvert would always be loyal to him and his heirs. He might have sent his friend to the tower. Instead he created him a baron in the Irish peerage, with lands in County Longford. Then, because the new Lord Baltimore had always wanted to found a colony in the New World, the king gave him a huge land grant on the Avalon peninsula in Newfoundland.

Colonists were sent out, and Sir George later followed with his new wife and family only to discover that Newfoundland was not a particularly hospitable place in which to settle. The winters seemed to last from mid-October until well into the month of May. There was virtually no time for crops to grow and be harvested. The fishing was excellent, and would prove a profitable venture, however the French began to harass Avalon. Calvert wisely sent his family south to Virginia, and spent the winter in his colony. When the spring came he was relieved to find himself still alive. He sent the king a letter explaining the difficult situation, and departed to join his wife in Virginia. He had sadly realized that Avalon was not the colony he wanted to found.

Once reunited with his family in Jamestown he set about to find a more hospitable territory where he could make his dream of a colony where all religions were tolerated equally come true. While he was welcomed in Virginia by his friends, he was also viewed with suspicion by many who assumed his faith would make him loyaler to his co-religionists from Spain far to the south of Virginia, than to his own countrymen. Ignoring them as best he could, George Calvert did look south for land, but while the climate was pleasant enough, there was no suitable deep water anchorage for the English ships that would bring supplies and colonists from England. By now a letter from the king was awaiting him in Jamestown ordering him to return home to England.

Before he might receive this missive, however, Calvert looked to the north of Virginia, exploring the Chesapeake region. What he saw excited him greatly. There were great sheltered bays, and harbors with tides that ran no higher on an average day than two feet. The bays, one running into another, were fed by numerous rivers and streams, some of them navigable quite far inland. The waters abounded with fish, shellfish, ducks, and geese. In the great forests lining the Chesapeake were turkeys, deer, and rabbit. There were bushes of edible berries, and fruit trees. He recognized a great number of hardwood trees that would build houses and ships. George Calvert, Lord Baltimore, believed he had found his colony, and it was a paradise.

Returning to Jamestown he found the king's letter, and immediately returned home, leaving his second wife and children behind. His goal was to obtain a grant for the lands about the Chesapeake area, for this was the perfect place for his colony. In England James I was dead, but Charles I, his son, was equally fond of Lord Baltimore. He thought his father's old friend and faithful servant looked tired and worn, and attempted to turn his mind from the New World. But Charles I finally saw that George Calvert would not be dissuaded until he could found this colony of his which he had been talking about for years. As for religious toleration, the king was doubtful such a thing could be obtained, but let George Calvert try if he must.

Lord Baltimore was granted by royal decree the land: *to the true meridian of the first fountaine of the River Pattowmeck.* Created Lord Proprietary, his rights over this territory were virtually royal. He could make laws. Raise an army. Pardon criminals, confer land grants, and titles. And then King Charles gave his father's old friend an especial right not even granted to the Virginia colony. Lord Baltimore's colony was allowed to trade with any country it chose to trade with; and in return, the king would receive one fifth of any gold or silver discovered in the colony, and be paid annually a quitrent of two Indian arrows.

As the charter was being drawn up for the new colony the king gently suggested that, having no name yet, Lord Baltimore might like to name it after the queen. George Calvert agreed,

a twinkle in his eyes. *Terra Mariae* was therefore entered
into the Latin charter as the colony's name, but it was immediately called by its more familiar English appellation,
Mary's Land.

Lady Baltimore and the children were sent for, but after a
quiet voyage their vessel was wrecked off the coast of England
with no survivors. Lord Baltimore was devastated. He had
lost two wives, and several of the children. Exhausted, worn
down by his many years of hard work, and saddened beyond
all measure, George Calvert, Lord Baltimore, died suddenly
on April fifteenth, 1632. Two months later the royal charter
was issued to the second Lord Baltimore, Cecil Calvert, a
handsome young man of twenty-seven.

At Glenkirk, James Leslie had learned all of this news—
sent to him by his stepson Charles Frederick Stuart, the duke
of Lundy—even as Kieran and Fortune prepared to go south
to England. "I doubt ye'll be able to sail this year," he said,
"but ye'll nae know that until ye speak wi Lord Baltimore.
Ye'll go to Queen's Malvern first, and Charlie will know
what ye're to do next. I dinna know these people, but since
they're connected wi the court, Charlie will."

James Leslie and his wife had decided they would not be
going south to England for their usual summer visit with
their family. The duke felt he had been away from his lands a
year, and would not travel again so soon. Jasmine was only
just recovering from her childbirth of seven months ago. She
did not want to take a bairn as young as Autumn on another
journey. The trip home had been all she would dare with the
precious infant upon whom she doted so greatly. Fortune
and Kieran would go alone to England.

Now as the day for their departure came near the duchess
of Glenkirk grew sad. When her second daughter had gone
she would have no children left at home but Patrick Leslie,
but he was sixteen, and while he loved his mother, and tolerated her concern, he considered himself a man. And her wee

Autumn Rose, who was growing so quickly Jasmine could almost feel life speeding by her, and she was helpless to stop it.

Fortune sensed her mother's mood, and attempted to cheer her. "She's only a baby, Mama. 'Twill be years before she leaves you. You can devote yourself to her as you never really could to the rest of us. I think Autumn is very fortunate to have you, Mama."

"Aye," her mother answered, brightening a bit. Fortune was very astute, but then she had always been the practical child. When she and her siblings were young I was at court, Jasmine thought. I did not have the time for them I shall have for this daughter. "I will miss you," the duchess of Glenkirk said softly.

"I will miss you, Mama," came the reply. "On one hand I am so excited to be going to the New World, but on the other I am a little afraid. It is such an adventure, and as you know I have never been one for adventure. I did not ever plan to have one. Yet here I am, setting off into the unknown with my darling Kieran. If only people would tolerate each other's religions, I should have never had to leave Ulster." She sighed deeply. "Do you think this Mary's Land will really be a place of toleration, Mama? What if it isn't? Where will we go then?"

"You will come home to Glenkirk where we will protect you," the duchess said firmly. Then she took her daughter into her arms, and they hugged one another. "You know, Fortune, that you and Kieran will always be welcome here. *Always!*"

It was so difficult leaving, Fortune thought, the day they departed Glenkirk. There was a strong likelihood that she would never see this childhood home of hers ever again. An ocean would separate them, and having crossed it once, Fortune was not certain she would have the courage to cross back over it again. As she had always said, she was not one for adventure, and yet what was this she was doing? This place they were going to was a wilderness. There were no castles, no houses, no towns, or shops. How would they survive? Yet what other choice did they have?

Fortune put on a brave face, and said good-bye to all those whom she loved. Her stepfather, James Leslie, her mother, Jasmine, her brother, Patrick, her baby sister, Autumn. Her mother's lifelong servants for the first time since she had known them were teary. They were, she noticed for the first time, growing older. I will never see them again, she realized suddenly. She put her arms about Adali, her mother's majordomo. There were no words to say what was really in her heart. He hugged her wordlessly, then turned away, but not quickly enough for she had seen his tears. Rohana and Toramalli hugged and kissed her, and unable to help themselves wept fulsomely.

They left Glenkirk, Fortune's great train of possessions behind them, protected until they reached Queen's Malvern by an armed troop of Leslie men-at-arms. The trip was, as it usually was, uneventful, but for Kieran, Rois, and Kevin it was as much of an adventure as their voyage from Ulster had been. For Fortune it was just another trek into an English summer.

Charles Frederick Stuart, the duke of Lundy, was awaiting them on their arrival at his home, Queen's Malvern. The estate had been given to his great-grandparents by Elizabeth Tudor, and passed on to him with the blessing of his grandfather, King James. It had therefore cost the canny king nothing to bestow a dukedom upon his first grandchild, a bargain he well liked. Charlie, as his family called him, was a tall, slender young man with auburn hair, and the Stuarts' amber eyes. He looked far more like his father, the late Prince Henry, than he did like his mother's family. He would be twenty in September, and was as polished a courtier as his Great-Uncle Robin Southwood, the earl of Lynmouth, had been at his age.

"You're looking particularly lush and well satisfied," he

greeted his elder sister with a wicked grin. " 'Tis obvious marriage agrees with you, Fortune." He kissed her heartily, and gave her a hug.

"A Stuart first, as Mama likes to say," she responded with a chuckle. "Here is my husband, Kieran Devers. Kieran, Charlie, the not-so-royal Stuart in the family."

The two men clasped hands, sizing one another up, and immediately decided they liked one another.

"Henry will eventually be over from Cadby," Charlie told his sister, and then said to Kieran, "the revered eldest brother of us all."

They moved into the house, and into the family hall where the servants were quick to bring refreshment. Settling themselves about the fire, for the June day was chill, they talked.

"Papa said you would know how to contact Lord Baltimore," Fortune said to her brother.

"He's at Wardour Castle down in Wiltshire," was the reply.

"How do we get there?" Kieran asked.

"Fortune will remain here," Charlie said. "You and I will ride down in a few days' time. I'll send ahead to gain an appointment with him, for this expedition of his is extremely popular, and he is besieged by those who are interested in going. Many, of course, are only interested in gaining lands, and then leaving them to their colonists while they return to England to live well. Cecil Calvert, like his father before him, wants responsible colonists who will remain in Mary's Land. I think you will qualify, and that, along with your ability to support yourselves, will weigh heavily in your favor. And of course because I am the king's dear nephew, and want a place for you," he teased them both.

"And we have our own vessels," Fortune said. "I'm going with you, Charlie. You aren't going to leave me behind while you two have all the fun, little brother."

"Wardour will be no place for a woman," he protested. "An important expedition is being set up there. It will be full of men, Fortune, and you are a respectable married woman now, for God's sake."

"Doesn't Lord Baltimore have a wife, Charlie?"

"Aye, Lady Anne Arundel," was the answer.

"Is she there?"

"Of course! It's her father's home," he replied.

"Then I shall go," Fortune said. "You're a courtier, Charlie, and you don't really know a great deal outside of the court. And my husband is a country gentleman from Ulster, unfamiliar with English ways. I have to go. I'm the only one of us with a practical nature, and we'll need my skills at negotiation."

"She's right," Kieran said with a chuckle, "but I'll not mind her company at all, Charlie."

The young duke thought a moment, and then he grinned. "Damn me if you aren't correct as always, sister. I'd forgotten that you are the sensible one among us. Aye, come along, but we're going to ride, Fortune. No servants, and no fancy clothing. Wardour at Tisbury is several long days' ride from Queen's Malvern. Perhaps on the way back we'll go by way of Oxton, and see India and her family."

"Ohhh, I should like that!" his sister responded enthusiastically.

They sent word to Cadby to Henry Lindley that they were leaving for Wiltshire, and would see him when they returned. Rois and Kevin were left in the care of the Queen's Malvern servants, and the trio rode out one fine June morning. Kieran was surprised to find how capable his wife was in caring for herself. He had not realized it before, and it struck him suddenly how little he really knew Fortune. They reached Wardour Castle several days later. Fortune had never seen a building such as Wardour before. It was hexagonal in shape, and its Great Hall was laid out over its entrance.

Cecil Calvert greeted them personally. "Charlie! 'Tis good to see you, my lord. The king is well?"

"I haven't been at court in a month," Charlie replied.

"I've come today to ask a favor of you, Cecil. This is my sister, Lady Fortune Lindley, and her husband, Kieran Devers. Kieran was heir to a lovely little estate in Ulster until his English stepmother decided her son, Kieran's half-brother, would make Mallow Court a better master."

"You're a Catholic?" Lord Baltimore said, his look sympathetic.

"Aye, my lord, I am," Kieran said quietly.

"They want to go with you, Cecil," Charlie said.

Lord Baltimore looked distressed. "We already have more people than I had anticipated," he said.

Now it was Fortune who spoke up. "We have our own ships, my lord," she said. "My own two trading vessels. The larger I'll use for our transport. The other I intend using for the horses. We have colonists, too. Fourteen men of whom five are farmers, two fishermen, two weavers, and one each, a blacksmith, a cooper, a tanner, a shoemaker, and an apothecary. The five farmers have wives, and several children among them. All are healthy, devout, and of good character. And we have a physician, Mistress Happeth Jones, plus my two servants. We can provision all our people as well as the ship, my lord. Please, let us come with you. There is nowhere else for us to go, for while my husband is a Catholic, I am an Anglican. They say you will practice toleration of all faiths in your Mary's Land. It would seem the perfect place for us."

Cecil Calvert looked at the lovely young woman before him. While she was dressed for riding, rather outrageously in doeskin breeches, her garments were expensive, and elegant. Her hands were the hands of a lady. Her speech refined. "It will not be an easy place to settle, Lady Lindley," he told her. "You will have to build your own home, and it will be nothing, I will wager, like that which you are used to for it is a wilderness. There are other dangers too. Some of the natives are not friendly, and as prone to war as the French and the Spanish, although I hope to negotiate a peace treaty with them. You must bring everything that you need with you, and if you find you are in need of something you do not have, you will have to do without it. You will be bereft of your family, for I know from Charlie that yours is a large family. You will not see your brothers and sisters for years, if indeed you see them ever again. Are you truly certain that you would make this great journey, and live in this new world?"

"Aye," Fortune told him bravely, "I am, my lord."

"I would consider it a debt owed you, Cecil," Charlie Stuart said meaningfully.

Lord Baltimore waved his hand. "Nay, Charlie, I am happy to offer your sister and her husband a place in my colony. They are just the kind of people I truly want. They will make something of the land given them, and they will remain to build the colony. Come with me now to my privy chamber. I will tell you what is involved, and what you will get in exchange." He tucked Fortune's hand in his. "I remember you, and your sister, India, at court. You were two of the prettiest young ladies there at the time. You departed, leaving behind many broken hearts." He led them along a stone corridor, finally ushering them into a paneled room where a fire was burning merrily.

Lord Baltimore settled his guests, sitting with them. "Now," he said, directing his gaze to Fortune and Kieran. "For every grant of land made by me, an oath of fealty must be sworn to me as the colony's Proprietary. You will receive a thousand acres for every five men you bring with you. As you are bringing fifteen men you will be given three thousand acres, Master Devers. I will want twenty pounds for each man transported. The women and children will not be charged. Each male colonist will receive a hundred acres for himself, and if he has a wife, one hundred acres for her in addition. Fifty-acres is assigned to each child over the age of sixteen years. They will pay twelve pence quitrent each year for every fifty acres. You will pay twenty pounds quitrent yearly.

"Each of your people must have a minimum of two hats,

two suits, three pairs of stockings, shoes, one ax, one saw, one shovel, nails, one grindstone, one spit, one gridiron, a pot, a kettle, a frying pan, and seven ells of canvas. The women, of course, will take gowns, and not suits. Each man will need a musket, ten pounds of powder, ten pounds of lead, bullets, and goose shot, as well as a sword, a belt, a bandolier, and a flask. Your people, both men and women, should learn how to shoot for they will not be able to depend solely upon the gentlemen in the expedition for protection."

Kieran nodded. "What kind of food supplies shall we stock?" he asked.

"Flour, grain, cheeses, dried fish, meat, and fruit. Casks of beer, cider, and wine. And seed. You will be given a list of what to bring for we must get through a winter and spring before we will be able to eat off our own land," Lord Baltimore said.

"Then you intend sailing this year?" Kieran was surprised. Both his father-in-law and Charlie believed Lord Baltimore's expedition could not set off until the next year. They would have to send to their people and tell them to prepare. Monies would have to be dispatched to Rory Maguire for the supplies. "When?" There was so much to do.

"Autumn. 'Tis not the best time to travel, but we have no other choice. Unlike my father, I seem to have enemies who would prefer Mary's Land not be settled."

The representatives of the Virginia colony were in particular most vexing. They complained to the king that by allowing the Mary's Land colony to come into existence they would lose both land and settlers. They complained that Cecil Calvert was setting up a colony where all people, even Catholics, could worship in freedom. Then they started rumors that only Catholics would be allowed in Mary's Land. They lobbied hard to get King Charles to rescind Lord Baltimore's charter. He listened to them all, but he remembered George Calvert's faithful service to his family. And, too, his young Catholic queen pleaded privily with him to ignore the malcontents.

"The charter will stand," the king told his wife. "I think the Calverts dreamers to believe they can actually make a place in this world where all people, no matter their faith, can be welcome. Human nature being what it is . . ." He shrugged. "But perhaps it is possible," the king concluded. "We will pray for their success."

Nonetheless Calvert's detractors continued to work behind the scenes to destroy Lord Baltimore's dream. Cecil Calvert realized he could not, at this time, go with his colonists. He put his younger brother, Leonard, in command, and his even younger brother, George, was made the colony's deputy governor. Jerome Hawley and Thomas Cornwallis were named to assist the Calverts as commissioners. The preparations continued for an autumn departure. Kieran and Fortune returned to Queen's Malvern to prepare. There was no time for visiting India at Oxton.

Back at Queen's Malvern Fortune realized that her moon link had been broken. She was with child. The knowledge put her in a quandary. She knew if her husband learned of her condition he would not allow her to go to Mary's Land until after their child was born. Had she been India, she would have kept the secret, but she was not India. She was the practical child, and yet . . . she sighed.

"What is it?" her brother asked as he came upon Fortune sitting upon a stone bench in the Queen's Malvern gardens. He sat by her side, and took her hand in his.

"I have a problem to solve," Fortune said. Her fingers worried her dark green silk skirts.

"Are you having second thoughts about leaving England?" he queried her. He didn't really understand the passion she and Kieran had for going. Catholics lived in England. Not easily, but they did.

"Mary's Land is where my husband and I belong," Fortune

said to Charlie. "I have never really felt at home anywhere, and neither has Kieran. We know Mary's Land is where we must go. That is not my difficulty, little brother."

"Then it can only be you have not told your husband about your expected child," Charlie said.

Fortune was astounded. *"How did you know?"* she gasped.

Charles Frederick Stuart laughed aloud. "How many children does Mama have? I was the fourth. Five have followed me, Fortune. I know when a woman is with child. When is the babe due?"

"I don't know," she admitted, and when he chortled, she said, "Don't you dare to laugh, Charlie! I always expected Mama would be here when I had my first baby. I thought it would be she who explained to me how long it took for a child to grow inside a woman. What am I to do?" She stood up, and began to pace the gravel path.

"When was your link with the moon broken, sister?" he asked.

Fortune looked askance at him, but said, "I have had no show of blood since we left Glenkirk."

His handsome brow furrowed a moment, and then he said, "Probably very early spring, but we'll write to Mama. In the meantime you must tell your husband, Fortune. He has to know."

Fortune debated with herself as to how she would inform Kieran that she was expecting their first child, and just how she would convince him nonetheless to let her travel to Mary's Land with their party. Yet she couldn't seem to get up the courage to tell her husband. She knew what he would say. He would insist they remain in England until the child was born, and able to travel in safety. After all, wasn't that the decision her parents had made last year in Ulster? And Autumn was Mama's ninth baby, not her first. Perhaps she would wait until they were at sea to tell him. Yes! She would apprise him of her condition then when it was too late to turn back. It was the perfect solution. God's boots, Fortune thought to herself. I am more like Mama and India than I ever realized. So she said nothing, and astutely avoided her brother's questioning looks.

She awoke one morning ravenous, and dressing, hurried to the family hall to join Kieran and Charlie in breaking their fast. She ate with enthusiasm. A bowl of oat stir-about with dried apples and heavy cream. Fresh bread smeared with butter and topped with a wedge of sharp cheddar. Two hard-boiled eggs, liberally salted, and topped off with a mug of sweet cider. Suddenly, however, her stomach rebelled. It rolled, and gurgled loudly, and then before Fortune could even stand up, she vomited her breakfast back upon the high board with a groan.

Both men looked somewhat horrified, and jumped up lest they be sprayed with her spew.

"Sweetheart, are you all right?" Kieran asked her, concerned.

Before Fortune might answer her husband, however, her brother spoke up. "You haven't told him, you vixen, have you?"

"Told me what?" Kieran demanded, looking from his wife to his brother-in-law.

"She's with child," Charlie burst out before his sister might concoct some believable tale which he would then have to either agree with, or end up calling her a little liar. "She was planning to tell you."

"When?" Kieran said dryly. "When we were at sea?"

"Aye," Fortune said in a tiny voice. "It seemed best."

Kieran snorted. "You would endanger yourself and our child merely to have your own way?"

The servants were now hurrying to clean up the mess, and the two men brought Fortune down to the fireside. Rois, who had seen what had happened, brought her mistress a mug of peppermint tea.

"Sip it slow, m'lady," she advised. "It will settle your belly. Then I will bring you some dry bread."

Fortune sat down in a tapestried chair. Looking up at her angry husband she said, "Will you go to Mary's Land without me, Kieran?"

"Of course not!" he almost shouted at her.

"Which is why I did not tell you," Fortune replied.

"You are not making any sense, Fortune," he told her.

"Aye, I am, if you will but hear me out, and stop roaring at me, Kieran Devers. I will not be howled at!" Then she burst into tears, sobbing piteously.

He was totally bewildered. She was in the wrong, and now she attempted to wheedle him with her tears. Well, he would not be manipulated by his fine lady. What she needed was a spanking, and had she not been with child, he would have given it to her.

"Women's emotions are outrageously sensitive when they are with child," his brother-in-law said calmly. "Give her a moment, and it will pass," he chuckled. "Fortune, stop weeping, sister, and tell us your reasons for being so secretive."

Fortune sniffled, but then she managed to contain herself. "If we do not go to Mary's Land with the first ships," she said, "we shall not get the best lands available. We need to be among the first! We are not influential milords, speculating with a new colony, Kieran; we are among the few of the colonists of wealth who will remain in Mary's Land, and build the colony. Most of the nobles going, if indeed they are even going and not simply sending their agents, hope for a quick profit. They will populate their lands with whoever they can, and then resell those properties to the highest bidder.

"We are bringing over horses next year. We need open meadows for them. We cannot spend our time clearing forests. If we are among the first colonists we will get those meadows, and shall receive our lands from Lord Baltimore himself. If we wait, we shall be forced to purchase those lands from others. We have to go, Kieran! We cannot remain here!"

"Why not?" he demanded. "There are Catholics in

England. Could we not purchase a home here, and live quietly?"

Fortune shook her head. "You know the condition under which Catholics live in England. And the Puritans gain more power every day. Even the king isn't entirely safe from their matterings, and everything the queen does is criticized. And why? Because she is a Catholic. You think me selfish for wanting to go even though I am with child. Mistress Jones will see me safely through my travail, and I am not afraid. Yet you, too, are every bit as selfish as I am."

"Me? How?" He was astounded by her accusation.

"You have told me yourself that your faith is not particularly strong, and that you clung to your Catholicism because it was all you had left of your mother. I think you also did it to irritate your stepmother. You gave her the perfect weapon to use against you so that she was able to steal Mallow Court from you. Mallow Court had one thousand acres, and Maguire's Ford was another three thousand. We might have been a power in Ulster, and certainly in Fermanagh, Kieran, but that you sought to cling to the past, and argue about religion like the rest of them. I love you, Kieran Devers. I gave up a great estate for you, and never have I had a moment's regret. I am to bear your child in early spring. If you do not want me to travel to Mary's Land under those circumstances I will remain here in England; but by God, husband, you shall go with that expedition, and claim us our three thousand acres of well-watered and fertile lands! You are a man now, and have great responsibilities to bear. I am not Lady Jane. You can no longer hide behind your faith, using it to excuse your pride, Kieran Devers!"

He was speechless, and even when Fortune got up, and left the family hall, he could not find the words to stop her.

"Your first dressing down, I presume," Charlie said with a small attempt at humor.

Kieran nodded.

"The women in this family have tempers it is best not to rouse. They are intelligent, and proud, Kieran. My sister is correct when she says you have to go to Mary's Land even if she can't right now. It is no longer just you and Fortune. You have all those people back at Maguire's Ford depending on you to lead them to the New World. You have a child coming. You cannot run away from your duty now, I fear."

"How did one so young learn so much?" Kieran said, finally regaining his powers of speech.

"I had good teachers. My great-grandmother, Lady de Marisco. My mother, and stepfather. And, by nature, my lineage has afforded me great opportunities. One grows up quickly in a royal court, Kieran, particularly if you wish to survive and prosper. Being the king's nephew was never enough for me."

"It's all so strange to me," Kieran admitted. "I never understood the kind of family I was marrying into when I fell in love with your sister. We are so provincial by comparison, but I never realized it until I came to England. The moment I saw Fortune I knew I had to have her, and yet now, I wonder that I have not bit off more than I can chew. Am I a man who can carve out an empire in a new world? I wonder. Will I disappoint Fortune if I cannot? And our child? What of our child?" He ran a big hand through his dark hair in frustration.

"First of all," Charlie said, "you must understand that *all* the women in this family work *with* their men. They have this rather irritating knack of bearing and raising their young while managing their affairs quite successfully. Accept this rather strange gift that God has bestowed upon you, Kieran. Sit down with my sister, and decide how you will manage the business of colonizing your bit of the New World. Understand that you must go, and she must stay to have the child. She will come next year. By that time you will have a house built for them. You would not want to stay behind, and leave the responsibility of building a home for your family to others. There is nothing in this that cannot be managed, my friend," Charlie concluded, putting a comforting hand on his brother-in-law's broad shoulder.

"I have no other choice than to take your advice," Kieran

said. "I pray you are right, Charlie. I do not like leaving Fortune."

"Mother will come, or better yet, India. Fortune was with her when she had her first child. Get her to tell you the story sometime." He grinned at Kieran. "Are you now over your shock? I don't imagine it was easy learning you had wed such a virago."

"I am not a virago," Fortune said, coming back into the hall. "How can you say such a thing? Kieran certainly knows better."

Her husband grinned. "Of course, I do, my love," he agreed. "Charlie and I have had a fine talk. We need to sit down and decide just how we will manage this voyage if you are to remain behind."

Fortune smiled at them both. "I knew you would see reason, Kieran," she murmured. "I am so glad that Charlie explained everything to you. Now, we have much to do, sir, and not a moment to waste!"

Charles Frederick Stuart, duke of Lundy, grinned over his sister's red head at his brother-in-law. The message was very clear. You see, it said. All you have to do is follow her lead.

Chapter
15

They sent word to Maguire's Ford as quickly as they could that the men planning to go with them be ready to board the *Cardiff Rose* in the next few months. Rory Maguire was sent a list of exactly what each man would need as had been provided by Lord Baltimore to the Deverses. The only woman in the party who would be allowed to go would be Mistress Jones, the physician, for her services could prove invaluable in those first months. She was advised to bring not only her dried herbs, roots, and barks, but plants and cuttings as well, for they did not know what plants would be available to her for her remedies in the new colony of Mary's Land.

The other women in the party, and the children, would remain in Ulster until the following summer when the *Cardiff Rose* would return for them, and then travel in company with the *Highlander,* the vessel which would contain the horses, and other livestock. It was planned that over the winter a house would be built for the Deverses as well as the others so that when the women arrived they and the children could be properly sheltered from the elements.

Once the men reached their destination on the far side of the sea, they would buy in Virginia oxen, a milk cow, and a horse for Kieran. That way come the spring they would be able to plow. They had already heard the Virginia colonists were not particularly friendly, being jealous of Mary's Land's special status. Fortune knew, however, that enough coin could overcome most reluctance, and advised her husband to make the best bargain he could, but to obtain what he needed at any price for their success, or failure, depended on it.

"You are so sensible," he told her one day as they went over a list of what had already been obtained. "I am sorry you cannot come with me, sweetheart."

She smiled up at him. "I want so very much to go with you," she said, "but I realize now it is better I don't. You must place your entire concentration on preparing our estate to be profitable, Kieran. I would be a burden to you, for you would fret over me in my current condition."

He placed his hand on her belly which had only recently begun to round slightly. "I hate that I will not be here when our son is born," he replied. "I remember my da, God assoil him, saying that the midwife took me from my mam's womb, and placed me directly into his hands. I wish I could be here to do the same thing, sweetheart." He caressed her stomach tenderly. "My son," he said, almost awestruck.

"Our child," she corrected him gently. "This could be a lass or a lad, Kieran. I care not as long as the bairn is healthy."

He kissed her mouth softly. "I agree, Fortune." He kissed her again, and this time his kiss was a bit more passionate. "Just think. This time last year we were falling in love."

She laughed, and it was a happy sound. "You are the most sentimental man I have ever met, Kieran Devers," she told him. "I knew I was right to love you even if it did cost me Maguire's Ford."

The summer ended. Jasmine, along with her baby daughter, Autumn Leslie, came south to England to Queen's Malvern. The duke and his eldest son would remain at Glenkirk, but the duchess could not be dissuaded·from being with her second daughter when she was with child. As Autumn was almost a year old now, she was able to travel more comfortably. Kieran felt better knowing Fortune's mother would be with her when their child was born.

"You are both wise," Jasmine said, "to have delayed Fortune's going. With first babies one can never be certain when they will come. It is better that Fortune remain here with us. Charlie will be off for court shortly, and we will have Queen's Malvern all to ourselves."

Charles Frederick Stuart celebrated his twentieth birthday. His brother, Henry Lindley, marquess of Westleigh, his older sister, India, countess of Oxton, and her husband, Deveral Leigh, came from their homes to help the not-so-royal Stuart commemorate the occasion. Jasmine looked about the hall that night. Here were her four eldest children. Once they had been so close. Now they were all grown, and making a great fuss over Autumn Leslie, the youngest of them all.

She looked at her Stuart son. "You are your father's image," she told Charlie. "He was twenty when he died. Thank God you have a stronger constitution. When he was born in Scotland they treated him like some Indian idol in my native land. He was carried about by his servants until he was four. He told me once that when they left him alone for the night he would creep from his bed, and run up and down his room. If he had not done so his poor legs would have been as weak as his baby brother's. Your poor Uncle Charles was less venturesome, and had a terrible time learning to walk. You may notice, Charlie, that even today he strides with an odd gait."

"I wondered where that had come from," Charlie replied. "You were older than my father, Mama, weren't you?"

"By three and a half years," Jasmine said, "but no one thought a great deal about it. I think they were relieved he had finally taken a mistress, thus proving his manhood. You know the rumors that always swirled about your grandfather, King James." She smiled, and patted his hand. "And you, my son? Has any lady yet stolen your heart?"

Charlie flushed. "I am the king's nephew. No matter I was born on the wrong side of the blanket, I am still his nephew, and the ladies are always most kind," the not-so-royal Stuart replied, a twinkle in his eye.

"Too bad Mama wasn't married to Prince Henry," Henry Lindley observed. "You'd be king now, and a better king, I think, than poor old royal Charles. If there is one thing he's certain of, 'tis his stature, but he cannot make any decision having to do with governance without mulling it to death. And do not dare to disagree with him. He takes neither suggestion, nor criticism, lightly."

"He is not a bad king," Jasmine defended the monarch.

"Aye, he is," the marquess of Westleigh said, "even if he does mean well, Mama. Still, at least our Charlie is spared Henrietta Marie as a wife," he chuckled. "An overproud, and pious little Catholic. Her very existence causes difficulties."

"*Henry!* Remember that your brother-in-law is a Catholic. I did not raise you to voice, or even consider, such prejudice," Jasmine admonished her oldest son.

"Mama, I am not anti-Catholic. I am practical, and speak the truth," the marquess said. "I would say the same if she were a pious little Puritan. Extremism is not healthy for a country, or its government. England is changing, and I am not certain I like the change."

"The English have shown a one-sidedness in religion for centuries," Kieran spoke up. "Perhaps not the people, but its rulers."

"The people too," Henry Lindley said fatalistically.

"I thought you had all come to celebrate my natal day," Charlie said with a grin. "I don't want to discuss politics, or religion. We are together as we will never be again. Soon our sister will leave us for this new world of hers. I want to eat, and drink, and reminisce tonight. Do you remember when we all fled to France because my grandfather, King James, and my grandmother, Queen Anne, decided that Jemmie Leslie was the perfect husband for Mama?"

"And it took him two years to find us because no one would tell him where we were," India laughed.

"Until Madame Skye hinted so broadly that he would have had to be a dunce not to find us, and he did," Charlie chuckled.

"He only found us because he followed our great-grandmother to France when she came to tell Mama our great-grandfather had died. But," Fortune said, "Papa was just the right husband for Mama, and the perfect father for us!"

"Except when he is so bull-headed that he cannot be reasoned with at all," India said.

"God's blood, India," Henry Lindley said to his eldest sister, "you're not still holding a grudge against poor Glenkirk? I thought you had forgiven him long ago. He did what he thought right."

"Oh, I've forgiven him," India replied, "but I was just remembering how he almost cost Dev and me our firstborn."

"I'd rather think of our childhoods," Fortune said. "What times we had when Mama was at court, and we got to stay with Madame Skye and Grandfather Adam. Remember the black pony he got you, India?"

India giggled. "I had been begging for that pony since you were born," she said. "In fact I remember telling him I should rather have a black pony than a baby sister. Do you remember when you were three, Fortune, and you managed, although to this day we don't know how, to clamber on that pony's back? Then you backed him from his stall, and rode out into the stableyard crowing with your accomplishment."

"And you were furious that I had dared to ride your pony,

and so the next day Grandfather Adam bought me a dappled-gray pony with dark spots on his rump. I called him Freckles."

"How did you get up on my pony?" India asked her sister.

"Henry helped me," came the mischievous reply.

"Henry?" India was astounded, and looked to her brother.

The marquess of Westleigh laughed, chagrined. "I didn't expect Fortune to go out into the yard," he said, "and she was so eager to be on that pony's back. I was terrified that Mama would find out. So I slipped from the stables through the rear entrance, and pretended to be just as surprised as everyone else when she rode out. Fortune never told on me, for which, sister, I am to this day thankful."

Surprisingly their mother laughed at the tale. "How lucky you all were to have one another. My poor wee Autumn will grow up like an only child. The youngest of her Leslie brothers is twelve years older than she is. There is no one left at Glenkirk now but Patrick, and at sixteen he is more interested in lasses he can bed than in a baby sister." She smiled at her four eldest.

The next day Henry Lindley returned to his home, Cadby, even as his sister, India, and her husband left for Oxton, and Charlie was off to join the court. By evening only Jasmine, her two daughters, and Kieran remained at Queen's Malvern. There was a melancholy about the wonderful old brick mansion. Fortune and Kieran were keeping to themselves, and Jasmine understood. Too soon they would be parted. Then came word that the Mary's Land expedition would be sailing from Gravesend in mid-October.

"It's ridiculous to go all the way to London when the *Cardiff Rose* is berthed in Liverpool. You will travel there, Kieran," Fortune said, and her mother nodded in agreement. "The ship will sail to Dundalk to pick up the colonists, and you can meet Leonard Calvert's ships off of . . ." She looked puzzled. "Where, Mama?"

"Cape Clear, off Ireland," Jasmine said quietly. "The Mary's Land expedition will pass that way as they cross the Saint George's Channel going out to sea."

"We'll have to send a messenger off in the morning to Lord Baltimore," Fortune said, "to confirm these arrangements. And one to Maguire's Ford so that our men will be in Dundalk at the proper time. And the messenger has to return from Lord Baltimore so that you will have time to ride to Liverpool. I will go with you."

"Nay," Jasmine said firmly to her daughter. "I will go, but you must say your good-byes to Kieran here. We cannot be bothered with a coach to convey you, and you should not make such a long journey a-horse. It is far too dangerous, Fortune, and you want a healthy child who will be able to make the long and dangerous trip to Mary's Land next summer."

"I agree, madame," Kieran Devers said quietly, and looked to his wife. "Fortune?"

For once Fortune saw the wisdom of her mother's argument without disagreement. She nodded, reluctantly. "I cannot argue with either of you, but oh, I wish I were going with you, Kieran."

The following day all the messengers were dispatched, and for the next few weeks the couriers came and went. Rory Maguire sent word that he would have the Irish colonists in Dundalk at the appointed time. The time grew nearer for Kieran Devers to leave his wife, and Fortune began to feel a dread such as she had never known.

"Are we mad?" she asked him. "It is such a long and dangerous journey across a vast ocean. What if the ship encounters a storm? What if it sinks? I will never see you again!" she wailed, and burst into tears, clinging to him, and soaking his nightshirt with her weeping.

"What other choice do we have?" he said quietly. "We have been over this a hundred times, Fortune. The New World is our destiny. There is nothing for us in this old world, darling." He stroked her disheveled red hair soothingly.

"I can become a Catholic," Fortune said. "I was baptized one. Then we can go to France, or Spain to live. We could live at Belle Fleurs, Mama's chateau. Grandfather Adam has family nearby at Archambault, Kieran. We could be happy there!" She looked up hopefully at him.

He sighed. "Perhaps you could be happy, Fortune, but I could not. I have my pride, and it has been difficult enough for me to swallow it these past months. I know that there are those who think I wed you because you are a great heiress, and not because I love you. Aye, I have a small inheritance thanks to my father, but my small wealth is nowhere near yours. In the New World I will build us a life, and a great estate. Perhaps not as great as the one we gave up, but I will do it myself, and no one will look askance at me. I never before considered what anyone thought of me, but then I married you, my love. I will not be a husband who lives off his wife's wealth! Nor will I have anyone think it of me, or of you. We will make our way together, Fortune, and we can only make it in the New World. *Not here. Not in England. Not in Ireland. Not in Spain, or France. In Mary's Land!* Do you understand now, my love, why I must go?"

"I never knew you felt this way, Kieran," Fortune answered him. "What I have is yours, darling. Let no one say otherwise. If it will make you happy, I will sign it all over to you!"

He chuckled. "Nay, sweetheart. I do not want your wealth. Your family is right to see that its women have their own. Besides, that is not the point, Fortune. As you have your pride, I have mine. A man must make his own way in the world." He caressed her tenderly. "What has happened to my practical little wife?"

"I don't want you to leave me!" she began to sob again. "I would rather be with you to share your fate than left behind here in England to have our child all alone!"

"You will not be alone," he said in reasonable tones. "You will have your mother with you, my love."

"I don't want Mama! *I want you!* "

Jasmine had warned him that Fortune's condition would cause her to act in an unreasonable manner at times. Here

was his beautiful wife who had instructed him to go to
Mary's Land to obtain the best land in the first wave of
colonists now wailing at him. He didn't know what he could
possibly say to her under the circumstances, and so he decided to take a tack he had never before taken with her.

"You cannot have me unless you wish to destroy all our
chances to succeed, Fortune," he told her sternly. "You have
said yourself our chances of success depend on obtaining the
proper land for our horses. If I do not go now, how can I do
that? You will survive without me to hold your hand. Didn't
India have her firstborn in a mountain hunting lodge with
only her two servants to help her? Having a baby is a most
natural thing for a woman. Now, behave yourself, Fortune."

She was astounded by his reprimand. "How can you
speak to me like that?" she demanded, suddenly angry.

"How can I not when you behave like a spoiled child?" he
countered, thankful she was no longer weeping.

"I shall never forgive you for leaving me," Fortune announced in regal tones. "You are being horrible, Kieran."

"When you arrive in Mary's Land next summer and find a
fine house awaiting you, and crops planted, and meadows of
lush grass for our horses, you will forgive me. I go for you,
Fortune, and for our child. Can you really be angry at me for
that?" He tipped her lovely face up so he could look into her
eyes.

"Yes!"

"Really?" he wheedled her, brushing her lips softly with
his own.

"Yes!" She glowered at him, but her lips were twitching.

"Truly?" He kissed her with a barely concealed hunger,
pushing her back amid the pillows on their bed, and unfas-
tening the ribbons on her nightrail so he could nuzzle at her
ripening breasts. She sighed, not answering him, and he
began to kiss the swell of soft creamy flesh. She was so deli-
ciously tempting. He fondled her bosom with a big hand,
then leaned forward to kiss her closed and shadowed eyelids.
"Have you any idea, Fortune, of how much I am going to

miss you, my darling? A woman, I am told, loses her desire as she grows full with her babe, but a man has no such luxury. If anything I find you more exciting than ever before."

Her blue-green eyes opened, and she said, "Then you had best make the most of the few days you have left with me, my husband. You will not, I know, be unfaithful to me, will you?" She drew him back down into her arms, and nipped his earlobe. *"Will you, Kieran?"*

"Nay, Fortune," he told her. "I will not be unfaithful to you." He gently rolled her on her side, and pushed up her nightrail.

She sighed as he entered her ever so gently. Who on earth had told him that silly old wives' tale about a woman losing desire when she was with child? Perhaps later she might, but certainly not now. She pressed herself back against him, purring as he moved within her, his hands caressing her belly, her breasts, teasing at her sensitive nipples. "You will miss me," she taunted him wickedly; then she gave herself over to the pleasure he was creating between them.

"Aye, I will," he groaned, straining to bring them to a state of blissful oblivion; and when he succeeded they sighed in unison, replete with their shared satisfaction.

They spent the next few days in a haze of passion, and then it was time for Kieran to leave Queen's Malvern for Liverpool. Fortune had managed to overcome her last-minute trepidation. She stood upon the front stoop of the house, offering her husband a traveling cup. He drained it down, gravely handing her back the silver goblet. Then reaching down he pulled her up to kiss her a final time. "It is all for you, and the babe," he said softly. "I love you, Fortune. Pray for our success, sweetheart. God willing, I shall see you next summer in Mary's Land." He set her back down again, and without another word swung his mount about to move down the driveway, Kevin following.

"Mama!" Fortune called, and Jasmine turned. "Come

home quickly, and give him what wisdom you can before you leave him."

Jasmine nodded, and then followed after her son-in-law.

Fortune turned back to the house, unable to see them ride out of sight. Mama would not be back for a week or more. She was virtually alone, but for her good Rois. "I hate this," Fortune muttered to herself, and then called to her maidservant to keep her company. She expected that Rois was no happier than she was with this situation. Rois came, red-eyed from weeping. "Don't cry, or I'll cry too," Fortune said. "I'm just as sad as you are, Rois."

"They had to go, I know," Rois sniffled. "Kevin says if we're to have a future we must own our own land, and we can't in Ulster. Still, why now? Now when I'm expecting our first bairn!" Then she began to cry again.

"You're having a baby too?" Fortune wondered why she was so surprised. "When?"

"A wee bit after you, m'lady," Rois admitted.

"Does Kevin know?" Fortune asked her servant.

Rois shook her head. "I was afraid to tell him lest he not go, and he was so intent upon it I didn't want to spoil his chances."

Fortune began to laugh. It was all so absurd. She had married the wrong brother because she loved him, lost her dowry in the process, and now was left behind *enceinte* with an *enceinte* serving woman while their husbands went off to seek their destiny. If this scenario had been presented to her two years ago she would have scorned such a fate for the practical and sensible Lady Fortune Mary Lindley. "Well, Rois," she said, "I think we have no other choice but to hope our men have great success in their endeavors. We'll keep each other company while our bairns ripen. Can you knit? I've never learned how, but I can sew a very fine seam. Let's make our babies some wee gowns. 'Tis as good a way as any I can think of to keep ourselves occupied."

Young Mistress Bramwell, the assistant housekeeper, went to the storerooms and brought back some lovely cam-

bric and the sewing supplies that they would need. There
were even old paper patterns from which they could cut the
infant garments. Rohana came to help them for she had not
gone with her mistress. For the next week they spent their
days cutting and sewing. Baby Autumn came, and crawled
about their feet, playing with the scraps of material that fell
to the floor.

Eight days after she had departed Queen's Malvern
Jasmine returned with her escort of Glenkirk men-at-arms.
"They've sailed for Ireland," she said. "The wind was fair,
and the seas calm. Don't look so worried, my poppet," she
told her daughter. "I was six months coming from India, and
I managed to arrive safely."

"He should already have reached Ulster, and taken on the
colonists," Fortune replied. "They are probably even now
sailing toward their rendezvous with Leonard Calvert. He
has surely embarked by now."

And indeed Lord Baltimore's expedition had departed
Gravesend, but they did not get far. Cecil Calvert had been
wise to remain in England. His enemies were spreading rumors that his two ships, the *Ark* and the *Dove,* were actually
sending nuns and soldiers to Spain. Lord Baltimore had to
go to court to defend himself, and his expedition. His vessels
were stopped by a royal naval ship, and forced to put into
Cowes, on the Isle of Wight. There they sat for almost a
month before finally being allowed to proceed on their journey. The master of the *Ark,* knowing that the *Cardiff Rose*
was waiting off Cape Clear, had sent word to Kieran Devers
via an outbound ship. He explained the delay, suggesting
that the *Cardiff Rose* proceed to Barbados where they would
await Lord Baltimore's expedition which would shortly follow.

On November twenty-second the colonists bound for
Mary's Land departed at long last. England was hardly out
of sight when they were caught in a violent storm, but once

it had passed they had perfect weather for the rest of their journey to Barbados, so perfect that the *Ark*'s captain remarked upon it. He had never known such a smooth crossing. The single violent storm they had encountered had, however, separated them from their traveling companion, the smaller pinnace, the *Dove*. They could only hope she had survived the gale, and would meet them in Barbados as the *Cardiff Rose* was to do.

Kieran Devers and his companions sailed across a cloudless blue sea facing the unknown. Day after day the sun shone brightly down on them. The further from Ireland they got, the warmer the air grew. The weather was so fair, and the voyage so smooth, that Mistress Jones and Taffy brought their plants topside, making a small enclosure for them in the bow area of the deck. After six weeks, the *Cardiff Rose* made landfall in Barbados where they would await the rest of the expedition.

The governor of the island, Sir Thomas Warner, was careful in his welcome. The *Cardiff Rose* was a member of the O'Malley-Small trading company, and therefore of some small import. Nonetheless it was filled with Irish Catholics. Not enough to cause him any difficulty, but he was indeed concerned. He tendered an invitation to Kieran and the ship's captain for dinner so he might learn more. Kieran gave his colonists leave to visit the island, but warned them they must cause no difficulty, or they would be sent back aboard and forced to remain.

"We must await Lord Calvert. I would be far more comfortable doing it ashore than aboard ship. We still have a long way to go. Any man found drunk will not be allowed ashore again until we reach Mary's Land." Then Kieran Devers went with Captain O'Flaherty to the governor's home.

They were greeted cordially, and sat down to table. Kieran was fascinated by the long bunches of yellow cucumber-shaped growths hanging from trees outside the governor's dining room.

Seeing the direction of his gaze the governor chuckled. "Bananas," he said. "They are called bananas. Peel away the yellow outer skin, and inside is a sweet fruit not unlike the taste of marmalade. I'll give you some to bring back aboard ship."

"We're remaining on the island while we await the arrival of Lord Baltimore's expedition, my lord. If we have your permission, of course," Kieran answered him. "We have been at sea for weeks, and are not sailors used to the water. My men are mostly farmers."

"Where are you bound for, if I may ask?" the governor inquired.

"Lord Baltimore's new colony of Mary's Land," Kieran told him.

" 'Tis only for Catholics, I am told," Sir Thomas replied.

"Nay, sir, Mary's Land is for all men of goodwill, be they Catholic or Protestant," Kieran told him earnestly. "None will be persecuted. That is why we are going, my lord, but many who travel with Leonard Calvert are Protestants."

"Don't like the idea of a Catholic colony," the governor grumbled. "We've got too much trouble with the Spanish here as it is."

"Mary's Land is *not* a Spanish colony, my lord. It is an English colony. We are all loyal subjects of his majesty. Did you know that my wife's half-brother is the king's honored nephew?"

"Indeed?" The governor looked a bit skeptical.

"Lord Charles Frederick Stuart, the duke of Lundy," Kieran said. "They call him the not-so-royal Stuart."

"Ah, yes, I recall something about Prince Henry having a bastard," Sir Thomas responded. "The mistress was a pretty wench as I remember now. Dark hair, and eyes like the turquoise sea."

"My mother-in-law, the duchess of Glenkirk," Kieran said, "although she was not wed to James Leslie when she was the prince's beloved friend."

"You're welcome to remain on the island itself as long as

your people don't cause us any difficulties," the governor told Kieran.

"Thank you, my lord," Kieran said politely, and turned his attention to his meal.

"Nicely done, sir," Captain O'Flaherty said softly with a wink. "The family would be proud of you."

Kieran looked at the captain, and the eyes twinkling back at him were familiar. "God's blood!" he swore softly. "You're one of them, aren't you?"

"Ualtar O'Flaherty, son of Ewan, grandson of the great Skye, great-grandson of Dubhdara himself," was the smiling reply. "Your wife and I are cousins, although I have never had the pleasure of meeting her or any of her nearest kin. I only met my grandmother, Skye, twice in my lifetime. My father is the Master of Ballyhenessey in Ireland. I'm the only one of his sons who felt the urge to go to sea. My grandmother saw to it that I could have my heart's desire as she did for several of my cousins. Various of us have been master of the *Cardiff Rose*. She's a fine, safe vessel. Mostly I've been on the Mediterranean run. We call in at various times at Algiers, San Lorenzo, Marseilles, Naples, Venice, Athens, Alexandria, Istanbul."

"Why didn't I know who you were?" Kieran wondered aloud.

"Was it important to you, sir?" Captain O'Flaherty asked.

Kieran laughed. " 'Tis a strange lot, this family I've married into, Ualtar O'Flaherty," he said.

"Aye, sir, and that's a truth," the captain agreed cheerfully.

It had been early December when they reached Barbados. They kept their Christmas there. There was no priest to celebrate the mass for them, so they sang songs and said their prayers quietly. A feast was arranged for the men on the beach where a pit was dug, and a large pig was purchased in the marketplace for roasting. A platter with bananas, muskmelon, pineapple, and watermelon was served along with roasted yams. Other than the pig, these were foods unfamiliar to the colonists. They tasted them reluctantly, and then discovering that they were good, ate with enthusiasm.

In early January the *Ark* reached Barbados, and was welcomed by the men aboard the *Cardiff Rose.* As Kieran Devers and his men before them, those aboard the *Ark* were amazed and enchanted by the exotic and brilliant flowers and trees growing on the island. The raucous and wildly colored birds were also fascinating. A mass of thanksgiving was held aboard the *Ark* which was attended by all the Catholics. The Protestant colonists went ashore to attend the governor's church.

Over the next few weeks they loaded up the vessels with seed corn, potatoes, and as many other food supplies as they could find room for, squirreling them away in every available nook and cranny. The water barrels were all refilled. To their delight the *Dove* arrived in the harbor along with a large merchantman, the *Dragon.* When the storm had hit, they had returned to shelter in a safe English harbor until it passed before beginning their journey again. Everyone who had started out with Leonard Calvert's expedition was now accounted for, and they were now ready to head north for Mary's Land. The governor of Barbados was openly relieved to see them go. He, like so many others, could not rid himself of the idea that English and Irish Catholics were loyal to their Catholic brethren in Spain rather than England's Protestant king.

They reached the Virginias in March. Although Lord Baltimore had advised against having anything to do with the Virginians, whose representatives at court were doing all in their power to stop the Mary's Land colony, Leonard Calvert had a message for Virginia's governor from the king, as well as some gifts for him that he wished to personally deliver. The colonists stayed nine days in Virginia, and the Virginians were extremely cordial much to Governor Calvert's surprise. When they left they took along a local fur trader, Captain Fleet, to serve them as a translator with the Indians, and a guide, for he knew the Chesapeake country well.

As their ships traversed Chesapeake Bay, the colonists stood at the ship's rails viewing their new home for the first time. The forests were magnificent, filled with both hard and soft woods. Kieran Devers knew he had finally come home, and was astounded by the certainty and confidence he felt in his heart. How he wished that Fortune had been able to come with them so they might see it for the first time together; but when she did come, he would have a home ready for her. He knew she was going to love it every bit as much as he already did. He hurried to his cabin to write her a letter. Once they were settled, the *Cardiff Rose* would be returning back to England, and he wanted it to carry his thoughts to Fortune. He had written them down each day so she could share all she had missed. He wondered if his son was born yet.

They made their first landfall on an uninhabited island that they called St. Clement. The Indians that had lined the shores to the east and the west the past few days were gone now. A tall cross made from newly felled tree trunks was planted. Governor Calvert's priest, Father White, said a solemn mass. Afterward Leonard Calvert took possession of Mary's Land in the name of God, King Charles I, and his brother, Lord Cecil Baltimore. It was the twenty-fifth day of March in the year sixteen hundred and thirty-four.

And on that very day at Queen's Malvern Fortune went into labor shortly after midnight. Her child was, by all calculations, late by at least a week. Fortune was thankful her mother was with her for poor Rois, about to have her own child, was of no use at all.

Jasmine took one look at the young maidservant's face as she entered her daughter's bedchamber, and said, "Get out! Send Rohana and Toramalli to me at once."

Rois sent the duchess a grateful look, and scurried out as best she could, given her own girth at the moment.

"Jesu, it hurts!" Fortune said. "I never realized how much it would hurt. When India went into labor, I rode off to fetch you and Papa. Owww! How long will it take, Mama?"

"Get up," Jasmine said. "We'll walk together for awhile, and see if we can speed up your travail, poppet. Alas, I'm sorry to tell you that bairns being born are neither practical or sensible. They come when they come, and that is the truth of it."

" 'Tis not particularly encouraging, Mama," Fortune muttered.

The bedchamber door opened, and Jasmine's twin servants entered the room.

"Young Bramwell would like to know, my lady, where you would like the birthing table set up," Rohana said.

"Bring it in here and set it by the fireplace. And see the cradle is brought as well as water, cloths, and swaddlings," Jasmine said. She was beginning to be assailed by memories. Her son, Charlie, had been born here at Queen's Malvern. His father, Prince Henry, had been with them. At first he had stood behind her, bracing her shoulders, encouraging her with soft words, massaging her distended belly with gentle hands. He seemed to have an instinct as to what to do, although he later admitted he had never before seen a child born. And when it was obvious that Jasmine was about to deliver, he had called Adali to take his place, and gone around the table, pushed her grandmother Skye aside, and birthed Charlie with his own hands. Jasmine felt the tears coming, and turned away quickly. Henry Stuart had been such a sweet man.

"Mama!" Fortune cried out. "I do not think I can walk another step. The pains are getting worse, and they are coming so quickly now."

It was now almost dawn, and Fortune had been laboring to bring forth her child for several hours now.

"Let us help you onto the birthing table," Jasmine said.

Fortune struggled onto the table with Toramalli's aid while Rohana went behind her to brace her shoulders.

"I saw your mother born, and your brothers and sisters," Rohana said. "Now I am to see your child born, my lady Fortune. I am so sorry you will be leaving us. I will not get to see the other children you will bear that fine young husband of yours."

"I hate him!" Fortune shouted. "How could he do this to me, and then go galivanting off to the New World while I am left to suffer like this? Owww! Will this child not be born? Mama, it's been hours!"

"You sound more like India than Fortune," Jasmine said. "I told you the child will come when it comes, and not before."

Several hours passed, and in midafternoon the baby's head finally appeared. Jasmine encouraged her daughter to push forth the child. Slowly. Slowly. The full head and the shoulders appeared. Then with a mighty push the child slid from its mother's womb. Its eyes flew open to meet those of its grandmother, and then opening its mouth the child howled with outrage.

"It's a little girl," Jasmine said, sounding simply delighted.

"It is?" Fortune was exhausted, and relieved. "Let me see her, Mama." She held out her arms.

Jasmine put the baby into her daughter's arms, and Fortune shrieked.

"She's all bloodied, Mama! Is she injured?"

"Birthing is a bloody business as my grandmother once told Prince Henry," Jasmine replied. "We'll clean her up in a minute. She's fine. A healthy little lass. Just listen to her cry, bless her."

Fortune looked down at the red-faced infant in her arms. Her small face was scrunched tightly with her anger, and her eyes were closed although her mouth was wide open as she roared, apparently affronted. "Shhhh, baby," Fortune ventured her first words to her child. The baby suddenly ceased crying, and opening her eyes looked directly into her mother's eyes. Fortune felt a sudden jolt, and was instantly filled with an overwhelming love for this child. "Her eyes are blue," she said wonderingly.

"All babies' eyes are blue," Jasmine said dryly. "Surely you remember that, being my third eldest, poppet."

"She's bald," Fortune observed.

"The girls usually are," Jasmine replied. "There's a bit of reddish fuzz, however, see." She gently touched the baby's head. "What are you going to call her?"

"Aine," Fortune said. "I'm going to name her after Kieran's little sister. I didn't expect a lass, Mama. I thought I was to have a son, and I was going to name him James, after Papa, but somehow I just know this wee lass of mine should be called Aine. Aine Mary Devers is what I shall baptize her." She kissed the baby's small head. "And I shall baptize her a Catholic, for I know her father would want it."

"You can't bring a priest into your brother's house considering his position," Jasmine said. "She must be baptized in England's church. When you and Aine get to Mary's Land, Fortune, you can do whatever you please. Here in England, however, you will follow the law of the land even as the queen does. Is that understood?"

Fortune nodded.

"Now let me have my granddaughter back for she must be cleaned, and you have yet to give me the afterbirth. We will plant it beneath an oak tree on the estate so that Aine Mary Devers will always be strong." Jasmine took the child, and gave it to Toramalli. Then she encouraged her second daughter to finish the business of birthing. And when mother and newborn were properly cleaned up, Fortune tucked into her bed, Aine in her cradle by the fire with the faithful Rohana seated next to her to watch over her, Jasmine brought her daughter a strengthening drink.

Slowly Fortune sipped it down. She was suddenly so worn, and very, very sleepy. Her eyes closed, and Jasmine just caught the half-empty goblet as it was about to fall from Fortune's hand. She smiled down at her child. How the years had flown, but she was grateful that she had been able to be with Fortune at this time. Soon her child would be gone from her. It was unlikely they would ever meet again for, Jasmine thought, I am not of a mind to cross any more oceans. She caressed Fortune's smooth forehead lovingly, then she crossed the chamber to look at her new grand-daughter. The child was fair even as her mother had been. Kieran Devers wouldn't be disappointed, and there would be plenty of time for sons when Fortune got to Mary's Land.

"Watch for a bit, Rohana," she said to her serving woman. "I'll send Joan, or Polly to relieve you in a little while."

"Yes, my lady," Rohana replied. "She's a fine little lass, isn't she? I'm sorry we won't get to see her grow up."

Jasmine sighed. "I am too," she replied, "but Aine has her own fate, and only time will tell us what it is."

Chapter
16

"Mama! Mama! The captain of the *Cardiff Rose* is here!" Fortune called excitedly. "Oh, sir, we thought you should never come! Tell me how my husband is, *please!* When are we to leave for Mary's Land?" She whirled about. "Rois! We must start packing!"

"Captain O'Flaherty? I am Jasmine Leslie," the duchess of Glenkirk said as she came forward, her hand outstretched.

Ualter O'Flaherty took the elegant hand, and kissed it. "We are cousins, madame, having the glorious Skye O'Malley in common for a grandmother. As we have never met, I wanted to come personally to deliver Kieran's messages to his wife, and to you. I hope you will forgive my unannounced arrival." He bowed smartly, and smiled at the two women, thinking that his cousin Jasmine's beauty had not been exaggerated. The garnet red gown she wore certainly complemented her dark hair and exotic turquoise blue eyes. And Kieran's wife was equally beautiful with her red hair, and blue-green eyes so like his own, so like Skye O'Malley's.

"You are more than welcome, Cousin. You must be one of

my hardly-ever-seen Uncle Ewan's sons, are you not?" Jasmine asked.

"His youngest son, and next to last child," the captain said.

"Tell us of Mary's Land," Fortune said.

"I think we should offer our cousin some refreshment first, and ask him to sit by the fire," the duchess told her daughter. "June is such a fussy month. Warm one minute, and cold the next. It has been raining for three days now. It must have been a chilly ride."

"Being at sea teaches one to get used to all weather, especially the inclement, madame," he replied with a smile, taking a goblet of wine as it was offered to him.

They sat down by the blazing fire in the hall, and the captain handed Fortune a large packet.

"What is it?" she wondered aloud, taking it from him.

"Your husband kept a daily record of his experiences, and he has sent it to you along with a letter, my lady Fortune," Ualter O'Flaherty said. He sipped the wine appreciatively.

"Is he well?" Fortune asked softly.

"He was in the best of health and spirits when I left him, my lady. The crossing was the best, I am told by the other captains more familiar with an Atlantic crossing, that any of them had ever had. The Virginians welcomed us, and the land that has become Mary's Land is beautiful beyond measure, but your husband's diary will tell you everything you need to know, my dear lady. We have brought back a cargo of salt fish from the Plymouth colony, which we called in on during our return journey, as well as beaver and fox furs. It will make the round trip a profitable one for you, my lady."

"You will remain with us for a few days, Cousin," Jasmine extended the invitation.

"I would be honored, madame," he answered her.

Fortune tore open the packet as they talked. It was a great temptation to read Kieran's letter first, but instead she began to read the journal of his travels, knowing he had written it in order to make her a part of the voyage she could not take, but soon would. She read the afternoon through, and the servants were setting the high board for the evening meal when she finally opened her husband's letter. She read it through, swearing softly under her breath as she did. Then she turned to Captain O'Flaherty.

"Do you know what is in this letter, Cousin?" she asked him.

"I do," he said.

"And you agree with my husband's assessment of the situation? Has he not made the situation a bit worse than it actually is? I expect Kieran wants everything perfect for me when I arrive, but it doesn't have to be perfect, sir," Fortune said.

"Nay, my lady Fortune. He has not equivocated in the least. Mary's Land is a wilderness, and the western shore where its first settlement is, is a forested region. There is much work to be done to make it habitable for civilized folk. The few women who came aboard the *Ark* and the *Dove* are putting up with a great deal of hardship."

Fortune pressed her lips together, irritated. This was not what she wanted to hear.

"What is it?" Jasmine asked her daughter.

"Kieran doesn't want us to come until *next* summer," she said. "The land has not yet been divided, and he claims they are living in an Indian village with the savages. I knew I should have gone!"

Jasmine looked to Captain O'Flaherty.

"We only arrived in late March," he began. "The main expedition was delayed on the Isle of Wight for over a month. Governor Calvert sent word to the *Cardiff Rose,* which was waiting off Cape Clear, to go ahead and meet them in Barbados. We took the southern, and rather roundabout route because of the unreliability of late autumn weather."

"A wise precaution," Jasmine agreed.

"The *Ark* did not arrive until January. Then the *Dove* straggled in ten days later. By the time we had taken on fresh water and supplies, and sailed through the Caribbean, and up the coast past the Spanish colonies, it was already spring. We stopped in at the Virginias, remained for several days, and then went on to Mary's Land. It was on the twenty-fifth day of March the colony was founded."

"Aine's birthday!" Fortune said.

"Aine?" He looked puzzled.

"Aine Mary Devers, my daughter," was the reply. "The child I remained to bear," she explained. "I bore a lass on March twenty-fifth, and Rois, my serving woman, Kevin's wife, bore a son, Brendan, two days later on March twenty-seventh."

"Your husband will be delighted," Ualter O'Flaherty said. "He fretted a great deal about you, and the bairn. I can't wait to see the look on his face when I tell him."

"I shall tell him myself," Fortune said.

"Wait, poppet," her mother said. "I want to know more about the living conditions in Mary's Land right now. Cousin?"

"The colonists found a village of Wicocomoco Indians on a small river north of the Potomac. The governor liked the region, and asked permission of the local chief to settle there. The area is well-watered and has a suitable deep water anchorage for seagoing vessels. The Indians have been having difficulties with a larger tribe, the more war-like Susquehanocks. They had been planning to move their village to another location. They agreed to share the village with us in return for our protection until they could relocate. The settlers are living in Indian wigwams, which are made of grasses, mud, sticks, and animal skins. It's primitive, and it's rough. When the Indians have finally gone, the colonists must build a fortification first with a guardhouse, a palisade, and a storeroom for the food. Such work requires all the men working together. No one can begin to build themselves a house until the fort is raised.

"Even now the *Cardiff Rose* is onloading more supplies for the colony. The governor has given orders that no more women, and certainly no children, be brought over until next year when the colony is on a more stable footing. Your husband was going down to Virginia to purchase livestock and poultry for everyone when I left. His men are working hard. Mistress Jones and Taffy have been a godsend to the colony. That is the truth of what is happening, Cousin."

"If the governor has given orders that you cannot go, Fortune," Jasmine said, "then you cannot. It is just that simple. You can either come home with me to Glenkirk, or remain at Queen's Malvern. I know Charlie will not mind if we stay. I will remain with you, of course, until it is time for you to go, poppet."

"How can you bear to be so far for so long from Papa?" Fortune said. "Nay, Mama, you must return to Glenkirk."

"Your father will not mind an English summer as long as he is back in Scotland for the grouse hunting season," Jasmine chuckled. She had no intention of leaving Fortune. While this second daughter had never been as willful as her first, she would not put it past Fortune to dash to Liverpool and stow herself, Rois, and the babies aboard the *Cardiff Rose. It was not going to happen.* Her daughter would wait until Governor Calvert said it was time for the other women and children to come to Mary's Land. "You had best write to Rory Maguire so he may tell the women what is happening. Explain the primitive living conditions, and that they are to prepare to leave next summer," the duchess suggested.

"I still think Governor Calvert is being too damned cautious," Fortune complained.

Jasmine smiled blandly. " 'Twill be better for the bairns this way," she reasoned.

"But not for Rois and me," her daughter grumbled beneath her breath. "I miss my husband in my bed, and Rois misses Kevin, too."

Both Jasmine and Ualter O'Flaherty laughed at this frank comment.

"I'm happy to see the women in this family remain hotblooded," the captain remarked, and then chuckled richly as Fortune blushed.

* * *

James Leslie came down from Glenkirk to join his wife and daughters. Holding his new granddaughter in his arms he approved of her fully, and said so. His youngest daughter hid her face behind her small hands each time she saw her sire in the first two weeks he was at Queen's Malvern. Then suddenly one day Autumn bestowed a sweet smile upon her father, and they were friends. He was very relieved for he had developed a very soft spot in his heart for this wee lass of his own blood. He had not known either India or Fortune when they were this small.

"I want you to come home with me in September," he said to his wife one evening as they sat together in the hall.

"I'm afraid to leave Fortune alone," Jasmine said. "I fear she will seek out the first ship sailing for the New World, and try to join Kieran. She misses him terribly."

"She is a grown woman," the duke said. "I will gain her word of honor that she will wait for the *Cardiff Rose* to take her next year, darling Jasmine. I want you back at Glenkirk. If you and Autumn remain here, my wee lass will forget me again. I cannot stay, and leave Patrick alone so much. He needs our guidance if he is to one day take my place. You must come home."

"Nay, my Jemmie, I must stay. Once Fortune is gone from me, when shall I see her ever again? Autumn is just going to be two. Go back to Glenkirk in September, and come back to us before Christmastide. Patrick is a man now, and can manage alone without you. Can you go back to Scotland at summer's end knowing you will never again see Fortune? We need you with us, my love. 'Tis only a few months."

He acquiesced as she had known he would. The summer came, and in late August the duke of Glenkirk returned to Scotland, promising to come back in December. Charlie had joined them over the summer. Now he returned to court to support the king in his never-ending battle with the Puritans. They were growing stronger every year, and openly disapproved of everything about the king, and his French Catholic

queen, despite the fact she had already borne her husband and
the kingdom four children, of which three were living, two
being boys, and was again expecting a child. Even the baptism of each prince and princess in England's church did not
satisfy them. Parliament had been dissolved several years
prior, but the Puritans still grew more difficult and condemning of the king.

In October a gentleman came riding up to the front entry
of Queen's Malvern. He introduced himself as Sir Christian
Denby, and told them he had just inherited a small estate
nearby.

"I did not know that Sir Morton Denby had a son," the
duchess remarked, taking in the measure of the young man
before her. He was dressed quite simply and severely in
black with a starched white collar.

"He did not, madame. I am his brother's younger son.
Uncle was generous enough to leave Oakley to me, as my
elder brother will inherit our father's holdings one day.
Having come to inspect my estate, I thought I would call
upon my neighbors."

"I am sorry my son, the duke of Lundy, is not here to
meet you, Sir Christian," Jasmine said. "His uncle, the king,
requires him at court much of the year. I am the duchess of
Glenkirk, and this is my daughter, Lady Lindley."

Sir Christian bowed, then accepted a small goblet of wine
offered him by Adali. "You live here, madame?" The query
was bold, but Jasmine chose to be amused rather than offended. Obviously this young man was attempting to get the
lay of the land. He could only do so directly as he was not familiar with the surrounding area.

"Only in the summer months, sir. My home is in
Scotland, but my daughter has been here while her husband
is in the New World. Since she cannot join him until next
year I have decided to remain with her and her infant. I have
brought my youngest child with me for she is too young to
be separated from her mam. And your wife, sir? She is with
you?"

"I have not yet had the pleasure of connubial bliss, madame," he told her, and Fortune swallowed back a giggle. "Finding a wife in this day and age is not an easy task. I wish a lady who will be content to remain in the country. She must be godly in her devotions, modest in her dress and speech, obedient to my will, able to run my household properly, give me well-mannered sons and daughters, and have a respectable dowry. I find many of today's young women irreverent, flighty, and far too bold."

"You are a Puritan then," Jasmine said pleasantly.

"I am," he replied half-defiantly, as if he expected her to render some sort of criticism.

"We are Anglican," Jasmine noted.

"Your husband is in the Virginias?" Sir Christian turned to Fortune, who had Aine in her lap at that moment.

"Mary's Land, sir," Fortune said.

"The Catholic colony? The king should have never allowed such a thing, and would not have but for the wicked intrigues of his queen and her friends! Your husband is a Catholic then."

"My husband is a Catholic," Fortune replied, "but Mary's Land is a place where all men and women of good will may live in peace. Most of its colonists are Protestants, sir."

"So they would have you believe, madame, but we know the truth. Lord Baltimore hopes to invade the Virginias, and gain them for the Spanish who are his allies," Sir Christian said venomously.

Fortune laughed aloud. "That is the most ridiculous thing I have ever heard, sir. You are a fool to listen to such rumors, and it is wrong to repeat such false gossip."

"Then why, madame, if I may be so bold, are you not with your husband?" Her antagonist's black eyes were brazenly questioning.

"Because, sir, there is currently no decent housing for us. I go in the spring, by which time that situation will be remedied."

Sir Christian looked at Aine. Reaching out he tipped her tiny chin up. "Your babe will be raised a Catholic?"

Aine took one look at the man and burst into tears.

"Take your hand off my daughter, sir," Fortune said quietly, and then she comforted the baby softly.

"We are pleased to have met you, sir," the duchess said, dismissing Sir Christian as politely as she could.

He arose. "How can you allow your own grandchild to be raised a Catholic?" he said low.

"You are, sir, far too brazen with your queries, and out of your depth, I fear," the duchess of Glenkirk said.

With a sketchy bow Sir Christian Denby left the hall.

Aine had at last stopped crying. "What an unpleasant man," Fortune remarked. "I hope we do not have to see him again."

Autumn Leslie celebrated her second birthday at the end of October. Jasmine and Fortune then journeyed two days overland to Cadby to meet the young woman Henry Lindley was considering as a wife. He would not tell his mother her name, teasing her in their correspondence that it was to be a surprise. And indeed it was. Henry Lindley had chosen for his bride Cecily Burke, daughter of Lord Burke of Clearfields, his mother's uncle. Cecily was three years younger than Henry; a beautiful young woman with her father's dark hair, and the family's blue-green eyes. She was Padraic's and Valentina's youngest daughter.

"But how . . . ?" his mother queried Henry, truly surprised.

"I know," he said. "We hadn't met since we were children at some great party at Queen's Malvern. I went to court last winter at Charlie's behest, and there was Cecily, a maid-of-honor to the queen because she speaks such perfect French. I fear, Mama, it was love at first sight. I have been to Clearfields several times, and Cecily and her family have been here at Cadby a number of times."

"And you never told me!" Jasmine didn't know if she should be angry or not, but Fortune laughed.

"Why Henry, I should have never taken you for a romantic," she teased her big brother.

"Ohh, Cousin," Cecily said quickly, "he is most romantic!"

They all laughed at the ingenuous remark by the bride-to-be.

"Uncle," Jasmine turned to Padraic Burke, "could you not have said *something?* You are still capable of writing, and do not look either infirm or slow of wit to me."

"What was I to say?" Lord Burke demanded. "I could be certain of nothing until this son of yours asked my permission. He was quite concerned because they are cousins, but they are not first cousins, and so I feel the consanguinity is of little import. But tell me, Niece, what your opinion is on this matter?"

"I am content with my son's choice, although actually Cecily and I belong to the same generation, Uncle, for you are my mother's older brother," Jasmine noted.

Cecily Burke laughed, and her eyes twinkled. "Then," she said mischievously, "the children Henry and I have will be his generation, will they not, madame?"

"God's blood!" the marquess of Westleigh said, which caused his family to burst into great laughter.

A party was held to celebrate the betrothal, and to Fortune's surprise Sir Christian Denby was there. Attaching himself to Fortune he remained by her side all evening, although she attempted to dismiss him coolly.

"You should not be unescorted, madame," he told her.

"I am in my brother's house," Fortune replied.

"Your neckline is far too low," he said, but he could scarce take his eyes from her cleavage.

"Does the sight of my breasts disturb you, sir?" she mocked him. "You are free to look away, I assure you."

"How can I when you display your wares so boldly for all to see," he responded. "Are you seeking to take a lover in your husband's absence, madame? I am told your mother once displayed such proclivities."

Fortune gasped, shocked, and not certain for a moment that she had heard Sir Christian correctly, but then he spoke again.

"Was she not Prince Henry's whore, madame?" he said.

Fortune slapped her companion as hard as she might, but aware of the place, she then turned and walked away. Immediately Henry Lindley was at his sister's side.

"What has happened?" he demanded.

"Why did you invite *that* man to your house?" Fortune asked.

"He is the cousin of one of my neighbors, and new to the vicinity. He is wife hunting, and my neighbor thought such a gathering at Cadby would be an ideal place for Sir Christian to observe the local belles. What is the matter, Fortune? Why did you slap the man?"

"Because he has insulted me, and he has insulted Mama as well, Henry." Then she went on to tell her brother what Sir Christian Denby had said to her. "He is a Puritan, Henry. I should not have him in the house, but you must not spoil Cecily's night by causing a scene and escorting the black-guard from your house. Just keep him away from me!"

Back at Queen's Malvern Sir Christian Denby paid them another call, pushing past the servants into the hall where Jasmine and Fortune sat. "I have come to tender my apologies to you both," he declared.

Fortune stood up. *"Get out!"* she said angrily. "How dare you invade our home without invitation? You are not welcome here, sir!"

"It is only my concern for you, a woman alone, madame, that causes me to behave so," he said.

"I am hardly alone, sir. My mother and my sister are with me. I have a daughter. The house is full of servants who have known me all my life, and my stepfather will be shortly coming down from Scotland to spend the months until I leave with us. *I am not alone!"*

"I must speak with you alone, Lady Lindley. I fear for your child. You must not raise her Catholic lest you condemn her sinful soul without hope of salvation, and into an eternal hellfire," Sir Christian Denby said earnestly.

"If you believe that, sir, then I feel very sorry for you," Fortune said angrily. "What sort of God do you worship? My daughter is innocent of any sin, as are all bairns. *Get out!* Do not come back!"

"Adali," Jasmine said quietly. "Escort the gentleman from the house, and see he is not allowed entry ever again."

"Yes, my princess," Adali replied, coming abreast of the unwelcome guest and conducting him swiftly from the hall.

"My God!" Fortune said despairingly. "What makes people think like that, Mama? Why is there such hate in the world for another faith, another clan? I will never understand such thoughts!"

"Nor I, nor did your grandfather," Jasmine said quietly. "I suppose we must pity Sir Christian, who certainly does not live up to his name."

"He frightens me, Mama. And his harping on Aine's salvation. He spoke of it to me at Cadby before he insulted us. I do not want him anywhere near my child. He is evil!"

Personally Jasmine agreed with her daughter, but she said nothing, instead soothing Fortune as best she could. She advised Adali, however, that her granddaughter was to be watched carefully at all times.

James Leslie came down from Scotland just before the twelve days of Christmas began. Henry came from Cadby with Cecily and her parents, for it had been decided that the young couple would wed on December thirty-first in the chapel at Queen's Malvern. The celebration made for a happy time, bringing back to them all the many family gatherings that had once been held at Queen's Malvern in the time of Skye O'Malley and her husband, Adam de Marisco. The family chapel, that had seen several weddings in its day, was warm with winter sunlight. Little Autumn Leslie preceded the bride in her first public duty.

Reaching the altar rail, she suddenly turned about and said in a tiny piping voice, "Mama, where do I go now?"

A chuckle arose from the assembled guests, and Charles Frederick Stuart, home for Henry's wedding, quickly picked his baby sister up and said softly to her, "Why into my arms, my lady Autumn, is where you go now." And when Autumn smiled sweetly at him, Charlie wondered if perhaps he shouldn't start giving thought to finding a wife himself, but as swiftly decided that perhaps he was still too young. After all, Henry was practically twenty-six, and he was only just twenty-two.

The winter set in, and while the days were once again growing longer, the winds were cold, and the snow blew gustily about the house on many a day. Still, by the time Aine Mary Devers celebrated her first birthday there were daffodils in the gardens of Queen's Malvern. In all the time since Captain O'Flaherty had come calling last summer, there had been no word at all from Kieran. Still, Fortune knew her time in England was coming to an end. Then one day they had a visitor.

"I am Johnathan Kira," he introduced himself. "I am in charge of the family's business in Liverpool, my lady." It was Jasmine to whom he spoke. "I am informed by our people in Ireland, that your daughter's vessel, the *Cardiff Rose,* was sighted a hundred nautical miles, or perhaps slightly more, off Cape Clear a week ago. I thought I would come to Queen's Malvern to see how I may be of help to Lady Fortune now that she is about to leave for Mary's Land, and also to ask a favor."

"What is the favor, Master Kira?" Fortune inquired.

"First a question or two, my lady," came the smiling reply. "Is it really true that Mary's Land is for all men, no matter their faith? And if that is so, would you allow my second son, Aaron, to travel with your party? If there is a place where he will not be persecuted, then the Kira family is of a mind to set up a branch of its business in the New World. Would a Jew be welcome in Mary's Land?"

"I can only tell you what I know myself," Fortune said. "Lord Baltimore himself told us that *all* people, no matter their religious faith, would be welcome in Mary's Land. If that is so, then surely there is a place for your son, sir. I will be more than happy to offer him passage on the *Cardiff Rose* when I sail. Your family has done business with my family, and my stepfather's family, for many generations."

"I thank you, my lady," Johnathan Kira bowed.

"Ye'll stay wi us the night," the duke said.

"I am grateful, my lord, for your hospitality," came the reply. "However, you must not be offended if I eat only the foodstuffs I have brought with me. Our dietary laws are quite strict, and when I travel I must bring my own food lest I violate them."

"What will your son do aboard ship then, sir?" Fortune asked him. "We will be at sea several weeks."

"He, too, will bring his food with him. When and if he runs out, he will do his best to keep to our code. In extraordinary circumstances it can be forgiven when a man must break the law," Johnathan Kira explained to Fortune. "Besides, Aaron is young, and his conscience does not often trouble him over any matter." He smiled at her.

Adali hurried into the hall, and going to Jasmine he bent and whispered in his mistress's ear. Jasmine grew visibly pale.

"What is it?" the duke asked his wife.

Jasmine looked to her daughter, anguished. "Rois has been found in the garden where she was with the children. She was unconscious. Brendan was safe in his basket asleep, but Aine is missing."

"Oh, God!" Fortune cried, jumping up.

"Is Rois conscious yet?" the duke demanded of Adali.

"She is coming around, my lord, but the blow to her head was a hard one. 'Tis fortunate she wasn't killed, I think. We have carried her into the house, and Polly is sitting with her. Brendan yet slumbers."

"Sir Christian Denby," Fortune said angrily. "I shall kill him when I find him, *and I will!*"

"What?" her mother said. "What is this you say, Fortune?"

"Aine has been stolen by Sir Christian Denby. I am certain of it! All he has done in the time we have been acquainted with him is fret that my daughter would be raised a Catholic. The man is a fanatic, Mama. You, yourself, recognized that."

"You canna accuse him wiout proof, lass," the duke told her.

"What kind of proof would you have me bring before you, Papa? My instinct tells me it is Sir Christian. Who else would take Aine? *And why?* Are the women of this region so bereft of bairns that they would dare to steal mine? Or perhaps you think it gypsies? There have been none hereabouts. *It is that man!* Every fiber of my being tells me this is so, Papa. You must mount a party of your men at once and find him, and my child," Fortune said angrily. "I will ride with you."

"Your daughter is most certainly correct," Johnathan Kira said quietly. "My lord, if you will allow me to speak. There have been rumors about this man for some time now."

"Rumors of what sort?" the duke asked.

"Infants, and small children, my lord. Catholic, Anglican, even a Jew or two, all who have disappeared while Sir Christian Denby was in the vicinity. Usually these have been the children of unimportant people who had neither the power, the authority, or the wealth to complain or seek their children out. It is said these children are placed with loyal Puritan families to be raised *properly.* I believe Lady Fortune's instincts to be absolutely correct in this particular instance. With your, with her permission, I should like to ride over to Oakley to speak with the gentleman in question."

"What can ye do to help us?" the duke demanded.

"Let us say, my lord, that I may have a small influence with Sir Christian. Time is of the essence, my lord. He will not have yet had time to dispose of your granddaughter. There are no Puritan families in the near vicinity. He will have to take her somewhere else. It is too late in the day for him to begin his travels, my lord. Let me help, if indeed I can."

Before James Leslie might say another word, Fortune said, "Go, Master Kira. Go now, and bring my daughter back."

Johnathan Kira bowed politely to Fortune, and then, turning, hurried from the hall.

James Leslie smiled a cynical smile as he watched the man go. The Kiras were an amazing family. He didn't doubt for a moment that if Sir Christian Denby had Aine in his custody, she would be returned to them this very night. "Adali," he called. "Send some of the men to escort Master Kira, and give him the protection he may need."

With a matching smile of irony, Adali moved quickly to obey.

Johnathan Kira was not surprised to shortly find himself amid a troop of Leslie clansmen. He nodded politely to their captain, and then continued silently on his way. He was a tall, spare man of indeterminate age with dark hair, a dark beard, and fine dark eyes. He wore dark clothing of a most fashionable cut. Those who did not know his smile found him rather intimidating. It was a trait that served him well. Within the hour he was at the front door of Oakley Hall. Dismounting he ordered his companions to await him, and then knocked loudly upon the door.

The door was opened by a liveried servant. "Take me to your master," he said sternly.

Cowed by Johnathan Kira's air of authority the servant obeyed, showing the dark-clothed visitor into his master's library. Just as they entered the room the cry of a child was heard from above stairs.

Johnathan Kira smiled knowingly to himself, and pushing the servant back into the passageway he closed the library door behind him, saying as he did, "Good evening, Sir Christian."

His host looked up, startled, then jumped up from his chair where he had been reading a tract on the Bible. "Kira! What are you doing here? My loan is not yet due. I will pay you when it is."

"I have come for Aine Devers, Sir Christian," Johnathan Kira said without dissembling. "Give me the child to return to her family, and you and I will have no difficulty."

"I do not know what you mean," Sir Christian said, not looking directly at his uninvited guest.

"Ahh," Johnathan Kira replied, "you are going to be foolish. How lamentable. You are fortunate the maidservant is not dead, only injured, else you would hang for murder. If you had taken her child, there would have been far less of an outburst, for the little boy is a Catholic of two Irish parents. Aine Devers, no matter her religion, is the grandchild of a duke, and the niece of several wealthy noblemen, one of whom is the king's nephew. You cannot hope to get away with this particular kidnapping."

"Get out of my house!" Sir Christian blustered.

"Your house?" Johnathan Kira laughed darkly. "Until you pay us back, Sir Christian Denby, it is not your house. I am well within my right, Jew I may be, to call in the loan we have made you. If I do, what will you have then? A worthless title, a mountain of debts, and nothing else. Is your possession of this child worth all of that? How will you help your fellow Puritans to lobby against the king if I strip you of the small power you possess right now through us? Fetch the child at once, and give her to me. If you do not, I shall open the door of this house to the duke's men who have accompanied me this night. They will search, and they will find the child, whom I have already heard crying on an upper floor. Then the matter becomes a public one, and you, sir, are ruined. *If,* however, you give me the child now, the matter re-

mains private, and we will not call your loan in for some time to come. I have said all I will on the matter. Bring me the child!"

"Devil's spawn!" snarled Sir Christian. "You dirty Jews are all the devil's own!" Then he pushed past Johnathan Kira, saying brusquely, "Follow me, and you shall have what you came for this night!"

With a small smile of triumph Johnathan Kira walked after his host who, going to the foot of the house stairs in the square entry foyer, called up to some nameless soul to bring the baby down to him. The order was quickly obeyed, and a serving woman came into view carrying Aine Devers.

Sir Christian took the baby roughly from the woman, and thrust her into Johnathan Kira's arms. "Here is the child who is now doomed to roast in eternal hellfire!" he spat at his antagonist.

"Thank you," Johnathan Kira said calmly. "And if you read your Bible correctly, Sir Christian, you would discover that we Jews are called God's *chosen* people. It is also a fact that Yushua of Nazareth, whom you call Jesus, was also a Jew. Good evening to you, sir." Johnathan Kira walked from the house with his prize, and handed her up to the Leslie captain. "Let us return to Queen's Malvern now," he said. Then he chucked the baby under the chin. "You have had quite an adventure, little one," he remarked. "Well, you are safe now, and on your way home to your mother, praise Yahweh!"

"Ma-ma!" Aine said forlornly. "Ma-ma."

He smiled a kindly smile at her, transforming his usually severe features. "Yes, Mistress Aine. You are going home to your mama."

They rode back through the spring twilight, the smells of newly turned earth, early blooming bushes, and flowers, cleansing the air and tickling their nostrils. Fortune was awaiting them at the door, and snatched her child down from the captain's arms, clutching Aine to her bosom, and sobbing softly.

"Ma-ma!" Aine's small voice was now happy.

"Aye, baby, I am your mama, and you are safe home." She kissed Aine's red head. Then her eyes went to Johnathan Kira. "Your son need only come aboard the *Cardiff Rose* with his personal supplies of food. Everything else he will need will be supplied for him, I promise you. You will transfer immediately one quarter of my funds to his care, Master Kira. And when we are settled in Mary's Land, another quarter is to be transferred. The other half I will leave here in England. You and your son will have my everlasting friendship for what you have done this night. But how?"

"Sir Christian inherited a tumbled-down house, my lady, with his title, but nothing more. He needed funds to restore the house, and invest in a venture that would make him independent enough that he might attract a wife with a good dowry. He came to the Kiras, and now he is in our debt. He had to decide whether he would lose everything he had gained this night, or return your child. Fortunately he chose wisely."

They walked back into the house. "Thank God you were here with us else I might never have regained my daughter without violence," Fortune said softly. She kissed the baby again, and handed her to Rohana to put to bed.

"Your serving woman?"

"She regained consciousness, and told us that Sir Christian and another man, probably his servant, had attacked her. The first blow they hit her with did not render her unconscious, and she saw them. She tried to scream, and they hit her a second time, but she recognized them," Fortune explained. "She will, with rest, be all right, thank God. I do not know how I would have told her Kevin if anything had happened to her. Come into the hall and have a goblet of wine. You can have it, can't you?"

"In my own cup," he chuckled.

"How long have our families been associated?" Fortune asked him curiously. "It has been many years, hasn't it?"

"Aye," he told her. "Your stepfather's revered ancestress, a great and powerful woman, made friends with my revered ancestress, Esther Kira. The two women aided each other in many ways, and through the influence of one, the other grew powerful and wealthy, too. That, I am told, is how it all began over a century ago. Then your mother's grandmother began dealing with us, and we found that she, too, was a woman of great intellect, honor, and ethics. That was over seventy years ago. Then parts of the two families intertwined in marriage, continuing to deal with the Kiras. It has, my lady, been a successful collaboration."

"May it continue to be so in the New World," Fortune told him sincerely with a smile.

"Amen," Johnathan Kira intoned. "Amen to that, my lady."

Chapter
17

Once again Fortune stood at the rail of the *Cardiff Rose* watching with interest as the landscape of her new homeland came into view. The beauty of it was so incredible that she almost wept. There was this strong feeling of belonging that she had never before experienced. Kieran had been right. *This was home.* It was unlike anything she had ever before seen. The bays through which they now sailed were huge. The waters very, very blue. Above her the sun shone in a cloudless sky. How different from their departure from England a month and a half ago.

The late spring day had been gray and rainy, and Fortune Lindley Devers had found herself suddenly afraid. She stood with her mother, and the only father she had ever known upon the ship's deck prior to their departure. Jasmine's eyes were red with evidence of weeping although she now seemed calm and in control of herself. Even James Leslie was unusually silent as he held Aine in his arms.

"We'll have to cast off soon, Cousin," Ualtar O'Flaherty

said as he joined them. "The tide will shortly be with us." Then he moved away to give them the privacy they so obviously needed.

"Ye'll come back one day to see us," James Leslie said suddenly.

Fortune felt the tears pricking at her eyelids. "I don't think so, Papa," she told him. "I am not brave, or venturesome, like Mama and India. Once I cross the ocean safely, I shall remain where I am, I fear. Remember," she said, giving him a weak smile, "I am the practical and sensible daughter."

"If you had been sensible," Jasmine said almost bitterly, "you would not have fallen in love with Kieran Devers." Her heart was breaking with the certain knowledge that she would never again in her lifetime see this second daughter of hers and Rowan's. Fortune would be as gone from her as surely as Rowan had been gone all these years. Jasmine could feel the anger welling up in her. Then she swallowed it back. It was not Kieran's fault, or Fortune's fault that this situation had come to pass. It was the fault of ignorant and narrow-minded people who could not accept anyone who was in the slightest manner different from them. People who wanted everyone to look alike, to think alike, to worship alike. Joyless souls who could not accept a God of love, but must have a condemning deity of fire and brimstone to worship. She pitied them, but at the same time Jasmine silently cursed them, for it was their intolerance that was causing her daughter to go.

"Mama." Fortune touched her sleeve. "It is time, Mama. You and Papa must go ashore now. We must say good-bye."

Jasmine turned stricken eyes to her daughter. *No!* the voice in her head cried out, and then Fortune spoke again.

"I am so grateful for you and Papa, for all the good times we have had together. I shall always remember it, Mama, even if I grow to be an old lady. Do not grieve for me. I am doing what I am meant to do. I love Kieran. I will love our new life in Mary's Land. I will send you letters each time the

Cardiff Rose makes the journey between there and here. You will hardly notice I am gone. I know that you want me to be happy, Mama." Then Fortune put her arms about her mother, and embraced her tenderly. "Farewell, Mama. Always remember that I love you, and Papa, and all my family here. Do not forget me." She kissed her mother's cheek. Drawing away from Jasmine she bid the duke of Glenkirk an equally tender farewell. "Thank you, Papa, for taking Rowan Lindley's last daughter, and loving her as your very own." Then she kissed him too, quickly turning away lest her own emotions overcome her and she lose what small courage she had, and they all dissolve into a paroxysm of sorrow.

The warm breeze touched her cheek, and Fortune brought herself back to the present. Her eyes were teary with her memories. Their crossing from England had been a relatively easy one. There had been no serious storms, and only a few gray days of drizzling rain. They had first stopped in Ireland to pick up the women and children from Maguire's Ford and Lisnaskea who would be traveling with them. The *Highlander* had already departed Ulster several days earlier with the horses and other livestock they would be taking to Mary's Land. Still, Rory Maguire was there in Dundalk to greet her, having escorted the colonists himself.

"So, lassie, and yer finally off on yer great adventure," he said, kissing her cheek. "Where is this daughter of yers now? I would see her, Fortune Devers."

Rois came forward with the two children, and Rory's eyes lit up at the sight of them. He took Aine into his arms.

"Ahh," he said softly, "she's a fine lassie, Fortune." Then, as an afterthought, he said to Rois, "Look to the gangway, Rois. Here is yer grandmam. Come aboard, Bride Duffy, and see the fine great-grandson yer lass has had."

"Did you bring the whole village?" Fortune teased him as they walked the deck with Aine.

"Well, Fergus had to drive one of the wagons that brought the women and children, and their goods and chattels. Nothing would do but Bride would come along with him," Rory chuckled, and when he did, Aine laughed too. "So you find that funny, do you?" He tickled her, eliciting even further laughter. *His granddaughter!* His eyes devoured Aine eagerly, then swept to Fortune. *His daughter.* 'Twas the last time he would see them, and he had been unable to resist the opportunity to do so. He sighed. Part of him wanted her to know the truth, but he could not, would not destroy her identity to soothe his aching heart. There was always the possibility she would hate him for it. Better the secret remain his burden.

"How are my brothers doing?" Fortune asked him.

"Well," was the reply. "Adam is a man of the earth without a doubt, and Duncan continues to be the scholar. They are both well-liked."

"And the peace holds in Maguire's Ford?"

He nodded. "But nowhere else in Ireland. 'Tis getting worse, Fortune, and it will continue to get worse until the English are gone from our lands."

"Kieran's brother, and his family?" Fortune asked. "I would bring him what news I can."

"Sir William continues his tyrannies from his sickbed. His misfortune has not softened him, but rather made him more vicious. He will, I fear, live to be an old man. It is rumored that even his mother and wife are now afraid of him. As for his daughter, he barely acknowledges her. 'Tis sad, but the man will forever be bitter over losing you, and over losing the use of his legs."

Fortune considered now if she would tell her husband Rory's news, or simply say nothing. A flock of geese flew over the ship's bow towards the western shore. Fortune smiled happily. Soon! Soon she would be in her husband's arms, and it had been so damned long! She wondered what awaited them, for there was no evidence of any civilization along the forested banks of the great bay. They would be landing at St. Mary's Town, the Calvert's settlement, this day. It couldn't be soon enough.

The other women were crowding the rails, peering at the landscape.

"It's all trees."

"Do you see the wild Indians?"

"I don't know which will be worse. Protestants or Indians."

"It's pretty enough."

"Ulster was pretty."

" 'Tis a chance to live in peace, and have our own lands. That's enough for me to leave Ulster!"

"Will there be a priest?"

"Aye, so they say."

"Thank God for that!"

Fortune listened, half-amused. It was good to know these women had been just as nervous as she had been about the voyage, and its eventual end. What would her new home be like? Had the *Highlander* made the crossing in safety? All of her wordly goods, along with the horses, had been aboard the smaller vessel. And what little the other colonists had was spread between the two vessels. She wondered what Kieran would say when he saw Aine. With God's blessing she intended giving her husband a son as quickly as possible. None of Mama's special potion for now.

"Look!" one of the women suddenly cried out. "I see buildings!"

"There's a church spire!"

"Praise be to God!"

Ualtar O'Flaherty came down from the wheel deck where he had been standing, and smiled at the women. "Well, now, lassies, if you intend looking yer best for yer men, you had best go below now. We'll be shortly landing at St. Mary's Town." Shooing their children before them, the women disappeared below.

Aaron Kira came to join them. " 'Tis a wild place, m'lady.

I wonder if there is any business to be had here. Time will tell."

Over the water came the sound of a cannon booming.

"They've sighted us," the captain continued, "and have signaled all their citizens that we'll be docking soon." He turned to Fortune. "Well, Cousin, yer almost home. Kieran will be eagerly awaiting you, I know. It's a very different place yer coming to, Fortune, and you must be prepared. He'll have a house built by now, I know, but it will not be the kind of house you're used to at all. Later, you will have a better one, but this first home will not be at all what you may have envisioned. The conditions are still very primitive."

"You frighten me, Ualter," she answered him.

"I don't mean to," he answered her. " 'Tis just that your new home will be nothing like Queen's Malvern, or your stepfather's castle, or even Erne Rock. 'Twill appear more like a large, rustic cottage."

"As long as I don't have to live in a wigwam as the settlers did last year," she told him. Then she smiled. "This is not the old world, Ualter. I know. 'Twill all be very new, but one thing will not be new. The love Kieran and I have for each other."

"Yer a brave lass," he said.

The *Cardiff Rose* sailed gracefully into St. Mary's crescent-shaped harbor, and docked shortly thereafter. Fortune and Rois stood holding their children in their arms, their eyes scanning the crowd on the wharf below. About them the other women and children crowded, some of them already weeping with the sight of their men. The gangway was lowered, and Captain O'Flaherty escorted his cousin and her party ashore, but there was no sign of Kieran. Then Kevin appeared, enfolding Rois and Brendan into his arms, his eyes wet with his tears of joy. Fortune waited while they greeted one another with kisses and caresses, Kevin admiring the son he had never seen. Brendan was not certain if he should cry or not at the sight of this big man who was hugging him so hard. Finally Kevin realized that his mistress was waiting silently. He broke away from Rois, and bowed to Fortune.

"Welcome to Mary's Land, m'lady. You'll be pleased to learn that the *Highlander* docked over a week ago. The horses are already settled in their meadow, and yer goods are safely at Fortune's Fancy."

"Fortune's Fancy?" She looked puzzled.

Kevin grinned. " 'Tis what the master calls the estate, m'lady," he told her. " 'Tis a fine house we've built for you, and the wee lass."

"Where is my husband?" Fortune asked. "Is he all right? Why isn't he here to meet us, Kevin?" Her lovely face was concerned.

" 'Tis that troublesome indentured wench, m'lady. She's been told a hundred times not to wander into the forest, but she did this morning, and managed to get herself lost. Many Moons, the old Wicocomoco medicine man, brought her back, sobbing and howling that she was going to be scalped by the Indians. The master didn't want to leave her alone under the circumstances. He knew you would understand, m'lady."

"Poor girl," Fortune said, but she was not feeling any sympathy at all for this nameless indentured servant who had disobeyed Kieran. Perhaps when the mistress of Fortune's Fancy came home at last the girl could be guided, and learn to behave herself.

"I've brought the wagon, m'lady," Kevin said, interrupting her thoughts. "The ship's crew have loaded the goods you brought on it, and we had best get going. We're about five miles from the town."

"What of the other colonists?" Fortune asked him. "And Master Kira?"

"Their men know where to take them, m'lady," was the reply. "Master Kira, opposite the docks, that small house there"—he pointed—" 'tis been purchased for you, along with an indentured man." Aaron Kira thanked Kevin, kissed Fortune's hand, and bid her farewell before turning to go to his own establishment.

Kevin helped his mistress and his wife up onto the hard wooden seat of the wagon. Each woman held her child. Then climbing up, he signaled the horses to be on their way. Within minutes he and Rois were chattering away. Fortune listened briefly with half an ear, and then her thoughts turned to a husband who would remain with a hysterical servant rather than go to greet the wife he hadn't seen in almost two years. She wondered why she had bothered to dress in her finest gown for him. It seemed to her that Kieran had more care for a servant than his own wife. Had she made a mistake in marrying him? Had she made a mistake in coming across an ocean, and away from her loving family? She would soon find out. If he had changed she would return with Captain O'Flaherty to England in a few weeks. She wouldn't stay where she wasn't wanted or loved. Her fingers brushed the rich blue silk of her gown. The warm breeze blew the feathery white plumes in her hat, and brushed her cheek.

Kieran saw her seated up on the wagon's bench as it came up the dirt drive of the house. The blue of her gown was neither dark nor light. The deep snow-white linen collar edged in lace stood out against it. She wore leather gauntlets trimmed with fine gold lace. He had never seen her in a hat. She was so very elegant. Why on earth had she married *him?* Why had she traveled all this way to live in this primitive place? Did she still love him? Then he saw the small child, not even a baby, seated in her lap, and garbed identically to her mother. Kieran Devers felt his heart contract, and then seemingly crack. He could scarce find his voice when the wagon finally stopped before him.

"Kieran!" He had forgotten how sweet the sound of her voice was. She smiled, and then said, "I feared for your safety when you did not come to the ship to meet us. Will you not welcome us home, sir?"

"God's blood, I have missed you!" he burst out. The look in his dark blue eyes was burning, and she instantly forgot all her previous doubts, as did he at the sight of her face.

Rois plunked her son in his father's lap, and snatched Aine from her mother, singing a favorite ditty to the startled baby so she would not cry, and her parents could greet each other properly. Rois could well imagine her mistress's hurt that Kieran had not come to the ship.

The master of Fortune's Fancy lifted his wife down, drawing her into his arms, and kissing her passionately. His lips burned against hers. He felt his desire boiling up, and he wished they might slip away to make love for the next week, or two. Her arms about his neck, she pressed herself as tightly against him as she could, sighing with undisguised pleasure as he kissed her mouth, her face, her eyelids over and over again until her knees grew weak, and she cried, "Stop, my love!"

"I have missed you," he said in his deep voice. "I thought I knew how much until this moment. Now I realize I knew nothing, and my longing for you was inconsolable. Welcome home, my darling! Welcome home to Fortune's Fancy!" Then he was kissing her again, and she was reveling in his passion for her. It was going to be all right.

"Ma-ma!" Aine's small voice piped out, and there was a distinct sound of annoyance to it. Who was this man who was taking her mama from her?

Kieran and Fortune broke apart, laughing happily, and turning Fortune took her daughter from Rois, and handed her to Kieran.

"This is your papa, darling," she told her daughter.

Aine's eyes surveyed the big man holding her. She put her hands over her face, and then slyly surveyed him through her splayed fingers. "Pa-pa?" she said, tasting the word carefully. Then she began to squirm, demanding, "Down! Down!"

Kieran put the child down.

"No want Pa-pa," Aine said in firm tones, and turning, clung to her mother.

His face was surprised, and then heartbroken. "She doesn't like me," he said, stunned.

Fortune laughed, and turned her daughter over to Rois. "She isn't used to men in her life, that's all. Mama and I lived by ourselves at Queen's Malvern most of the time. When Papa was there he was more interested in courting Autumn, for he adores her, than in fussing over Aine. Our daughter will grow used to you in time, Kieran. Ignore her, and she will come to you, my darling. Now, I want to see my house!"

She stepped back from him, and looked at her new home. It was a story and a half high, constructed from lumber, with three brick chimneys, and a wooden roof. She was pleased to see the windows were of glass with heavy shutters flanking them. Captain O'Flaherty had been correct when he had said it would be different than anything she had ever known, or lived in. It certainly was.

"There's a cellar beneath the house," Kieran said in an effort to elicit some sort of opinion from her on the dwelling. "We'll replace the house eventually with one built of brick, but for now we can just make enough brick for chimneys."

Fortune nodded. Finally she said, "How big is it inside?"

"It has four rooms on the main floor, plus a buttery and small pantry," he told her. "The servants sleep on the upper floor which is not particularly big. Kevin and Rois have their own cottage nearby."

"Servants?" She was surprised, and then she remembered the indentured woman who had kept her husband from her. "How many?"

"In the house three bondwomen, and in the barn four bondmen," he replied. "I purchased them in Virginia last year."

"Are not bondservants transported criminals?" she asked him.

"Some are," he answered her, "but many have been convicted of ridiculous offenses. Then there are those who have assigned themselves into bondage because after seven years of servitude they are freed, and given their own lands. Mrs. Hawkins, who is our cook, could not pay the physician who attended her dying husband. He had her transported. Dolly, who I bought to look after Aine, is a Catholic. Comfort Rogers, the maidservant, was caught stealing bread to feed her siblings. The four men I purchased to help in the fields and with the livestock are all Puritans. Those are their crimes, but they're welcome in Mary's Land. They are all good workers. I would not bring dangerous criminals into the house, my darling. God! You are so beautiful even in that silly hat with its white feathers." He kissed her again, this time hard, and quick.

Fortune laughed up at him. "This hat is all the fashion in London now. I shall be the envy of every lady in the colony."

"Come into the house, my love," he entreated her, taking her by the hand.

They entered the dwelling so Fortune might inspect it. She was somewhat taken aback to find that inside the walls were rough wood with mud set between the boards to help keep out the wind and rain. However, there was a center hallway that ran the length of the building. The floors were unfinished wooden boards. Thank heaven she had brought India carpets with her, Fortune thought. On the left side of the hallway was their bedchamber. On the right side was a salon. Behind their bedchamber was a tiny second bedchamber, access to which could only be gained through their room. Then running across the entire back of the house and at the end of the hallway was a large keeping room off of which, and almost as an afterthought, were the buttery and pantry.

"The walls have to be plastered at once," Fortune said firmly. "It will be much too cold in winter for Aine, and for me. The floors must be sanded and polished. Where is the furniture I brought with me?"

" 'Tis in the salon but for the bed which I have already set up," he told her, a meaningful look in his eye.

Fortune blushed, but it was a blush of pleasure, and of anticipation. If her husband was eager for her, she was equally eager for him. "The furniture will remain where it is until we plaster the walls. It will not look suitable against the rough boards."

"We will begin tomorrow before the summer damp sets in," he promised. "Come, and meet the house servants," he said, and they walked back to the room where three women were waiting for them.

One was plump and smiling with twinkling brown eyes. This was Dolly, who would watch over Aine. Fortune liked her at once. She curtsied to Fortune very politely.

"Do you know how old you are, Dolly?" Fortune asked her.

"I was born in the year they tried to blow up the Parliament," Dolly answered. "I don't hold with such things, m'lady."

Dolly would be thirty then. "Good," Fortune said, and her own voice was filled with laughter. "I don't hold with such things either. Will you mind having more than one bairn to look after? I plan on having more, and for now you will also have to watch over my Rois's lad. He is two days younger than my daughter. They can both walk and are inclined to get into mischief."

"I can manage," Dolly replied. "Had two of my own before the sickness took them, and my man in the prison."

Fortune felt tears spring into her eyes, and she reached out and comfortingly touched Dolly's hand. Their eyes met in a moment of understanding, and Fortune smiled at the woman.

"Here is Mrs. Hawkins, my darling. Without her we would not eat half as well as we do," Kieran said.

Fortune turned her attention to a tall, big-boned woman, who curtsied to her. "I can see how well fed my husband is, Mrs. Hawkins. I am grateful for your obvious talents."

Mrs. Hawkins smiled, and her teeth were every bit as big as the rest of her. "Thank ye, m'lady. I've a nice big turkey roasting on the spit for yer dinner, and I'm happy to serve ye."

"And this is Comfort Rogers, who keeps our house for us," Kieran said. "She had a bad fright this morning."

"So I have been told," Fortune replied dryly, looking over the bondwoman with a critical eye. Where the other two women were older, Comfort Rogers was barely out of her childhood, and she was very pretty with sandy-colored hair, and blue eyes. "Do you know your age, Comfort?" Fortune was frankly quite curious. The wench had a sly look about her.

"I be born in the year the old queen died, or so I was told," Comfort Rogers said. "Me mam died with the eighth baby, and me dad run off soon after. I be the oldest, and was transported for stealing bread to feed me brothers and sisters."

"What happened to them?" Fortune asked the girl.

Comfort shrugged. "Don't know," the girl said, seemingly unconcerned.

"And don't care," Fortune heard Mrs. Hawkins mutter under her breath.

"You will not wander into the woods again, Comfort?" Fortune fixed a stern gaze on the girl.

Comfort didn't answer. She just stared at Fortune.

"You have not answered me, Comfort," her mistress said.

"Didn't mean to get lost," Comfort replied. "I was looking for berries for Master Kieran's breakfast."

"Do not go into the woods again unless you have someone with you who can find their way back to the house," Fortune said firmly.

"You can't tell me what to do," Comfort said boldly. "Only the master can give me orders."

Before Kieran might remonstrate with the girl Mrs. Hawkins whacked her hard on her bottom with a large wooden spoon. "Mind yer manners, ye little London trull. This be the mistress of the house, and the house belongs to her, and all in it. It is she who will tell ye what to do, and ye will do it, Comfort Rogers, else she sell yer bond elsewhere, which I'm thinking would be a good idea." She turned to Fortune. "She can clean, I'll give her that, but she has no respect for her betters, m'lady. Didn't learn it in her own home, if indeed she ever had a home, and a mam she remembers."

"Master! Ohhh, master," Comfort howled, and flung herself at Kieran, clinging to him. "Don't let *her* send me away! *Please don't!*" She turned her head to look at Fortune.

"Now, now, lass, just do your work, and mind my good lady wife," Kieran said, "and we'll have no problems. Mrs. Hawkins knows the lay of the land. The house is indeed my lady's. Your loyalty should be first with your mistress." Kieran patted the girl on the shoulder, and untangled her from his person.

Fortune slipped her arm through her husband's. "You will call us when dinner is ready," she said to Mrs. Hawkins, ignoring Comfort.

"Yes, m'lady," came the prompt reply.

"Dolly, follow along, and come meet the children," Fortune said.

"Cow!" Comfort said when her master and mistress had gone.

"Ye'd best behave, wench. Her ladyship will be patient to a point, but then ye'll find yerself in a kettle of hot water. The master ain't for you, and he ain't never going to be," Mrs. Hawkins said.

"If she really loved him she would have come with him when he arrived in Mary's Land," Comfort said. "It's been almost two years since they've been together. Why didn't she come sooner if she loved him? Do you see how he looks at me? He wants me. I knows men."

Mrs. Hawkins sniffed scornfully. "Yer a fool, Comfort Rogers. The master don't look at you in any special way, if indeed he has looked at you at all. Her ladyship didn't come at first because she was with child. Then Governor Calvert ordered that no more women and children come until there was decent shelter for them. We had no choice in the matter being bondservants, but the master wanted her ladyship and his babe safe." She smiled slyly. "There'll be another babe born in this house within a year, I can tell you. Tonight, and for many nights to come, master will be plowing a good furrow with his lady."

Comfort glared at the older woman. "I hate you," she said.

Mrs. Hawkins cackled, pleased to have tweaked the uppity wench's temper. The girl was trouble, and had been from the start. Sadly the poor master couldn't see it, but then men were never very clever where women were concerned. But the mistress had seen it right away. Comfort Rogers would not get her own way with the master now.

Dolly and the children took to one another almost at once, leaving Rois free to help her mistress unpack a few things.

"I'll live out of the trunks until we get the plaster done, and the furniture properly placed," Fortune told her serving woman. "Let's go and see the cottage Kevin has built for you."

Rois's new home was located within sight of Fortune's Fancy. It had two rooms, and a loft. The floor was packed dirt. There were two fireplaces and three windows covered with oilpaper, each with its own shutter. A small dormer window had been installed in the loft. The heavy wooden door was hung with stout iron hinges. Rois walked about her new home, well-pleased, nodding at the small brick oven built into the side of the main fireplace, and the iron pot arm that could be swung about above the iron grate. The cottage, however, was empty for Kevin had not dared to place his wife's furniture which stood out in the yard.

"Let's bring it inside," Fortune suggested. "You can't leave it out in the night air." She picked up a small wooden chair.

"Oh, m'lady, you shouldn't be doing that," Rois cried.

Fortune smiled at her servant. "And who else is there to do it if we don't, Rois? I haven't been raised to be so fine a lady that I can't bring a small chair into a house. Come on!"

Working together the two women lugged several chairs, a trestle table, and a wooden settle into the main room of the cottage. Then they brought in the bed with its head, foot, and rope springs. Looking for his wife, Kieran Devers saw what the two women were doing. Calling to Kevin, they joined their wives, putting the bed together, bringing in the mattress and featherbed, as well as Brendan's large oaken cradle, which was set by the small hearth in what was to be the bedchamber.

Suddenly Rois stopped, and looking distressed said, "What am I to cook for dinner? I have no pots unpacked yet, or food to feed us."

"You'll eat with us," Fortune said quietly. "Mrs. Hawkins said she was roasting a turkey."

"But, m'lady, it isn't proper that we sit at table with our betters," Rois worried. "What would yer mam say? What would my grandmam say for that matter? It isn't right."

"Rois," Fortune said patiently, "this isn't England, or Scotland, or Ireland; and Fortune's Fancy certainly isn't a castle, or the fine mansion it will be one day. This is Mary's Land. I will wager my husband hasn't been sitting in isolated splendor all these months at his meals. He's eaten with Kevin, and whoever else came to table." She looked to Kieran, and he nodded. "You see," Fortune said. "Now, no nonsense about it. In time I'll have an elegant room for dining, but for now it is the keeping room for all."

Mrs. Hawkins had roasted a large bird that she served with yams that had been baked in the coals, new peas, fresh bread, butter, and cheese. Afterward there was a dessert made of dried apples and honey. Fortune ordered that a small barrel of October ale that she had transported be broached for them to enjoy. The four bondmen sitting at the far end of the trestle, thanked her. They had not tasted good English beer in a long time. The two mothers cut tiny pieces of turkey to feed their children along with mashed yams, and bits of bread and cheese. Both Aine and Brendan already had a few teeth, and were eager to use them. Dolly proved most helpful, giving her mistress and Rois opportunity to eat while she kept the two little ones amused. Comfort Rogers, however, did not sit at the trestle for Mrs. Hawkins had her busy helping to serve the meal.

"When do I get to eat?" Comfort whined. "There'll be nothing left by the time *they* finish."

"If there's no turkey, you can have a nice bowl of corn mush," Mrs. Hawkins said cheerfully. "It'll fill you up right enough."

The meal over, the bondmen departed for their quarters in the barn. Kevin picked up Brendan, who was already half asleep, and putting an arm about Rois headed for their cottage.

"I'll put the wee mistress to bed, m'lady," Dolly said. "She's asleep already, bless her."

"Thank you," Fortune said.

Kieran reached out, and took her hand in his. "Come," he said. "I want to show you about before the sun sets."

They walked out, and Fortune saw that the house was set on a small bluff above the bay. She could see the meadows with the horses, and at least two fields planted with some kind of crop. The air was soft with early summer, and it was so different than England. And far warmer too, she noted.

"I have so many questions," she said. "What are we growing in those fields?"

"Tobacco," he told her. "It's an excellent cash crop for us, and we need it for Mary's Land is not quite the civilized society it will be one day. The horses we raise are not the sort

to pull wagons, but rather the kind a gentleman or a gentle-
woman would ride, or race. Perhaps we shall sell some of
our animals into Virginia, but not yet."

"Are we growing food?" she asked him.

"Aye, for by Mary's Land law we must. There are three
crops the Indians have introduced us to besides corn. There
are beans, squash, and pumpkins. And we have found our
seed grows in this soil. Peas, carrots, beets, marrows. And
native yams, of course. 'Tis a bounteous land."

"When we rebuild the house with brick," Fortune said, "it
must face the bay. The view is so beautiful. I have never before seen anything like it." She turned, and looked up at him.
"Thank you for our home, Kieran."

"I have missed you so very much," he said softly, his fingers touching her face gently. "How many nights I lay awake
longing for you, Fortune, wondering if this place we have
come to would suit you as it suits me. Can you be happy here
in Mary's Land, so far from your people?"

"You are my people," she told him. "You, and Aine, and
the other children we shall have. Aye, I will miss my family,
but as long as we are together I can bear it. As for this place,
it is where I belong. Where you belong. I felt it as we sailed
up the bay from the sea to St. Mary's Town. I knew it deep
within me. This land called us, Kieran."

The sun was setting behind them, and the stars beginning
to come out above them as they walked back to the house
hand in hand.

"I am going to have a bath," Fortune announced. "Somewhere among all my possessions is a large oak tub. Have the
men find it and fill it for me. It can be set up in our bedchamber. I shall go and find Mistress Hawkins so she will set
the water boiling. I haven't had a bath in six weeks, Kieran,
and my skin is sticky with the sea wind, and the salt. I must
have a bath. And then"—she smiled at him seductively, and
knowingly—"we will have to become reacquainted, sir."

He grinned happily at her. "I'll see the tub is found,

madame. I may even join you, or play the maid, whichever will
please you."

Fortune laughed happily. It was beginning to feel as if
they had never been apart, and she could see from the eager
look in his eyes that he felt the same way too.

The tub was found, and set up in the bedchamber.
Buckets of water were brought to fill it. Finally they were
alone. A small fire burned in the corner fireplace for the
evening air had turned chill. The curtains were drawn. The
candles flickered softly. Kieran knelt before his wife who sat
on the edge of their bed. He pulled her boots off, and then
rolled her stockings down her legs, remembering first to
slide the rosetted garters off. Fortune stood, and turned her
back to him. He unlaced her bodice as she undid the tabs
holding her skirts up. The skirts and bodice were carefully
laid aside upon a chair.

Fortune now stood facing him in her chemise and petticoats. The petticoats were swiftly discarded. Raising her
arms she gathered up her flaming red hair, and pinned it atop
her head. He could see the outline of her breasts as she performed this simple task, and felt his desire rising. Reaching
out he deliberately began to undo the narrow pink ribbons
holding the halves of the chemise together. When the fragile
cambric garment was undone at last, he pushed it over her
shoulders so that it fell to the floor. Then he stepped back, and
breathed a sigh of pure pleasure.

"God's blood, lass, you are surely the most beautiful
woman I have ever known." His two hands clasping themselves about her waist he lifted her up slowly, lowering her
just enough so he might kiss her moss rose nipples.

"I must bathe," she protested softly.

His tongue began to lick at her flesh. "You're salty," he
said with a small chuckle. Then he ceased his teasing, and
set her down in her tub. Kneeling by her side he took up the
washing cloth, and soaping it began to smooth it over her
back and shoulders, using his big hand as a cup to rinse her.

Then one arm. The cloth slid down the silken skin from neck to hand. He rinsed her, and kissed each fingertip. The second arm was identically served, but this time he sucked on her fingers slowly, and with deliberate meaning.

"You are a poor maid," she said low. "You have washed neither my neck, or my ears, Kieran Devers."

In reply he bent and placed a kiss on the nape of her neck before running the soapy cloth over it. "You have always had the most graceful neck, and tempting nape, madame," he murmured. The hand holding the cloth dipped below the water, surfaced, was wrung out, and then gently scoured each small ear, the lobe of which he kissed as he finished.

The cloth was moistened, and squeezed out again. He soaped it lavishly, and wiped it across her chest, sliding beneath the water to cleanse her ripe breasts, teasing the nipples with the flannel cloth until they puckered and thrust forward in the warm water. "Stand up," he said in a thick voice.

"I can do the rest," she assured him. Her heart was beating wildly. The look in his eyes was so passionate.

"*Stand up!*" he repeated through gritted teeth.

Fortune stood.

From his kneeling position he almost looked like a supplicant at the foot of a goddess, and he felt like one. He had promised her he would be faithful, and he had been. He had not lain with any woman since he had last lain with his wife. *His beautiful, seductive, lush wife.* Kieran was almost trembling with anticipation. His manhood was already rock hard in his breeches with his desire for Fortune. He wondered if she felt the same way, and looked up into her face.

When their eyes met Fortune felt the prudently banked fires in her loins spring up and threaten to suffocate her in the conflagration. She could actually feel her nipples thrusting and tingling with anticipation. Her legs felt weak, and yet she stood straight as the cloth laved gently over her belly, and down each shapely limb. Her blue-green eyes never left his dark green ones. She could not have, even if her very life depended upon it, looked away. The look overwhelmed her with its hungry craving, its intense need, its blazing desire.

His finger spread her nether lips open to his view. For a long, hot moment he stared at the sweet flesh filling his gaze. Then the cloth swept over it, washing, teasing, making her long for him even as he longed for her. She whimpered as he leaned forward and began to tongue her. She felt heat licking at her center of being. *"Kieran!"* She half-sobbed his name as his hands cupped her buttocks drawing her into a most intimate conjunction with his lips.

The taste of her! The scent of her! It maddened him with lust. How many months? How many years since he had last held her in his arms? Had made passionate love to her? He rubbed his cheek against her belly, his fingers digging into the flesh of her derriere as he forced back the lust that threatened to consume him. He wanted it perfect tonight of all nights. They had waited for so long, and now within their own home he would take her slowly, and with love. He stood.

Fortune's fingers clumsily began to unlace his shirt. Her hands were practically shaking in their eagerness. She pushed the fabric from him, her lips touching his heated skin. She felt a chill as the night air touched her wet body, and remembered she was standing in her tub. Bending she kissed his chest and belly frantically. She was aching to possess him. This love play was utter torture. Her fingers fumbled at his breeches, and he laughed, helping her, but then she swore impatiently.

"You've still got your damned boots on," she said, straightening up, and glaring at him.

In reply he pulled her close again, but this time his fingers sought her out. "You're an eager wench," he said softly, and two of his fingers pushed themselves into her sheath.

Fortune shuddered with pure pleasure. "Ahhh, yes!" she sighed.

The fingers thrust deliberately, tauntingly into her fevered body, and Fortune squirmed frantically to make the conjunction between them even closer than it was, her fingers tangling themselves in his dark hair, pulling at it to force his head down, and then their lips met in a hungry kiss, their tongues frantically playing. She shivered as a frisson of pleasure was released by his teasing fingers.

"There, you delightfully greedy little bitch, that should hold you for a moment or two while I divest myself of the rest of my clothing." The fingers slid from her body, and looking into her sloed eyes he put them into his mouth, murmuring appreciatively. "You taste quite delicious, my darling lass."

She couldn't move for the longest time. She stood there in the warm water of her tub enjoying the wonderful feelings of pure pleasure that he had unleashed in her. *It had been too long. But it would never be that long again,* the voice in her head assured her.

His back to her, he drew off the remainder of his garments. "Now, wife," he said to her, "it is your turn to bathe me."

"Kieran, I am dying for you," she pleaded with him.

"As I am for you," he replied, and turned about.

She moaned lustfully at the sight of his manhood, fully engorged with his hunger for her, thrusting out from its nest of black curls.

"You must learn the fine art of compromise, Fortune," he told her, climbing into the tub. Seating himself carefully, he pulled her down.

Fortune gasped with both surprise and pleasure to find herself impaled on his love lance as he seated her opposite him.

"Now, my love," he said calmly, handing her the flannel washing cloth, "wash me." The dark green eyes gazed at her.

She could hardly breathe as she attempted to ply the soft cloth over his chest. The sensation of him filling her was so terribly acute. He throbbed with desire within her hot, tight sheath. She ached. She was both hot and cold at the same time. Finally, drawing a deep breath, she washed him with an almost grim determination, leaning over his shoulders to wipe at his broad back. The slightest movement she made was so intense that she was close to shrieking her need for him, particularly when he began to fondle her breasts, playing in leisurely fashion with the sensitive globes, tweaking at the nipples until she begged him to cease, or she would shatter into a thousand pieces.

In response he lifted her off his love lance, and stood, drawing her up with him. "I remember another time like this," he said softly as he stepped from the water, and drew her out as well. Taking the large towel on the rack by the fire he dried her as she frantically took the edge of the towel to dry him. "Enough," he said finally, and pushed her onto the bed.

Fortune didn't need further instructions. She opened herself to him immediately, crying out with undisguised pleasure as he entered her with a single, smooth movement. *"Yes!"* she almost wept. *"Yes!"*

It was almost too much. When her legs wrapped themselves about him Kieran shuddered with delight. He delved deeply into her soft welcoming passage, thrusting again, and again, and again. The walls of her love channel closed about his manhood, tightening, releasing, tightening, releasing until he could no longer bear it, and his long pent-up lust for Fortune exploded in a rush of boiling love juices so profuse that she could not contain it all, and it oozed from her body to dampen the lavender-scented sheets. *"I love you!"* he cried out to her.

"As I love you," she sobbed. "Oh, my darling, never leave me again. Until this moment I did not fully realize how desperately I had missed you, and how much I needed you, Kieran."

They kissed hungrily, passionately, their lips mashing frantically as if they could not get enough of each other.

"I want more," he growled in her ear.

"Oh, please, yes!" Fortune answered him, as their bodies uncoupled for a short time. *"More, and more and more!"*

He laughed, and brushed a lock of her hair that had come undone in their passionate encounter. "For some reason, my love, I do not find that prospect unpleasant. We shall never be parted again, Fortune."

"Never!" she agreed.

Chapter

18

The walls of Fortune's Fancy were plastered. The floors were sanded, and then polished. Tapestries were hung. The India carpets were laid. The furniture Fortune had brought from England was set about. The Irish colonists were invited to a celebration at Lammastide by their sponsor, Kieran Devers. They came to eat, and to drink, and to dance. They stood solemnly as Father White, Leonard Calvert's Jesuit priest, blessed Fortune's Fancy. The feeling of community was strong.

Mistress Happeth Jones, the physician, brought Fortune a special gift of two rosebushes. "I brought a dozen from Ireland," she explained, "and they have taken to this climate well. Come and see me soon, m'lady, and I will give you a strengthening potion for you and the babe you are now carrying. There will be a number of births come next spring." Her brown eyes twinkled behind her spectacles. "It would seem all the husbands were happy to see their wives again, m'lady."

Fortune laughed happily. "Say nothing to Kieran yet. I am

going to tell him today. My Rois is also expecting. Isn't Mary's Land the most wonderful place, Happeth Jones?" She was happy. She could not ever remember being happier in her entire life.

This New World of theirs seemed blessed. Its earth was fertile beyond measure. In the fields the Oronoco tobacco grew. The large dark leaves with their pointed tips, like fox ears, would soon be ready to harvest. In the gardens the corn was high, and the vines from the squash and pumpkins grew together so thickly that you could not see the earth beneath them. The beans, growing on their poles, had produced bounteously all summer long. Everything grew well. The seeds from the carrots, beets, and peas had produced generously, not just in crops, but in seed for the year to come. The lettuces did better in the spring, and they would grow more come the autumn. The cabbages were already green and round. They grew yams, and a small crop of what was called potatoes. These, they had learned from the Indians, could be kept in cold storage most of the winter, and provided tasty nourishment when roasted in the coals, or boiled.

In the forests around them turkeys and deer were plentiful. The bays were filled with ducks and geese. The waters alive with fish of all kinds, as well as shellfish like oysters and clams. There were crustaceans such as crabs and lobsters. Kieran saw that each of his people donated a portion of their harvest to the general storehouses. The rest they stored themselves. The Indians showed them how to grind the corn into a flour which could be used to make bread and cereal.

Comfort Rogers did not like the Indians. She said she was afraid of them, afraid of their curiosity about her sandy-colored hair. Fortune, on the other hand, was not afraid. She willingly let down her long red hair for inspection, snipping tiny bits of it to give the Indian women for souvenirs. They rewarded her with a new name, which translated into English meant *Touched-by-Fire.*

"You'll wake up some morning with your scalp missing,"

Comfort said meanly to her mistress, in an attempt to frighten her.

Fortune laughed. "They are only curious," she answered. "After all, their women are all dark-haired. They have never seen hair like ours that is light, or red. Why do you fear them?"

"Dirty creatures," Comfort replied meanly. "And they look at me outta the corner of their devil's eyes. I know what they're thinking. They're wondering what it would be like to be on top of me, swiving me, hearing me scream as they hads their way with me."

"They have beautiful women of their own," Fortune responded. "I think, girl, you have allowed your imagination to run away with you. I believe we must find you a husband, Comfort. You are obviously ripe for bedding. Perhaps a strong man in your bed would make you feel safer."

"Already picked my man out," Comfort said boldly.

"Have you?" Fortune was not surprised. "Who is he?"

"Master is the man for me. You'll not be able to live in this New World long. You'll go home to England soon enough, and then I'll have the master for my man. You're too much of a lady to survive here. You're a soft, pampered bitch, and you don't deserve him, but I do. And when I gets him between my legs he'll forget you right enough!"

Fortune slapped the girl hard, astounded by her brazen words. She had known that Comfort had a *tendre* for Kieran, but thought it just a youthful infatuation. After all he had bought her bond, and treated her with kindness and decency. "Mary's Land is my home, Comfort, and my husband will *never* be your man. Nor will he ever leave me under any circumstances. We have a child. I am expecting another. I think I must speak to the master about you. Perhaps you would be happier elsewhere than at Fortune's Fancy."

"He won't sell my bond to another," Comfort said smugly. "The master likes me. I see how he looks at me even if you don't."

"Go and polish the furniture in the salon," Fortune snapped. "It is full of dust, and you have been neglecting your duties."

That night as she lay in Kieran's arms she said to him the words he had been longing to hear. "I am with child again, my love."

"Will you give me a son this time?" he asked, as if she could actually guarantee his wish.

"Aye," she said blandly. " 'Tis a lad I carry this time. I know it in my heart. It is not as it was with Aine."

"When he is born," Kieran said, "I shall give you the moon, and the stars, and anything else your heart desires, Fortune mine."

"I should like a down payment on your rash promise," she half-teased him.

"Name your wish, wife," he urged her.

"I want you to sell Comfort's bond to another," Fortune replied.

He was only half surprised by her request. "What has the wench done to displease you, Fortune? I know she is infatuated with me, but she's still just a sixteen-year-old girl, and her life has been so hard. Surely you're not jealous, sweetheart?" He caressed her breasts lovingly.

"There is nothing girlish about Comfort," Fortune said. "She is as old as Eve, and has the cold heart of a whore. Do you know what she had the temerity to say to me today?"

He was almost afraid to ask, but he did, and was somewhat shocked by the answer.

"She has not been doing her housework, and Mrs. Hawkins says she will not help in the kitchen unless absolutely driven to it. She disappears for hours on end, and no one seems to know where she is. She is a discordant note in our home, and I don't want her here, Kieran. I am already affected by the new life growing inside of me. I cannot, I do not, want to cope with the wench."

"It will not be easy to find someone to purchase her bond," he said thoughtfully. "I bought her in Virginia, and the price I paid for her included the cost of her passage.

When her term of indenture is up, I must give her fifty acres of land, an ox, a gun, two hoes, a skirt and waist of penistone, shoes, stockings, a blue apron, a linen smock, two linen caps, and three barrels of corn. I don't know if there is anyone here who will have her."

"Then take her back to Virginia, and sell her," Fortune said irritably. "Or better yet, we'll give her a purse, and send her back to England on the *Cardiff Rose* next time she returns. Who is to know she was transported for theft? She certainly won't tell them else she be thrown back in Newgate. With a purse she can set herself up in a little shop, or find a husband to quell that itch that is consuming her."

"Let me see if I can find someone to purchase her bond from me," Kieran said. "I dislike losing the entire investment, and she has worked off two years of her bond already. I'll not get full price for her, Fortune."

"I don't care if you get nothing for her. If someone can be found to take her, sign her bond over to them gratis. I just want her out of our house!" Fortune said.

"When the harvest is in, I promise you," he said.

The tobacco was cut in September and hung in the curing house to dry. Then it was tied into bundles, and packed into hogsheads for shipment to England on the *Cardiff Rose*. The O'Malley-Small trading company now had a small investment in tobacco which was to prove highly profitable. The *Cardiff Rose* would also take barrels of corn to England. The colony was growing more than it needed, and a cash crop was always welcome. The garden crops were gathered in, the root crops and the cabbages stored in the cellar for winter use. The men went hunting for deer and fowls to be hung and kept for winter's meat. The *Highlander* returned with three milk cows, two team of oxen, two dozen hens, and a rooster.

Around them were signs of the coming winter. The geese were flocking in great cackling groups that filled the waters of the bay. The trees were turning colors. The maples gold and red. The oaks red and russet. The beeches and birches a wonderful rich gold, almost the same color as the dried tobacco. And Fortune began to bloom with the evidence of her coming child as did her serving woman, Rois.

One afternoon as the two women sat outside the house sewing new garments for their children Comfort Rogers came into view. There was an almost slatternly look about her today. There were pine needles in her hair, and she had a look about her that caused Rois to say, "I wonder who she's been lying with, m'lady."

"God's nightshirt!" Fortune swore. "If she gets herself a big belly Kieran will never be able to get rid of her, the little bitch!"

"Is he going to sell her bond?" Rois asked. "I'm glad! You should see her eyeing my Kevin. Rubs up against him every chance she gets. I'd like to scratch her eyes out, but I'd not make a scene and embarrass you, m'lady. I'll not be sorry to see her go! The bondmen gossip to the other men, and 'tis said for a ha'penny, Comfort Rogers will spread her legs without argument."

Fortune closed her eyes, and swore softly to herself. Then opening them she looked directly at Rois and asked, "Why didn't you tell me this before? The girl is, as I suspected, a trull. We have to get rid of her, and the sooner the better!"

"I can't find a buyer to take her bond," Kieran admitted to his wife when pressed about the situation that evening.

"The wench is lying on her back for any and all, Rois tells me," Fortune said angrily.

"I know," he admitted unhappily. "That is why I can't get anyone to take her bond. No decent woman will have the wench in her house. I'm sorry, sweetheart. I only meant to give you servants as you have always had. I didn't want you to be unhappy in Mary's Land."

Shaking her head ruefully Fortune cuddled her husband on her breasts. "What a coil," she said. "Well, there is no other choice. We will have to send her back to England with a purse to keep her. I cannot have her whoring from our home. It will bring us into disrepute if we appear to be allowing it, and how can we stop her short of shackling her?" She paused. "Perhaps we should so she can't run off all the time where we cannot find her. I think we should have her whipped, and put in the stocks. That will show everyone that we do not condone her bad behavior. Then we will shackle her ankles so she cannot roam."

"It's harsh," he said, "but I agree. The *Cardiff Rose* is back one final time this year. When she sails for England Comfort Rogers will be aboard her, I promise you, Fortune. We can't be bothered with such a wayward wench."

Fortune called her servants together the following morning. "I am well aware," she began, "of the bad behavior of some of you. You are put on notice that I will not tolerate it any longer. I will sell the bond of any whose behavior is not Christian, or proper." She looked sternly at the four bondmen, who, though they professed the Puritan faith, had been as dissolute as anyone else. "Comfort Rogers, you are not to leave the house without my permission. Do you understand me?"

Comfort glared sullenly at her mistress, but was silent.

Fortune did not press the issue. The decision had been made concerning Comfort's fate.

"About time," Mrs. Hawkins said to Dolly, the nursemaid. "I wouldn't be surprised to see her gone, and sooner than later."

"Do you really think mistress will sell her off?" Dolly asked.

"If they can find someone to take the jade," Mrs. Hawkins said. "I'm sick unto death of hearing how *master* looks at her. The wench needs a good beating, I tells you."

"She probably wouldn't mind if master administered it," Dolly giggled. "Owww!" She rubbed her arm where Mrs. Hawkins had smacked her with a hard wooden spoon. "What was that for?"

"You mind yer tongue, Dolly," the cook warned. "The mistress loves her man dearly, and he, her. I'll not listen to such talk, and shame on you who are in charge of the little ones."

"I didn't mean anything," Dolly said, stricken.

"I know," Mrs. Hawkins soothed her, confident she had restored order. "Now be a good lass, and run along. I've a brace of ducks to clean and stuff for tonight's dinner."

Standing in the shadow of the keeping room's outside door, Comfort had listened to the two women. Mrs. Hawkins was an old cow, and Dolly too soft and stupid. When I'm mistress of this house, Comfort thought, I'll send them both packing. I'll be the one selling their bonds. Master Kieran will never send me away. He loves me except he can't admit it because of *her*. His hoity-toity lady wife with her flaming pate, and white, white skin. *I hate her!* What is it the Indians call her? Touched-by-Fire. That's it! I wonder if some big buck with his red-brown body would like rummaging between her milky thighs. Ohhh, she'd scream, she would. If she weren't around Master Kieran would turn to me. *I know he would!* Says I can't leave the house without her fine lady-ship's permission, does she? I'll show her! I'll go where I like, and when I like. I'll have no bitch like my old mistress back in London ordering me about. I showed that one, and I'll show this one!

She needed to get away from the house. She needed a man stuffing her full with his want, but now the menservants would be chary of her, Comfort realized. Damn her lady-ship! What difference is it to her that the men were swiving me? I wasn't hurting nobody. Ohh, it's all right if her, with her belly, gets serviced, but not poor me. Well, I'll fix her soon enough, the bitch!

"Mistress Fortune." Prosper, one of the bondmen, was speaking.

Fortune looked up from the chair before the house where she and Rois were sewing infant garments. "Yes, Prosper, what is it?"

" 'Tis Comfort, yer ladyship. She's going off into the woods again. We saw her from the fields."

Fortune jumped up. "That damned girl! She'll get lost again."

"Nay, yer ladyship," the bondman said. "Comfort knows the woods hereabouts better than any. Every bit as good as the Indians."

"Does she?" This was rather interesting news. Was it possible that Comfort had deliberately pretended to be lost the day they arrived? "Show me where she is," Fortune said. "Rois, go and tell Kieran I have gone after the troublesome bitch, and that tomorrow she goes into St. Mary's to the stocks, and for a whipping."

"She'll come back, m'lady," Rois said. "Don't go after the wench."

"She's deliberately disobeyed me, and in front of the others," Fortune said. "If I do not fetch her back myself, I shall lose control of my household." Turning, Fortune followed the bondman.

He led her to the edge of the tobacco fields, pointing out the path that Comfort had taken. "I'll go with you, mistress," he said.

"Nay," Fortune replied. "She will not have gotten far, and I want to bring her back myself. Cut me that switch, Prosper."

He obeyed, handing it to her with a small grin.

Stepping into the woods Fortune followed the barely visible path. About her the leaves were brilliant with their late October color. They fell silently around her, and yet the path seemed clear enough for a distance. Ahead of her she could hear Comfort singing a little ditty, and recognized the tune as "The Miller of Dee." Fortune increased her pace, but she could not seem to catch up with the serving girl. Then she suddenly realized that she hadn't heard Comfort's voice in the past few minutes. Where had the damned girl gotten to? Fortune wondered.

Comfort could hear someone following her. Was it one of

the men? she thought excitedly. She hid herself in the brush long enough to discover her pursuer. Seeing Fortune picking her way through the undergrowth Comfort felt a surge of disappointment. Then an idea struck her. She began to sing again, leading her fine ladyship on deeper and deeper into the forest. She crossed a small stream, and hid herself again, watching as Fortune forded the small watercourse, and continued onward. With a smile of triumph Comfort turned back. Her rival had chosen her own fate. She would soon discover herself lost, and she would not be able to find her way back out of the forest. But I will be there for the master, Comfort considered, smiling to herself as she walked out of the woods, and across the fields to the house.

Fortune suddenly realized she couldn't hear Comfort's voice anymore. She also could not hear the sound of footsteps padding ahead of her. She stopped. All around her the forest was thick with trees and other growth. I have to go back, Fortune thought to herself. She turned about, and attempted to retrace her footsteps, but while the path had seemed so obvious going into the woods, it was not as definite now that she needed to find her way out. Ahead she heard the sound of water. The stream she had crossed! But as she came upon it she wasn't certain it was the same stream. The one she had crossed was silent-running. This one sang and chattered as it tumbled over its streambed of rocks.

Panic began to set in. *I'm lost!* she thought, frightened. Fortune stood stock-still. She was suddenly afraid to move in any direction lest she become even more lost. I haven't been walking that long. I can't be *that* far from home. But which direction do I take? Oh, God! I don't know! She began to cry. She was lost in this New World forest, and no one was ever going to find her. Aine would be orphaned, and the son she was certain she carried in her womb now would die with her. Crumpling to the soft floor of the forest she wept herself into sleep.

"Touched-by-Fire, awaken," she heard a deep voice calling her.

Fortune awoke, and scrambling to her feet found herself face to face with a tall, elderly Indian. She gasped.

"Do not be afraid, Touched-by-Fire. I am Many Moons, the medicine man of the Wicocomoco."

"You speak English?" Fortune was amazed.

He smiled a small smile at her. "Your medicine woman, Glass Eyes, taught me, as I have taught her our tongue."

Glass Eyes? Of course! Happeth Jones with her spectacles! "I am lost, Many Moons. I followed a disobedient servant into the forest, and became lost. Can you guide me back to my home?"

He nodded. "It is the girl with the corn-colored hair you followed? She is a very bad person, Touched-by-Fire. She has brought sickness to several of our young men who were tempted by her. She let them use her as a man will use a woman. Then they became sick."

"Her name is Comfort, although she is anything but," Fortune said, walking by the medicine man's side. "My husband is going to send her away. She claims to be afraid of your people. I am sorry she has brought illness to your men. Perhaps Mistress Jones, Glass Eyes, can help you. I am grateful that you found me, Many Moons. I do not think I could have found my way out of the forest without your help." Fortune could see the trees thinning, and past them the tobacco fields. The sun was close to setting. She had obviously been in the forest most of the day. She was very lucky, she realized.

"Fortune! Fortune!"

Her name was being called. "I'm here," she cried back, and then she exited the woods, running into Kieran's open arms.

"I thought I had lost you," he said, kissing her hungrily.

"You almost did, but thanks to Many Moons—" She turned. "He's gone! Oh, Kieran, I wanted you to thank him, too. The Wicocomoco medicine man who is Mistress Jones's friend found me, and led me out of the forest. Do you know what the Indians call her? Glass Eyes!"

"Why did you go into the forest?" he asked her as they turned to walk back to the house.

"I scolded the servants this morning for their behavior, and then I told Comfort she was not to leave the house without my permission," Fortune said. "Of course she did, deliberately disobeying me. Prosper saw her crossing the fields into the woods. He came to tell me. I followed the wench, but she must have discovered I was coming after her. She disappeared, and I couldn't see or hear her. Then I realized I was lost. I wandered about a bit, gave in to a bout of vapors, and then Many Moons found me," Fortune concluded breathlessly. "I'm starving, Kieran!"

"Mrs. Hawkins will have dinner ready soon. Rois came and told me you had gone into the forest. By the time I learned where you had gone, you had vanished. I skirted the edge of the woods all afternoon calling you. We were just about to send to the Indian village, and ask for their help. What the hell was Comfort doing in the forest?"

"She knows it well, I have learned. She is also not one bit afraid of the Indians despite her claim. She's been lying with several young bucks, and has infected them with some sort of disease," Fortune told her husband. "Did Rois say I wanted her sent to St. Mary's tomorrow?"

He nodded "I've shackled her, and put her in the buttery," he told his wife as they entered the house.

"Ohh, m'lady, thank heavens yer back!" Rois cried as she ran to greet her mistress.

"It's all right now, Rois," Fortune assured her serving woman, "and tomorrow we dispose of Comfort Rogers."

"Good riddance!" Rois said bluntly.

In the early morning the weeping Comfort was brought from the buttery, and put into the wagon. Kevin would go with his master to St. Mary's Town. As the vehicle moved off from the house, however, Comfort shrieked irrationally, "He's taking me away, you bitch! We're going to be together, and yer going to be left alone! I knew he wanted me. I knew he loved me, and not you!"

"Bitch!" Rois muttered.

"I feel sorry for her," Fortune replied. "Not so much that I want her about, but I still have pity for her."

In the evening when the men returned, and they were all, servant and master, settled about the trestle in the keeping room, Kieran Devers explained that they had all had a narrow escape. He and Kevin had reached St. Mary's in good time. He had brought the bondwoman before the governor, requesting that she be put in the stocks and whipped for her misbehavior. He was prepared to afterward give her into the keeping of Captain O'Flaherty, to be returned to England.

Comfort was forced screaming into the stocks in the public square, her blouse ripped down its back, and then given ten lashes for her immoral and lewd behavior, as well as her disobedience to her master and mistress. She would remain the day in the stocks, going aboard the ship in late afternoon before the evening tide. Kieran and Kevin having seen the bondwoman properly punished went about the business of seeing the hogsheads of tobacco loaded aboard the *Cardiff Rose*. Then they went to see Aaron Kira, pleased to learn he had been accepted in St. Mary's, and his money-lending establishment was thriving.

"What do I do with the wench when we get back to England?" Ualtar O'Flaherty asked his cousin's husband when the cargo had been finally loaded, and the three men sat in the captain's cabin eating a meal.

"Give her the purse I gave you, and send her on her way. She doesn't dare go back to her old haunts lest she be caught, and rearrested. She's only served two years of her bond, but we can't sell her bond to anyone, her reputation is so foul. I don't want her around my family. She lured Fortune into the forest, and then left her there, lost. My wife was rescued by one of our Indian allies. Frankly I wouldn't care if you threw her overboard in midocean, Ualtar. It's no more than she deserves, the conniving bitch. Keep her shackled, and under lock and key lest you find her spreading her legs for your crew, and have a mutiny on your hands. She's a wicked bit of goods."

There was a knock on the cabin door, and it opened to reveal the cabin boy. "Gentleman to see Master Devers, sir," he said, and stepped aside to allow the man with him to enter the cabin.

"I am Kieran Devers," and he arose, holding out his hand.

"Anthony Sharpe, Master Devers. You have in your possession a bondwoman named Comfort Rogers?"

"I do, but not for long," Kieran replied.

"I have a warrant for her arrest, sir. She is an impostor, a convicted felon who was due to hang for murder. She switched places with a dead woman in Newgate who was to be transported. No one would have known but that she angered another woman who was also about to be transported. Lay with her man, the bold wench did. Quite a randy lass, I am told," Anthony Sharpe said with a small grin.

"I purchased her bond over two years ago," Kieran said. "Why has it taken so long for her to be claimed by the government?"

"The woman she angered could get no one to listen to her until she got here to the New World. She came later on a different vessel. This woman's master heard the story, believed his bondwoman, and notified the authorities. Then word was sent back to London. A small reward was offered amongst the felons in Newgate, for many of the same people there for debt were still there, for any information as to what had happened to Comfort Rogers. Money do be an excellent restorative of memory, sir. We learned that Comfort Rogers had died, and her identity had been taken by one Jane Gale."

"What did this woman do?" Kieran asked.

"Killed her mistress, she did. Was convinced that her master was mad in love with her, and killed the wife to get at him," came the reply.

"Was he? Did he lead the girl on?" Kieran inquired.

"Nay, sir, 'twas all in the lass's head," Anthony Sharpe said.

"My God, Kieran, you are fortunate she did not kill your wife," Ualtar O'Flaherty said, and then turning to Master Sharpe explained what had happened to his cousin only the day before.

"Aye, sir, your lady is indeed a lucky lass," was the observation.

"The wench is in the stocks," Kieran said. "We were just going to fetch her now." He did not say that he had been planning to return Comfort Rogers, or Jane Gale, or whatever her name was, back to England simply to be rid of her. "What will you do with her?"

"Take her back to England," was the answer. "I'll have to find a ship that will have room for me, and my prisoner."

"I will be leaving tonight with the tide, and I have room for you," Captain O'Flaherty said quickly. "Yer passage will be a free one, Master Sharpe, for my cousin, who is distantly related to the king, would expect me to aid his royal authorities. I'll send some men to fetch the wench from the stocks."

"We'll go with them," Kieran said. "I would, however, like to see your warrant before I leave the ship, Master Sharpe."

"Of course, sir," came the response, and reaching into his doublet he drew forth the parchment, handing it to Kieran.

Accepting the official-looking document, Kieran opened it and read it. It was indeed a warrant for the arrest of the convicted felon, Jane Gale, also known as Comfort Rogers, female, aged sixteen, hair flaxen, eyes blue. Folding the warrant back up Kieran returned it to Master Sharpe, and turned to Captain O'Flaherty. "You have my wife's letter for her mother, the duchess. We will see you in the spring. I hope the tobacco sells well on the London market. Godspeed."

The two men shook hands.

"The family will be delighted to learn of the new bairn," the captain said. "God bless you all Kieran, and my love to Fortune."

* * *

"So Ualtar has sailed for England with Comfort Rogers in chains," Fortune said as her husband finished his tale. "God help her."

"You can say that after all the trouble she caused?" he said wonderingly. "Your heart is much too good, sweetheart." The others about the trestle murmured their agreement.

"I am no fool, Kieran, as you know, but see how auspiciously fate has dealt with us. Until we came to Mary's Land each of us was besieged in our own passage through life, and yet we kept moving forward. That was what Comfort Rogers was trying to do. Move forward. Be loved. But, alas, she did not know how. I have been loved my whole life, and you, despite your mother's death knew that your father and siblings loved you, even if your stepmother did not. What kind of a life did that poor creature have, I wonder, that caused her to become so wicked? Babies are born innocent. It takes terrible deeds to turn them into evil people. Aye, she tried to kill me, and to steal my husband, but tonight I am safe at Fortune's Fancy with you by my side, while she is on her way back to England to be hanged. God help her, Kieran. God help her!"

He looked at her with his dark green eyes filled with love and admiration for this woman he had found to be his wife. Lady Fortune Mary Lindley Devers was truly amazing. "I love you," he said. "I loved you yesterday. I love you today, and I will love you forever though time itself ceases to exist. We are home, Fortune. Home in our Mary's Land. *Home, and besieged no more!*" He stood, drawing her up, and took her into his arms. Then he kissed her with all the passion in his Celtic soul, and Fortune knew he was right. They were home.*Home, and besieged no more.* It was a good feeling!

Author's Note

Mary's Land is, of course, the state we know today as Maryland, and its founder, George Calvert, the first Lord Baltimore, was a man so far in advance of his time that we haven't yet caught up with him. He dreamed of a world where all people could worship as they chose to worship. Freely, and without being constantly besieged by intolerance. Human nature being what it is, we aren't there yet, but like George Calvert, I have hope, because I believe that with God, or the Creator, Yahweh, Allah, or whatever you choose to call the Celestial Actuary, all things are possible.

If you have comments on *Besieged* that you want to share with me, please feel free to drop me a note at P.O. Box 765, Southold, NY 11971-0765, or at bertricesmall@hotmail.com. I'll eventually answer. Good reading, and God Bless from your most faithful author, Bertrice Small.